THE FIRST HUNTER

The Eternity Road Book 1

LANA MELYAN

Copyright © 2019 by Lana Melyan
All rights reserved.
No part of this book may be used or reproduced in any manner whatsoever without written permission except in the case of brief quotations embodied in critical articles and reviews.
This is a work of fiction. Names, characters, places, and incidents are products of the author's imagination or are used fictitiously and are not to be construed as real. Any resemblance to actual locales, organizations, events, or persons living or dead is entirely coincidental.

Lana Melyan

www.lanamelyan.com

*Dedicated to my grandfather,
after whom I named
my First Hunter, my Captain,
my Keeper of the Book, Samson.*

Chapter One

THEY GALLOPED *through the dark woods and came out to a meadow that glowed silver in the moonlight. The young woman stopped her horse abruptly, and the hood of her cloak fell, revealing long, fair curls. She sniffed the air and rolled the axe in her hand. 'We are surrounded.'*

Amanda put the pen down. It was late. Yawning, she dropped the notebook on the floor and slid down under the duvet. As soon as her head touched the pillow, she was asleep.

She was falling through total darkness. The next moment, she jolted at the impact with something soft, and her eyes flew open. Sitting up, she brushed her back against a rough, wooden headboard. She felt awake, but the surrounding view was unfamiliar.

Amanda looked at the nightstands with oil lamps on them, one on either side of the bed. There was also an old dresser and a mirror with blurry, yellow spots. The walls were covered with faded, bulging wallpaper.

I must still be dreaming.

Her heartbeat rose, drumming against her chest. Where was she? Just a second ago she had been at home, writing in her bed.

She swung her bare feet onto the cold, dusty floor. After a moment of hesitation, she went to the door and stuck out her head. There was a hallway with three more doors and a staircase leading down. Amanda tiptoed to the first door and put her ear to it.

No sound.

Peering in the keyhole, she saw the outline of a chair.

What am I afraid of? she thought. The situation was strange, but it didn't seem dangerous. Holding her breath, she carefully put her hand on the rusty door handle and pushed it.

Nobody was inside. She checked the other rooms, and they, too, were empty.

Downstairs, Amanda came upon a large living room with old-fashioned furniture, a big fireplace, and high windows covered by heavy curtains. The walls were stained with mildew, and there were spider webs in every corner. To her right, she could see the front door.

"Hello? Is anybody here?" she asked in a small voice.

She turned to the front door and pushed it, but it wouldn't open. A key stuck out of the keyhole. She glanced behind her and saw only her own footprints in a thick layer of dust. Everything said that nobody had visited this place in a long time.

Amanda unlocked the door and stepped outside. Tall grass covered the big front yard, surrounded by woods on all sides. No gate or road. In the middle of the yard was a dried up fountain with the statue of a baby cherub. Amanda ran down the porch stairs.

"Hello? Is anybody there?" she cried.

All she heard was the rustling of leaves coming from the woods. Goosebumps from the morning chill popped out on her arms. Only then did she realize that all she was wearing were her night shorts and a top. She hugged herself and headed back to the house to search the rest of it.

As soon as she stepped inside and closed the door, a wave

of dizziness hit her. She dropped down in a big, leather armchair. In the same second, the armchair and the floor disappeared beneath her, and she fell into a big, dark, endless hole. Amanda's scream echoed around her as she fell.

When she opened her eyes, she was still screaming. But now she was back in her own bed, in her own bedroom.

Breathing heavily, Amanda looked around.

"It was a dream," she murmured.

Still shaking, she took the duvet and threw it around her shoulders. A knock on the door made her jump.

"Amanda, honey, are you alright?" she heard her dad's voice.

"I'm fine, be right down," she replied, trying to sound normal.

"Okay. We'll wait."

Wait for what? she wondered. She never ate breakfast, he knew that.

Amanda felt weak and tired as if she had carried stones all night. She got out of bed and opened the window. It was a sunny spring morning, full of the sweet smell of blooming lilac. The light, cool breeze tickled her face. She closed her eyes, took a deep breath of the fresh air, and headed to the bathroom.

A quick shower warmed and relaxed her. But she couldn't forget the dream. It had been too real, and she could still smell the dust.

As Amanda headed down the stairs, she heard whispering in the kitchen, and when she came around the corner, she saw her father and Melinda standing side by side in front of the kitchen table.

"You look weird, people, you know that?"

"Happy birthday to you, happy birthday to you..." They started singing and stepped aside. Behind them was a cake with eighteen candles sinking into the icing. "Happy birthday, dear Amanda, happy birthday to you!"

"I forgot…" Amanda laughed. "I forgot my own birthday."

Her dad pulled her in and kissed her forehead. "Make a wish, honey."

Amanda considered the candles for a moment and blew them out.

"What did you wished—"

"I am not telling you what I wished for, Melinda," smirked Amanda, settling into a chair beside her father.

"Right. We don't want to jinx it." Melinda turned to the coffee maker, poured a cup of coffee, and handed it to Amanda.

Melinda, a slender African-American woman of around fifty, had been their housekeeper for the past nine years. Always curious, she never missed a chance to ask questions.

"I can't believe that I forgot my birthday," Amanda shook her head. "It's because of that creepy, stupid dream."

"What dream?" Melinda leaned forward on the table and narrowed her eyes.

"Is that why you screamed?" asked her dad.

Amanda nodded, taking a sip from her cup.

"What was it, dear?" Melinda asked again. "What did you see?"

"Okay, well… I was all alone in an old house covered with dust, in the middle of nowhere. I couldn't find anybody, and believe me, that was already scary enough. But then I fell in a big dark hole. That's when I began screaming. What do you think it means?" asked Amanda and both, she and her father, looked at Melinda.

"It was just a silly dream. Forget about it." Melinda looked at Amanda's father. "You are going to be late, Lindsey."

"Yeah, I've got to go." Lindsey pulled himself up and

reached for his coat. "Honey, you said that you don't want to have a party, are you sure?"

"Yeah, don't worry about it."

"I promise I'll sit in my room, quiet as a mouse." He adjusted his tie. "Or I could meet some friends."

"Are you looking for an excuse to go out?" Amanda teased.

"No, no party. But I'll have fun, I promise."

"All right, then." He picked up his briefcase from the floor, grabbed his car keys, and headed to the door.

Amanda's cellphone rang. She scooped it up and looked at the screen. It was Hanna.

"Where are you? We're going to be late."

"Hello to you, too," Amanda chuckled. "I'll be there in a minute."

She grabbed her bag, took the apple handed by a smiling Melinda, and ran out.

THE MOMENT AMANDA closed the door, Melinda's smile disappeared. She hurried upstairs to Amanda's room and carefully removed the duvet. There, on the fresh, white sheets, were clumps of dust and a few small pieces of grass.

"Oh, God," Melinda gasped. She reached for her cellphone and dialed a number. "Craig, it's me."

Chapter Two

WHEN HANNA'S car broke down yesterday, she and Amanda made arrangements for the girls to ride together. Amanda drove down Oak Street and spotted Hanna standing outside in the shade of white acacia. As soon as the car stopped, Hanna threw herself in.

"Relax," said Amanda with a grin. "We are not that late."

"I know. Close your eyes."

"What? Why?"

"Close them, please."

"Okay."

Hanna took Amanda's hand and placed what felt like a hexagonal box into her palm.

Amanda opened her eyes. The box was covered with old, vinous velvet. She lifted the lid and saw a silver bracelet. It consisted of eight small coins connected to each other by tiny golden loops. The coins had a golden roman number and a golden circle with many small holes around each number. Amanda studied the eighth coin.

"This one doesn't have a number," she pointed out.

"It's a clasp. Happy Birthday," Hanna said softly. "It's from me and my brother."

"Craig? You're kidding, right?" Amanda smiled shyly. "He doesn't even like me".

"You always say that. I told you, he doesn't talk to us much because he doesn't want to bother us."

Amanda looked closely at the bracelet, turning each coin. It was handcrafted and didn't look like something found in a regular store.

"Do you like it?" Hanna asked.

"It's old and valuable, isn't it?"

"Yes, it's very old and valuable. You're not going to sell it, are you?" Hanna said trying to sound serious, and looking straight into Amanda's eyes.

"Silly. It's just . . . you're giving it to me."

"Craig and I want you to have it." Hanna squeezed Amanda's hand.

"Thank you." Amanda hugged her, put the bracelet on, and started the engine. "Okay, history class awaits." She took a bite of the apple and drove.

The radio was on, and when "Bad Things" came on, they both sang along with Jace Everett.

"Do you like the TV show?" Hanna asked.

"This song is from a TV show?" Amanda took another bite of the apple.

"It's about vampires. You like vampire movies."

"I like Buffy. I like how she kicks their asses."

"Can you put down that damn apple and hold the wheel with both hands?" grumbled Hanna.

"What? I'm eating it. You know what they say, right? One apple a day —"

"Yeah, but if you crush your skull, I don't think your apple will save you."

"Calm down, everything is under control."

Amanda stopped the car on the school parking lot, and they both got out.

"There she is," said Hanna and nodded to the side, where Kimberly sat on a bench in the shadow of a big oak, looking annoyed and impatiently tapping her foot on the grass. When she saw Amanda and Hanna, she got up and dashed toward them.

"What took you so long?" she said, passing right by them.

"Where are you going?" Amanda spread her hands.

"Wait," said Kimberly, heading to her car.

Hanna glanced at Amanda and shrugged.

Kimberly came back with a beautifully wrapped package in her hands. She handed it to Amanda, beaming.

"Happy birthday! Open it."

They sat on the bench as Amanda unwrapped the present.

It was a framed picture of the three of them, taken last summer. They had picnicked at their favorite spot beside the lake outside of town. Amanda and Kimberly offered to give Hanna a ride on their hands. They took each other by the wrists and Hanna sat down and put her arms around their shoulders. They took her right to the water to throw her in. But she grabbed them by their necks so tightly that all three of them collapsed into the lake. They stuck the camera on a fallen log and snapped a picture of themselves sitting around a small fire, wet from head to toe, laughing. Kimberley had written in one corner, *Friends forever.*

"I had forgotten about that," said Amanda.

"Me, too," said Hanna, still grinning.

Amanda pulled Kimberly into a hug. "That's so sweet, thank you."

"We prepared everything, and we're going there today after school."

"We are?"

"Yes, just the three of us, to celebrate your birthday. Or,"

Kimberly quirked an eyebrow, "did you want to invite somebody else?"

"Like who? Him?" smirked Hanna. She nodded toward the school entrance. "Look who your boyfriend is talking to."

Amanda and Kimberly turned their heads. Alec Stafford, a tall, blond guy, was talking to his ex-girlfriend, Debra Gordon as she flirtatiously smiled at him.

"He is not my boyfriend, you know that," said Amanda indifferently.

"The whole school thinks he is," said Hanna.

Kimberly shrugged. "They're just talking. At least she's not pulling his hair. That's good, it means—"

"That they remained friends? Please." Hanna chuckled. "Look at her. Does she look like a friend?"

"What's wrong with you?" Kimberly gazed at her, frustrated.

"What's wrong with both of you?" Amanda got up, and the three of them headed for the school building.

Amanda opened her locker and pulled out the history book. She looked into the small mirror attached to the door and ran her fingers through her long, dark-brown hair.

"I'm sorry," said Hanna, looking at Amanda's back. "It's just she always flirts with him when you're around."

"First of all, she's a flirt, not he, and second— I don't care." Amanda turned to face Hanna. "He is not my boyfriend. People can walk together and talk to each other and not be a couple."

"Maybe. But the way he looks at you . . ." started Kimberly and stopped, her gaze drifting a few inches above Amanda's head.

"Hello, girls," said a voice behind Amanda.

"Hello," said Kimberly.

Amanda turned around. "Hi, Alec."

"Kimberly, are you coming?" said Hanna in a sharp tone, walking past them.

"Yep," said Kimberly, following her.

Alec leaned on the lockers. "Hanna doesn't like me."

Amanda didn't know what to say, because he was right. "She's just in a bad mood. Her car died," she improvised.

Alec chuckled.

The bell rang. Amanda hugged her history book as they moved along the corridor.

"I was going to ask if you have any plans for this Saturday."

Amanda thought for a few seconds. "No. Not yet. What's up?"

"Party, at my house."

"Is everybody invited?" She looked at Kimberly and Hanna arguing far ahead.

"If by 'everybody' you mean Hanna," he said, tracing her gaze, "then, yes."

"She will come, you know." She looked at him sideways, smiling.

"I know." He smiled as well. "It's okay, I'll wear my football gear."

"I have to go," said Amanda as she spotted Mr. Hancock, the history teacher, at the end of the hallway.

"See you," said Alec.

Amanda caught up to Hanna, who was talking to Sarah about the essay due next week and sat behind her. Kimberly sat on the left from Amanda's desk and stared out the window with a bored face until Mr. Hancock walked in and shut the door.

Amanda looked at her bracelet and touched it with her fingertips. Craig wanted her to have it. Was that so? Why? Maybe Hanna only included him because it was valuable and she was afraid that Amanda wouldn't accept it if it had been just from her. Or maybe it had belonged to somebody from their family, and she couldn't give it to her without having Craig's permission. Then again, why give it to her?

She liked Craig a lot. Her heart began to pound every time she looked at his blue eyes or if his strong hands accidentally touched her. But to him, she was just Hanna's friend. He never gave her any reason to hope.

She often dreamed about him, and it was always the same dream. She stands in the middle of a green field. Suddenly, out of the dark forest surrounding the field, Craig appears. He runs towards her, and when he finally reaches her, he looks deep into her eyes and says, "Eleanor."

Amanda always woke up then. And every time she felt such a disappointment. He wasn't running across that whole field for her—he was running because he thought she was somebody else. Who was Eleanor? Amanda had known Craig for three years now, and she was sure he didn't have a girlfriend.

Mr. Hancock asked a question, and Hanna's hand flew up. She loved history. It was her favorite subject. She was always ready for class. But somehow, her book still looked as new at the end of the year as it had been at the beginning.

"What do you do with it?" Amanda had poked fun once. "Keep it at the right temperature and turn the pages with sterile gloves?"

Hanna said she liked to surf the web and read outside of school to get her information.

Mr. Hancock asked another question, and Hanna's hand shot up again.

"Anybody else?" said Mr. Hancock, slowly moving his eyes from one student to another. But there were no more hands in the air. He sighed.

"Can't wait to read your essays," he said and pressed his lips together.

He walked to his table, leaned on it, crossed his arms over his chest and looked at Hanna.

"Yes, Ms. Kaylan."

Hanna pushed her dark-blond curly hair behind her ears. Even from behind her, Amanda could tell she was enjoying the moment. Amanda smiled at Kimberly, who chuckled in response. When Amanda turned her head back, she saw Mr. Hancock moving toward her. The moment Hanna stopped talking he looked at Amanda.

"Do you want to add something, Ms. Shane?"

"No, there's nothing to add, she was very comprehensive," said Amanda without hesitation.

"It's very important to hear your opinion," he said sarcastically. "Because, as I noticed, you were very interested in the subject and didn't miss a word during the class." He stared at Amanda, but his small round eyes weren't angry.

The bell rang.

"Very good, Ms. Kaylan," said Mr. Hancock.

Hanna put her book in the bag and pulled her vibrating cellphone out of it. Her expression changed as she looked at it, becoming serious.

"What is it?" asked Amanda, distinguishing Craig's name on the screen.

"It's nothing," said Hanna. "Ah, I forgot, I wanted to ask Mr. Hancock . . ." She looked back, but he was already gone.

"Calm down, the class is over," said Amanda, rolling her eyes.

"Thanks to Mr. Hancock, you noticed," said Kimberly. "It looked like you were far away from here, flying in your dream bubble."

"I would be, if *Ms. Granger,*" Amanda threw a sideways look at Hanna, "didn't burst it every minute with her popping hand, attracting everybody's attention to us."

"What were you dreaming about, anyway?" Hanna asked, as they headed to the exit.

"I wasn't dreaming, I was thinking."

"Aha! I knew you could do that."

"Very funny."

"Thinking about what?" asked Hanna again.

"About what I am going to wear to the party on Saturday."

"What party?" Hanna and Kimberly asked together.

Chapter Three

AFTER CLASSES, all three of them jumped into Kimberly's Ford and drove to the lake.

The day was warm and sunny, and the windows in the car were open. Kimberly slipped in a CD, which contained improvisations of the Birthday Song performed by various artists. When the second song began, Amanda said, "Thank you, girls," pushed eject, and turned on the radio.

They parked the car on the shoulder of the road, took the small bag Kimberly and Hanna had prepared the day before out of the trunk and headed to the lake.

They walked on a well-trodden path between the trees and came out to the open space on the lakeshore. The place looked welcoming this time of year. The forest on the other side of the water was mirrored in its calm surface. A willow tree on the slope dipped its fresh foliage right into the lake as if drinking from it. It was quiet, and only the chirping of birds disturbed the silence.

"If you think that this place is too dull for a birthday party, we can still go to a club," Kimberly said, dropping the bag to the ground.

"It's perfect," said Amanda, treading the small dock.

"We should take a swim, don't you think?" asked Hanna.

"No," said Kimberly, kneeling on the grass. "It's a nice day, but the water is still cold." She pulled out the marshmallows.

"I'll go get some twigs for the fire."

"I'll come with you," said Amanda, and after a minute, they disappeared behind the bushes and trees.

When they returned with their hands full of twigs, they saw Kimberly standing in between the trees on the opposite side of the clearing, peering at something.

"Kimberly," called Amanda.

"Guys? There you are," she said, walking back. "I thought you were over here."

"Didn't you see where we went?"

"I did. But then I heard noises from that side." Kimberly pointed her thumb behind her shoulder. "I thought you'd come around to scare me."

"Why didn't we think of that?" Amanda smiled at Hanna.

But Hanna didn't smile back. She was looking in the direction Kimberly had pointed.

"What kind of noises?" she asked, squinting.

"Rustling of the bushes. And I think I heard a whisper."

"It could be people like us, just walking around," Amanda said.

"Usually people come here by car." Hanna threw the twigs on the ground. "And I didn't see any cars at the shoulder except ours."

"Are you scared?" Amanda raised one brow. "Sometimes you are so tough, Hanna, but sometimes you're such a chicken."

"She's a tough chicken," Kimberly chuckled.

"I'll go check." Hanna frowned as she left.

"Do you want us to come with you?" Amanda called after her.

"No, stay where you are."

"Ma'am, yes, ma'am," murmured Amanda.

"She is so weird sometimes." Kimberly pulled out of the bag the matches and a piece of paper. "Like, remember that night at your house, when she heard some voices in your backyard and said she saw shadows? She ran down there at two o'clock in the morning to check." Kimberly crumpled the paper and stuffed it under the twigs. "A normal person would just close all doors and windows, draw the curtains, turn off the lights, and peek from the safety of the house." She lit the paper.

"I don't think she's afraid of anything—" started Amanda, but Kimberly interrupted her.

"She's nuts. That's why she never had a boyfriend."

"Kimberly, she has a boyfriend, you know that," said Amanda skewering the marshmallows.

"Yes, but have we ever seen him? We know he's in Florida and she visits him sometimes, but he never comes here." Kimberly stared at Amanda with excitement. "Maybe she's a lesbian?"

"What?" Amanda burst out laughing.

But Kimberly was too fascinated by her theory to let it go. "Maybe HE is a SHE, and Hanna doesn't want us to know?"

"I am not a lesbian, Kimberly," came Hanna's voice from behind her.

"Are you sure about that?" Kimberly grinned as she turned to look at her. "'Cause if you're gay you can tell us. We're your friends."

Hanna rolled her eyes.

"I just wanted to make sure we're safe here."

"Safe? Of course, we're safe. What can be dangerous here?"

"Do you know how often people disappear in places like this?" Hanna sat down beside the fire.

"Then why did you go out there alone?" Kimberly stared at Hanna, waiting, but Hanna didn't answer.

"What did you see?" Amanda asked. "Did you find anybody?"

"No," said Hanna, staring at the burning twigs. "Whoever it was, they're gone now."

"Good job, Miss Marple. Now can we relax and have fun? Wasn't that the plan?" Amanda handed each of them a marshmallow skewer.

"Yep."

Kimberly retrieved three cans of soda. They each took one and chinked them together.

"So, we are going to a party," said Hanna.

"Let's hope it will be fun," muttered Kimberly, twirling her stick over the fire.

"Why shouldn't it be fun?" Amanda asked.

"Maybe because we don't have boyfriends or dates," said Kimberly flatly. "I broke up with James two months ago, Hanna's boyfriend is God knows where, while you have the best guy at school but keep him as a friend. I hope you'll at least dance with him. Then I can promise all my dances to Hanna." She looked at Hanna with a big marionette smile.

"That will be a dream come true," Hanna cleared her throat.

"There will be other guys there," Amanda said. "Like Alec's entire football team, and not all of them are taken."

"And, of course, those who are not are the most attractive and interesting ones," said Kimberly, throwing another sarcastic smile, this time to Amanda.

"Alec is not taken," said Amanda. "You like him, and I think he likes you too. Just ask him for a dance and work your charm."

"He likes me because I'm your friend. When you're not around, all we have to say to each other is 'Hi.'"

"You know stuff about him. He plays football, and photography is his hobby. Just start somewhere, and maybe he will take over."

"Amanda, everybody knows how he feels about you. And you want me, your best friend, to be the one who . . . but if you just want me to distract him . . ."

"Kimberly, I think you got a little bit distracted yourself," Hanna chuckled. "Your marshmallow is in the fire."

Chapter Four

AMANDA STOPPED the car at Hanna's front yard.

Hanna and Craig moved to Green Hill three years ago. The grand house they lived in belonged to their rich uncle, who took them in after their parents died on a boat trip when a storm struck. It happened many years ago.

Amanda looked at Craig's Jeep in the garage and turned off the engine.

"I'll come in for a second. I want to thank Craig for the present."

"Craig," Hanna called from the doorway, as they entered the house.

"I'm here," he answered from the kitchen.

Amanda and Hanna walked into the kitchen to see Craig standing with his arms crossed, staring at a big map on the table. A few locks of his dark, soft hair fell over his forehead, touching his frowning eyebrows.

"Hi," said Amanda.

He looked up, and his blue eyes met hers. Amanda's pulse started knocking into her bracelet.

"Amanda, hi." Craig's face brightened.

Amanda approached the table and looked at the map. All she could see were mountains and forests.

"Going somewhere?" She nodded toward it.

Craig smiled.

"This is the state map," he said. "Just trying to find new places. To hike."

"Did you find any?" asked Hanna, spotting a few red marks in the forested areas.

"Not sure." They exchanged a glance. "I'm working on it."

"I like hiking," said Amanda. "My dad and I—we used to hike a lot."

"Hanna likes it, too. When I find a place, we can go together."

"I'm in," said Amanda.

Craig folded the map and pushed it aside. "You're back early," he said, looking first at Hanna then at Amanda. "I thought you were celebrating."

"We were." Amanda nodded. "But it started raining."

"We were at the lake. Just the three of us," said Hanna. "We offered her to go someplace where we could have some beer, but she declined."

"I have a better idea." Craig went to the fridge and pulled out a bottle of champagne. "She will not decline this."

No, she wouldn't. Amanda was happy that he gave her a reason to spend more time around him, especially now, when he was being so unusually talkative.

Amanda watched them while Craig opened the bottle and Hanna busied herself with putting glasses and strawberries on the table. She was always amazed by how different they looked. Hanna was the absolute opposite of tall, dark-haired, and blue-eyed Craig with her dark-blond hair, brown eyes, and arched chestnut eyebrows. The only similarity was that they were both beautiful. Amanda supposed that they looked like their parents, but she couldn't say for sure. She had never seen any pictures of them; in fact, she never saw any pictures at all. She didn't know what Hanna and Craig looked like when they were small. Their uncle never visited them and Amanda didn't know how he looked, how old he was, or if they had any other relatives. Hanna never spoke about it and Amanda never asked.

Craig handed a glass of champagne to Amanda. Then he took his own and stepped closer—so close she could feel his breath on her face. Her whole body weakened as she looked at him. The glass of champagne became heavier in her hand. His eyes looked deep into hers, just like in her dream, and any second now she expected him to call her Eleanor.

"To your eighteenth birthday, Amanda," he said.

Amanda took a deep breath. Craig and Hanna raised their glasses.

"Thank you, guys."

Amanda took a big gulp, hoping it would relax her and hide her nervousness. Hanna chortled and took a big sip, too. Amanda glanced at Craig, who was watching them. He only had a taste and put his glass down. Amanda felt disappointed.

"Somebody has to drive you home," said Craig, and his lips parted in a breathtaking smile.

Amanda thought this smile seemed different. Not because of the champagne, which was spreading warmth throughout her body. It was different, because, this time, his eyes were smiling, too.

Craig added more champagne to their glasses.

"Now, tell me, what did you do at the lake? Did you have fun?" He put the bottle down and gestured to the chairs, taking a seat.

"It was interesting," started Amanda, "and a little bit mysterious."

"What do you mean?"

"I think somebody was following us," said Hanna.

Amanda caught the expressive look she exchanged with Craig.

"I don't think it was that dramatic," smirked Amanda.

"Why, what happened?" Craig stared at Hanna.

"Amanda and I went to collect twigs. When we came back, Kimberly said that she'd heard rustling and whispers in the bushes. I went to check." She paused.

"Did you see anybody?" asked Craig.

"Yeah, I saw two men."

"What?" Amanda put down her glass. "I asked you the same question, and you said that nobody was there."

"It's your birthday. I didn't want you to worry. They were leaving, anyway."

Craig stood up, put his hands in his pockets, and slowly walked to the window.

"Is that it?" he asked.

"No. When we were leaving I saw them standing in between the trees behind us, watching."

These words surprised Amanda even more; she hadn't seen anybody.

"What did they look like?" asked Craig. The cheer was gone. His voice was cold.

"Young, dark sunglasses, heads covered with hoodies." Hanna took a sip from her champagne. "And very pale."

Craig gave Hanna a questioning look. She nodded.

Amanda couldn't understand why Craig was asking all those questions in such a serious tone.

"Craig, what's going on? Do you know those guys?"

"No." His expression softened. "I just want to be sure that you three are safe."

They went out to Craig's Jeep so he could take Amanda home. She felt nervous, as they drove. Never before had she been so close to him one-on-one. Now, when he was right beside her, she wanted so badly to touch his hand and look into his eyes. She glanced at him, and he met her eyes. Then he turned off the radio.

"I'm sorry if I made you uncomfortable back there." He ran his fingers through his hair.

"You didn't. Craig, you don't have to worry about Hanna. She's tough. She can take care of herself."

"I know. But I want to ask you something."

"Yes?"

"Please, don't go to places like the lake, or the forest. Stay close to people until I find out who those guys are and why they were following you."

"Okay, we'll be more careful." She still thought he was overreacting.

"Here we are," said Craig, stopping the car in front of Amanda's house.

She unfastened her seatbelt and turned to him.

"I actually stopped by because I wanted to thank you for the present." She put her hand on the bracelet.

"You're welcome." He took her wrist and stroked it with his warm thumb. "It looks beautiful on your hand."

His touch made Amanda's heart beat much faster and she had to watch her breathing.

"And even if Hanna talked you into it," she continued, "it's nice to know . . ."

"No, it was my idea."

She blushed at this unexpected answer. It was dark in the car and she hoped he didn't notice. She looked down, afraid that her eyes would give her away, that he would see in them how happy his words made her.

"Thank you," she breathed out. "I like it very much."

"We hoped you would."

"And thank you for the ride." She opened the door. "Good night, Craig."

"Good night."

Amanda heard him wait until she'd walked into the house and closed the door behind her before driving away.

"Amanda, honey?" Her dad came out from the kitchen.

"Hi, Dad."

"I see somebody drove you home," he said, sounding worried.

"Yeah. That was Craig, Hanna's brother."

"Why? What happened, are you alright?"

"Dad, I'm fine. Everything is fine." She headed to the living room.

"Then where is your car?" He went after her.

"Oh, that?" Amanda smiled to herself. "The car is fine too." She dropped onto the couch. "I left it at Hanna's. She'll bring it back tomorrow before school." But her father still wore a question mark on his forehead, so she added, "I had champagne."

"And Craig?"

"He didn't, so he could drive me home."

"Very thoughtful of him." The question mark disappeared. "They're good friends."

"Yes, they are. Look at what I got from them." She held out her hand.

"It's beautiful." Her dad leaned down, took her hand, and looked at the bracelet closely. "And it seems to be handmade." He walked toward the cabinet and pulled out a small, light beige box. "I also have something for you." He handed it to Amanda.

The box contained a white gold necklace. A pendant in the outline of a big drop hung on the chain. At the bottom of the drop was a small flower. Tiny diamonds covered both.

"Oh, Dad, it's gorgeous." She hugged him tightly. "Thank you."

"Let's try it on." He took the necklace out of the box and put it around Amanda's neck.

She went to the hallway mirror.

"It's beautiful."

"I'm glad you like it." He walked up to her. "I was worried. I'm getting older, thought I'd lost my taste."

"You? Getting older? No, Dad. You are young and handsome, and you are the coolest dad ever."

"Okay, that's the alcohol speaking," he said, but a tender smile appeared on his face. He put his hand around Amanda's shoulders. "Let's go. I just made tea, and your cake is waiting for you." She took his waist, and they shuffled to the kitchen.

It had been a long day. Amanda lay down on her bed and closed her eyes. All she could think about was Craig. She remembered his touch, his smile, and his voice echoed in her mind. It probably didn't mean much. It was her birthday, and he was just trying to be nice. But still, he wasn't only worried about Hanna—he was worried about her, too. And when he drove her home, he didn't leave until he knew she was safe.

What had made him so worried? Why did Craig ask all those questions when they were already home safely? It seemed Craig and Hanna knew something Amanda didn't. And Hanna, she became so different, so serious and grown-up.

Amanda shook off those thoughts. She didn't want to think about it right now. She put one hand under her cheek and the other on the bracelet and fell asleep.

Chapter Five

CRAIG'S EYES followed Amanda as she left the car. The moment she entered the house and closed the door behind her, he gripped the wheel and drove home at full speed.

"Hanna!" he called from the hallway.

"I'm here."

Hanna's voice came from the living room. He found her curled up on the couch.

"Are you out of your mind?" he said furiously.

Hanna blinked.

"Craig, I know I should—"

But Craig went on.

"Two leeches prowling around you and you say you didn't want her to worry?"

"Craig, I'm sorry—"

"You should have dragged them into the car and left instantly! What were you thinking?"

"Listen," Hanna shouted back, "I can't act like that every time. They already look at me like I'm some freak."

"Your purpose here is to protect her. We are here to keep

her safe. Hanna, she turned eighteen tonight. This is it, this is the moment we've been waiting for."

"Craig, they're not going to hurt her. They need her, too," she said, her voice now calm.

"But they can take her away, and by the time we find them, it could be too late." He sat beside her. "And think what kind of danger we're putting Kimberly in every time. She can become an innocent victim."

"I know," Hanna sighed.

They sat in silence for a minute. Then Craig stood up and headed upstairs to his bedroom.

"Good night, Craig," said Hanna.

Craig looked at her.

"I crossed the line today. I was too nice to her. I shouldn't do that."

"You didn't do anything wrong. She's in love with you, I can see that."

"I can see it, too," he said. "But right now, she's just a girl who doesn't know anything. I want her to know first."

He stepped into his bedroom and walked to the open window without turning on the light. The sky was clear now, and only a pleasant smell of wet grass reminded of the past rain. He took off his leather jacket, threw it on the bed, and lay down.

He remembered Amanda's smile, her soft hand, and flushed silky cheeks. It was so difficult to keep cool, to hide his feelings when her warm brown eyes looked at him. He wanted to press her to his heart and bury his face in her long, brown hair. Imagining that, his chest filled with pain. The image reminded him of another, almost the same—he was pressing to his heart a young woman with long, brown curly hair. But that picture was from his distant past. The woman's name was Eleanor. She was dead. Craig, his face buried in her hair, was crying and screaming, because the pain of this loss was unbearable and probably would have killed him, had he been able to die.

∽

YEAR 1669

It was the year 1669. The mount Etna erupted in Sicily. The citizens of Catania didn't leave the town, truly believing that its defensive walls would protect them. A huge amount of ash, like black snow, covered streets and roofs. The destructive lava got closer and closer, demolishing everything in its path.

When the first houses started burning, the people, overcome with delayed panic, tried to run as far as possible. The luckiest ones, who had carriages and wagons, sped out of the city, leaving behind hundreds of others crying for help.

A young man was giving a hand to his mother and father to climb into a carriage when he saw an old woman with two little girls clutching her legs, standing on the small balcony of the burning house. He was the last passenger the carriage waited for. The coachman, who was barely holding his restless horses, yelled at him, *"Veloce! Veloce!"*

The young man put one foot on the step, hesitating. Then he looked at his mother and said, "I need to do something. Don't worry about me, I'll find a horse. I'll be right behind you." Stepping back, he yelled, "Go!" to the coachman. The moment he slammed the carriage door, the horses raced.

"Craig! No! Craig!" his mother cried.

"Come back!" called his father.

But Craig threw one last glance after the speeding carriage and ran to the burning house.

Saving the girls wasn't a problem. They were small, and the woman, holding them by the hands, hung them over the balcony and dropped them into Craig's arms.

The problem was the woman herself. Craig didn't speak

Italian, and he tried to gesture for her to drop down too. But the woman wasn't looking at Craig, with his hands up, ready to catch her. She was looking at the girls, telling them something, and desperately waving them away from her.

Craig didn't have much time. The whole house was on fire, the roof beginning to fall apart. He started to climb, clinging to hot protrusions which could crack at any second and let the flame out.

He reached the balcony and begged, "Please, Signora, please." She let him help her over the railing. When he lowered her down, he saw two men on horses riding toward them through the crowd. One of them jumped down from the horse and hurried the girls away from the house. The other man rode closer to the balcony and said something to the woman that made her finally let go of Craig's arm, which she had been clutching with both hands, and drop down onto the horse.

As the man led the horse away, Craig lifted his leg to climb over the balcony. In that moment, a heavy object hit him over the head. He fell down. Searing pain rushed through his body, and all sounds became distant. He smelled burning hair and fabric. He pushed himself up but was knocked over again, this time on his back. From the portico, he saw a blurry picture—burning pieces of the roof cascading on top of him.

The first thing Craig saw when he opened his eyes was a torch hanging from the low ceiling and swaying side to side. The room moved with it, and the muffled sound of waves lapping against the wooden wall left no doubts that he was on a ship. He sat up and looked at his hands, then at his chest, then carefully touched his face and hair.

The last thing he remembered before everything went dark in front of his eyes, was the burning logs collapsing over him and the pain that came along with them. But now there were no traces of burns, no pain at all. The white shirt he was wearing wasn't his—it was clean and undamaged. Somebody had saved him, and that somebody was probably the man on the horse, although Craig could not understand how. And even if that man had saved him, how did he cure him so fast? Was it fast? He didn't know how long he had been lying here.

He stood up and took a few steps. For somebody who had been lying unconscious, he felt surprisingly well—no numbness in the feet, no dizziness, not even the slightest headache.

He didn't just feel good. It was more than that. He felt a rush of energy in his body, felt his loud heartbeat. Question after question popped up in his head, and he needed to find somebody to answer them.

He went out on the deck. The sky was covered with clouds but even without the moonlight, he could clearly see the endless surface of the ocean. The sharp, cold wind didn't bother him. Craig had always been energetic and athletic, but it was nothing compared to what he felt right now. Every muscle in his body screamed for action. He wanted to run, jump, fight, and do it all at the same time. He took a deep breath of the cold, wet and salty air. An inexplicable sense of freedom and power filled him.

Craig saw three men standing beside the wheel on the other end of the three-mast ship.

"Welcome onboard the Destiny," spoke a calm, deep voice behind him.

Craig spun around.

"Thank you, sir."

"My name is Samson. I am the captain of this ship."

Even though the man was without his hat and wig, revealing his shoulder-length brown hair, Craig immediately recognized him. As he'd thought, it was the man on the horse, the one who'd helped him save the old woman. He wore a white shirt and a leather vest, tightly bound to his strong body.

"How do you feel?" asked Samson.

"Very well, sir." Craig smiled. "Too well for somebody who should be lying dead right now."

"Good to hear," said Samson. "Your English is very good. I assume that you are not Italian."

"No, sir, I am not. My name is Craig Kaylan. I am from Scotland," said Craig, then added, "You don't look Italian yourself, sir."

"I was born in England," said Samson. He looked at the three men beside the wheel. Two of them started toward Craig and Samson. "Not now," said the Captain.

At first, Craig thought he was talking to him, seeing as he spoke in the same low voice. But then he saw the two men on the other end of the ship stop and walk back.

"They heard you? How can they? It's sixty feet between us," he said in astonishment. The creaking of masts and the noise of the waves made Samson barely audible even to him.

"Let's go inside," said the captain, pointing to the door.

They stepped into the cabin.

"Sir, I am very grateful to you for saving my life," said Craig. He approached the table and stood behind one of the six tall chairs around it.

"I'm glad I succeeded." Samson sighed. "You were lying under burning wood and the house was about to collapse."

"It was very brave and noble of you. I hope you didn't harm yourself," Craig said.

"It's not that easy to harm me. Even then, I heal fast. It's you I was worried about. Half of your body was covered in burns. Your pulse was so weak you could have died at any moment. I needed to get you to the ship as quickly as possible."

Craig looked at his hands again and ran them through his hair.

"How long have I been here?"

"Two days."

"But, sir, that's impossible," said Craig.

His excitement increased. Samson, who could probably tell, waited patiently for the next question.

"Sir, you just said that it's not easy to harm you," said Craig. "What does that mean?"

Samson glanced at Craig, then walked to the chest of drawers. He took out a sheet of paper, rolled it, and lit it off the torch. As the fire grew, he put his hand around it and held it there until almost all of the paper had burned. He squeezed the rest and threw it away.

"Look," he said, extending his hand.

Craig leaned over and looked at the hand closely. It wasn't red, not even pink. It wasn't damaged at all.

"Is it an illusion?" he asked.

"Illusion?" Samson smiled, bemused, and cleared his throat. He walked back to the chest of drawers. This time he pulled out a big knife and handed it to Craig, "Does this knife look real to you?"

Craig took it. First, he tried to bend it, and then he tested the blade on his thumb.

"Yes, it is real," he said warily.

Samson took the knife. He put his hand on the table and stuck the knife through it.

Craig's stomach clenched. Only a few beads of blood spurted from the cut. When Samson pulled the knife out, it was red but the wound wasn't bleeding—it healed right in front of Craig's wide eyes, and in a few seconds, it was gone. Craig was stunned. He closed his mouth and swallowed.

"Who are you?" His brow furrowed. "Or, what are you?"

"I am human," said Samson folding his hands behind his back, "but I am different than others."

"How different?"

"As you saw, I can't be harmed. That means that my friends and I, we can't die. Besides that, we are also very strong and have powers."

"Powers," Craig repeated thoughtfully. "Is healing people one of them? How did you cure me?"

"No, I don't have healing powers." Samson bowed his head and began walking back and forth.

"Sir?" called Craig.

Samson stopped.

"There was only one way to save you," he said, looking straight into Craig's eyes. "I made you one of us."

Craig's mouth went dry. His next words came out as a whisper.

"What did you do to me?"

"I am sorry that I didn't give you a choice before I turned you."

"Turned me? What did you do to me? How did you do it?"

Craig looked at Samson, suddenly remembering the legends about the powerful and immortal vampires who looked human. How people tried to hunt the creatures, but they were too fast and too strong, and the hunters ended up dead. According to legend, to turn somebody into their kind, the vampire had to first drink the victim's blood and then feed the victim the vampire's blood. Most of the victims had bite marks on their necks. Craig's hand flew up to his neck, inspecting his artery.

"You are not a vampire," said Samson.

Craig realized that even if he had been bitten, the trace would have been gone by now, same as the rest of his wounds.

"Vampires don't have a heartbeat. Put your hand on your chest."

But Craig didn't need to. His heart was beating so loudly that the sound plugged his ears.

"Then what am I?" he asked angrily.

"Vampires are monsters," said a soft voice behind him.

Craig turned around and saw a young woman ascending the same stairs that had led him to this room. She was in her night robe, her gorgeous black hair flowing down her shoulders.

"Yes, we have powers and we are immortal," the woman continued, "but we are humans, and our purpose is to hunt down those monsters and destroy them. We are Hunters. There is a lot more out there than just vampires. There are also werewolves, demons, and other beasts." She looked at Samson. "How am I doing for my first time, my love?"

"Remarkable." Samson smiled.

"I thought you might need some support." She walked to him and leaned back on his chest. She was almost as tall as Samson, her head coming up to his cheekbones.

"Definitely. You see, my charm doesn't work on him the way it works on you." He hugged her and kissed her hair. Then he looked at Craig. "This is my wife, Gabriella. She became one of us only fifteen years ago, and you are the first transformation she's witnessed."

"Fifteen years ago," repeated Craig. He looked at her, trying to guess her age. "How often do you . . . do it?" he asked.

"It happens very rarely. It's not easy. I can't simply bring anybody," said Samson, letting go of Gabriella.

"Does it mean that you turned me not because I was dying, but because you chose me?" asked Craig.

"Yes. I couldn't let you die. We need people like you."

"People like me? What's so special about me?"

"Your question only proves that I made the right choice," said Samson. "You are a very brave man. You sacrificed your young life to save an old woman. It doesn't happen every day, and we are not always around when it does."

"Then I should consider myself lucky," said Craig bitterly. "How rare is it? I mean, how many are you?"

"With you, we are now six. The last one before Gabriella, I turned eighty years ago."

Craig stared at him. "How old are you?"

"I am twenty-nine."

Craig narrowed his eyes.

"And I've been twenty-nine for the last four hundred and fifty years," added Samson.

Craig looked at Samson's forehead, then his eyes slid down to Samson's neck and hands before they froze on the knife still lying on the table.

"This can't be true," he whispered.

"I know you're confused," said Samson, stepping forward. "But you'll be all right. You just need time."

"Excuse me, but right now I need some air," said Craig, and he stepped outside.

His excitement was gone. Half an hour ago he was happy to be alive, but now he doubted it was true. All he had seen and heard in that room couldn't be real.

And what if it was happening, if it was real? Wasn't it a better option than lying dead under a pile of ashes?

Then why did he feel like this? Craig closed his eyes and turned his face against the wind.

The door behind him opened, and Gabriella walked out to stand beside him.

"Listen, I just wanted to say that if you need help to understand things, we are here for you. We will help you through this difficult time," she said gently.

Craig looked at the three men at the other end of the ship.

"Can they hear us now?" he asked.

"No. We can only hear Samson, and only when he wants us to. Not too far, a couple of miles or so."

"A couple of miles?" Craig's brows raised in disbelief.

"Yes. And he can hear us, too."

"Why did Samson turn you? What were you dying from?" He stepped back and sat on the small stairs.

"I wasn't dying," said Gabriella, and sat beside him. "I became one of them at will."

"You chose this?" Craig looked at her in bewilderment.

"Yes," she said, and he saw a glint of happiness in her black eyes. "Samson and I, we fell in love, and I wanted to be with him forever. I was nineteen. Samson told me that I was young, that I didn't know what I was asking for. He explained to me that I would never age. I'd never have children and a proper family. I insisted, but he said that I needed more time to think about it. He turned me when I was twenty-three."

Craig sighed. He was twenty-three too, and he would never grow older.

"Did you ever regret it?" he asked.

"Not even a minute. Our life is full of adventures, and I have the opportunity to experience them with someone I love more than anything in this world. Of course, it's not easy to defeat the monsters. They are strong as well, and they can hurt us. But we heal fast. Not as fast as Samson and Fray, but fast."

"Why, what is the difference?"

"They are the First Ones; they were turned by Higher Powers," said Gabriella. She stood up. "The sun is rising. I need to change and give orders for breakfast. We were up all night, and everybody is dying of hunger."

"Wait, just one more question." Craig stood up, too. "Does that mean there's no way to die at all?" As Craig asked this, he realized how much the question bothered him.

"There's always a way, even for the immortal," said Gabriella.

Craig found it strange, but he felt relieved.

He returned to the cabin and joined Samson in front of the window. They stood in silence for a few minutes, watching how the crests of the now-calm waves sparkled in the rising sun. Its majestic ascent announced the beginning of a new day of a new life.

"Where are we going?" Craig asked in a low voice.

"Home."

"Where is that?" Craig's eyes squinted, looking far into the ocean.

"In America." Samson sighed, probably predicting the next question.

"What about my family?"

"Your mother and father will receive a letter, informing them that their son died a hero, saving people's lives."

Craig lowered his head and closed his eyes.

"I am sorry," said Samson.

Craig nodded, then turned around and went back to his room.

Chapter Six

TODAY

WHEN CRAIG WOKE up in the morning, he realized he'd fallen asleep with his clothes on. He took a quick shower, put on his jeans and a fresh shirt, and went downstairs. From the kitchen window, he saw that Amanda's car hadn't moved, which meant Hanna was still at home. He turned on the coffee machine, grabbed his cellphone, and dialed a number.

"Samson, hi."

"Hello, Craig. Any news?"

"Yes. They're here. They're watching her."

"You'll need help. I'll send Ruben. Be careful, they're not stupid. They know who you are, and they know that you're near helpless right now."

"Samson," said Craig quietly, "people are going to die."

"I know," sighed Samson. "But if we succeed, we will finally be able to help them. Did you find the place?"

"I'm working on it, but there's not much to go on. All Melinda said was that it's an abandoned house in the middle of nowhere."

"Let me know if you find something."

"I will," said Craig, and he hung up.

"Was that Samson?" Hanna appeared in the kitchen doorway.

"Yes. He's sending Ruben."

"That's good." Hanna slung her bag on a chair and sat at the table.

Craig poured the coffee into two cups and handed one to Hanna.

"I don't get how they knew we'd be at the lake," said Hanna, sipping her coffee. "They got there before us. How did they know?"

Craig leaned on the countertop.

"That's my question," he said, looking at Hanna's puzzled face. "Did you tell anybody where the three of you were going?"

"No. We wanted it to be a surprise for Amanda, and, since she's been with us the whole time, we didn't speak about it at all. We only told her yesterday in the parking lot. Nobody was around."

"And before that? When you and Kimberly were planning the surprise, where did you do it?"

"At school. Kimberly dragged me into the bathroom and said she had this idea... The bathroom was empty."

Craig heard a note of doubt in Hanna's voice.

"Are you sure it was empty?"

"Craig, they're vampires. They were wearing long hooded leather jackets at the lake and stood in the shade. How would they get into a school bathroom in the daytime?"

"Before sunrise," said Craig. He drank from his cup and moved to sit across from her.

"I'll check the school basement. If they were spending the night—or daytime—at school, it's the best place to hide," said Hanna.

"And I'll check the most suspicious places around Amanda's house. We need to find them. We have to know how many there are, who they're talking to. They'll try to blend in, make some connections with people around you, to make them their eyes and ears in the daytime. Did Amanda tell you anything about her dream?"

"No." Hanna shook her head.

"I need to know more about the house."

"Okay. I'll try to pry out some details."

She stood up.

"Hanna, be careful. I know there's not much you can do right now, since you can't fight them. But, if something happens—make a scene, attract people's attention."

"Don't worry, I'll be able to protect her. I still remember some tricks, and I always have this." She took out of her bag a custom-made gun. It had five barrels with wooden spikes inside them.

∾

ON HER WAY to Amanda's, Hanna tried to find a non-suspicious way to ask her about her dream. Maybe she could pretend she'd had a nightmare herself.

She smiled when she saw Amanda standing on the sidewalk, an apple in her hand.

"How did you sleep? Were your dreams healthy?" asked Hanna as Amanda slid into the car.

"Oh, yes. Nothing like yesterday."

"Yesterday?" said Hanna, pretending to be surprised.

"Didn't I tell you? I had this horrible nightmare," and Amanda told her about her dream in every detail.

As soon as they arrived at school, Hanna began looking for an opportunity to sneak away and check the basement. The right time came during the lunch break when they went to the school cafeteria. Kimberly was talking to Nicole Price, who shared a few classes with the three of them, while Amanda was cornered by Alec on her way to the vending machine. He started going on about his photography website. As much as Hanna disliked Alec, right now she appreciated him keeping Amanda busy.

Hanna passed the lockers and turned into the empty corridor. Assured that nobody was watching her, she opened the basement door. As she stepped in, she pulled out her gun. Moving slowly, she tried to listen for voices, but the muffled humming of pipes running along the ceiling distracted her.

Carefully shifting her feet, she reached the next half-open door. Hanna held her breath and looked into the gap. The basement was filled up with school inventory. Not far from the doorway was a tall stack of chairs. She slipped in behind it and peeked around. Convinced that there was nobody inside, she lowered her gun and took a deep breath.

She decided to check the place for clues. A table with three chairs caught her attention. As she came around the desk loaded with books, she stumbled on something and flew forward. Before her chin could hit the corner of the big wooden box in front of her, she stopped herself with her hands. Straightening up, Hanna glanced back.

She had stumbled over the legs of the janitor, Mr. Sullivan, lying in front of the desk. Hanna's eyes stopped on the bloodstains on the collar of his shirt.

"Oh, no," she whispered and crashed next to him. "Mr. Sullivan." She shook him by the shoulder. "Mr. Sullivan," she called again. When she leaned closer and turned his head, she saw two small holes on his neck. Then she looked at his hands and found a pair of holes on each of his wrists.

In her three hundred and thirty years, Hanna had witnessed a lot of pain, starting with her childhood. But she had almost forgotten how it felt to find a dead body, to be too late to save a life.

∽

IN 1693, when Hanna was eight years old, a troll attacked the small Norwegian village in which she lived with her mother, father, and two older brothers. There were only seven houses in the forest clearing, and most of the residents were women and children. The elder ones fought back, trying to protect their children, to give them time to run away.

But Hanna's brothers didn't want to run. They stayed to help their parents fight. Hanna, hiding behind the trees, half-buried in the snow, watched as the giant monster killed her family one by one. When everybody was dead, the troll, crushing roofs and windows, headed to the woods.

When he was far enough away, Hanna came out from her hiding place. She stood in the middle of the clearing, surrounded by the bodies. She found her mother and sat beside her, holding her hand and crying silently.

She didn't know how long she had been sitting before three men on horses galloped into the village. The strangers stopped their horses and jumped off. Blood was everywhere. It looked like a flame on the white snow, sparkling under the rays of the rising sun. Their faces darkened as they looked around, and they spoke angrily in a language Hanna didn't understand.

It was Craig who saw her first. He said something to Samson, who walked to her, got down on one knee, and took her ice-cold hands in his. Hanna saw sorrow in his eyes. Still holding her hands, he got up, and she stood up, too. He spoke, but she didn't understand. Then he pointed, first toward the houses, then toward her, and said "hus." She looked at her house and what remained of the roof, and the two of them went inside.

Samson took a blanket from the bed, covered her small, frozen body, and spoke to her. Hanna asked him to repeat those words to her a couple of years later when she had learned English. What he'd said was they'd come from a distant country and it had been a long journey. He was very sorry they arrived too late to save her family.

They had to leave to kill the troll. But before they left, Samson gestured for her to stay in the house and wait for them, that they would come back for her.

They did, and they took her with them.

They arrived at a wharf and climbed on the deck of a big ship, where a beautiful woman with black hair and a fine gown waited for them. When she bent down to Hanna, she smiled a bright and welcoming smile. Little Hanna couldn't understand why her eyes were full of tears.

After months of travel, their ship moored at an empty shore. As they stepped onto it, Samson touched the air and said a few words. Right before Hanna's blinking eyes, an arch appeared. With her mouth open, she looked up at Samson, who beamed back at her, took her hand, and walked through it.

What she saw before her was beyond her childish imagination. Between two hills stood a castle with a tower. Green bushes and colorful flowers surrounded it. A fountain and statues decorated the large front yard. When they reached the entrance, she saw a carved symbol on each side of the massive brown front door—a circle with a star in it.

Hanna thought that she was in a fairy tale, which became even more vivid when she stepped inside. Fascinated, she took in the sight of the marble floors and high ceilings, large, foreign plants in pots and statues, the furniture with carved legs and golden handles, the silver candelabra, and a heavy iron chandelier.

The black-haired woman with the beautiful name—Gabriella—whom Hanna liked very much—walked her through the second floor. It had dark wooden walls and carpets. Gabriella opened one of several doors in the corridor and showed Hanna her room.

The castle became her home. She was surrounded by love and care.

Everybody brought her presents, and very soon, her room was filled up with toys and books. Gabriella became like a mother to her. She brushed her hair, dressed Hanna like a doll, read her books, and taught her English. Samson taught her to ride a horse, and they often went riding together. To the rest of the family, she was their sweet little sister.

Hanna liked to spend her evenings in the library. She found it to be the most magical place in the castle. The large room had a wide fireplace with sculptures of eagles on each side, a long, massive table, and a big globe mounted on a round, wooden stand. It had only one tall, arched window. The rest of the walls were topped with shelves full of books. She could spend hours curled up in a big soft armchair, reading.

She loved to hear the stories when the whole family gathered around the fireplace after a hunt. Hanna always begged Samson to give her the powers. She wanted to become one of them, to be part of the mission. She never forgot that one of those monsters had killed her family, and she didn't want such a thing to happen to anybody else.

The years passed, Hanna grew up, and on her eighteenth birthday, Samson made her wish come true.

∽

HANNA WAS A HUNTER, and she never forgot it. But it had been a long time since she'd killed her last vampire, since she had seen somebody killed by one. The past three years in Green Hill, she'd lived like an ordinary girl who went to High School and had girlfriends, and she'd gotten used to that life.

But now the vampires were here. They'd come after her best friend, and this body on the floor was her wake-up call.

Hanna staggered to the bathroom, washed the blood from her palm, and returned to the cafeteria. It was almost empty, but Amanda and Kimberly were still there. They had already eaten and sat at the empty table, waiting for her. Without taking any food, Hanna approached them, dropped her bag on the table, and sat on a vacant chair.

"Where have you been? Is everything all right?" asked Amanda with a grin on her face. "You look like you just met my not-boyfriend Alec."

"Let's go," said Hanna sternly and stood up.

The girls didn't move.

"You didn't eat anything," said Kimberly, "Aren't you hungry?"

"No."

"Hanna, what happened?" Amanda asked, seriously this time.

Hanna sat down again.

"Nothing happened. I just don't feel very well." She pressed her hand to her stomach.

"Then maybe you should go home and lie down."

"Actually, you know what, maybe I'll skip biology. I'll eat something, and then I'll go to the library. Meet me there after classes. Just tell Ms. Finch that I have a bad stomach ache and I'm in the bathroom. Okay?"

"Okay," said Amanda.

After they left, Hanna waited until the bell rang before grabbing her bag and running toward the parking lot.

∽

ON THEIR WAY out of the cafeteria, Kimberly, looking at Amanda sideways, whispered, "I bet she was exploring again."

When they arrived at the classroom, Mrs. Finch wasn't there yet. Amanda and Kimberly decided to wait for her beside the door, not wanting to tell her about Hanna's stomach problems in front of the whole class. When Ms. Finch came over and they told her that Hanna was in the bathroom, she forced a smile.

"Are you sure about that?" she asked. "Because I just saw her starting her car."

"But she said . . ." Kimberly blushed with anger.

"Guess the school's bathroom wasn't good enough for her," said Ms. Finch.

On the way to their seats, Kimberly threw a look at Amanda, which translated as "I told you so!"

∾

ONLY WHEN HANNA had started the engine did she see Ms. Finch crossing the parking lot a few steps away from her car. Positive that she had been spotted, she hesitated. It meant that Amanda and Kimberly would soon learn of her lie. But she was too overwhelmed, and she needed to see Craig and tell him everything. To sit two hours in biology and pretend that nothing had happened would be torture. She took off.

Hanna could live with the fact that her friends thought she was a freak, and the way things were going would only reinforce that opinion. What she couldn't afford was losing their trust. She couldn't tell them the truth, and that left her with one option: to come up with a new plausible lie.

Hanna parked the car and released a sigh of relief when she saw Craig's Jeep in the garage. She walked through the front door and spotted Craig, already hurrying toward her.

"Hanna, what's wrong? You drove like crazy."

"Did I? Sorry, I was in a rush. I need to tell you something."

"Where did you leave Amanda?"

"Don't worry, she's in class. I'll be back before it ends."

She went to the living room and dropped on the couch.

"What did you want to tell me?" Craig asked, following her.

"I checked the basement."

"And?"

"And I found a body. It was our janitor, Mr. Sullivan."

Craig gritted his teeth. He put his hands in his pockets and began pacing in front of her.

"Did you check—" he started his question, but Hanna interrupted.

"Of course I did. He was bitten in three places—on the neck and on the wrists."

"Did you tell anybody?"

"No. But I left blood marks on the door and the handle. I figure the other janitor will notice and they'll find him faster."

Craig stopped.

"You didn't leave any fingerprints, did you?"

"No. I used my palm." Hanna nervously pushed her hair behind her ears. "Do you think they'll come back?"

"No. I think they already found a new place. If they had wanted to come back, they wouldn't have left the body."

"That's good," sighed Hanna. "Craig, I know I said that I can protect Amanda, and I'll do everything possible to keep her safe, but I don't think I can stand against the three of them by myself."

"Three? How do you know there's three of them?"

"Because they set up a desk and three chairs."

"Hmm." Craig sat beside Hanna. "And you don't think it could be the students who did that?"

"No. Mr. Sullivan checked the basement regularly to make sure that nobody smoked there. And, hello, three bites."

"Well, now we know there are three of them."

"For the time being."

"I looked around Amanda's house but didn't find anything."

"I smell coffee," said Hanna unexpectedly.

They moved to the kitchen. The big map was once again unfolded on the table. This time the red marks were placed along the big and small roads outside of town. Hanna poured herself a cup of coffee and sat at the table, in front of the open laptop placed on top of the map. Google Map showed a house beside a field.

"You're looking in the wrong places," said Hanna, taking a sip from her coffee. "You were right before. Go back to where you started."

"The forest?" asked Craig.

"Yes. It's a two-story house, surrounded by woods. She didn't see any gate or road. But it has a fountain. Maybe that will help you make it out." Hanna took another sip and stood up.

"Thank you, it will," said Craig, "At least now I know what I'm looking for."

"Craig, I still don't understand. You're looking for a house she saw in a dream." She spread her hands. "Why?"

"We'll talk about it later."

"Yeah, I've got to go anyway."

Craig walked her to the door.

"And, Hanna," he said softly, "You are not alone. I can't revolve around the school much. It'll look weird. But Ruben is coming tonight, he'll help you. Kimberly, she doesn't have a boyfriend, does she?"

Hanna saw a gamesome smile on his face.

"Why? You don't want them—"

"Why not? He is young and—"

"He is a hundred years older than you."

"You know what I mean. It will give him a reason to hang

around the school when we need him and, at the same time, he will watch after her. Being your friend is putting Kimberly in big danger."

"What if she falls in love with him? He's a handsome guy. His black eyes and his black curly hair, and he's funny—girls love that."

"We'll tell him to hold his horses. Go." Craig smiled.

Hanna parked the car at the school parking lot. Nothing had changed during her absence, and it bothered her. Of course, she could go to the principal herself and tell him that she saw something on the basement door that looked like blood. But, by doing so, she could draw too much attention to herself. The police taking her to the station for questioning was not an option; she couldn't leave Amanda unprotected for that long.

There wasn't a single cloud in the sky, and Hanna thought it'd be much safer to take Amanda and Kimberly out of the school building, which now seemed so unwelcoming and dangerous to her. That's why she chose to not go to the library.

Avoiding running into Ms. Finch, she went to the end of the hallway. Her hands crossed over her chest, she leaned against the wall behind the big potted lemon tree.

Hanna hadn't been able to come up with a new lie like she planned, so she decided to tell Amanda and Kimberly as much of the truth as possible. They were going to find out that Mr. Sullivan was dead anyway. She'd tell them she found him. If they asked her any questions, she'd improvise.

The bell rang, and Amanda and Kimberly came out of the classroom.

"I didn't lie to you," Hanna said, cutting their incredulous looks. "I really was feeling ill. But it wasn't because of my stomach. Well, my stomach did hurt, but it wasn't because . . ." Seeing the confused looks on their faces, she said, "Let's go outside and I'll explain it to you."

Wading between the students and their backpacks down the cramped front stairs, they came out to the schoolyard.

"I was taking the biology notes to my locker," started Hanna as soon as they sat on the grass, "when I saw red marks on the floor. They looked like blood. I followed the marks—"

"You don't say," chuckled Kimberly.

"Kimberly, believe me, this is not funny," said Hanna angrily.

"Kimberly, wait," said Amanda. "Then?" she asked, staring at Hanna.

"I followed those marks, and they led me to the basement. I went downstairs and found Mr. Sullivan . . ." She paused only for a second, and Kimberly seized the moment.

"That's something we've never seen before."

"Kimberly, shut up!" Amanda said exasperated, then turned back to Hanna. "And?"

"And he was dead, lying on the floor all covered with blood."

"What?" Kimberly's face became serious in a second. "How?"

"What how? I don't know how," lied Hanna. "I got scared and ran away."

"Did you tell the principal or any of the professors?"

Now came the improvisation part.

"No. What if they think that it's me, that I did something to him?"

"What? No, they're not that stupid," said Kimberly, sounding supportive, to Hanna's surprise. "You would never hurt anyone."

"You're just a girl," added Amanda. "Mr. Sullivan is . . . was . . . a strong man. You couldn't hurt him even if you wanted to."

Hanna felt guilty again because that was a lie as well. She wasn't just a girl, and they had no idea what she was capable of. That she had killed things in her life much stronger than Mr. Sullivan. But in one thing they were absolutely right—she would never kill a human.

"No, wait," said Amanda suddenly. "What if he was shot?"

"See, that's what I'm saying. I don't know how he died." Hanna sighed. "They'll find him sooner or later, though it's horrible to think that he is lying there dead and nobody knows about it."

"That's why you left? You couldn't stay at school knowing he's there?" asked Kimberly.

"Yes." Hanna nodded. "There wasn't time to tell you, the class was starting, and I drove home, to Craig."

Hanna noticed that at these words, Amanda's look softened.

"I understand," said Amanda.

Chapter Seven

YEAR 1669

CRAIG RETURNED to the room where, just a little while ago, he had woken up happy that he was alive. But now that happiness was long gone. He sat on the pallet with his head down, thinking about his family, which he could never see again. He imagined the moment when his father would read the letter to his mother, brother, and two little sisters, and his heart throbbed with pain.

But he was alive, and he was here, on this ship, among people he'd never met before. And he wasn't even sure if they were people, if they were human beings. But whatever they were, he didn't think they were evil. Samson and Gabriella seemed nice. And now that he was one of them, he didn't feel any different, he didn't feel evil. He was the same Craig, except for the blood boiling in his veins, the rush of energy, and muscles that grew and stretched with every minute.

He paced the room, trying to put himself together. They would call him to breakfast soon, and he had to be ready to meet the rest of them. Samson said he couldn't just turn anybody, which meant they were normal people, once chosen like Craig himself.

The proof came a few minutes later. Somebody knocked.

"Come in," said Craig, folding his hands behind his back.

The door opened, and a young face, framed in black curly hair, looked out from behind it.

"Hello," the face said.

"Hello," said Craig.

The young man stepped inside.

"I'm Ruben."

"My name is—"

"Craig. I know, I already asked," said Ruben, beaming. His black eyes were full of excitement, and Craig could not help but smile, looking at his happy face.

"It is very nice to meet you," he said.

"It's nice to meet you, too," said Ruben, stepping closer. "I waited the whole night for your awakening, we all did."

"Thank you," said Craig.

He wondered what Ruben's story was, how did he become a Hunter.

"Samson was very worried about how you would take it," said Ruben. His smile shrank, and he shifted from foot to foot. "You were unconscious, and he never got the chance to ask you for permission. I hope you're all right."

"I think I'll be fine." Craig looked down.

"Ruben!" Gabriella called from upstairs.

"Coming!" Ruben yelled, sticking his head out the door. Then he looked back at Craig. "Breakfast is ready. We better go before the potatoes get cold, or she'll bite my head off." He made it just one step before turning back again. "That was a joke."

"I hope so," said Craig, then asked, "What are potatoes?"

"Oh, that's her new discovery, and now she makes us eat them at least once a day."

The table was set up according to rules of etiquette, except it didn't look like breakfast. In Scotland, for breakfast they usually had porridge, cheese, eggs, jam, and buns with tea. This table had everything on it—chicken, fish, cold meat, cheese, vegetables, fruits, and something light yellow, shaped like an egg. Potatoes? Judging by the steam coming from them, Ruben's head was safe.

Gabriella was now wearing a satin gown, and her hair was neatly gathered. She politely invited everybody to sit, and when they took their places, two chairs remained empty.

"Breakfast is ready," said Samson, taking a piece of meat.

Craig realized he was talking to the men beside the wheel on the other end of the ship. When two seconds later one of them entered the room, Craig's wide-open eyes moved from one to another and stopped on Samson.

"You can do it, too. Move fast. You just don't know how, yet," said Samson.

The man, who seemed only a few years older than Craig, walked to the table and looked at him.

"My name is Riley," the man said.

Craig stood up.

"I'm Craig. Craig Kaylan."

They both sat down. Riley took the place beside Gabriella, opposite to Craig.

"How do you feel?" Riley asked.

Craig paused. "I don't know yet."

"Is he in shock?" asked Riley, turning to look at Samson.

"He's doing fine," said Samson.

"How did you feel when you woke up surrounded by strangers who told you that you are immortal, that monsters are real and you have to kill them?" asked Craig with a little edge to his voice.

Riley looked very confident, his tall muscular body reflecting power. It was very difficult to imagine that something could put him in shock.

"I knew that monsters were real. I wanted to fight them,

and receiving power and immortality was a priceless gift," said Riley.

"Let's eat, the potatoes are getting cold," said Gabriella, and everybody reached for food.

"Fray and I met Riley in 1456 in the forests of Ireland," said Samson, cutting the meat. "He was tracking down a werewolf, but he didn't know there was more than one. There were three of them, and he was lucky we were tracking them, too.

"We'd never met anybody like Riley before, somebody who not only believed that monsters exist but who would go against them all alone. He didn't have powers, not even proper equipment to protect himself. All he had was a silver knife, which was indeed the right weapon against werewolves. When I looked at Fray—you'll meet him later—I knew that we were thinking the same thing, that we could trust him, that we could make him one of us. We made him the offer, and he took it willingly. He said that he had heard stories about us that we were just a legend, but he always believed we existed. He was the first one we turned."

"I realize it could be difficult for you, and I didn't mean to . . ." Riley shrugged. "I was concerned if you were all right."

"Thank you," said Craig.

"I didn't know anything about monsters before they told me," said Ruben, adding a chicken leg to his plate.

"Ruben is from Cilicia. He was seventeen when I turned him. It happened eighty years ago," said Samson.

"Eighty-two," corrected Ruben.

"You are still a little boy," said Gabriella teasingly.

"I am not a boy," said Ruben, pulling his black eyebrows together. "I am sixty-one years older than you."

"Ruben was on a cliff, trying to save his falling horse," continued Samson. "We saw him from the hill and hurried to help. But by the time we reached the cliff, he wasn't there; he had already fallen. His legs and spine were broken, blood was running from his head, but he still had a pulse. Were his actions heroic? No, they were stupid. But he was young and daring. I decided to give him a chance and have never been sorry. He is a very good Hunter."

Ruben raised his eyebrow, looked at Gabriella, and loudly cleared his throat. Everybody smiled.

Finished, Riley stood up.

"I'll replace Fray," he said.

The door closed behind him, and it took only seconds for Fray to enter the room. He walked right to Craig and extended his hand.

"My name's Fray."

Craig stood up and took his hand. Noticing that nobody was saying his last name except him, he said, "I'm Craig."

Fray looked to be the same age as Samson. His blue velvet waistcoat was unbuttoned, and Craig stopped his eyes on the big dagger hanging under a wide belt. He couldn't see the dagger itself, only the sheath, which looked interesting. It was dark brown covered by golden text. Craig could see it clearly but couldn't read it. The letters were unfamiliar to him, mostly looking like symbols.

"There is no need to wear that on the ship," said Samson, catching Craig's look.

"I always have it on me, you know that," said Fray in a deep voice and then took his place at the other head of the table.

"Nobody is going to attack you here, it's just us," said Gabriella.

"How do you know?" Looking at Gabriella, Fray pointed his hand at Craig. "He just got his powers. Who knows what he's capable of?"

"Who? Me?" said Craig, glancing from one to another. He remembered Gabriella telling him that Fray and Samson were the First Ones, and it didn't matter how strong Craig was now,

Fray was experienced and definitely much stronger. He smiled. "I hope you'll help me find out."

"First lesson in two hours," said Fray.

Fray was waiting for Craig on the dock with his feet shoulder-width apart and his arms crossed.

"Are you ready to discover your new self?"

"Yes," said Craig, thinking it would be good to do something, to distract himself from the heavy thoughts of his family, of his ostensible death which disconnected him from his previous life with no chance to look back.

"You'll like it," Ruben's voice said behind him.

Craig stepped closer to Fray.

"Tell me what is going on with your body. What do you feel right now?" asked Fray.

"I can feel my blood," said Craig, musing. "It's warm. I feel it running through my veins."

"That is temporary. Soon you won't notice that."

"I can see and hear much better. I also feel my muscles. I don't seem to have changed much outwardly, but my muscles are stretching. I feel them getting harder and stronger every minute."

"Those two days, you were unconscious because your blood was changing. That process is finished, but the transformation of your body is still in progress. That will take a little longer. You have to start training because you have to know how to use your strength when you need it and how to master that power in regular life. Hit me." Fray unfolded his arms.

It's not that Craig hadn't expected it. He knew what Fray had meant when he said he would train him, but he didn't feel comfortable doing it with everybody watching them. He lifted his hand and hit Fray in the shoulder. Fray swayed and took a step back, which actually surprised Craig since he'd put no effort into that blow.

"I didn't say pat me, I said hit me," said Fray, "Haven't you ever fought before?"

"I have, but not without reason."

"Aha." Fray thought for a second. "Stand here." He pointed at the shipboard. "And look there." He pointed to the opposite shipboard. "Jump from here to there. Jump as far as you can."

Ruben chuckled.

"Silence," yelled Fray.

Craig looked at Ruben, then at the rest of them. Everybody was smiling. He felt confused. The distance between the two shipboards was around twenty feet. He didn't know how far he could get. Not fully transformed yet, he figured he would have to try harder to make it more than halfway.

Craig took a step, then pushed off with all his might and jumped. His body came off of the deck and flew with a speed he hadn't expected. He twirled his arms and legs in the air, trying to stop himself, but it didn't help. He plopped into the cold water a few feet away from the ship.

When Craig came up to the surface, he saw all of them looking down at him and laughing. They threw him a rope ladder, and he climbed up to the deck.

"Now you have a reason." Fray smiled at him. "Go change. We'll continue later."

"Ruben, give Craig dry clothes," said Gabriella.

Craig went downstairs into his room.

A few minutes later Ruben came and handed him the clothes.

"He's done that to all of us," he said, still smiling. "You're lucky it was just water. When he did it to me, I ended up with my face in manure."

"Is there anything else I should be aware of?" asked Craig, taking his shirt off.

"Oh, yes, his fists. You have to hit him. He will make you

do it anyway. You already have enough power to make him fly across the deck. Use it. Of course, he'll hit back, but he'll also teach you to protect yourself."

"Why did you do it, Ruben?" asked Craig suddenly.

"Do what?" Ruben didn't understand.

"Kill yourself. You knew that you could die trying to save your horse, but you didn't let him go. Why?"

"Because I was a cavalryman," said Ruben calmly, now sounding much older. "My horse was my friend."

Yes, they were people, just like him. They had been chosen because of what they had done, because of choices they had made, and he, Craig, had to accept the fact that he was one of them now.

"You're a good man, Ruben."

"You're a good man, too. You saved three lives."

Yes, he had. He just hoped his family would understand that he did what he had to do and would forgive him.

"Is Samson going to train me as well?" asked Craig, changing the subject.

"We'll all help, but mostly it will be Fray. You see . . . these long trips by ship . . . Fray doesn't like them. We all like our fight-free time when we can finally relax, but he gets bored. He wants to train you himself. It will keep him busy."

"Can't wait to get busy myself."

Craig was overwhelmed by what had just happened to him. The jump he had made was amazing, almost a flight. He couldn't wait to find out what else could he do? What other skills did he have? He looked forward to the next training session.

One evening about three weeks later, when Craig was going to bed, Samson stopped him.

"I'm very delighted to see how quickly you learn," he said. "Do you enjoy your lessons?"

"Thank you, sir. I like them, and I want to learn more. I want to be ready when I meet my first monster."

"Glad to hear that." After a short pause, Samson asked, "How are you doing, Craig, how do you feel? Is it getting any better?"

"It's easier in the daytime," said Craig quietly. "But at night, when I think about my family . . . It's not because I'm dead to them. People die. It's just that when they do, they don't feel the pain they've caused their loved ones, and they don't miss them."

"There's nothing I can say to make your pain go away. Only time can do that. I know; I've been through it myself." Samson pointed to a chair, inviting Craig to sit. "Fray and I were friends. We were in Egypt, crossing the desert, and we got lost. After three days without water, we couldn't move anymore. We were dying.

I woke up first and saw Fray lying on the ground a few feet away. Then a man appeared out of nowhere and told me he had saved us. He said that I was chosen for a very important mission. He told me what I needed to know, gave me, among other things, a book, and teleported the still-transforming Fray and me to a castle. He said that the castle was invisible to anybody else, and only we could see and enter it. He also said that we could live in it, that it was ours now. And then, after putting this great responsibility on my shoulders, the man disappeared.

"You see this mark?" Samson pushed the sleeve up to the elbow on his left arm, showing the mark to Craig. It looked like Fray's dagger. "Fray has it too. It appeared on our arms after the transition as a sign of the First Ones.

"When Fray woke up, I told him what had happened. We were as lost and confused as you are now.

"I, like you, had millions of questions, but there was nobody around whom I could ask.

"We were in the middle of nowhere. As the man had said, it was a good place where we could hide from the rest of the world and keep our existence secret, to stay a legend. Later, we came across the Pueblo people, who tried to kill us in every possible way. We let them try everything, and when they didn't succeed, we became their gods.

"We learned from the book I received from the man all we could about our powers and mission, then chose the ten strongest Pueblo men and sailed our ship to England. I visited my hometown and watched my family from a distance. It was so painful that I never came back during their lifetime."

Craig who listened carefully took a deep breath. He had wondered what Samson's story was, but never dared to ask.

"The man said you're the chosen one. What did he say about Fray?" asked Craig.

"He said that it's up to me to decide, that I could keep him if I trusted him, or he could stop Fray's transformation. And I kept him, which wasn't as easy a decision to make as it seems. I didn't know what his reaction would be, if he would want it. But thankfully, he never complained."

They sat in silence for a moment.

"I think it's time to show you something," said Samson. "Remember you asked me how did I turn you?" He stood up, took the torch from the table, and said, "Come with me."

They walked to the dark corner beside the stairs and stopped in front of a big mahogany chest. A golden lion rested above the keyhole as if guarding the chest. On the lid was a golden circle with a five-pointed star in it.

Samson opened the chest, and Craig saw a big open book. It didn't look like any other book. It wasn't printed, but handwritten in burgundy ink. The cover of the book, sticking out from under the thick layer of heavy yellow pages, was made of iron and fastened to the bookrack by metal clasps.

"This is the Book of Power," said Samson, turning one

page after another. "This is where your power and immortality came from, with my help, of course." He turned another page and said, "Look."

Craig looked and saw a depiction of the symbol that was on the lid of the chest.

"This is a pentacle," continued Samson. "It's a symbol of harmony, health, and great mystical powers. We're using it to fight evil but, unfortunately, many people use it to create it."

"What's this?" asked Craig, pointing at the colorful feather beneath the pentacle.

"This is the feather of a peacock tail. It symbolizes changeability, the process of transition of a subject from its beginning until its full transformation."

Craig looked at the left page, covered by what looked like small symbols, written in gold. They resembled the ones he'd seen on Fray's dagger.

"What kind of language is this?" he asked.

"The kind that can be read only by the Keeper of the Book."

Now he pulled up the sleeve on his right arm and showed Craig another mark, which looked like an open book.

"Which means me," said Samson, "This mark the man put on my arm himself. The Book contains only a few pages like this one; the rest you'll be able to read. It will tell you who we are, what our mission is, who we fight, and how. It will help you find some answers."

"And nobody else knows what is on the golden pages?" Craig asked.

"No, nobody. They only know the meaning of one of the pages. And I'm going to explain it to you, too. It describes the process of the transformation. It taught me how to turn people. All I need from the person I'm turning is a few drops of their blood. I drip it into the pentacle. Then I have to read the golden text on this page, which is different every time.

What those words will say depends on the blood and its owner. And then I connect that person to the Book by putting my right hand above those two symbols and my left hand on his chest. Two rays of light will come out of the Book and go right into his chest. One ray is blue—it's the power, the other ray is red—it's the immortality."

"This golden text, what does it say, does it tell you something?"

Samson took a deep breath.

"I think that's enough for today. But, before I close the chest, I want you to put your hand here." Samson pointed at the pentacle and the feather.

Craig looked at Samson, then at the symbols again, and slowly lifted his hand and did what he was told. The Book was warm. Its pages, which looked heavy from the side, were soft, and Craig's hand plunged into them like a head plunges into a feather pillow. He squeezed them slightly, and he could swear they squeezed back. The energy flowed from the Book to his hand and went through his entire body, connecting them to each other. At that moment, Craig's hand felt a distant intermittent signal, like it was suppressed deep inside that warm, soft, welcoming Book. The signal confused Craig and made his heart beat faster, his breathing heavier. The signal—the pulse. He jerked his hand back.

"It's alive," he gasped.

"Yes, it's alive," said Samson. "And here is the first and most important rule you must remember—the Book cannot be closed."

"Why?"

"Because he who closes it will die. The Book will kill him and take back the power from the rest of us. You see these clasps?"

Craig nodded.

"Only one of us can close the Book. But once it's closed, it will remain closed because, right now, there's nobody among us who will be able to open it again."

Samson closed the chest and put the torch on the table. Craig was deep in his thoughts and he didn't know how long they stood in silence before Samson spoke again.

"You understand how important this Book is and how much we all depend on it. Showing it to you, I am showing you my trust."

"Thank you, sir." Craig respected this courageous and noble man. Yes, Samson hadn't been able to give him a choice, but he had saved his life, given him power and immortality, his trust and support. "I will not let you down," he said, looking into Samson's eyes.

"I know." Samson walked to him and put his hand around Craig's shoulders. "You don't have to call me sir. We are family and we call each other by name."

A week later, standing with Samson on the deck of *Destiny*, Craig saw an ancient castle sublimely towering on the beautiful shore.

"Welcome home," said Samson.

Craig heard a noise behind them. He turned around and saw Fray, Gabriella, Riley, and Ruben smiling at him.

Chapter Eight

TODAY

IT WAS ALREADY DARK when Craig heard the hiss of braking wheels.

"You kept the car," he said, meeting Hanna in the hallway.

"Yes, to be sure that she's not driving anywhere alone." She headed to the kitchen. "I told her our cousin is arriving tonight and I have to pick him up from the station because you have a meeting with your imaginary website guys."

"You could have actually done that, you know," a voice called from the living room. "Then you would've saved me from that cracker in the taxi who kept telling me how young I am and how I don't know anything about life."

Hanna turned around and saw Ruben standing in the kitchen doorway. She ran toward him and clutched her arms around his neck.

"Oh, God, I am so glad to see you."

"I hope it's because you missed me." Ruben hugged her back tightly.

"Of course I missed you. I miss all of you." She stepped back. "You look different."

"It's my new haircut."

"It's gorgeous. It makes you look older."

"I am older. Look." Ruben took his driver's license out of his pocket and handed it to Hanna. "I'm nineteen now. And you say we can't age."

"Really?" said Craig.

Ruben had changed his age before, but he always made himself younger so he could stay longer in one place.

"Samson said that we probably won't need any more high school kids and I can choose any age possible for me."

"Congratulations," laughed Hanna. "Now you can go to college!"

"Funny."

"Does this mean I don't have to buy beer for you anymore?" smiled Craig.

"No, brother, at least not in Europe. Just whisky and vodka."

They laughed.

In the living room, Craig pulled a bottle of whiskey out from the cabinet and three crystal glasses. Hanna settled comfortably on the couch, and Ruben sat down on the big, dark-red velvet armchair in front of her.

"Okay," said Ruben. "I know how things are here in general, Samson kept me updated. Fill me in on the details and tell me what your plans are for me."

"We know that at least three vampires are watching Amanda," said Craig, handing each of them their glasses and taking his place in another armchair. "I want you to help Hanna keep an eye on the girls, to be beside her if something goes wrong. That's why I think it would be very handy if you become friends with Kimberly."

"Kimberly? She's the other girl, right?" He looked at Hanna. "Your and Amanda's friend?"

"Yes," said Hanna. "And you have to promise me that you'll keep yourself together. Keep your charm under control."

"I promise. Is she pretty?"

Craig chuckled.

"It's not funny." Hanna scowled. "If you break her heart, I'll kill you."

"I said I promise. When are you going to introduce us?"

Craig smiled. Hanna gazed at him sideways, then looked at Ruben.

"You'll meet her tomorrow after school. The day after tomorrow, we're going to a party, and I'll make sure she invites you to go with her."

"Good," said Craig quickly before Ruben could react to Hanna's "making sure" part of the plan. "Where is the party?"

"At Alec Stafford's house."

Craig's face drained. Hanna had told him about Alec. She had also told him that Amanda didn't reciprocate his feelings. But the fact of his existence bothered Craig.

"He knows how much I hate him, and he invited me only because he knew that Amanda wouldn't go without me."

"Who is Alec?" asked Ruben.

"It's not important," said Craig, throwing a warning look at Hanna. She closed her already open mouth. "The important thing is to be careful at that party. Do not rely on the fact that it's a private house. You know teenagers, they'll invite anybody, even someone they met only once." Craig and Hanna gazed at Ruben.

"Or never met at all." Ruben grinned.

"Exactly," said Craig.

Hanna's phone rang from the kitchen.

"It's probably Amanda." She ran to get it.

"I am glad you came," said Craig quietly. "I don't remember the last time she laughed."

"It has been tough for you guys. I know, been there."

"It has been tough for Hanna. Amanda is just a regular mortal girl. Anything can happen to her—illness, car crash, or some other stupid accident. People are so fragile. And now that the vampires are here… she's freaking out."

"Yes, too much responsibility."

"She was just asking if I made it in time," said Hanna, returning from the kitchen. She sat back on the couch. "I said everything's okay and I'm on my way back. This lying," she moaned, "it's killing me. I have to lie to them all the time, make things up. I'm always afraid I'll get lost in my own lies."

"We're almost there, Hanna," said Ruben. "One way or another it'll be over soon. Let's just hope that this time we'll succeed, that it's really her."

"It's her," said Craig and sipped from his whiskey.

"Are you absolutely sure about that?" Ruben asked.

"What if you feel like that because she looks like Eleanor?" said Hanna carefully. "Because you want it to be her?"

"No." Craig stood up. "I know it's her. Samson said he can feel it, too." He poured more whiskey into his glass. "I found about a dozen houses which match Amanda's description. Tomorrow I'm going to check a few places on the west side." He looked at Hanna. "Sorry I didn't tell you before. You already had too much to worry about. The thing is that this dream Amanda had, it might not be a dream."

"What do you mean?"

"Melinda thinks she's been in that house. That she was teleported there."

"What? They can't do that, can they? And I tore myself to pieces trying to keep her safe."

"I'm afraid Melinda is right. It explains why they didn't touch you at the lake. They have other plans. This way it's more secure, nobody will oppose or follow them."

"If that's so, why didn't they keep her?"

"Melinda says it's impossible. To teleport somebody from a distance, you have to be a very powerful witch or warlock, but even then, you can't transfer a person too far and keep them there too long. She thinks this was just a test, to see how it would go. Melinda put some protections up in Amanda's room. She's not sure if it's going to prevent the whole process, but it'll make it much more difficult and short-lived. That's why you two have to be watchful. If they see that it's not working, they'll try to kidnap her, or who knows what their plan B is."

"You think that house—that's the place where everything is going to happen?" Ruben asked.

"Yes. Whether they kidnap her or teleport, they'll take her there. That's why it's very important to find it as soon as possible," said Craig.

"What time is it?" asked Hanna.

"It's nine," said Craig, checking his watch.

Hanna took the remote from the coffee table and turned on the TV.

"The body was found in the school basement by Monika Wilson, the school assistant janitor," said the anchor of the evening news. "As Wilson says, she was polishing the floor when she saw bloodstains on the basement door. The cause of death of the janitor James Sullivan has not yet been determined . . ."

"They're probably feeding right now," said Hanna. "And we're just sitting here doing nothing."

"Hanna, there's not much we can do, you know that," said Ruben.

"I know, and that's what pisses me off. If we had our powers, we would never have let this happen right under our nose."

Craig leaned back and closed his eyes. Those words brought back painful flashes of memory, two vivid images. The first one was Eleanor's dead body in his arms, and the other— the closing yellow pages of the Book of Power.

"Yes, we don't have our powers, and they know that," said Craig, opening his eyes. "We could still kill them. It wouldn't be easy, but it can be done. Only, if we killed one, they'd bring five more, and we can't be distracted right now. Amanda is our priority. We have to keep the situation calm for as long as possible."

∼

CRAIG WOKE EARLY the next morning. He took a bottle of water from the fridge, grabbed the printed maps, and went to his car. The sun was up but the street was still quiet—the morning stir hadn't started yet. He sat in the car and rolled down the window on his side, letting in the cool air.

Craig threw the bottle on the passenger seat and studied one of the maps. The first house he would check was fifteen miles away from the town and about hundred yards into the woods. The map didn't show any road toward it, and all he could see was a roof and a small open space in front of it.

Starting the car, he pulled out of the driveway and headed for the main road. When he reached the place at the edge of the woods, he stopped but didn't get out of the car. According to Hanna, Amanda hadn't seen any roads or gates around the house, and right now Craig was looking at a gravel trail between the trees. Maybe the trail didn't go all the way to the house? Shifting into gear, he drove up.

But the road didn't end. He saw an old one-story house ahead. In the place where Amanda said there was a fountain, a car sat instead. Craig turned around and drove back.

The next house was eight miles away. After a ten-minute drive, he turned to a narrow, unpaved road going up a hill. The road ended abruptly, and Craig saw a track stretching into the forest on his left.

Grabbing the bottle, he got out of the car and moved forward, sticking to the trail.

The sunlight hardly penetrated through the dense foliage,

and the air was moist and chilly. The trail ended at a large barn, which had a horseshoe nailed to its wall. The place was old and deserted. Craig released a disappointed sigh. He went closer. The wide gate wasn't locked, and he threw it open. A loud rusty squeak pierced the morning silence.

Implements for horses were everywhere; a broken saddle lay on the ground, bridles and ropes hanging on the stall door. He stepped to the pile of hay, took a small bunch, and pressed it to his nose. A flash of nostalgia warmed his heart. That scent reminded him of his horse, his black Frisian steed that he hadn't ridden in a long time. The horse was at the castle. Even though the castle was only thirty miles away from Green Hill, he didn't visit it. He didn't want to leave Hanna alone.

Craig walked to the small decrepit annex on the right of the barn. He peeked into the window but didn't see much through the muddy glass. The only chair on the porch looked sturdy enough, and he sat on it and took a sip of water.

He thought about Amanda. He always wondered what would happen if she suddenly uncovered the truth about him and Hanna. What would happen if he just told her? Eleanor had known from the first moment they'd met, and it hadn't frightened her. But times were different, circumstances were different, everything was different.

Chapter Nine

YEAR 1833

ONE AUTUMN EVENING the Map showed a monster too near some private estates only twenty miles from the castle. Craig and Riley straddled their horses and hurried to the forest adjacent to that area.

The Map was a part of the Book, without which it wouldn't be possible to know where the danger was. It wasn't attached to the Book, but Samson, who always took the Book with him when they left the castle for a long time, kept the Map in the chest so they wouldn't forget it if they took off urgently.

Samson checked the Map two or three times a day to see if there were any changes. The witches were the messengers. Centuries ago Samson and Fray, traveling from country to country, gave the most powerful and most trusted of them a spell to call the hunters, and the witches passed that knowledge on from generation to generation.

Performing the spell, the witch had to drip a few drops of her blood onto the earth. A red stain would appear on the Map in the area where the blood had fallen. The number of drops depended on the number of monsters and victims. The more monsters or victims, the more drops, and the bigger the stain grew.

Sometimes, witches tried to fight the monsters themselves. The local ones, whom Samson knew personally, were advised to call hunters immediately, without taking any chances and risking their lives.

This time, the Map showed a speckle, which probably meant that it was only one monster and that somebody might be injured. The big full moon hanging above the hill left no doubts that the creature was a werewolf.

"The scent is all over the place," said Riley when they reached the spot. "Look at the manor. People are still outside at this late hour."

Craig saw a couple of men talking on the porch. A few carriages stood on the front yard. Horses were snorting and shaking their heads, seeming disturbed.

"It looks like the house is full of guests," said Craig, "We need to go down there to make sure that the werewolf is not around them."

"Let's split up. You go down to the left and check the backyard, and I'll check the other side," said Riley, and he rushed away.

Craig headed to the large garden behind the house. When he got closer, he saw two ladies sitting on the bench under the bright moonlight. He jumped down from the horse and moved forward. Peering into the darkness between the trees, he listened for suspicious noises, but all he heard were the muted sounds of a piano and the conversation of the two young ladies, sitting on a bench.

"That's good news," said one.

"Yes," said the other with a sigh.

"Then why are you sad, Eleanor?"

"I am not."

"Tell me what's wrong."

"Kate… It's not what… It's not how I imagined my life."

"You did the right thing. It will get better."

But the lady named Eleanor didn't say anything.

"Let's go before they start looking for us," said Kate.

"You go. I would like to stay for a while."

That's not a good idea, thought Craig. *She needs to go inside.* He stepped noisily toward the bench, hoping to scare her away. He even broke a few twigs on purpose.

But Eleanor didn't move. Her eyes were fixed on the full moon. He hesitated for a moment, then approached her from the side.

"I am very sorry, miss…" he started, looking at her dark curly hair.

She turned her head, her expression a little startled.

"I didn't want to disturb you," he continued.

She stood up.

"Who are you?" she asked, stepping closer.

"I am. . . from around here. I was…" Their eyes met, and Craig forgot what he was going to say.

"How come I've never seen you before?" She smiled.

A heavy, husky breath sounded behind Craig. Frowning, he turned his gaze to the bushes at the far corner of the house. In between the foliage of jasmine, he saw two glittering yellow eyes. Eleanor's eyes followed his gaze.

The werewolf extended its forepaw, which had big hooked fingers with long claws. It took a step forward and snarled, baring its teeth.

"What's that?" Eleanor whispered, turning a wide-eyed look at Craig. "Is that a . . . ?"

The wolf jumped. Craig, who anticipated the move, in a flash shoved Eleanor aside and jumped toward the beast. He knew she would notice his unusual moves, but he didn't have time for discretion. He clutched the beast in the air, and they fell to the ground and rolled. The wolf lurched at Craig's throat. Craig struggled to clamp its jaw shut with one hand, pushed it back with another, and kicked him away. Ripping Craig's clothes with one paw and scratching his face with another, the wolf flew back, hit a tree, and fell down. But it instantly sprang to its feet, stretched out its body, and again leaped toward Craig.

Craig stepped forward and hit the oncoming wolf in the chest with his fist. That blow sent the beast a few yards back. Craig plucked his silver knife out of its sheath and, when the wolf was ready to attack again, Craig launched forward and struck it through its heart.

Eleanor cried out. The beast roared first, then howled a dog's howl and fell to the ground.

Craig hurried to Eleanor's side. She was now clinging to a tree, petrified, pressing both hands to her stomach.

"I'm sorry I pushed you. I had to. And I am sorry you saw the fight," he said.

"That was intense," she breathed out.

"I tried to warn you," said Craig offering his hand. "You should go inside."

"I'm fine, but you . . . you're bleeding." Eleanor looked at Craig's face. She touched his cheek, and blood seeped into her delicate glove.

Craig's inner voice told him to leave. He felt his wound pulling shut, but he just stood there, not able to look away from her. He looked at her brown eyes, blinking with long, velvet lashes, at her parted mouth, at her silky curls.

A weak, crackling noise behind him distracted them. Eleanor looked over Craig's shoulder and gasped.

"It's human! Oh, God, it's human!"

As the werewolf died, he had transformed back to his original form. Craig, knowing that it would happen, shouldn't have let Eleanor see it.

She moved closer, but Craig stopped her, standing in her way.

"He is not just human, he is a…"

"Werewolf," Eleanor whispered. "People were talking. They were saying that somebody saw something in the woods that looked like a werewolf. And this one—he didn't look like an ordinary wolf. He was twice as big and he had fingers, and I don't think a wolf can stand on its hind legs like this one did when he attacked you."

Craig couldn't believe his own ears. Her tone of voice—there was no fear. She was excited.

"I see you found it." Riley's voice came from between the trees.

"Yes," said Craig. He walked toward the werewolf, now in its original form of a middle-aged man. He pulled the knife from his chest and put it back in the sheath.

"I'll take care of this," said Riley, coming closer.

He looked at Eleanor then turned to Craig with a questioning expression on his face.

"It's fine," said Craig.

Riley lifted the man's body, slung it over his shoulder, and walked away.

"I need to go as well," said Craig to Eleanor. He stayed in the shadows, keeping his distance so she wouldn't see his healing face. "But I have to ask you not to tell anybody what you just saw."

"What's the point? They won't believe me anyway." She stepped closer and looked at Craig with fascination. "Your wounds are healing." She touched his cheek again. "If I tell this to anybody, they'll think I'm crazy." She looked at the dry blood on her glove and asked, "What are you?"

"You don't have to be…" Craig was going to say "afraid," but it was obvious she wasn't. Instead, he just said, "I am human."

"Of course you are," she said, looking deep into his eyes. "You are more human than anybody I've ever met. But you are also more than that. What are you?"

It was pointless to lie, and he didn't want to, but their existence was secret, and it was important to keep it that way.

"I can't tell you," he said.

"You can trust me."

Craig looked at Eleanor's glowing eyes and shook his head. "I'm sorry. I have to go."

He moved to leave, but she touched his arm, stopping him.

"If you change your mind, there's a lodge in the woods, not so far away from here. Tomorrow afternoon…"

At that moment, the sound of the piano grew louder. Somebody came out of the house. Eleanor glanced to the open door. When she turned back, Craig was gone.

"I'll be waiting for you," she said quietly.

Craig heard her. Standing beside his horse, he watched as a man twice Eleanor's age approached her.

"My darling, what are you doing here? We missed you. Let's go inside." He offered her his hand.

∽

WHEN CRAIG and Riley returned to the castle, only Hanna was awake. She showed up at the library door in her night robe.

"How did it go?" she asked, hugging a book.

"Fine," said Craig.

"Except we had a witness," said Riley, looking sideways at Craig.

"When I found her, the werewolf was already there. There was nothing I could do," said Craig in a detached way. Then he added, "She's not dangerous. She's different."

At those words, Riley and Hanna exchanged a curious glance.

"Different?" Riley raised one brow, "Different how?"

"Just different," said Craig, annoyed. "Can we talk about it later? I'm tired. I'm going to bed." As he climbed up the stairs, he felt their piercing looks on his back.

The large fireplace in Craig's bedroom was kindled. Its fire lit the room and made the shadows of the furniture dance on the walls. Craig pulled aside the heavy curtains, letting the bright moonlight in, and looked far into the ocean. He thought about Eleanor, he wondered if she would go to that lodge tomorrow. If she did, if he knew she was there, waiting for him—would he go?

A desire to see her again washed over him. He already knew where the lodge was, having found it on his way back. She wanted to know who he was. Was the reason she wanted to meet him again just curiosity? He remembered that surprised and delighted look on her face when she saw him, and that was before the fight, before she realized he was not like others, not an ordinary human being. He knew that if he met her, she would ask questions. Was he ready to answer them?

Craig was a hundred and eighty-eight years old. He had had many different women in his life before, but only once did he reveal to a woman who he really was. It was a hundred and fifteen years ago, her name was Bethany, and she broke his heart. She said that she loved him, but the kind of life Craig offered wasn't acceptable for her.

Craig hated himself for being so stupid, thinking that Beth or any other girl would accept his conditions, that somebody would love him as much as Gabriella loved Samson, willing to give up everything for him. From then on, he'd closed his heart and shielded it from such painful and destructive experiences. Perhaps he wouldn't be like Fray, who had too much fun in that area, and not like Ruben, who was very amative, but more like Riley, who had women but never sustained relationships.

But something happened that night and his shield, which had protected him for more than a century, melted under the warmth of Eleanor's eyes. Was he in danger of falling in love again? Even so, the circumstances were different. Eleanor had learned that he was unusual, and it did not scare her at all.

Craig was very quiet at breakfast the next morning, and it didn't go unnoticed.

"Are you alright, Craig?" asked Gabriella.

"I'm fine, just didn't sleep much," answered Craig, avoiding her eyes.

"You didn't have any complications yesterday, did you?" asked Samson, looking first at Craig, then at Riley.

"Actually, it went well, we arrived in time," said Riley, swallowing his food. "The wolf was in the backyard of a manor, and there were people outside."

"Did it hurt anybody?"

"Yes. One man was injured, but he wasn't from that house. I found him not far from it, on a tree. His legs had deep scratches and he'd lost a lot of blood, but he wasn't bitten."

"Are you sure about that?" Fray scoffed. "Or you are just so sensitive that you didn't dare to kill him?"

If a human were bitten by a werewolf, at the next full moon he would transform into a werewolf, as well, and there wasn't any way to stop that process. There was no cure against it. Fray killed them right away, without bothering to find out if it was a scratch or a bite.

"I can tell a scratch from a bite. Not everybody is like you, ready to finish people off just because they're bleeding," Riley snapped in reply.

"I'm doing the right thing," said Fray aggressively. "You can never be sure about how they got injured. We've made this mistake before."

"It's better to fix the mistake later than to kill an innocent man. I thought our mission was to protect people, am I wrong?"

Fray squeezed the silver fork in his hand, then threw it on the plate. Kicking the chair aside, he stood up and stormed out of the room. A moment later, his horse galloped out of the yard and up the hill.

"Samson, he's always so angry. You have to talk to him, find out what's bothering him," said Gabriella.

"I tried. Several times. He doesn't want to talk." Turning to Riley, he changed the subject. "You said there were people outside. Did they see the wolf?"

Riley glanced at Craig, then at Hanna, and then reached for his glass of water.

"I don't know." He drank the water and put the empty glass back. "It was Craig who took down the wolf."

Craig took a deep breath.

"There was a young lady in the yard," he said, leaning back on the chair.

"How much did she see?" asked Samson in a serious tone.

"The wolf scratched my face right in the beginning, and by the time I had dealt with him. . . She saw my wound heal.

"Don't worry," said Samson. "I'll ask Emily to erase her memory."

Emily was a witch who helped them sometimes. If Emily erased Eleanor's memory, she would forget him and everything that happened last night.

"No," said Craig quietly, staring at his empty plate. "Don't." He looked up at Samson and saw that everybody's eyes were fixed on him.

"Oh, Craig," whispered Gabriella, looking at him fondly. "After all these years."

"I know. But this time it's different. She knows. After all that happened in front of her eyes, after what she saw . . . it didn't frighten her. She wants to meet me. If she hasn't changed her mind, of course."

"I don't think she'll change her mind. I saw how she looked at you." Riley smiled broadly.

"You saw her?" asked Ruben.

"I was there, too, if you remember?"

"But you just said—"

"Is she pretty?" interrupted Hanna.

"I was there only a minute, but I saw her. She is very beautiful."

"I have to go." Craig stood up.

"I hope it works out for you," said Samson.

Craig nodded and left.

When Craig arrived at the familiar forest, it was still early, and he got off of the horse and walked the rest of the way. Yellow but not yet dry, the leaves covering the forest floor softened his footsteps. The horse snorted, scaring a scarlet tanager. The bird stopped singing and turned its little head to one side then the other, listening before taking off and disappearing behind the foliage.

Eventually, Craig reached the lodge. He led the horse to a tree and hung the bridle on a broken branch sticking out of it.

He opened the lodge door and looked inside to make sure nobody was there.

Then he heard a mild clop. Sitting sidesaddle, Eleanor looked at him with a compelling smile. She wore a sky blue gown with pink and dark blue flowers at the edge of the skirt and a dark blue cloak. Her dark-brown curls fell over her shoulders.

Eleanor stopped her horse right in front of him, and Craig held out his hands. He gently took hold of her slim waist and helped her down. When he put her on the ground, she looked into his eyes.

"I turned around and you were gone."

"That was rude. I'm sorry, but I had to."
"I understand. Mr.. . . ?"
"My name is Craig."
"Thank you for saving my life, Craig," she said and stepped closer.

Craig's heart hammered.

"Thank you," he whispered, putting his arms around her. She didn't resist.

"For what?" she asked. Her eyes still fixed on his, she put her hands on his chest.

"For coming. I was afraid that you would change your mind over the night. After what you saw yesterday."

"From the moment I saw you, it was like I found something I was sure was mine, something I have been looking for a long time. What I saw after made that feeling even stronger."

Pulling her to his chest with one hand and brushing her silky curls with another, he kissed her. She shivered in his arms when their lips met and leaned closer.

∽

THEY SAT in the lodge on the soft, fleecy bearskin, Craig with his back against the wall and Eleanor resting her head on his chest. He kissed her palm, then slowly turned her and kissed her in the corner of her lips, which were the color of ripe raspberries.

"Eleanor, what you saw yesterday. . . There is more about me that you should know."

He lightly touched her cheek, and his lips followed his fingers.

"I supposed so. There is something I have to tell you too." Her lips smiled, but her eyes didn't. "Let's leave all talking for tomorrow." She ran her fingers through Craig's hair and kissed him.

Craig couldn't stop smiling the whole way back. He felt relief and breathing became so easy like somebody had opened spare valves in his lungs. With a slow trot, the horse approached the castle where Riley, Ruben, Gabriella, and Hanna were playing football.

"Somebody looks happy," said Riley, looking at Craig.

The moment Craig jumped down from the horse, all four of them surrounded him.

"She came," said Gabriella, delighted.

Craig took the ball and threw it to Riley, who kicked it toward Ruben. Gabriella grabbed Ruben, pushed him away, and took the ball.

"Gabriella, that's cheating," Ruben chortled, catching Gabriella by the hand and pulling her back.

She laughed and pushed the ball to Hanna with the tip of her foot.

Craig looked up at the castle where Samson watched Gabriella from the long stone balcony, a joyful smile on his face.

"When do I turn her?" Craig heard Samson's voice. He sighed in response.

The next morning, Craig left right after breakfast. She wanted to tell him something. Her eyes were serious when she said it, and it sounded a little bit alarming. But, whatever it was, it didn't matter, as long as it wasn't goodbye. All he wanted was to see her, to be with her. He hoped that she wanted it, too.

They were lying on the bearskin with Craig holding Eleanor in his arms when he told her the truth. The same truth he told Beth a hundred and fifteen years ago. Now, after meeting Eleanor, it seemed such a stupid mistake. His heart was open again. He didn't care if Eleanor would hurt it. From now on, it was hers.

When Craig finished talking, he sat up and leaned against the wall in order to see her face. Eleanor sat up, too.

"You asked who I am. Now you know," he said, looking at her.

Two tiny tears slipped down from the corners of her eyes.

"You almost died saving that woman. Is that why Samson turned you? Because you were dying?" she asked.

"No," said Craig, wiping her tears with his thumb. "He turned me because he chose me."

"I would choose you as well." She smiled and leaned forward to kiss him.

"I thought you already had," whispered Craig against her lips. In response, she kissed him again.

"How did he turn the others? Did he turn them when they were dying, too?" She asked, pulling back.

"No. Only Ruben. Riley, Gabriella, and Hanna were changed by will."

"And Samson agreed? Why? Did Gabriella and Hanna do something heroic too?"

"No," said Craig. "It's not like that. All stories are different. Hanna was eight when all her family was killed by a troll. She grew up in the castle, and Samson was like a father to her. He turned her when she became eighteen. She asked him to. She has destroyed many trolls since then."

"She must be very brave." Craig heard notes of esteem in her voice.

"Yes. She is our brave, sweet sister."

"She was my age," said Eleanor. "Almost. I will be eighteen in the spring."

Craig was amazed at how easily she took it. She wasn't pretending or trying to be polite. Her interest was absolutely genuine.

"What about Gabriella? What is her story?"

"Gabriella's story is as old as the world." Craig paused,

then looked at Eleanor's expectant eyes and said, "She and Samson—they fell in love the moment they saw each other. Gabriella is Samson's wife."

When Craig had told her the story, he skipped Gabriella's part on purpose. He thought that it might alarm Eleanor, make her feel obligated somehow, that it would sound like a hint he didn't intend to give and scare her away. He didn't want that to happen. All he wanted was to be with her, to see her as often as possible.

"Wife?" Eleanor asked quietly and her eyes froze.

Craig's heart stopped beating for a moment.

"But it wasn't easy," he said quickly. "To turn Gabriella, Samson waited for four years," he said hoping it would calm her down. But Eleanor's next questions didn't sound like she was scared of anything.

"Why?" she asked. "Why did he wait that long? He wasn't sure about his feelings?"

"No, he loved her very much," said Craig.

"Gabriella didn't want to? Or maybe it was some other serious reason?" she asked, persistently seeking an answer.

"No, she always wanted to. She loved him so much that, even knowing about all the consequences, she insisted he change her."

"Then it was nothing." She looked down and spread her hands. "Nothing was stopping them," she whispered. Her hands fell to her sides and when she looked up again, her eyes were full of tears.

Craig's pulse was probably visible by now. Did it mean what he thought it meant? Her questions sounded like she wanted to know what it took to become one of them. It seemed that she would, but something was stopping her. Was it possible that Eleanor, after seeing him only three times, was so in love with him that she wanted to be with him forever?

"Eleanor," he said carefully, "Are you saying that you would…"

"Oh, Craig, I wouldn't even think a minute. But . . ." Suddenly she closed her hands over her face.

Craig's heart sank. He was right. When she opened her hands, her face was calm, but tears dropped one after another from her eyelashes.

"I need to tell you something. It may change your feelings for me, but please, promise you won't disappear, at least without saying goodbye."

"Eleanor, nothing." He moved closer to her. "Do you hear me? Nothing is going to change my feelings for you."

"Craig, I am married."

"No," murmured Craig. Something snapped inside him. He leaned against the wall and closed his eyes. The words "don't disappear without saying goodbye" echoed in his head. Was this the goodbye he was afraid of? Did this mean that he had to leave and never come back?

He remembered the conversation between the two voices on the bench that first night. He stared at Eleanor, who didn't move an inch and whose eyes were still full of tears.

"But you don't love him," he said.

"Of course, I don't love him," said Eleanor, wiping her cheeks.

"Then why did you marry him?"

"I did it for my family." She took a deep, heavy breath. "My father owned a sawmill, and a year ago, he was on the verge of bankruptcy. We nearly lost the house before Richard McLane, his distant relative, and a very influential person, offered him his help."

"And then Richard asked you to marry him," said Craig with a cold voice.

"Yes. My father said if I refused, Richard might destroy us. I have two little brothers, what would happen to them? And I had to say yes to the man, who is only a few years younger than my father, and whom I'll never love."

"Is that the man who came after you that night?"

Eleanor nodded.

"Eleanor, you have to leave him."

"I can't. If I could, I would stay right here with you, I would go with you anywhere you wanted." She hugged him as hard as she could. "But I can't."

"I can help you." Craig pulled back.

"You can't, Craig. You don't understand—"

"Eleanor, we are rich. I am very rich and I can help you. And I'll not ask you for anything in return. You can do whatever you want, whatever you decide. If you want to stay with your family, I'll still be here if you want me to."

Eleanor, who was holding Craig's hands, let go of him and sat back, motionless, looking into nowhere. Craig was confused. He thought hard, trying to figure out which of his words brought up such reaction.

"You could do that?" she said indifferently.

"Yes. Eleanor, what's wrong? What happened? If you don't like my offer, just say so."

"Your offer is perfect," she said in a stony voice. "It's just two months too late. Craig, I'm pregnant."

"Oh God," whispered Craig, "Of course. How could I be so stupid?"

Eleanor stood up, put the cloak around her shoulders, and walked to the fireplace.

"I should have told you yesterday," she said, staring at the flame, "but I just wanted that day to be perfect, to be mine, to keep it as a gift."

Craig looked at Eleanor and thought about that little heart beating inside her, and it didn't matter where it came from because it was she who would give it life, bring it into this world.

"Forgive me," she said with unbearable bitterness in her voice.

"Forgive you?" He flashed forward and stopped behind her. "For what? he said, turning her around, "For being human? For loving your family? For sacrificing yourself for them?"

"Craig, you're hurting me."

Only then did he realize he was holding her arms too tightly and almost shouting.

"I'm sorry," said Craig, lowering his voice and letting go of her. "I just—"

"It's all right. You're overwhelmed, you're angry, I understand that."

"I'm not angry. I'm just trying to explain . . . Eleanor, I can give you many things, I can give you anything you want, but your pregnancy—it is something that you would never have with me. You are going to have a child—how can I be angry about that?"

"Is that true?" Tears started dripping from her eyes again. "I mean, could you really give me anything I want?"

"Anything. Eleanor, what do you want?"

She looked at him with eyes full of pain.

"Eleanor, just tell me what do you want."

"I want you."

"Eleanor." The wave of emotions swept over Craig.

He kissed her wet eyes, his lips slipped down to her smooth cheek, and then he felt the tender push of her lips to his.

Chapter Ten

TODAY

NONE of the six locations Craig checked had matched the description, and he was driving back. He wondered what excuse Hanna and Ruben had come up with in order to keep Amanda and Kimberly close by.

He drove into the garage. Amanda's car was parked on the driveway. Craig looked at the kitchen window, but the low sun reflected in it so brightly that he barely saw the frames.

"Craig, you're back," said Hanna the moment he showed up in the kitchen doorway.

"Hi," said Craig.

"Hi," chorused the others.

Ruben stood bent over Kimberly, who was sitting at the table and staring into the laptop screen. He straightened and looked at Craig with an unspoken question in his eyes. Craig shook his head slightly and Ruben nodded, pressing his lips together.

"What are you up to, guys?" asked Craig.

"We're making dinner," said Hanna.

Craig looked at Amanda, who tortured a tomato, trying to cut it for salad.

"Do you want to help us?" asked Hanna. "I'm putting the fish in the oven, Kimberly and Ruben are looking for a sauce recipe, and you can help Amanda cut the vegetables. Then maybe we'll be able to use them today."

"Hey, I'm doing my best." Amanda looked up at Craig, smiling, and he smiled, too.

"I'll be back in a minute, I'm just going to take a quick shower," he said. As he turned around, he knew Amanda was watching him. Those brown eyes were always watching him when he wasn't looking. And he wanted to look back so badly.

He had waited all this time, but he couldn't and he didn't have to stay away from her any longer. She wasn't a child anymore, she was eighteen. He wanted her to know who she was first, and there weren't many days left until she would find out. But he couldn't let, in that short time, somebody like Alec Stafford win her heart because he was there for her, because he didn't ignore her, or because she didn't want to be alone. Craig wouldn't avoid her anymore. He would start with small steps.

After the shower, he pulled on a fresh shirt and hurried downstairs. Ruben and Kimberly had found a recipe and stood beside the oven, looking into a small saucepan, talking and giggling. Hanna was taking out plates and glasses, and Amanda had advanced to cutting a cucumber.

"Let me help you," said Craig, taking the knife out of her hand.

"Thank you, you're a savior," said Amanda with relief.

Craig felt her eyes on him. He looked at her and their eyes met.

"Guys." Hanna turned to them. "Are you done with—" But she looked at Ruben, who was staring at Amanda and Craig, too, and grinned. "It's okay. The sauce isn't ready yet."

Amanda looked away.

"Yes, it is," said Kimberly, trying the sauce from the tip of the spoon. "And it's even edible."

Craig quickly sliced the cucumber.

"We're done, too," he said, shifting the vegetables into a bowl.

∼

"IT WAS NICE, we should do it more often," said Hanna as the girls were leaving after dinner.

"Thanks, guys." Kimberly turned to Ruben. "I had a really nice time."

"I'll drive you home," said Ruben, already holding Craig's car keys.

"Come back soon." Hanna gave him a look. "Don't make your girlfriend jealous."

"You have a girlfriend?" asked Kimberly.

"I have a girlfriend?" Ruben asked, raising his eyebrows. "I did, but she got old and died." He looked at Hanna with a teasing smile. "Like the rest of them."

"Your cousin is so funny," Kimberly laughed.

To Craig, it sounded like a splash of relief. He chuckled along, looking at Hanna who gazed back angrily.

"Hanna, can I have my car keys?" asked Amanda.

Hanna dug them up from her bag and glanced at Craig. He took them.

"I'll drive you." He put his hand around Amanda's waist and led her outside.

She shivered slightly at his touch.

"Craig, it's my car, I know how to drive it," she said.

Craig didn't react to her statement. "Ruben, pick me up on your way back," he said to Ruben, who already stood beside the jeep.

"He doesn't know where I live," said Amanda.

"Ask Kimberly," he added to Ruben without looking at

him, then opened the passenger door and said, "You can't go home alone, it's too late."

"Even by car?"

"Even by car. What is it, Amanda? You don't want me to drive you? Then Hanna can."

"No. You know that's not it." Her eyes looked deep into his.

"I know," said Craig softly.

"It's just . . . you're too worried."

"I am," he sighed.

They got in the car and took off.

It was almost midnight, and the streets were dark and empty. Craig's eyes were fixed on the road. He wondered how he could tell Amanda that she was in danger without scaring her.

"You didn't have to ask Ruben to come after you. You could go back in my car," said Amanda.

"No, your car has to stay in front of your house. Don't drive it. Don't go anywhere alone."

If those vampires had orders to abduct her, even those few steps from the car to the door were too risky.

"What is it, Craig? Is this because of those two guys?"

"Yes. Tomorrow Hanna will pick you up."

"Is her car fixed already?"

"It wasn't broken."

"She lied to me?" Amanda shook her head. "Why?"

"Because I told her to, and because she's trying to protect you," said Craig calmly.

"How can Hanna protect me from two guys?"

"She can, she knows how."

"What about Kimberly?"

"As you can see," Craig could not help but smile, "Ruben is watching after her."

"Is that what he's doing?" Amanda smiled, too. "Wait.

Hanna said her car was broken before we went to the lake, before she saw those guys."

"That was extra precaution. We know who those guys are and we knew that they would come."

"What do they want?"

"Sorry, I can't tell you more. But I'll tell you again—don't go anywhere alone. Stick with Hanna and Ruben and listen to them, please, they know what they're doing." Craig couldn't resist; he took her hand. "I don't want to scare you," he said after a short silence, "I just want you to be careful."

"I am not scared, Craig. I just don't understand what's going on."

Craig parked the car in front of the porch and turned to her.

"Everything's going to be all right. I won't let anything happen to you."

Their eyes met, but Amanda didn't blush and look down like last time; this time she held his gaze.

"I know," she whispered. "Though I don't know why. All this time, you haven't even noticed I exist."

"That's not true." Craig looked away. He didn't know what to say. He did avoid her, and if now he said she was the most important thing in his life, it would sound like empty words.

"That means I must be in real danger," said Amanda, and in the light of the streetlamp, Craig could see her pupils dilate. "But I'm not afraid," she continued. "Somehow I know you'll do anything to keep me safe. It's important."

Those words made Craig's heart jerk. He leaned forward and took her by her arms.

"We will."

Amanda's eyes froze.

"Craig, I feel weird. It's like I know something, but I don't know what it is."

He hugged her and kissed her temple. He knew he was the one that brought up those feelings by getting closer to her.

"Kimberly has nothing to do with this. They're after me, aren't they?" she whispered into his ear. "They need something from me." She pulled back. "What do they want, Craig?"

But Craig didn't say anything. His heart trembled, and only one thought pulsed in his head: it's her, it's really her.

∽

RUBEN STOPPED the car in front of Kimberly's house. They had chatted the whole way, but suddenly an uncomfortable silence fell between them. Just to break it, he said, "Your parents are probably waiting for you," and glanced at the windows.

A lonely dim light shone from the entrance hall.

"No. They're not home," Kimberly said. "They left today with my little brother to visit my stepfather's parents."

"And you didn't go with them?"

"No. I never do."

She smiled, but Ruben heard sad notes in her voice.

"You're alone, and you're not having a party?"

"This is my stepfather's house. He would never allow it."

"I'm sorry," said Ruben.

"I'm not. I had a very nice evening with my friends, and I wouldn't change it for anything."

"I had a nice time, too," said Ruben, looking into her dark glittering eyes. And it wasn't difficult to understand what they were telling him, what she expected him to do next, what any other guy would do.

But it wasn't as easy as it seemed. Ruben wasn't an ordinary guy, and Kimberly was Hanna's friend. Ruben looked down at her lips and then his eyes moved up again. He pushed back her smooth ginger hair with his fingertips and kissed her cheek.

"Good night, Kimberly," he said.

The gleam in her eyes extinguished.

"Good night, Ruben," she said quietly and got out of the car. But then she turned around. "We're going to this party tomorrow. Would you like to come . . . with me?"

"With pleasure." Ruben was glad that she still wanted to see him.

She walked to the house, and he watched her until her long ginger hair disappeared behind the door. Then he sighed and drove away.

When Ruben arrived at Amanda's place, he saw Craig and Amanda standing beside the car. He turned off the engine, not wanting to rush them.

"Ruben is here." He heard Amanda's voice through his open car window. "Go, don't worry, I feel better now."

But Craig didn't move.

"I'm sorry, I shouldn't . . ."

"No, it's not your fault. I had those dreams and I always knew they had a meaning, that they were trying to tell me something, and the things I said... It came to me when I looked into your eyes. You just made it clear that you're a part of them."

"I'll keep my distance if you want."

"No. I think I know why you've been avoiding me all this time. It's because of your secret. I still don't know what it is, but at least I know you had a reason. It makes me feel better."

Craig nodded and bowed his head. They stood in silence for a few seconds, and then Amanda said, "Good night, Craig," and went inside.

Ruben hadn't meant to listen, but it was so quiet outside that he heard every word. She knew something, and now he was curious how much.

"What happened?" he asked the moment Craig sat in the car.

"She knows," muttered Craig, still immersed in his thoughts.

"Knows what?"

"She doesn't know who she is or what her mission is, but she knows that they're after her, that what they want from her is important. She also knows we'll protect her."

"But how? What did you say?"

"Nothing. She just looked into my eyes and started talking."

"Then you were right; it is her." Ruben swallowed. If he had doubts before, now the comprehension that everything was going to change hit him.

"Yes," said Craig, "it is her."

Ruben saw the bliss in his eyes.

∾

THE LIGHT in her father's study was on.

"Hi, Dad," Amanda said, leaning on the doorway.

"Hi," he said, taking off his glasses.

"You shouldn't have waited up," said Amanda, looking at her dad's tired face. "I sent you a message. You knew I'd be late."

"It's all right. I needed to get some work done, anyway," he said, closing the laptop. "How did it go? Was the dinner nice?"

"Yes." Amanda smiled. "Thanks to Melinda, I don't even know how to cut vegetables properly. But I got help from Hanna's brother."

"Hanna's brother? The guy who just drove you home again?"

"Dad," Amanda raised her brow. "Were you. . . ?"

"No, of course not. I heard the car, and when I saw that

you were not alone . . ." he said haltingly. "He seems attentive to you. Does he like you?"

"You don't have to worry, nothing is going on. He's a very noble guy."

"Okay, then," said her father, turning off the table lamp. "It's time to sleep." He put his hand around Amanda's shoulders, and they left the room.

"Dad, did we have psychics in our family?" Amanda asked, making it sound like an innocent curiosity.

"Psychics? I don't think so. Why?"

"What about dreams? Did you ever have predicting dreams?"

"I had one before your mom died. And your dream, when you told it, sounded familiar, and then I remembered I had a dream like it when I was about your age. I remember the house. And there was a fountain outside."

"Yes, that's right," said Amanda, getting excited.

"And there were books in the house."

"Books?"

"Yes. There was a room, a library, and one of the books was very interesting. It had an iron cover and a lock on the side. I tried to open it, but I couldn't."

"Book," said Amanda, trying to remember.

"I don't know if it was a predicting dream, but if you had the same one, then maybe it means something."

"It definitely does. I just don't know what," she said, opening her bedroom door. "Good night, Dad."

"Good night, honey."

Amanda walked to her dresser and took a picture of her with her young mother out of a drawer. She was nine years old when her mother was diagnosed with cancer. Everything happened quickly, and two months later, she died. Nine years had passed, but Amanda's memories about her were still vivid; her soft touch, her beautiful smile, her tender voice. And cookies. Amanda still remembered that delicious smell of baking coming from the house when her mother made those oblong, straw-colored cookies that melted in your mouth.

Amanda also remembered the day when she saw a woman she didn't recognize sitting beside her mother's bed at the hospital, telling her something quietly. When the woman left, her mother told her father that after her death, she wanted him to hire the woman until Amanda turned eighteen.

He did as his wife had asked, and they had never been sorry. Melinda took good care of both of them and the house. She was always there when they needed her, and after nine years, she had become part of the family. Only one question bothered Amanda: why did her mother want Melinda to stay until she'd turned eighteen? Was it Melinda's condition or hers? And what would happen now? Was Melinda going to leave them? Amanda hoped that Melinda would stay. After she got into college she would have to move. It would give her peace of mind knowing that her father was not alone.

She put the picture back and sat on the bed.

Something had happened tonight, something important, and Craig and Hanna were part of it. All this time, Hanna had known about these guys from the lake, she knew that they would come, and she didn't tell Amanda anything. Why? And what was that important thing they wanted her to do? Who the hell were they?

She subconsciously ran her index finger around the coin on her bracelet. She couldn't think of anything in her life that could bring about this mysterious stir around her. She wasn't even a member of any school club or any organization which could've attracted to her such unwanted attention.

She looked at the bracelet, and her finger stopped moving. The same warm feeling that she'd experienced when she looked into Craig's eyes washed over her. Craig. It had something to do with Craig. She didn't know what. It was as if somebody wiped her memory but left behind this brewing mixture of feelings, making her whole body groan.

She lay down on the bed, closed her eyes, and touched the spot on her head where Craig had kissed her. They had been so close today. She even felt his heartbeat when he hugged her. Did he really like her, or was his behavior the result of his concern for her? Or maybe it had something to do with his secret? She always thought he was special, different. To her, Craig himself was some kind of secret. Was she about to uncover it, to find out what made him avoid her all this time?

Amanda was tired, and all these questions made her dizzy. She pulled the blanket over herself and, recalling the pleasant feeling of Craig's arms around her, fell asleep.

Chapter Eleven

YEAR 1833-1834

CRAIG AND ELEANOR tried to be together as often as was possible. They left notes for each other inside a hollow tree on a forest path where Eleanor usually went for a walk. Eleanor wrote to Craig about the day and time when she would be able to come to the lodge, and Craig let her know when he needed to leave with the others to hunt.

Every time he came back after a fight, she asked him every detail, making sure that he wasn't badly injured, that he wasn't in pain. Though Eleanor knew Craig was immortal, he could feel that she was always worried about him.

"It's me who has to worry about you, not the other way around," he told her once when he came back from the hunt a few days later than he had planned and found her anxious. "Nothing is going to happen to me. The only way for me to die is if my family decides to kill me, and I can assure you that it's never going to happen because we all love each other."

"Then there is a way for you to die?" said Eleanor. "You never told me about it."

Craig immediately regretted what he had said. He had been trying to calm her and had only made it worse.

"How?" asked Eleanor. "Is there some kind of weapon?"

"Samson and Fray, they have these daggers. They got them from the man who turned them. Those daggers can kill any of us who Samson turned, but not them. They'll be badly injured, but they'll recover. The blade is covered with golden symbols. That's the incantation which breaks the enchantment, takes away the protection given us by the Book, and makes us mortal again."

"Was it Samson who enchanted the daggers? Can he give power to objects too?"

"No, the Man did. Samson can only give power to living things, to beings that have blood. He turned our horses to make them faster."

"What if somebody else found out how to read the incantations, could they use it?"

"It's impossible. Samson is the only one who can read those symbols, and the incantation doesn't work without the dagger."

"Have they ever killed anybody from your family?"

"No, of course not," Craig, who had been reclining on the bearskin with his head on Eleanor's knees, stood up.

"Then how do you know it can kill?"

"It's written in the Book." He crouched in front of the fireplace to add more wood. "Besides that, as I've told you before, Samson chooses people, but he can never be absolutely sure if the person is good, that he can trust them enough to make them one of us and bring them into our family. For example, if Samson turned somebody who was dying after he did something that seemed to be right in that moment, but then it didn't improve during the transition, Samson would use the dagger to stop the transformation."

"You mean he'd kill that person."

Craig nodded.

"But why?" asked Eleanor, "What does it mean 'didn't improve during the transition'?"

"If the person is good and there is no evil inside him, which means that he didn't deceive or kill anybody, wasn't cruel or violent, then the transition usually takes two days. But if their blood is dirty, as we call it, and the conscience is not clean, then the transition will take much longer, and after the fourth day passes, Samson stops it. To give somebody like that power and immortality is very dangerous. You never know how they will use it."

Eleanor didn't speak for a moment, then she suddenly said, "My conscience is not clean. I am married to a man that I don't love, and I am lying to him."

"What?" Craig rose. "Eleanor, I was talking about evil. You are not evil—you are joy."

Eleanor walked to him and put her arms around his neck.

"Try not to make them angry, all right?"

"I will do my best," said Craig and kissed her.

"I love you," she whispered.

"I love you too," he whispered back.

∾

IT WAS the beginning of December. Brown leaves on the forest floor were stuck to each other and hammered into the dirt by past heavy rains. The air was cold and moist. Craig had been arriving at the lodge early to warm it up.

They both knew that they'd need to think of some other way to see each other. Even though Eleanor didn't want to admit it, but because of her pregnancy it was becoming harder for her to walk all that way up the hill. And although her husband was usually at work and knew nothing about her walks, Eleanor's long absences in such unpleasant weather could arouse suspicion in the servants.

"Eleanor, I want to ask you something," Craig said once, "While you can still come here, would you like to meet

Gabriella and Hanna? They torture me every time I come home."

"They want to meet me? Really?" asked Eleanor. Her face glowed. "Why didn't you tell me?"

"If you don't feel comfortable about doing it, say so. You don't have to see them just to please me."

"I would love to. I always wanted to, but didn't dare ask."

"You can ask me anything, you know that. And you can tell me anything."

"There's not much I can do for you, but you can ask me anything, too."

"Can I?" said Craig. "Then why do you change the subject every time when I ask about Richard?"

"Because I don't want to think about him when I'm with you."

"Eleanor, all I want to know is if he's being nice to you. I want to know that you're safe with him and that he's taking good care of you. He's the one around you day and night."

"He's nice, you don't have to worry about that. And the good news is we don't see each other much. During the daytime, he's busy with work and his friends, and at nights. . . ." she looked at Craig with a smile. "You don't need to worry about them, either. I told him I don't feel comfortable sleeping in the same bed in my condition, and I chose the bedroom on the other end of the house."

"You did?"

"Yes. Very soon, I won't be able to come here anymore and this way, my bedroom window, which is looking into the backyard, will always be open for you."

"Thank you. Then I don't have to set vampires and werewolves on him to make his disappearance look like a horrible accident."

Eleanor laughed, and Craig was already kissing her.

Next time, Craig came with Gabriella and Hanna, who

immediately started asking questions about the baby and how the pregnancy was going. When the conversation turned to, "Craig has told us so much about you, he's so worried," Craig said, "I'll be around," and stepped outside.

When Gabriella and Hanna left, Craig walked Eleanor back. She looked happy.

Gabriella entered Craig's room the moment he got home.

"I just came to tell you that I like her very much. I'm glad you found the one you've been waiting for."

"I need to ask you something," said Craig.

"Yes?" Gabriella sat down on his bed.

"Do you think I am doing the right thing by keeping in touch with her?" he asked in a low voice.

"What do you mean? I don't understand."

"I mean if she's married and seeing another man . . ." he paused. "Her conscience is not clean, and it's my fault."

"You listen to me now," said Gabriella seriously. "I had doubts about her before. I wondered if she really would agree to turn in order to be with you, or if she just said it because she knew that it was impossible. Today, after I met her, my doubts are gone. She loves you so much she'll do anything for you. Life has been unfair to her, and if you are the one she wants to be with, if you're the one who makes her happy, then who cares about the conscience? She deserves to be happy, to love and be loved."

A short silence followed, and then Craig said, "Thank you."

"Oh, Craig." Gabriella stood up and hugged him.

"I can't live without her."

"I know."

∼

CRAIG VISITED Eleanor's bedroom as often as possible during the cold winter months.

The eleventh of March was Eleanor's eighteenth birthday. Craig came earlier that day to give her his present and spend a little bit more time with her. He found her sitting alone on the backyard bench, just like many months ago when he saw her for the first time.

"I know it's only been two days, but I missed you so much," she said.

"I missed you, too." He kissed her forehead then pulled out a vinous-colored, velvet, hexagonal box from his pocket. "I have something for you," said Craig, opening the box.

Eleanor looked into it and saw a silver bracelet and ring. The bracelet consisted of eight small coins connected to each other by small golden loops. Each coin had a golden roman number and a golden circle with holes around each number. The ring had a coin, too, but its golden circle had small diamonds sticking out of it instead of holes.

"Oh, Craig, they're so beautiful." Eleanor beamed. She took the bracelet and examined it closely. "It looks like yours. Your bracelet—it also has coins with numbers."

"Yes. Yours is for a woman, but for men . . . look." Craig stretched out his hand. "The same coins are placed on the rectangular silver plates to make the bracelet bigger. Same as the coin on the ring, remember?" And he pointed on his finger.

"Yes, I remember," said Eleanor and looked at the ring in the box.

"Eleanor, I know that you can't wear it. But I want you to keep it somewhere close. This is not just jewelry. We all have one, and it helps us communicate with each other. Each number on these coins represents us in sequence according to age. Samson is the oldest—he is number one, then comes Fray—he is number two, then Riley, and so on. I'm number six. If we want to call each other, we have to press the diamonds on the ring to the holes on the bracelet coin. If I want to call Riley, I will push the ring first to my number, then to his. That way he knows who is calling him. I'll push it once when I visit so you know I'm here. You don't have a number, but if you're alone and want me to come, push the ring to my number twice."

Eleanor took the bracelet and ring and looked at them.

"How will I know that you pushed it?" she asked.

Craig pushed his ring to the number six on his bracelet, and a green light shone out from the sixth coin on Eleanor's.

"Ah!" That little magic thrilled her, and she let out a short laugh. "Craig, but this one, this coin doesn't have a number."

"It's the clasp. The clasp is an emergency coin. If someone pushes that one, red light will come out from all coins at the same time. That means that they need help or something very bad has happened."

Craig noticed movement in the house and spoke faster.

"One more thing. When labor starts, push it three times. I want to know when it happens." He took her face in his hands and kissed her lips.

"I will. Don't worry, my love, I'll be fine. I'm strong."

"I have no doubt about that," he said quietly. "I just want to be near."

After the birthday, things became more complicated. A month before the delivery of the child, Eleanor's mother decided to stay and look after her daughter herself. She asked to put her bed in Eleanor's bedroom so she could be beside her day and night.

Craig stayed in the lodge all the next week, before he got a chance to see Eleanor, and as soon as the green light twice shone on his bracelet, he was standing in her bedroom and kissing her hands, her curls, her face and her tender lips.

"How do you feel, are you alright?" he asked, pulling back.

"Craig, I missed you so much, but there was nothing I could do."

"I know." He kissed her again. "I saw the doctor was here. What did he say?"

"He said everything is fine."

"I'll probably go home today. I haven't been there in a week and Gabriella and Hanna are worried about you. They are waiting for news. But I'll be back tomorrow night."

"Craig, I still have a month. You can't stay in the lodge all that time."

"I want to be close in case you need me."

"I always need you." She kissed him.

Everybody in the castle received the signals Craig and Eleanor sent to each other. To avoid confusion, Craig explained their meaning.

They already knew that Craig didn't come home all those days because he was waiting for the chance to see Eleanor.

It was around midnight when he entered the castle, and they all came downstairs except Fray, who wasn't home. He was hunting a couple of vampires in Virginia and didn't want to take anybody with him because he might stay there for a while.

Craig told them about Eleanor's mother's decision, and that she still had a month, and that the doctor said everything was fine. But even though everything seemed all right and Gabriella assured him it was too early to worry, Craig barely slept that night. He couldn't relax knowing that he was twenty miles away from Eleanor. The next morning, even though he knew he couldn't get too close to the house in the daytime, he left right after breakfast.

He reached the lodge, jumped down from the horse, and patted it on the back.

"Don't go too far, Gray," he said. He remembered Eleanor when she had asked, "Why did you call your black horse

Gray?" Then she answered her own question. "I know. It's because of his gray eyes."

Craig smiled. He patted the horse again and went down the hill. When he had walked almost halfway, the number six on his bracelet shone with green light three times. Craig's heart trembled. He stopped, looking at the bracelet in disbelief. Realizing that he hadn't sent the answer, he pressed his ring to the coin and ran.

Panting, Craig stopped as close to the house as was possible and stared into the open window. All he could see was the nightstand and the edge of Eleanor's bed. Eleanor's mother, the maid Luisa, who knew all about Craig and have been supporting them all this time, and one other female servant were walking in and out, making preparations. The doctor was nowhere to be seen.

When half an hour passed and the doctor still wasn't there, Craig decided to look in the front yard. He stood where there was a big open space between trees and he could view the road. Eleanor's father and husband walked back and forth, looking agitated. Richard was saying something, heatedly waving his hand, and Eleanor's father was nodding in response.

When the doctor, a thin tall man with gray hair, showed up in Eleanor's bedroom one hour later, Craig released a sigh of relief. The doctor gave some orders to the servants and closed the window.

After a moment, Craig saw all three men together with Eleanor's mother, coming out to the backyard. He sat behind the large oak, trying to catch every word they said.

"Mr. Douglas, yesterday you said that everything is fine. And she has still a month to go," said Richard, irritated.

"Premature birth happens often. A day ago, she was feeling perfectly well, there was no sign that the baby would come ahead of time."

"Is it dangerous?" asked Eleanor's father.

"The baby can be a little bit more fragile, require more attention and care."

"And Eleanor? What about Eleanor?" asked Eleanor's mother.

"She is doing well right now. I'll be able to tell more after I examine her."

"You examined her yesterday," said Richard.

"Mr. McLane." The doctor cleared his throat. "As you can see, things have changed since then."

The doctor returned to the house, and all Craig could do was wait.

Time passed slowly, making Craig more miserable with every minute. He had never felt so helpless in his life. Eleanor was going to suffer, and there was nothing he could do. He wanted to see her so badly—he wanted to jump into the window, take her into his arms, and tell her that everything was going to be all right. But he couldn't even do that.

It was getting dark. There was more ado in the room now. Richard paced in the backyard, and Eleanor's father stood with his hands folded on his back and periodically looking up at the window.

Then suddenly the door opened, and the doctor and Eleanor's mother rushed toward them.

Mr. Douglas began to talk, and Craig held his breath, afraid of missing a word.

"I'm a little bit worried."

"Worried about what?" Richard demanded.

"The thing is . . ." Mr. Douglas looked back at Eleanor's window and lowered his voice. "When I examined her yesterday, the position of the child was adverse, and it still is. We may have some complications."

"Oh, God," gasped Eleanor's mother.

"Quiet," grumped Richard. "Let's go inside."

Craig's temples throbbed. One question pulsed through his head: was Eleanor's life in danger?

During all those months, only once did the thought that she could die in childbirth cross his mind. He thought that maybe he could talk to Samson, ask him to turn her if such a thing happened. But to do so, Samson would have to unclasp the Book; he couldn't come here with the chest. And besides that, how would they get into the house, and how would they explain it to her family?

But that wasn't the reason he pushed all those terrifying thoughts away. Eleanor couldn't die. She was going to be a mother, and her child needed her. She had to live.

He didn't know how much time had passed, one hour or more, when he saw Luisa running toward the woods, her eyes searching between the trees. He showed himself, and she stopped before him.

"She said that you would be here," said Luisa. "She sent me to tell you that she loves you very much." She gave a weak smile, her lips trembling. "The baby is fine. It's a girl." She paused.

Craig's heart stopped beating. He could feel that she had something else to say and it wasn't good, but he was afraid to ask.

"The doctor can't stop the bleeding," she said, and tears dropped from her eyes, "Sir, she is dying."

"No, no. No." Craig tried to speak, but no words would come.

"She knows, and she says that she is very sorry."

"This is not happening," whispered Craig. His eyes started to burn, and everything blurred in front of them.

"They sent for a priest," Luisa sobbed. "I have to go, sir," and she ran back.

"No. I have to do something," he muttered, holding his head in his hands. He was confused, lost. He made a step back, then forward, and then back again. Then he looked at the bracelet. . . . But at that moment the air shifted behind him. He turned around and saw five horses standing ten feet away from him. Their owners were dressed in black and wore black masks. One of them held a big wooden case.

"You didn't think that I would let her die, did you?" said Gabriella.

Craig gulped the air. His mouth was open, and his lips shook.

"How? How did you. . . ?"

"We were in the lodge. We came after your number shone three times. Samson was listening and told us what's going on."

"It was Gabriella's idea," said Samson.

"You never know what can happen. We had to be prepared," said Gabriella, and Samson tapped the case.

"You unclasped the Book," said Craig, coming back to life and wiping his eyes with his sleeve. "But how are we going to do it?"

"We have a plan," said Samson and handed him the case. "You hold this and wait here. Tonight, Riley will be a vampire."

"What?" Craig looked at Riley and noticed him wearing a priest's clothes.

Riley smiled, showing big fangs sticking out of his mouth.

"How did you do that?"

"All questions later," said Samson, "Riley—go."

Riley put the hood on.

"Pull it down, I can see your mask," said Ruben.

Riley pulled it to the tip of his nose, dismounted, and went to the front yard.

"When Riley comes out from the window, it'll mean that his job is done."

"What is his job?" asked Craig.

"He has to scare everybody away from Eleanor's room. Then we all, except you, will go down there."

"Oh, God," gasped Hanna, "What if she dies before that?"

Craig stared at Samson.

"Few minutes don't change anything," said Samson calmly. "Her blood will still be fresh."

Craig took a deep breath.

"People might run outside. Gabriella and Hanna will keep them away from the backyard. When I call you, bring the Book through the window."

They heard screams. Short moments later, Eleanor's bedroom window swung open and Riley jumped down.

Samson, Gabriella, Ruben, and Hanna galloped to the front yard.

Riley stopped beside Craig. His mask and fangs were gone.

"How is she? Was she scared, too?" Craig asked.

"No. I immediately took the mask and fangs off. She smiled. She recognized me. She looks pretty bad. I told her that you'll come in a minute. God, you should see them running."

Craig heard the stirring in the front yard.

"What did you do?"

"I had to make them invite me in, because Samson said everything has to seem real in case some of them know how it works. When the old maid opened the door, she said 'Come in, Father,' before I even said anything. I took the hood off and growled and they saw my fangs. They started screaming, and when I jumped to the second floor, the servants ran, but the mother and father tried to come up, so I had to put extra effort to make them leave. Only the doctor was in Eleanor's room, and he ran out after them."

Riley sounded excited, but Craig felt sorry for Eleanor's parents.

"Everybody, stay where you are. Don't worry, we'll deal

with it." Craig heard Samson's loud voice coming through the open window. And straight away the same but now quiet voice said, "Craig, bring it."

Craig ran and jumped. Holding the case in one hand, he grabbed the window sill with the other, and lunged into the room. He looked at Eleanor, and pain shot through his heart. She was very pale, like there was no life in her at all, with big dark shadows under her closed eyes.

"Eleanor," he whispered, taking her hand and sitting beside her.

Eleanor opened her eyes. The moment she saw Craig, they began to fill up with tears.

"Craig," she said, her voice scarcely audible, "I'm so sorry."

Craig kissed her forehead.

"Everything's going to be fine."

"Step aside," Samson said behind him.

He stood up, and Samson took his place.

"Eleanor, I'm Samson," he said, taking off the mask.

"You," Eleanor sobbed and smiled at the same time.

"Do it, don't you see she's dying?" said Craig impatiently.

"Craig, she is conscious," said Samson. "That's why I have to ask her first."

"Then ask her." Suddenly, he froze and stared at Samson, "You think—"

"No. But I have to ask." He looked at Eleanor. "You know who we are, and you know that I can turn you. But, to do so, I'll need your permission. Eleanor, do you want to become one of us?"

Craig stopped breathing. He looked at Eleanor in anticipation.

She smiled.

"I'd be honored. Please, do it."

"With joy," said Samson. He stood up and punched the statuesque Craig in the shoulder.

Craig heard banging and crashing from behind the wall.

"What is that?"

"It's Ruben, fighting the vampire," said Samson. "Let's do this before he destroys the whole house."

Samson pushed everything from the nightstand to the floor.

"Wait," said Craig before Samson put the case on it. He opened the drawer, took out the velvet box, and put it in his pocket. "Now she'll be able to wear it."

Samson placed the case on the nightstand and unlocked it. The Book had already been opened on the essential page. Beside it lay a knife with a long narrow blade. Samson took the knife, then Eleanor's hand, and pierced her index finger. Eleanor blinked.

"Sorry, my love," said Craig, "but he needs a few drops of your blood."

Eleanor, who in the last minutes became even paler, just smiled weakly.

Samson, holding the knife beneath the wound, gently pushed it. Blood dripped onto the blade. Keeping the knife upright above the Book, he dripped the blood into the pentacle. Ripples emerged from the center of the symbol. The blood was gone, and, on the other page, the golden text began to sparkle, changing the text.

Craig looked at Eleanor, but she didn't look back. Her eyes were closed. The last weak smile was frozen on her face.

"Eleanor" Craig rushed toward her.

Samson shoved him away, sending Craig flying several feet to bang against the wall. He put one hand on the page with the pentacle and peacock feather and another one on Eleanor's chest. Two rays of light—one red and one blue—came out from the Book. Those glittering rays, denser than steam but much lighter than water, slowly stretched up into the air. Then, with full speed, they flew down to Eleanor's chest and dove inside her.

Craig moved forward, but Samson stopped him again.

"Wait, I'm not done yet." He took the knife. "Everything has to look real, believable." He stuck the narrow, pointed blade into Eleanor's neck.

"What are you doing?" yelled Craig, "Are you mad?"

"They must think she was bitten by the vampire," he said and stuck the knife in a second time, doing it quickly even though Eleanor couldn't feel anything. "Now she has two punctures on her neck, as it is supposed to be. Think for yourself. Her wounds will start healing, she will look better with every hour. It has to have some explanation."

"We're leaving her here?" asked Craig, confused.

"Yes. She can't just disappear. These people have a right to say goodbye to their beloved daughter."

"Of course they do. But, Samson, they'll bury her," said Craig with horror.

"And we'll dig her out," said Samson, closing the knife in the case.

"But… But, how long will that take? What if she wakes up in the grave?"

"I wouldn't let that happen. Trust me." Samson patted Craig on the shoulder.

Craig did trust him. He was sure Samson knew what he was doing. He had a plan, a plan which didn't look like something that was made up at the last minute.

"When did you come up with this plan?"

"Two hundred years ago when I turned Gabriella, except that she was only pretending to be dying," beamed Samson. "And Riley's fangs, which I made out of ivory, are the same fangs he had on him then." He went toward the door and put on his mask. "Take the case and go."

But Craig didn't leave. He wanted to hear what Samson was going to say to Eleanor's family.

"You can come in now; the vampire is gone," he said. Craig heard Ruben going downstairs and everybody else coming inside. "He came to the smell of blood," continued Samson. "I'm sorry to tell you this, but we were too late; the woman was already bitten."

Craig heard gasps.

"Oh no, my poor Eleanor," cried Eleanor's mother.

"What is going to happen now?" Richard asked. "Is it true that she might become one of them?"

"Yes. And if she does—you will all be in grave danger."

The last voice was unfamiliar. Craig looked through the gap in the door and saw the real priest standing beside Richard.

"That's why you must do everything exactly as I say," said Samson. "Check on her every hour. If you see that the bite mark is disappearing and she's getting better, it means she is turning. You have to keep her face covered and bury her tomorrow evening. Till then, she'll not be perilous, and you can all say goodbye to her. Father." He turned to the priest. "Please take care of her soul. We'll take care of her body after you bury her, take some precautions, make sure she doesn't wake up as a vampire."

Eleanor's mother sobbed, and Luisa was crying.

"How do you know these things?" The priest furrowed his bushy eyebrows. "Who are you?"

"We are hunters," said Samson in a certain and cold voice. "And I know this and many other things from experience."

"Then why are you wearing masks?"

"For protection. We have families. What do you think the vampires will do to them if they find out who we are?" lied Samson, then stepped to Richard and asked, "Is she your wife?"

"Yes," said Richard with a trembling voice.

"You should bury her tomorrow before dark. And do it properly," said Samson strictly. "What happened to her is not her fault." He walked to Eleanor's sobbing mother and father and said, much softer, "Don't be afraid of her, she is still your daughter. She is harmless until tomorrow night." He looked at everybody and added, "We will catch that monster."

Samson walked to the front door, followed by Ruben.

"I advise you to keep in secret what happened to her." Samson looked at the baby in the old maid's arms. "For her and for this child's sake," he said and left the house.

Craig knew Samson was trying to protect Eleanor, make them remember her as she was, not let the fear replace their love, and he was very grateful to him for that.

Two days later, Eleanor woke up in the castle.

Chapter Twelve

TODAY

AFTER EVERYTHING that had happened the previous evening, the last thing Amanda wanted to do was to go to Alec's party. But she also didn't want to break her promise. Besides, if Amanda didn't go, Hanna wouldn't go, and there would be no point for Kimberly and Ruben to go, either. And Kimberly was so excited about it. When she called this morning, all she talked about was Ruben said this and Ruben did that, and how much she liked him. Amanda didn't want to ruin it for her. She knew exactly how Kimberly felt because now that Craig had finally noticed her, she wished she, too, could tell everybody how happy it made her.

But she couldn't. Not yet. She wasn't sure if he did what he did because he liked her or because he was just worried about her.

The doorbell rang. Amanda checked in the mirror one more time before going downstairs. She ran her hands over her hips, making sure that her dark-blue, fitted dress didn't have wrinkles. Then she pulled back her hair.

"You look stunning," said Hanna's voice behind her. "Alec will faint."

"That's the plan," said Amanda, turning around. "And after I disable him, maybe you'll relax and have some fun."

"There is no 'relax' for me. It'll be one down, three to go."

"Three? What do you mean?"

"Nothing, it was a stupid joke. Let's go," said Hanna and stepped out of the door.

"Hanna, wait. You don't think that those guys will show up there, do you? And when did they become three?"

"You have nothing to worry about."

"Listen, I know that you're guarding me." Amanda rolled her eyes. "God, that sounds funny. But what can you do against three men? I don't remember you taking karate lessons. If you are going to pull their hair out, then I'm in." She grinned.

"You think this is funny," said Hanna, stepping back into the room. "If you see those guys, you better run in the opposite direction and take Kimberly with you."

"What if they hurt you? You want me to just leave you there alone?

"They can't hurt me, and I'm not alone. That's why Ruben is here."

"What does that mean, they can't hurt you? Why? Because you're so tough?" Amanda said. "Why didn't you tell me about these things? You're my best friend. I thought that we didn't keep secrets from each other."

"I thought so, too," said Hanna with a cryptic smile.

"What are you talking about?"

"Craig can't come to the party, but he'll be around. If something goes wrong, we'll let him know. Let's go, Ruben and Kimberly are waiting." She left the room before Amanda could speak again.

~

AMANDA SPOTTED Alec as she got out of the car, standing on the porch with a few guys from his football team. He walked to her with a bright smile across his face.

"Hi. I've been waiting for you," he said, then said hello to her friends.

"This is my date," said Kimberly, proudly taking Ruben's arm.

"I'm Alec." Alec reached out his hand.

"Ruben," said Ruben, taking it.

"Come on in, guys." Alec took Amanda by her waist and led her inside. "You look gorgeous," he said, leaning to her ear.

Hanna gritted her teeth. As they stepped in, their voices drowned in the bass of the loud music, and she was glad that she couldn't hear him anymore.

The party was already in full swing. The furniture in the large living room had been dragged aside, opening a big dance floor. It was crowded with people, mostly seniors from school.

"Let's sit there," said Hanna, nodding to the empty couch under the staircase.

Hanna, Kimberly, and Ruben passed the table loaded with snacks and plastic cups and dropped onto the couch.

Hanna looked away from Alec and Amanda as they talked on the other side of the dance floor. She gazed around the flickering sound lights, searching for unfamiliar faces.

"Who is that, in the gray jacket?" she asked Kimberly, looking suspiciously at the guy leaning on the wall apart from everybody, a blue plastic cup in his hand.

"That's Nicole's boyfriend," said Kimberly.

"Are you sure? I've never seen him before," said Hanna.

"That's because he's new. They started dating only a week ago, and he's not from our school," explained Kimberly.

"A-ha." Hanna and Ruben exchanged a glance.

"Why? Do you like him?" asked Kimberly with a teasing smile.

"Kimberly, believe me, I can do better than that," said Hanna. "And, as you know, I am spoken for."

"If I could meet the one you're spoken for at least once, it would help me remember."

Alec and Amanda moved toward them.

"Would you like a drink?" Alec shouted over the music. "Ricky is making mojitos in the kitchen."

"Thank you, that would be nice," said Amanda.

"Just friends, hmm?" said Hanna to Amanda after Alec left.

"Sorry, my plan didn't work," said Amanda, sitting next to her.

"Oh, it worked, all right."

"I don't understand why you hate Alec so much," said Kimberly angrily. "He's a very handsome and nice guy."

Ruben took Kimberly's hand and stood up.

"Kimberly, let's have some fun," he said and dragged her into the dancing crowd.

"I am sorry," Hanna sighed. "It's really not my business. He's not who I have to protect you from." She cracked a smile. "I'm sure you can deal with this one yourself."

Amanda watched Kimberly and Ruben dance.

"Kimberly likes him. She's so fascinated," she said.

"Yes, that's what scares me."

"Why? What now?" said Amanda, a little irritated. "Why can't you just be happy for her?"

"Amanda, you don't understand . . ."

The phone lying on Hanna's lap vibrated. They both looked at it. It was a message from her boyfriend, Ned.

"You see? You can have a boyfriend, and she can't?"

"Ah . . ." Hanna spread her hands, then dropped them helplessly on her knees. "I don't want her to get hurt. She'll fall in love with him, and very soon, Ruben will have to leave, forever."

"Why? It seems he likes her, too."

"I'm sure he does, but . . . I can't explain . . . it's complicated."

"He doesn't really have a girlfriend, does he?"

"No, it's nothing like that."

"I see, more secrets," said Amanda, pressing her lips together.

"Amanda . . ."

"Why can't you tell me, Hanna? As I understand, I'm part of that secret, too, and I have plenty of questions."

"And very soon you'll get all the answers. But not right now, and not from me."

Amanda sighed and looked around.

"Are they here?" she asked.

"No, not the two I saw at the lake. But I don't know what the third one looks like. And there can be others."

"Ladies," said Alec, appearing in front of them with three mojitos.

"It's not too strong, is it?" asked Amanda, taking one of the glasses.

"Absolutely not, trust me," said Alec, handing the second glass to Hanna and putting the last one on the small coffee table.

"Thank you," said Hanna. She took the glass, sipped from it, then looked at Amanda, "It's fine."

"As I said," Alec smiled. "And, Hanna, you can trust me too."

"Sorry, I didn't mean to . . ." she looked guiltily at Amanda.

Debra Gordon popped up out of nowhere and walked toward them with an artificial smile on her face. She wore a short red dress with frills around the waist.

"Hi," she said. "Nice party, isn't it?" And, without waiting for an answer, turned to Alec. "Come." She took his arm.

Alec threw her an annoyed glance. "I'm busy, Debra," he said, gently removing her hand from his arm.

"Mark wants to have a word with you."

"What is it?"

Debra shrugged.

"Sorry," Alec said to Amanda. "I'll be back in a minute."

"What is she now, a messenger?" said Hanna, looking after them.

It was funny to watch Debra trying to catch up with Alec, who deftly and quickly moved through the dancing crowd.

"Where did they go?" asked Hanna, bemused, as Alec and Debra suddenly disappeared.

"I don't know. This is a big house. I'm sure there are other rooms besides this one," said Amanda with irony.

"Then I have to check them." Hanna stood up.

But Amanda grabbed her arm and dragged her back.

"No. It'll look like you're spying on them. And besides, I'm here, not there, and you should stay with me."

A few minutes later Hanna saw Alec talking to the DJ. Slow music started. He walked to Amanda and took her hand.

"Shall we?" he said and pulled her along.

Now, when Hanna was alone, she read the message from Ned, saying how much he missed her and that he would be there soon. Hanna sighed.

Ruben came back and sat next to her.

"Where's Kimberly?" she asked.

"She's talking to that girl, Nicole. I asked her to find out a bit more about the guy."

"Didn't she ask why? She might think you like him." Hanna smirked.

"I said that he looks like some escaped felon I saw in the newspaper."

"She's not stupid, you know."

"No, she's not. She said it, too. But she said she'd ask for me."

"That's it, she thinks you like him," Hanna laughed. "Especially since you didn't kiss her yesterday."

"I have the whole night to fix that mistake." Ruben beamed.

Hanna elbowed him.

"Do you see anybody else who looks suspicious?" asked Ruben.

"No, and as long as Alec is far from the door, they can't get in."

"Then you can relax. This is a party and you deserve some fun. Come on, sis, dance with me." He stood up.

"Okay, let's dance."

Ruben kept an eye on Kimberly while they danced, and Hanna tried not to lose Alec and Amanda from her view.

∽

"THIS IS OUR FIRST DANCE," said Alec.

His voice was casual, but he looked into Amanda's eyes with a tender gaze. Kimberly was right, Alec was very handsome. Amanda noticed that he seemed different tonight, more relaxed and confident than usual.

"Yes," said Amanda, turning her eyes away.

"It feels nice," he said.

Amanda didn't say anything, but he was right, it felt nice. She hadn't had a date for a long time. It was nice to have somebody beside her who liked her and wanted to be with her. To know that she could put her arms around him if she wanted to, that she could call him anytime and he'd be there for her. She was in love, and she had all those feelings suppressed inside her. Except they weren't for Alec. And if she felt comfortable enough with him to loosen that choking pressure a little bit, then Hanna was right—she and Alec weren't friends. Deep down, she knew that but didn't want to admit it. Alec had been working his way to her for two months now, and he wasn't looking for friendship. To him, this evening was their first date, and she was sure he would try to take advantage of it.

When the music ended, he didn't let her go.

"I want to show you something," he said. "Come, it's in my room."

Amanda looked back at Hanna as she and Alec walked up the stairs. Hanna had stopped dancing and was staring at her with disapproval.

∽

"AND WHAT SHOULD I DO NOW?" said Hanna. "Go up there and guard the door?"

"Look." Ruben nodded toward the hallway on the right side of the front door. "There's a lot of movement over there."

"I know. That's where Alec went with Debra."

"I'll go check."

"No, I'll do it. You don't know how the vampires look. Kimberly is coming. Stay with her and keep an eye on the stairs," said Hanna and drifted away.

She went around the dance floor. When she passed a bunch of giggling students, somebody grabbed her arm.

"Hanna, hi!"

It was Sara. Judging by her glittering eyes, the cup of beer in her hand wasn't her first.

"Hi," Hanna said, grinning. "Having fun?"

"Oh, yeah. Great party, isn't it?" She pulled Hanna aside. "Listen, who is that guy you were dancing with? Is he your boyfriend?"

"Oh, no. He's my cousin."

"God, he is so hot. Can you introduce me?"

"Sorry, but he's taken. He's here with Kimberly."

"Damn it, all the cool guys are taken." She desperately shook her hand with the plastic cup in it. The beer splashed out on her skirt and shoes. "Dammit! Look what I did. I need a bathroom." She headed toward the hallway.

Hanna followed her.

"The bathroom is here?" she said disappointed. "Are you sure?"

"Yes, right next to the basement."

"The basement." Hanna bit her lip. "Of course."

∽

"NICE," Amanda looked around, pleasantly surprised.

Alec's room didn't look like a teenage football player's room. It was large and spacious. Except for his desk, which had some books and sheets of paper lying around the laptop, it was clean; things were in their place. He had pictures, books, cameras and lenses, and only a couple of football accessories on the shelves. The walls were covered not with posters, but with beautifully framed photographs and paintings.

"Not what you expected?"

"To be honest, no. I expected to see more football gear. I knew you liked photography, but I didn't know it was a priority," she said, stepping to the picture of an eagle soaring above the sea.

"Football helps me stay in good shape, but photography and painting are my passion."

"Are these all yours?"

"Yes."

"Where did you take this one?" Amanda asked, looking spellbound at the large image of a castle, captured at night in heavy rain.

"In England." Alec stepped closer to her.

"It's magnificent, and it looks so mysterious."

"Remember I told you about my website? It's done. Most of my work is there. I'll send you the link. Promise that you'll look at it. I'd like to know your opinion."

"Sure," said Amanda. "Do you want me to leave a comment?" she joked.

"No." He gently took her by the arms and pulled her closer. "I want you to tell me in person." His gray eyes pierced hers. "May seventeenth was your birthday. I have something for you. I hope you like it."

He let go of her and walked to the desk. A large framed picture leaned on the side of it. He lifted it and turned it around.

A thrill went through Amanda. It was a painting of her. In it, she walked alone down the empty park alley. Its trees and the ground were covered by yellow and red leaves. She wore dark jeans and a short black leather jacket, and a small bag hung on her shoulder. A breeze pulled back her long hair. She was smiling, the way people smile when they think that nobody is looking at them.

Amanda remembered that day. The park was far from school, and it was months ago before Amanda and Alec were even friends yet. That fact moved something deep inside her.

"Say something," he said. "You look sad. You don't like it?"

"I love it," said Amanda quietly. "I don't know how to explain. You know that feeling when something is so beautiful and so real that it makes you happily sad?"

Alec smiled.

"That was exactly my reaction when I saw you in that alley. That means you see what I wanted to show." He put the picture aside. "I'll take it to your place. I hope you'll hang it in your room."

"I will. Thank you."

He stepped to her.

"Amanda, I know you think of me as a friend." He hugged her, and his lips touched her temple. "But I have feelings for you. I thought that maybe if I told you, you'd look at me differently."

Amanda closed her eyes. She saw it coming, but the voiced version of his feelings confused her.

"I see you, Alec," she whispered. "You're interesting and attractive, but . . ."

She didn't know what to say.

"No, don't say anything." He pulled back. "You need time. Just promise me you'll think about it."

She didn't want to cause him pain, not today. Maybe she would wait until the end of school. After graduation, they would all go in different directions. He'd start a new life and forget about her.

"Okay, I promise," she said and stepped to the door. "Let's go before people start talking."

"Maybe we should give them something to talk about?" chuckled Alec.

"Come on." Amanda smiled and opened the door.

∼

HANNA WALKED down the basement stairs. The basement itself was a big room with a low ceiling, and it was buzzing with people. She greeted those sitting beside the stairs and stepped forward. About half a dozen boys and girls stood around a pool table, watching the game. Hanna's eyes moved from one face to another. Some of them she knew pretty well, others only vaguely. And then, farther, in the corner, she saw Debra sitting with three young men. Two of those three pale faces Hanna recognized immediately. The third one held Debra around the shoulders, his deep-set eyes staring at Hanna. She seethed with rage.

"You stupid cow," she grumbled through gritted teeth.

"Did you say something?" The guy standing beside her turned around.

"No, no." She stepped away from him.

The vampire hugging Debra sneered at Hanna. There was nothing she could do right now; she had to leave, but her legs were moving in the opposite direction of the exit.

"Hanna." Debra sounded surprised.

Hanna stopped in front of them.

"Did you want something?" asked Debra.

But Hanna didn't look at her. She kept staring at the smiling vampire.

"Your bills are coming, pal, you'll pay for everything you've done." She sneered back. "So smile while you can."

"Oh, will I?" The vampire let go of Debra and leaned forward.

"Do you guys know each other?" asked Debra, ping-ponging her eyes from one to another.

"You don't know who you're playing with," said Hanna, ignoring Debra.

The vampire laughed. "I know exactly who you are, and when the time comes, we'll see who wins."

"I know what you're hoping for. But it's never gonna happen."

"So you don't wanna fight? Why? Scared already?"

"Fight—that's when you go up against an equal. You'll always be just a bunch of leeches." Hanna looked at him despisingly.

The other two rose from their seats, but the third vampire raised his hand, stopping them.

"Aren't you forgetting something? You're nothing without one very special thing, and you don't have it." The vampire's thin lips curled into a confident smile.

They were attracting attention. The room was becoming quieter and quieter.

"Oh, I'll get it," said Hanna. "We'll get back everything that belongs to us." Looking at stunned Debra, she said flatly, "Have a nice evening," and walked away.

∽

RUBEN AND KIMBERLY sat on the couch. He drank his beer while she sipped mojitos.

"His name is Zac. He and Alec went to high school together," Kimberly said.

"To high school? I don't understand," said Ruben.

"To his previous high school. Alec isn't from Green Hill; he moved here only a year ago. Nicole said Alec introduced them when they ran into each other at a coffee shop. The next day, Zac asked him for her phone number."

"Thanks, Kimberly."

"Are you going to tell me what you need this for?"

"Hanna," said Ruben, spotting her. He put down his beer. "Is everything all right? You look disturbed."

"I think it's time to leave," said Hanna.

"Leave?" said Kimberly, shoulders slumping. "Why?"

"Kimberly, excuse us for a second," said Ruben. He pulled Hanna aside. "What happened?"

"They're here, in the basement, and I think that it's better if we leave."

"I got that part, but I know you better than you think. What happened, Hanna, what did you do?"

"Nothing," she said, looking away.

"Hanna," he insisted.

"Ok. We had a few words. I couldn't help it. He sneered at me, and it made me angry."

"And now you've made *them* angry."

"They killed Mr. Sullivan."

"And what do you think they'll do now?"

"They would do it anyways—they need to feed. And I think we should stop them."

Ruben glanced around and saw Amanda and Alec coming down the stairs.

"You're right. We can't leave all those young people unprotected. We need to fish the vampires out of here. But first, we have to take Amanda to a safe place."

Amanda and Kimberly conversed for a moment, then Amanda approached Hanna and Ruben.

"Kimberly said we're leaving. What happened? Are they here?" she asked.

"Yes, all three of them, and guess who they came with?"

"Who?"

"That moron, Debra."

"Debra? Guys, they're not going to hurt her, are they?"

"First we have to make sure they won't hurt you. Let's go," said Ruben, and the three of them returned to Kimberly and Alec.

"Kimberly." Ruben took her hand. "Sorry, but we'll have to go now."

"Guys, it's not even ten yet," said Alec. "Is something wrong?"

"Nothing's wrong," said Amanda. "Something came up. I'm sorry, Alec. We really have to go. You have fun, though," she nodded toward the dancing crowd.

"I am not much of a dancer," said Alec. "Mark asked me to play a round of pool with him. I think I'll take him up on his offer."

"Mark? Is that Debra's new boyfriend?" Hanna asked innocently.

"Boyfriend or date, I don't know, but, yes, that's him. She introduced us a couple of days ago."

"Hanna, we need to go. It was nice to meet you," Ruben said to Alec, and he and Kimberly headed to the front door.

"Bye," said Amanda, and she and Hanna followed them.

But as soon as they crossed the threshold, somebody called Hanna. They turned and saw Debra.

"Debra, are you alright?" asked Hanna, looking at her frowning face.

"Am I all right?" shouted Debra. "What was that all about?"

"Debra—"

"Those things you said. Why would you do that?" Debra kept shouting.

"Debra, listen to me," said Hanna calmly. "Those guys are very dangerous."

"They were nice to me before you came."

"They were nice to you because they need you. You better go home. You'll be safe there."

"You're worried about me?" Debra laughed nervously. "You better worry about yourself. You made them so angry. They left and are probably looking for you."

"They left?" Hanna stared at Amanda. "I didn't see them leave."

"Amanda," a voice called behind them.

Amanda and Hanna looked back. Two feet away from them stood Craig.

"Amanda, you need to get in the car." He put his hand around Amanda's back and led her to the street.

Hanna turned to Debra.

"I'm saying this for your own good, Debra, stay away from those men."

But Debra wasn't listening. Her eyes were following Amanda and Craig.

"Oh, my god," she whispered. All her irritation and anger

were gone. "Who is that guy?" she asked Hanna, with pleasant surprise on her face.

Hanna shook her head.

"She can't get enough, can she?" muttered Debra.

"What's that supposed to mean?"

"If she has that," Debra pointed after Amanda and Craig, who had already disappeared from view, "Why would she take Alec from me?"

"She didn't take him. Amanda and Alec are just friends."

"Friends, huh? Have you seen his photo collection of her? We dated for three months and he has only two pictures of me, and they're both with his football team."

Two guys having a beer on the porch chortled.

Alec walked out of the house. He looked sideways at the guys until they went inside. With his hands in his pockets, he stepped closer and stopped behind Debra.

"You talk too much," he said in a cold voice.

Debra flinched and looked back.

"I think you should go inside." He gazed at her.

She flipped her hair and left without saying a word.

"Sorry for that," said Alec to Hanna.

Hanna nodded and walked away.

She came out to the driveway and looked at her car across the road. It was empty. She turned to the left and peered into the darkness, then took a few steps forward. She had just spotted Craig's jeep in the string of parked cars when two men grabbed her arms from both sides. She glanced back and saw the familiar faces. Hanna jerked, trying to free herself, but the grip was too tight.

"Easy," she heard Mark's voice. There was a flash, and the vampire appeared in front of her. "Even if you did have your powers, you wouldn't be able to do much against the three of us."

"If I had my powers, you wouldn't even have a chance to speak your first word."

"Then maybe you're right. Maybe I have to seize my chances while I can," said Mark, and his fist slammed into her stomach.

Hanna cringed in pain.

∽

"WHERE'S HANNA?" asked Ruben the moment Amanda and Craig got into the car.

"She was right behind us," said Craig.

"Maybe she went to her car," suggested Kimberly.

"She was talking to Debra," said Amanda. "Debra seemed pretty angry. Guys, what happened?" She turned to Ruben and Kimberly, who sat in the back.

"I don't know," said Kimberly. "All I know is, while you were gone, she left, too, and when she came back she said we had to leave."

"Ruben," said Craig, "am I understanding this right? You were with Kimberly, Hanna was gone . . ."

"She was safe," said Ruben, predicting Craig's question. "She was upstairs, and I was—"

"Dammit," said Craig through his teeth.

"I'm telling you," said Ruben, but then realized Craig wasn't talking to him. His eyes were fixed at the street ahead, and the rest of them followed his gaze.

Two men held Hanna by her arms, and a third one appeared out of nowhere, spoke to her, then hit her in the stomach.

"Hanna!" screamed Amanda.

"Oh my God," Kimberly gasped.

Ruben hopped outside. Amanda grabbed the door handle,

but as soon as she opened it, Craig pulled her to him and Ruben shut her door.

The back door was still open. Ruben bent down and leveled with Kimberly's shocked face.

"Everything's going to be fine," he assured her, then closed the door and stormed away.

"Hanna will be fine, I promise," said Craig. "Amanda, listen to me. Whatever happens next—don't do anything rash. I don't think they know you're in this car."

"It's all because of me, it's my fault," Amanda muttered with trembling lips.

"I need to go there," said Craig, "Lock the doors. If anyone tries to get in, just drive away. Otherwise, wait for Hanna. Do you understand?"

Amanda nodded.

"I don't," Kimberly suddenly yelled. "What the hell is going on?"

"Kimberly, all questions later. And, please, keep your voice down, those guys have pretty good hearing."

∽

RUBEN DIDN'T WANT the vampires to see the direction from which he had come, so he snuck to the other side of the street.

"Let her go," he said in a cold voice, and all three men gazed at him.

"Or you'll do what? Slap me to death? Ruben, if I'm not mistaken?" said Mark.

"Hey, Mark," called Hanna.

The vampire turned around. Drawing on the two men clutching her arms, Hanna kicked him in the chest with both feet.

"Or we can do that," she said.

Mark staggered backward. Ruben, who was standing right behind him, kicked him in his back. Mark collapsed face down.

"Never turn your back on the enemy," said Ruben and kicked him once more, this time in the head.

Distracted, one of the vampires holding Hanna loosened his grip. Hanna jerked her arm and elbowed him in the nose. But the other one was too fast, and before her fist met his face, he caught it, pushed it down, and clasped his arms around her chest. The elbowed vampire swung his hand at Hanna, but Ruben was already there and hit him in the chest, then sent another blow to his nose. This time it cracked.

The vampire groaned, then snarled rabidly, baring his fangs, and his fist landed in Ruben's face. Ruben hit the ground.

Hanna made one more effort to get free, but the vampire holding her twisted her wrist upward. She doubled over.

"All right, you had your fun," said Mark in fury, jumping to his feet again. His face changed. His eyes glowed red, and fangs protruded from his upper lip. "Now it's our tu—"

Craig grabbed him around his neck from behind. His free hand pressed a stake to Mark's back.

"One movement and I'll stick it through your heart," said Craig through his teeth. "I have done this for centuries, and I won't miss, believe me."

Ruben rose and stood beside Craig. None of the vampires moved.

"Now, let her go," said Craig, looking at the one holding Hanna's hand.

The vampire obeyed.

"Go," said Craig, nodding to where his jeep was parked.

Hanna ran to the car.

∾

AMANDA SAW Hanna running to them and unlocked the doors.

"Hanna, I am so sorry. That was horrible."

"Are you all right?" asked Kimberly warily, "You look all right."

"I'm fine." Hanna started the engine. "Put your seatbelts on," she said and drove away, leaving Craig and Ruben behind.

"Where are you going?" asked Kimberly. "What about them?"

"They're big guys, they can take care of themselves," said Hanna.

"Can they? A minute ago Ruben was on the ground."

"I am doing what they asked me to do—taking you away."

"We have to call the police."

"No." Hanna looked at Kimberly in the rearview mirror.

"Why not?" asked Kimberly, who had her cellphone ready.

"Kimberly, put that phone down. They're my brothers, and I would never leave them in danger. I know you're scared, but you have to trust me. Nothing is going to happen to them."

"Hanna, Craig—He was holding something in his hand. It wasn't a knife, was it?" Amanda asked carefully.

"Relax. It was just a piece of wood."

"It's all because of me," said Amanda, shaking her head. "We shouldn't have gone to that party."

"You keep saying that. Why?" said Kimberly, spreading her hands in bewilderment. "What does it have to do with you?"

"You know it's not true," said Hanna. "You heard what Debra said. It's my fault."

"Debra? Debra said something? When the hell did that happen?" asked Kimberly.

But nobody paid attention.

"What was that all about?" Amanda asked Hanna.

"She wasn't exaggerating. I really made them angry. Sorry, lost my temper. God," Hanna moaned, "Craig will kill me."

Amanda looked back at Kimberly.

"It happened when we were leaving."

"Remember I asked Alec about Debra's new boyfriend?" said Hanna. "He was the one who hit me,"

"No," Kimberly gasped. "You think that it was Debra? That she sent them after you? You know, she might be a bitch, but she would never do something like that."

"No, she has nothing to do with it," said Hanna. She stopped the car in front of Kimberly's house and turned to her. "Are you still alone?" she asked before Kimberly could come up with another undesirable question.

"Yes, my parents come back tomorrow night. Let's go in."

The moment they stepped inside, Hanna's cellphone rang. It was Ruben.

"Where are you?" he asked.

"At Kimberly's. What happened? Is everything all right?"

"Everything's fine. We got away. Hanna, they're pretty pissed off, so it's best if you girls stay indoors."

"We will. Is Craig mad at me?"

"We haven't gotten to that part yet."

"At least I got them out of the house," said Hanna.

"Let's wait for the morning news. We'll see if it worked."

Hanna sighed.

"See you tomorrow," said Ruben, and he hung up.

"They're fine," said Hanna to the staring at her Kimberly and Amanda. "Slumber party?"

Chapter Thirteen

YEAR 1834

IN SPRING 1834, when a small, red mark appeared on the Map showing signs of trouble in Virginia, Fray, annoyed by everybody's big love and attention to Craig and all that stir around his pregnant Eleanor, gladly volunteered to go and find out what the problem was. He arrived in Lynchburg and met the local witch, Martha, who had summoned him. She told Fray an interesting story.

A well-known painter had knocked on her door about a week ago. He looked like he had been ill for a long time. He said he knew Martha was a witch and had come to her because nobody else would understand.

He said that a woman around the age of twenty-five came to him at night nearly a month ago and introduced herself as Ms. Murray. She asked him to paint her portrait and promised a good payment, but with one condition: he had to do it at her place and stay there until he finished his work. The painter agreed, and not only because of the money; the woman was very beautiful, and he imagined how magnificent the portrait would be.

She took him to a manor outside the town. He didn't know

which way they went; as soon as they got in the carriage, she drew the curtains.

As they walked into the house, he saw a few other people. They didn't look like servants, more like friends or companions, but they all obeyed her and listened to everything she said, which seemed weird to the man. He also found it strange that they never went outside in the daytime, no matter how good the weather was. They went for a walk only when it was very cloudy. When Martha asked him if they left the house at night, the painter said he didn't know. When it was getting dark, the woman would send him to his room. Then one of her men would bring him dinner, and he never remembered what he did after he ate it or how he fell asleep.

But even though the painter got more than enough time to rest, he felt very weak and got worse every day.

The painter was almost done with the portrait when, one night, he saw something that frightened him. He had been so weak the whole day he couldn't eat his dinner when they brought it. It was the first time it took a while before he fell asleep. His sleep wasn't as deep as usual, and after a short time, he was awakened by the neighing of horses and some bustling.

When he looked out of the window, he saw that two of the men who lived in the house were dragging a girl to the backyard. She struggled, trying to get free and making noises that sounded like suppressed cries. The painter was stunned. He didn't know what to do. He thought maybe he should tell Ms. Murray what he had witnessed. He walked out of his room and searched the first floor, but he didn't find anybody. Assuming that she was asleep upstairs, he decided to try to find out what those men wanted from that woman. Perhaps she was a whore, or she had stolen something from them? And if they planned to do something unsavory, he could threaten to wake Ms. Murray. These men obeyed her, after all.

He went outside and kept close to the bushes as he

quietly got around the house. He saw an outbuilding in the backyard. Voices, one of which was female and sounded familiar, drifted from the open door. The painter cowered behind the bushes and crept to the closest window, then looked through it.

What he saw confused him even more. In the middle of the mostly empty room, lit by about a dozen large candles, sat Ms. Murray. All her men stood around her. The girl was tied to a chair, and Ms. Murray looked at her with a delighted expression on her face. The girl stared back with pleading, tear-filled eyes.

"I like her. Good job, gentlemen," said Ms. Murray with a smile.

"We are glad to please you, Ma'am," said one of the men.

"I bet she tastes good, too."

The painter's mouth fell open. Was that a joke? Or was this some kind of game? Very stupid and very violent, but a game nonetheless?

"Gregor, did anybody see you?" Ms. Murray asked.

"No, Ma'am. She was praying in the church, all alone," said the man.

"I see." She stood up, walked to the girl, and pulled the gag out of her mouth. "Your God is so helpful." She laughed.

"Please, please, let me go, please," begged the girl. Her lips shook, and tears streamed from her wide-open eyes.

"Oh, sorry, dear, I can't. You see." Ms. Murray clutched the girl's jaw and pulled up her head. "I'm hungry and you're my dinner," she said with an evil smile. "And I'm going to have it right now. Untie her," she commanded, letting go of the girl.

The second the girl got free, she ran toward the open door. In a twinkling, Ms. Murray was standing right in front of her, even the painter hadn't seen her move. She grabbed the girl and pressed her to herself.

At that moment Ms. Murray's face changed. The painter

couldn't see every detail, but he was sure he saw fangs sticking out of her mouth, and something had happened to her eyes.

The girl screamed in horror.

"You're going to sing for me? So nice of you." Ms. Murray turned to her men. "Are you sure the painter is asleep? If he hears any of this, I'll have to kill him before he finishes my portrait."

The painter froze.

"I gave him his dinner more than an hour ago. I'm sure he's asleep," said the youngest of the men.

"Shut the door, just in case," she said, then growled and bent to the girl's neck.

The moment the door closed, the terrified painter headed back to the house as fast as he could. All he wanted was to run away from that place. But it was impossible—he didn't know where he was, and even if he knew, he wouldn't make it far; he was too weak.

He returned to his room. Shaking, he sat on the chair and looked suspiciously at his untouched dinner. To make the plate look like it usually did after he finished with it, he took the knife and fork and sliced everything into small pieces, then threw half of the food out of the window into the bushes.

The painter was sure that when he finished the portrait, Ms. Murray would kill him. But to his surprise, when the work was done a few days later, he was taken home and paid as promised.

When Martha told him they were vampires, he said that he had supposed as much, but he was afraid to share his story with anybody else. Even in a town like Lynchburg, which people called Satan's Kingdom, nobody would believe him.

"Was he really poisoned?" asked Fray after Martha finished the story.

"It was a very powerful soporific mixture, and I think it's the reason she let him go. His blood wasn't good. I gave him a potion, and when he came to me yesterday, he was feeling much better."

"He came back? Why? What did he want this time?"

Martha stood up, walked to the old cabinet, and pulled from its drawer a piece of parchment.

"He brought me this," she said, handing the parchment to Fray. "I told him I know people who can take the vampires down. He thought that this might help you find them."

What Fray was looking at was a drawing, from which a young woman looked back at him with her cold blue eyes. The ends of her black, arched brows were hidden under black wavy locks on her temples. The rest of the hair was pulled back and collected in a high bun. Her contoured lips expressed a barely perceptible, mysterious smile.

"Mesmerizing, isn't it?" said Martha.

It was, and that possessing gaze pierced Fray. The face had an attractive zest that brought up curiosity and excitement, both unusual for Fray. He looked at Martha on the other side of the table. The elderly witch stared at him, unblinking like she was trying to read his thoughts.

"Fray, she is evil," she said pointedly. "All I see behind that beauty is a coldblooded, evil bitch."

"Don't worry," Fray said, irritated, "I remember who I am and who I'm fighting against." He stood up and walked to the big fireplace made of river rocks. "Is there anything you can do to help me find the manor? Maybe some locator spell?"

Martha looked at the drawing.

"I'll see if I can locate her. If she's not too far, it can work."

She stood up and went back to the cabinet, smoothing her white apron. On its left side was a door. She took out a key from the small, narrow drawer and unlocked it.

"Take the parchment and come with me," she said.

She led him to a modest square room with only one small window on the wall opposite to the door. Under the window stood a chest of drawers with several figurines and crystal balls on it. The walls were lined with shelves filled up with dusty boxes, bottles, and jars. Some of them contained turbid liquids, others held powders and an array of dry herbs and flowers.

Martha put the parchment on the round table in the middle of the room and lit three candles around it. She took a jar with silver powder from a shelf and sprinkled a pinch of it on the drawing. Then she closed her eyes, held her hand above the picture, and began to whisper.

Martha froze for a few seconds, then began whispering again.

"Follow," she said, louder.

Under the eyelids of her still closed eyes, her irises moved from side to side. Suddenly, she gasped, and her eyes flew open.

"She's in the painter's house," said Martha, and hurried to the living room. "I think he's in danger. And she's not alone, there is a man with her."

Martha wrote down the address on a small piece of paper and handed it to Fray.

"Go, hurry."

Fray took it and left in a rush. He wasn't rushing to save the painter. He wasn't thinking of him. He wanted the woman. She possessed all the qualities he was meant to fight, and his duty was to destroy her. But, against all the rules, she was also the kind of woman, who attracted Fray the most. He rushed because he was seized with an irresistible desire not to kill, but to catch her.

But it didn't happen. When he found the house and entered the already open door, he was surrounded by a deep silence. The painter lay dead not far from the entrance, which probably meant a quick death. She was in a hurry. Why?

Fray felt her scent and followed it outside, but he lost the track only a few yards away from the door. The vampire smell was long blown away by the fresh spring wind. Frustrated, he stared at the dark, narrow, empty street and, admitting the fact that the woman was gone, he went back.

Martha stood with closed eyes beside the round table, her hand on the picture.

"I missed her," he said.

"I know."

"Can you find her again? Try to locate the manor."

"It is too late." She opened her eyes. "She's gone. And I don't think she's coming back."

"What?" Anger crossed Fray's face. "But why? What do you think happened?"

"I have no idea."

"First, she lets the painter go, and then she comes back after him." Fray was pacing and muttering. "Something happened. Something alarmed her." He stopped and looked at Martha. "Is it possible that she knew I was coming?"

"No. When she came to him, she was already prepared to leave, and everybody was waiting for her. I saw it."

"Then what scared her?"

"You can ask her when you find her. Something tells me you won't rest until you do." She handed him the drawing and gave him a cold look. "You forgot to mention the painter is dead."

"Yes, he is dead," said Fray, pretending he cared.

But he didn't fool Martha. Her wrinkled face didn't change its accusing expression. She blew out the candles and left the room.

"It's not just my fault," said Fray, following her. "Why didn't you call us earlier? What were you waiting for?"

"Because I didn't know," she shouted. "There were no bodies, no deaths under mysterious circumstances. People were missing, but I didn't know why."

"Don't worry, Martha, she'll pay for what she did." He rolled up the parchment and pointed it at the witch, who looked at him askance. "I can still track her down. It's not over yet."

But he was wrong. He didn't find her that day or even that year. All he found out was that Ms. Murray had been invited to look after the house, which belonged to an old, married couple, who suddenly left for France without informing friends or neighbors. He also found "France" in a grave behind the manor.

Chapter Fourteen

TODAY

AMANDA STOOD in the middle of a green field. Craig ran across it and stopped before her. Looking deep into her eyes, he said, "Eleanor."

Amanda woke up and groaned in disappointment. She pushed away the tickling ginger hair lying across her face, then looked at Kimberly's back on one side and Hanna, with her nose buried in the pillow, on the other side. She sat up and leaned against the headboard.

"How do you even breathe like that?" she asked, glancing at Hanna's curls outspread on the pillow.

Kimberly lifted her head and looked over her shoulder.

"With her ears," she said, and they laughed.

"I don't know, but as long as I'm not choking . . ." Hanna rolled over, "What time is it?" She took her cellphone from the nightstand. "Wow, it's long past my coffee time."

"Ok, I'll try to be a good hostess. Coffee will be ready in five minutes," said Kimberly, and with a lazy gait, she went downstairs.

"Five minutes at that pace?" said Hanna looking after her. "I think it's a bit optimistic."

"How do you feel?" Amanda asked.

"I'm fine. Stop worrying."

"Hanna, that guy hit you."

"It wasn't that painful. I have good abs."

"What if you meet him again and nobody's around to help you?"

"I am not afraid of him. Who I'm really afraid to meet right now is Craig. He'll kick my ass."

"I can't imagine Craig angry," said Amanda. She lay down again and stared at the ceiling. "But he is so serious, sometimes, and so thoughtful."

"You noticed," said Hanna quietly. She closed her eyes. "He has a lot on his mind right now."

"Hanna?"

"Hmm."

"Who is Eleanor?" Amanda asked carefully.

Hanna's eyes flew open.

"Eleanor? Why?"

"I had . . ." Amanda hesitated for a second, and then she continued, keeping her eyes on the ceiling, "I had a dream. In it, Craig looked into my eyes and called me Eleanor."

She sat up and glanced at Hanna, who sat up, too. She stared back at Amanda in astonishment, her eyes tearing up. But then a tiny smile appeared on her face. The reaction confused Amanda.

Hanna got out of the bed, keeping her back to it. After a moment, she sat at the edge of the bed and looked at Amanda.

"Eleanor was Craig's girlfriend," she said in a low voice.

"Was? What happened?"

"She died. It was an accident."

"Oh, that's so sad." Amanda thought of her dream. "Why does he call me Eleanor in my dreams?"

"I think it's because your eyes pretty much look like hers," said Hanna fondly.

Amanda could see Eleanor meant a lot to Hanna, too.

"You were close to her, weren't you?" she asked.

"Yes. She was like a sister to me."

"Oh, Hanna." Amanda sighed. "I'm so sorry. How come you never told me about her?"

She leaned forward and squeezed Hanna's hand. A ray of sunshine fell on her wrist through the open window, and she looked at the sparkling golden circles around it. The bracelet. Her heart skipped a beat. She let go of Hanna's hand.

"Because I wasn't ready to talk about her yet." Hanna stood up and turned around looking for her clothes, but it seemed that she was trying to hide her face.

Amanda gazed at the bracelet again.

"He loved her very much," she whispered stroking it.

A mix of feelings punched her in the chest and made it difficult to breathe. Stunned, she turned her back to Hanna and muttered, "I need the bathroom."

She ran to the downstairs bathroom. The second she shut the door behind her, tears gushed from her eyes. The pain in her chest was unbearable, and she let it out. To suppress the sound, she grabbed a towel and covered her face before she started sobbing. Otherwise, how would she explain this to Hanna and Kimberly? She herself didn't understand this outburst. She took the bracelet off and put it on the sink. Right now, she needed to find out what was causing these feelings, which one of them hurt the most—was it offense, or anger, or maybe disappointment, or loss—LOSS! She looked at the bracelet again. "Craig and I want you to have it," Hanna had said when she gave it to her. "It was my idea," Craig had said. Those words were the thin thread of hope that maybe he liked her after all. That thread was gone. Amanda had lost her only hope. Now she knew why he was nice to her, and if he ever again looked into her eyes, she'd know that it wasn't Amanda he was looking at, but his intolerably missed, forever loved, irreplaceable Eleanor.

Her eyes and the tip of her nose were red from crying. Trying to control her voice, she called out to Kimberly, who was not so far away in the kitchen.

"Yes," said Kimberly from behind the door.

"Can I take a shower?" Amanda asked.

"Sure. The clean towel is under the sink. I'll bring you my bathrobe."

A few minutes later after Amanda got out of the shower, Kimberly knocked on the door. Wrapped in a towel, Amanda opened it, and Kimberly passed her a bathrobe.

"Hanna left, you can come out now," she said in a casual tone.

Amanda cast a quick glance at her.

"Why did she go?" she asked, taking the robe out of Kimberly's hands.

"Craig called and said he needs his car. But you can't leave. She said she'll be back and drive you home herself," said Kimberly. On her way out, she added, "Hurry, the coffee is ready."

Amanda walked into the kitchen where Kimberly was waiting with two cups of coffee in front of her. As she sat across from her, Kimberly pushed one of the cups toward her.

"Amanda, what's going on?"

"It's nothing," said Amanda.

"It's nothing? You were crying." She took her cup, eyes still focused on Amanda.

"I don't know what happened. We were just talking."

"Did Hanna say something to you? Is it because of what happened yesterday?"

"No, it has nothing to do with that," said Amanda, sipping the coffee.

"Then, let me guess." Kimberly put her cup down. "Maybe it has something to do with Craig?"

Amanda stared at her.

"You think I don't know?"

"How? Is it that obvious?"

"To me it is. You stop breathing every time he looks at you. I was waiting for the day you'd tell me yourself. But you keep clenching your teeth together and suffering alone. Why?" asked Kimberly, her tone a bit resentful. "We've been best friends since we were nine. We never had secrets from each other. Why didn't you tell me?"

"I don't know." Amanda glanced at her. "Maybe because once you had a crush on him too. Three years ago, when they moved to town, we both fell in love with him. You told me first, and I decided to shut up. I didn't want to ruin it for you."

"Really?" Kimberly's look softened. "Sorry, I didn't know then. But it was ages ago. Why didn't you tell me later?"

"I don't know. I guess I just got used to that pain in my heart." She took a deep breath. "Remember what you said? You said that he was gorgeous but older, and he wouldn't notice you, that to him you were just a little girl, and he wasn't going to wait until you grew up to realize what an amazing woman you'd become."

They both smiled.

"But he is still alone," said Kimberly. "Isn't it strange? A guy like him alone. Who is he waiting for?"

Amanda's face grew sad again.

"Yesterday, he was pretty worried about you," Kimberly continued. "And the other time, at dinner, he was all over you and even drove you home. Isn't that a good thing?"

"I thought so, too, until now."

"Why now, what happened?"

"He's not waiting for anybody," said Amanda bitterly. "He had a girlfriend who he loved very much, but she died."

"Oh, no," gasped Kimberly.

"Hanna just told me. I think that's why he is so thoughtful all the time. Her name was Eleanor. Hanna said that she was like a sister to her."

"So it was a big loss for her, too."

"Yes, it was. That's why she didn't tell us, she said she wasn't ready. Did Hanna hear me crying?"

"No, she ran out like a maniac."

"She probably didn't want to make Craig even angrier."

They moved to the living room. It had modern furniture and matching curtains, a beautiful thick carpet and flowers on the coffee table, and altogether it looked nice, but it made Amanda feel like a short-time visitor.

Amanda, during all those years of friendship, had been in this room only a few times, and only when Kimberly was home alone. Amanda and Hanna didn't come here often because of Kimberly's stepfather, who was a very unpleasant man with a fake smile.

Kimberly never knew her real father. Her mother raised her alone. Money was always an issue. When David came into their lives that problem was gone, but many others came instead, and very soon Kimberly's view of David as a father figure vanished. He acknowledged her presence only when he needed a glass of water or his newspaper. Her mother didn't have much time for her anymore, and Kimberly told Amanda how greatly she missed those cozy evenings in their old house with hot chocolate and cookies, the times when it was only the two of them.

Five years ago, when her brother was born, it got even worse. She felt more alone and forgotten than ever. She told Amanda that if one imagined her family as a body, she was the appendix.

They sat on the couch, and Kimberly lit a few candles in an attempt to make it feel more comfortable.

"Kimberly," said Amanda, reflecting on their conversation, "If you knew about Craig, why did you keep pushing me to Alec?"

"Because I wanted you to move on, to have a life. Alec's a nice guy, and he's in love with you. Give him a chance, or, rather—give yourself a chance."

"I tried, and you know how it ended. I dated Kevin, hoping it would help me move on, and I just broke his heart."

"That was almost a year ago, and Alec is not Kevin. Alec is level-headed and has everything to make it work. Amanda, he's not just your friend; he loves you."

"I know." Amanda sighed. "I realized that at the party. Besides, yesterday I promised him to think about it."

"He told you about his feelings?" Kimberly shrieked with joy. "That's why he took you upstairs. Please, don't push him away."

"Kimberly, he's interesting and handsome, but I don't feel anything for him."

"Things can change. Have a date, or two, and see what happens. Maybe we can go on a double date?"

Amanda remembered what Hanna had said about Ruben, about his leaving forever.

"Did Ruben ask you out?" she asked.

"Not yet. But I think he's going to." Kimberly sighed. "That bastard hit him so hard. I hope he's all right." Her voice became soft and quiet. "I think I'm falling in love. He's so different and so special. Beside him, I feel special, too. He was so gallant yesterday, and he said I looked amazing."

Amanda's heart sank. She had to say something.

"Kimberly, you know he's just visiting."

"And so what? He was very nice to me. If he likes me, we'll keep in touch and, when he can, he'll come and visit again."

Amanda knew that whatever she said now would sound wrong. She had to talk to Hanna. Maybe she'd find a better way to explain it to Kimberly, as Amanda didn't know what she was explaining.

"Just be careful," Amanda said. "I don't want you to get hurt."

"Don't worry, I won't," said Kimberly, beaming.

∽

HANNA RAN out of Kimberly's house and threw herself in the car.

"God! What's wrong with me?" she yelled in fury the second she shut the door behind her. Amanda's expression as she looked at the bracelet was still in front of her eyes. Why? Why couldn't she keep her mouth shut? This was the second mistake she'd made in the last twenty-four hours.

There wasn't much time left. Very soon, Amanda would know the truth. Until then, her heart would be bleeding and she'd probably hate Craig.

Hanna cursed herself the whole way home. She knew that it would upset Craig, but she had to tell him. Maybe he'd be able to fix it somehow.

Hanna walked into the living room, where Ruben sat with a newspaper in his hand.

"Hi," she said.

"Hi," said Ruben. "You look tired. What happened? Hangover?"

"I wish. Is everything all right?" She nodded toward the newspaper.

"It's horrible," said Ruben folding it. "There's this grandma. She lost her cat."

Hanna heard steps and looked up at Craig coming down the stairs.

"How are they?" he asked.

"They're fine," said Hanna.

"We scared the hell out of them," said Craig, "Did they notice anything—the fangs, the faces?"

"No. Amanda saw that you had something in your hand and she thought that it was a knife. But I told her that it was just a piece of wood."

"Just a piece of wood," said Craig angrily.

"Craig, I know. I made a mistake."

"We're about to get our powers back after a hundred and sixty years of waiting, and we're all very excited," he said, his voice rising. "We're Hunters, and every time we see those monsters, we want to rip them apart. But you're three hundred years old. You should know how to control yourself. You know that it wasn't just a piece of wood," he shouted. "Do you know how difficult it was to not kill him? I almost started a war, and we can't afford it right now. It's only the three of us, and God knows how many they are. They have the Book, Hanna, and if they get Amanda, we'll lose both."

"I know that!" Hanna shouted back.

"Do you?"

Ruben stood up.

"Ok," he said, looking from one to another, "the emotions are out, and I hope you both feel better. What now?"

"Now I need to go," said Craig, still irritated. "I need to find that house."

He went to the kitchen and came back with a bunch of printed maps in his hand.

"The key," he said without looking at Hanna.

"It's in the car," she said, but when Craig walked to the front door she stopped him. "Wait."

Craig looked back.

"I think I made another mistake," she whispered.

Craig slowly walked back.

"I think I broke her heart," she said in a guilty voice.

"What did you do, Hanna?"

Hanna took a deep breath.

"She asked me about Eleanor."

Craig froze, and it looked like he'd stopped breathing. Ruben was stunned, too.

"She saw you in her dream. You called her Eleanor," continued Hanna. "I told her Eleanor was your girlfriend, that she'd died. And Amanda was sorry for you, for both of us. And then she asked why in the dream you called her Eleanor." Hanna paused.

"What did you say?" asked Craig, and his voice wasn't angry or irritated anymore, it was soft.

"I said it was because her eyes look like Eleanor's. Then she looked at the bracelet, and her expression changed."

Craig smiled sadly.

"She thinks I gave it to her because she looks like Eleanor."

"Craig, I'm so sorry. Her question confused me, and when she looked at me . . . God, those eyes . . ."

"I know. That's why I avoided them all these years."

"I handled it all this time, but I think you're right, I'm too excited, I need to pull myself together." Hanna sighed. "I need to get back and drive her home."

"No," said Craig, "Ruben can do it. I want you to take a nice bath, eat something, and watch some comedy. You've been under a lot of pressure. Take some time out."

"You should rest." Ruben nodded approvingly.

"I'll happily oblige. I couldn't look into her eyes right now."

"Don't worry," said Craig, looking at the sheets of papers in his hand, "we'll get that heart back."

Chapter Fifteen

YEAR 1841

IT WAS late evening when Fray, Samson, and Gabriella stepped off the train at the wet and cloudy New Castle railway station. Several people had gone missing in this small town of three-hundred residents. The witch, Helma, summoned them after two dead bodies were found with bite marks on their necks.

The moment Fray stepped onto the platform, illuminated by the poor yellow light of the lanterns, he saw her. He couldn't be mistaken. It was her—the woman he'd sought for seven years. She was passing by only fifteen feet away, and he, without knowing it, was already moving in the same direction.

"Fray, where are you going?" he heard Gabriella's voice.

He looked at her. "I'm . . ." he started. But he didn't have time to make up a reason; he was afraid to lose the woman from his view. "I need to do something," he said, glancing after the woman.

"There's no time for that," said Samson, eyeing the subject of Fray's attention. "We're here on business."

"I'll meet you at Helma's house," said Fray edgily.

The woman was moving in the opposite way of the small crowd of newly arrived passengers. When her silhouette disappeared behind the corner of the station building, he decided not to risk losing her. He flashed forward and caught up with her in a split second.

The sudden, short gust of wind didn't pass unnoticed. The woman stopped. When she turned around, her face didn't express fear or surprise, it remained impassive. But as she appraised Fray from head to toe, it changed.

"Who are you?" she asked, interest in her voice. "You're not from around here."

"What gave me away?" Fray smirked.

"You're dressed too well for this place."

"Then you're not from around here, either."

Fray's eyes moved from the small elegant top hat sitting on her gathered black hair, down to her velvet overcoat.

"Were you following me?"

"Yes."

"Why? What do you want?"

"What can a man want from such a beautiful woman?" he said, looking into her cold blue eyes framed by black lines of long eyelashes.

"Oh, that," she said in a casual voice. Then she raised her black arched eyebrow. "Why not? There's something different about you." Her eyes narrowed. "I can sense it. You look firm. You emanate power, and I like a strong man."

Oh, I can sense you, too, thought Fray.

"I'm staying outside of the town," she said. "It's not too far. You can come with me."

"And you're not afraid? I am, after all, just a stranger."

"What are you going to do? Bite me?" she laughed.

"Oh no, I don't bite." *I do other things*, he thought. "Allow me to introduce myself. I am Fray Wald." He bowed slightly.

"I'm Joanne. Joanne Murray." She turned around and went to a coach waiting for her.

Fray walked behind her on the dirty road, wet from the drizzling rain, a content smile on his face.

All that mattered to the family was the mission, but Fray didn't care anymore. He was tired of all the rules and obligations. They had this great power, and they could do so much more with it. They could create armies of immortals and subjugate towns and countries, build their own kingdoms instead of hiding who they really were from the world. But all they did was kill the monsters. When Fray shared his thoughts with Samson, Samson called them reckless and violent.

Fray knew there was nobody in the castle who would support his desire; which was why he spent a lot of time away from them. He wanted to have his own people who'd understand and support his ideas, who would be loyal to him. He'd been traveling, trying to find them among the mortals. He listened to their conversations, socialized with them, and watched their actions, hoping that when he found someone, he'd convince Samson to turn the man for him.

And once, Fray brought a man to the castle.

He'd found him in Texas. They spent a month together, drinking, playing cards, having fun with women. To see the man in action Fray provoked a fight, and after came to the conclusion that he had found what he was looking for.

He explained to the man who he was. To prove it, Fray showed him a few tricks. He told the man about his plans and made him the offer to become like him, to become his companion. Fray saw the darkness in him, and he knew that there was a possibility the transformation would take longer than two days and Samson would stop it. But he didn't care. He had to try.

Fray told Samson the man was his friend. He made up a story about how the man helped him kill werewolves and almost got killed himself. But he couldn't fool Samson. When the man was still transitioning on the fourth day, Samson approached Fray saying he couldn't wait any longer, that Fray probably didn't know the man as well as he thought. Then he pulled out his dagger and stuck it in the man's chest.

Fray's fists clenched and the gust of rage burned him, making his blood boil.

"Oh, I knew him," he snarled ferociously. "He was good, he was better than all of you, and he could have been my friend. But you killed him because you didn't like him, because he was different, because it was I who chose him."

"I did what I had to do," said Samson.

"This was the first time I asked you to turn somebody for me, and you killed him."

"You think that it's easy?" said Samson with anger. "He wasn't good, and I can't give that kind of power to someone who I can't trust."

"It's not him you don't trust, it's me. I don't trust you either. I'm a First One, too. I don't know what's on those golden pages, but I'm sure they have something for me."

"The Golden pages are meant only for the Keeper of the Book, and I've told you as much as I can."

"Fine. You keep your secrets, and I'll keep mine."

Fray had been sleeping with vampire women for a couple of centuries now, and it was one of his biggest secrets. He didn't care what the family would say if they found out. He would've left them long ago, but he still needed Samson. He was the only one who knew the contents of the golden pages, the only one who could turn people.

One day Fray realized that weak mortal women didn't attract him anymore. They were too breakable, and he always had to control his strength. He needed someone new, stronger, somebody with whom he wouldn't have to hold back.

That's when the idea to try a vampire crossed his mind. Of course, he could ask Samson to turn someone for him, but he had never met somebody with whom he wanted to spend eternity. Unlike Samson, he had never met the love of his life. Even if he did, the kind of women he liked would never fit Samson's rules. If only he could turn people himself. It would change everything.

He still remembered his first time, his first young vampire woman, and the distinction, the satisfaction. He found her at the graveyard. She was feeding, but he didn't intervene, didn't stop her. The night was dark, but Hunters, the same as vampires, had perfect sight. Standing at a good distance, he could appreciate her long, flowing hair, her shapely legs showing out from under the drawn-up hemline of her gown. When she was done and dragging her victim toward the tomb, Fray showed himself.

"Do you need help with that?"

She dropped the body and looked back, startled. But perhaps the fact that Fray was alone encouraged her. She smiled.

"Look at this gorgeous man. You look delicious."

"I'm glad you like me."

Fray approached her, looked into her black eyes, at her pale face. He put one hand on his dagger, grabbed her waist with the other, and pressed her to his chest.

"Mmm, you are strong," she said.

She slowly bowed and pressed her mouth to his neck. Fray raised up his head and closed his eyes, enjoying the touch of her cold lips.

"You should be careful. I might bite you," she whispered into his ear.

"You can try," he whispered back, pressing her to him harder.

She moaned. He knew that it wasn't from pleasure, but pain. As a result of her defensive reaction, her fangs pierced Fray's neck. He threw her away. She flew back, hit a tall gravestone, and fell down, hissing. Fray chuckled.

The woman looked at him in astonishment, wiping her lips with her sleeve as if something burned them.

"What are you? You're strong, but you're not a vampire. Are you a werewolf?"

"How long had you been a vampire?" Fray asked.

"Twelve years," she said, standing up.

She was too young and had probably never heard about Hunters. And she didn't need to; it would scare her, make everything complicated.

"I'm human. But very strong. You don't have to be afraid." He walked to her. "I just want to have fun." He grabbed her, lifting her up slightly and pressing her to the gravestone behind her. "You're very attractive." He leaned into her tightly, and his hand moved down her hip.

"Mmm," she moaned, closing her eyes, but then suddenly she hit him in the chest with both hands.

Fray bounced back and bumped into another, much lower gravestone and almost fell over it. He laughed.

"Oh yes. This is going to be interesting."

"You promise?" she said, standing with her hands on her waist and wiggling her hips.

Fray dashed to her, threw her on the grass, and sank his lips into her breasts.

It was a long and crazy night, full of new and powerful sensations. Fray woke up in the tomb, where she dragged him before daybreak. He walked out and stopped, looking around. Fray never was romantic, but even he couldn't ignore the beauty surrounding him.

It was the middle of October. Hardy, wild chestnut trees were just turning yellow. But maples stretching along the paths already covered the green grass with orange and red leaves. He noticed a short tree with deep purple foliage and looked at the grave beneath it. A sculpture of a raven was attached to its small headstone. Fray didn't understand why someone would put a raven on a gravestone, but he liked it.

That night was revolutionary for Fray, and not for its extraordinary sexual experience. Something had happened that night, something important. He, the Hunter, enjoyed the time in the company of a vampire, who he had been created to fight against, to hate, to destroy. He broke the rule. Standing in the silent graveyard, Fray smiled.

Usually, Fray killed his vampire lovers. But for Joanne Murray he had other plans. Her beauty wasn't the only reason he decided to keep her alive. He needed her.

Joanne Murray was a leader. She had her own team who obeyed her, and that was something Fray had always dreamed of. Vampires were powerful and immortal, too, and she could make as many of them as she wanted. Fray didn't know if he would ever be able to convince Samson to turn someone for him, and he needed a backup plan. Maybe with vampires he wouldn't be able to take over the world, but it would be interesting to try something new, something different.

Joanne Murray was also smart. That's why Fray couldn't find her. He'd been on the right trail twice, but by the time he got there, she was gone. Living a full social life, she knew when to disappear and how to cover her tracks. Every time Samson needed somebody to hunt down a vampire, Fray was the first to go, but it was never her.

And now, here she was, which meant that this time something had gone wrong.

Meeting her today at the railway station was a fluke. He had to take advantage of it immediately, because tomorrow when Samson found her, it would be too late.

∾

WHEN THEY ARRIVED at her manor, Fray saw a two-story house detached from other estates. As they came out of the coach, a young man opened the front door and waited for them to enter. He threw a quick glance at Fray and stepped to Ms. Murray to take her coat and hat. Fray also took off his coat and hung it on the man's arm.

"Where is everybody?" she asked without real interest.

"They are out, Ma'am," said the man.

"Bring us wine and you can leave, too." She turned to Fray. "How do you find this place?" she asked, moving her eyes from one side of the room to the other. "Do you like it?"

Fray glanced at the furniture upholstered with light green fabric, at the tightly closed lustrous taffeta curtains, and then looked at the floor.

"Hmm, nice carpet," he said, and then looked at Ms. Murray with a smile. "Where are the owners?"

She stared at him.

"I am the owner. Why would you ask such a silly question?"

"I'm looking at the wall, and there are two portraits of venerably aged people—a man and a woman," said Fray. "And yours is nowhere around. Where is it? I am sure you have one."

Her face brightened. "It's in my bedroom," she said coquettishly.

The young man came back with two glasses of wine on a silver tray. She took one of them and handed it to Fray.

"Thank you, Ms. Murray," he said.

"Please, call me Joanne." She took the other glass. "Let's go. I'll show you my portrait." She picked up one of the several candelabra standing around and led the way up the stairs.

She put the candelabrum on the nightstand.

"There it is," she said, looking at the wall opposite the bed.

In the portrait, she stood at full length and looked at Fray with her icy-cold eyes. Her black dress accentuated the paleness of her face, and her dark-red, insidiously smiling lips looked like blood on snow.

Fray was impressed by the grandeur of the portrait, but his face and the tone of his voice didn't change.

"Magnificent," he said, sipping his wine. "Who is the painter?"

"A well-known artist from Lynchburg, but I don't remember his name."

"Lynchburg? I knew a painter in Lynchburg." Fray watched her reaction. "He died seven years ago. Poor thing was killed. Drained of blood from his neck. What a strange way to kill somebody. I was curious, how did they do that?"

Ms. Murray's face darkened.

"You are a very interesting man," she muttered.

She put her glass beside the candelabrum and stepped to Fray, who now stood with his back to the portrait. She spun him around. Fray didn't resist. He tossed aside his glass. It crashed against the wall, covering the small white flowers on the sky-blue wallpaper with dark red. She hit him in the chest with both hands and collapsed against his body when he fell on the bed.

"Yes, you're right, Joanne," Fray smirked. "It's time to play."

"You ask the wrong questions, you don't get to play. You want to know how the painter was killed?" she whispered into his ear. "I'll show you."

She growled and her fangs pierced his neck. Fray laughed loudly and shoved her so hard she flew back and hit her portrait.

"That tickles," he said, lifting his head and leaning on his elbows.

He looked at her sitting on the floor. She stared back with her bloodshot eyes like an enraged predator, and thin spider veins covered her face.

"Who are you?" she asked, panting angrily.

Fray got up from the bed. When he moved toward Joanne, she jumped to her feet.

"I think you already know. Though there is no vampire alive who has met us, I'm sure you've heard legends about your most dangerous enemies," said Fray, impaling her with his gaze.

Joanne ran for the door. Fray caught her by the arm and pulled her back. She clawed at his chest like a wildcat.

"Don't be stupid. I'm faster than you and much stronger."

As Joanne's face normalized, Fray watched fear replace her fury. She jerked her arm free and walked past Fray to the other side of the room.

"How do you know about the painter?" she asked.

"I was there when you killed him, but I missed you," said Fray. "I was wondering, what made you come after him?"

"After my men took him home, they noticed birds gathering under the bedroom window, the one that was his when he slept in our house. The painter threw away the food—"

"That you gave him to keep him asleep." Fray nodded.

"You know? How?"

"Yes, I know. You couldn't drink his blood because it wasn't clean at the moment. Sure that he didn't know anything, you let him go. When you realized that he might be dangerous, you killed him. But it was too late. He had already done the damage you were afraid of, and I already knew about you," said Fray. He pulled from the inside pocket of his vest the drawing that Martha had given to him seven years ago. "I've had it with me all this time. Nice work," he said, showing her the picture. "I recognized you the second I saw you."

"How did you find me?"

"I have to admit that it wasn't easy. How old are you?"

"Two hundred and thirty-three," she said, proudly lifting her chin.

"I am not surprised you survived so long. You have been very careful. Usually, you don't leave evidence, but this time," Fray shook his head, "you left two bloodless bodies in the alley. And you're still here? That's not your style. What made you act so thoughtlessly?"

"Bodies? What bodies?" she asked. Then suddenly her look became savage. "That sneaky filth," she said through her gritted teeth and stormed downstairs.

But there was nobody in the house. The young man was gone, along with the coach.

"How dare he disobey my orders," she shouted in fury. "That's why he's been slipping away lately, avoiding company. I will rip his head off."

"You don't have to worry about that," said Fray, coming down the stairs. "That's why I'm here."

"So kill me." Joanne glared at Fray and walked up to him. "What are you waiting for? If you're here to kill us, then do it."

"Don't you think you deserve it? You're a killer. You've killed thousands of men, women, and children."

"People are our food. You think humans are better? Don't they do the same when they're hungry? They kill animals, don't they? First, they take milk from a cow, then they eat its babies, then they slaughter the cow itself. Nobody calls them killers." She went down the stairs again.

Fray folded his hands behind his back and stood there, thinking. He used to talk to his vampire lovers to learn more about their lives. He had a question for Joanne.

"If you died today, would you want to see the morning, to see the sunrise before it happened?" he asked, walking down the stairs.

"You mean if I want you to fry me? No, I prefer a stake through the heart," she sneered, but Fray could see the fear in her eyes.

"I mean, do you miss it? Also, you see, when people have

problems, or they are scared of something like you are now . . ."

"I am not afraid to die," said Joanne.

"Then in the morning," continued Fray, "when the sun comes up, everything seems so much easier and brighter, and the worry and fear go away. How is it for you? You can't enjoy the sun, you live in darkness and shadows all the time. It must be terrible; it's like living in never-ending horror."

Joanne laughed wildly.

"Humans are so stupid," she said arrogantly. "You are right—it seems easier. But in fact, nothing goes away. Daytime is the time when night raises its dark curtains and lets the performance begin. Real life happens at night. Night is the time where you hide all your secrets, your true feelings, your desires. It's the time when you can do things you would never do under the sunlight in front of hundreds of eyes watching your every move. At night you are who you are. Under the sunlight people are acting, showing off, pretending that everything is fine. Only at night do they become themselves, when their tired, exhausted brains resist fighting and let out their real thoughts—hate, jealousy, fear, temptation, and their thoughts about real love. The real love, and not the one which they have to fake under the sunlight, show it to the wrong people because they have to. This is the terrible life. To me, this is the horror. We, who sleep in the daytime, we are not like that. We are always real. We can be tricky and insidious, but we hate if we hate, and we love if we love. We do what we want to do." She sighed. "You want to know if I miss the sunlight. Yes, I miss its shine on the water, the beauty of nature in spring and fall. And, yes, I miss its heat, but not enough to burn under its rays. So, if you want to kill me painfully, then that's the way."

Fray listened carefully and suddenly a bizarre thought crossed his mind. If Joanne were turned by the Book of Power, the sun wouldn't be dangerous to her anymore; she would be able to enjoy its heat. Was that possible? It was. She didn't have a soul, but she had blood, didn't she? And that's all that was needed. The absence of the soul would make the process much longer, weeks probably, but then she would become invulnerable, like the Hunters. If only he had that power. Fray sighed and walked to her.

"Actually, I am here to save you," he said.

"Save me?" she asked. "Save me from whom?"

"I'm not here alone. There are two more Hunters with me. Tomorrow night at the latest, you'll all be dead. You're lucky I saw you at the station," said Fray, and his tone became serious. "How many men do you have?"

"Eight," said Joanne.

"You'll take one man and run. The rest will have to die. That'll convince the Hunters that the problem is solved. I'm sure you have someplace to hide. You'll tell me where it is so I can find you later."

"You're not doing this from the kindness of your heart. What is the price?" Joanne gazed at him.

"You and I will become partners and gather a new team. I will choose the people, and you will make them vampires. We will have as many men as we want and do whatever we want, and no Hunter will find us. You'll be safe with me."

"You, a Hunter, who exists to destroy us, want to create more vampires?" she asked in disbelief. "Why?"

"I have my reasons. I'll explain everything to you later." Fray clutched her in his arms. "I chose you, and I'm putting my faith in you. But if you try to trick me—the next time I find you, I'll kill you." He gazed at her.

He knew it wasn't easy for her to lose her freedom, but now, when Hunters knew about her existence, she didn't have a choice. She needed protection.

Joanne looked at him. She nodded, no doubt in her eyes, nothing but cold vampire prudence.

"We've still got time." He leaned closer to her face and said with sly smile, "What do you say, do I get to play now?"

She closed her eyes and took a deep breath. When she opened them again, they were burning with passion.

"Oh, yes. Can't wait to feel your power."

Chapter Sixteen

TODAY

A SMILE SHONE on Kimberly's face when instead of Hanna she saw Ruben coming out of the car. On one hand, Amanda felt relief that she didn't have to pretend that nothing had happened, but on the other hand, she felt anxious. Why would Hanna send Ruben? She listened to Ruben and Kimberly talk from the kitchen.

"Hi," said Ruben when Kimberly opened the door.

"Hi. How are you?" asked Kimberly. "I've been worried."

"I'm fine. See?" he pointed at his face. "No bruises."

"That's good, though a bit weird. That guy seemed pretty strong."

"Kimberly, I'm sorry for scaring you like that. I want to make it up to you. Would you have lunch with me?"

Amanda almost dropped her cup as she put it in the dishwasher.

"I'd love to." Kimberly beamed. "I'll need to change," she said, looking down at her shorts. She stepped aside from the doorway, "Come in."

Kimberly led Ruben to the kitchen and then went upstairs. Amanda sat at the table and fingered her bracelet.

"Hi," said Ruben.

"Hi." Amanda's fingers stilled. "Where's Hanna?"

"She's at home."

Amanda stood up and took a few steps towards Ruben.

"Is she all right?"

"She's fine. But after what happened yesterday, Craig thought it would be better if she had some rest. I'm your guard today and I am inviting you to have lunch with me and Kimberly."

"No, thank you," said Amanda gloomily. "And I don't need a guard."

"Yes, you do."

"Because of me, you're all in danger. It's me they need, not you."

"Amanda, it's not your fault, you don't understand . . ."

"Everybody keeps saying that," she said sharply. "So explain."

"I can't," said Ruben calmly.

"Why? You came here to keep an eye on Kimberly, you know what's going on. Why can't you tell me?"

"I know how you feel."

"How can you? You don't even know me."

Ruben's face softened.

"I know everything about you, and I want to protect you from the danger you're in. I know you have plenty of questions, but I can't answer them right now." He looked into Amanda's eyes. "You'll have to wait. Just trust us."

Amanda stared back. Suddenly a familiar churning sensation overwhelmed her. She clutched her bracelet and looked away.

"All right." She glanced at him after a moment and almost whispered, "But I have a question which you can answer right now. Why are you doing this? I mean, Kimberly. Hanna said you'll have to leave and never come back. Why are you giving her hope?"

Ruben nodded in acceptance of her question.

"You think she likes me?" he asked.

Amanda heard sad hopelessness in his voice.

"You know she does," she said.

"As you said, I'm keeping an eye on her. She doesn't know what's going on, and we can't just ask her to stay at home. It's better if she's with me than somewhere alone."

"Do you like—" started Amanda, but she heard Kimberly's footsteps and stopped talking.

"I'm ready." Kimberly stepped to Ruben and took his arm. "Let's go."

Kimberly called dresses her happy clothes, and she didn't wear them often. Usually, it was jeans or a skirt with a top. Now, she looked wonderful in a coral skater dress.

Ruben looked at her tenderly. Even though his lips didn't move, his face smiled. Looking at him, Amanda knew the answer to her unfinished question.

∽

"SEE YOU TOMORROW," said Amanda, and she shut the car door. But before she reached the porch, Ruben caught up with her.

"Amanda, if you want to go somewhere—call me. Otherwise, please, don't leave the house, not alone, not with friends, with no one else but one of us."

"Don't worry, I'll stay in my ward," she said sarcastically.

The front door opened, and Melinda stepped out. She and Ruben looked at each other, but neither of them said hello.

"Good," said Ruben, looking at Amanda again. "See you."

Amanda stepped inside.

"Is Dad home?" she asked.

"No, he's at the office," said Melinda.

"It's Sunday."

"Yes. But he's leaving tomorrow. Going to LA, remember? They're going to present their new bridge."

Amanda stopped in the kitchen doorway.

"That's tomorrow?"

How could she forget? It was such an important day for her father.

"Yes. So, as he said, they want to make sure that everything is all right. Are you hungry?"

"No."

Amanda grabbed a glass of water.

"You look tired. Did you sleep well? How was the party? Did you have fun?" Melinda spat out the questions while Amanda drank.

"Melinda, breathe." Amanda smiled. "The party was okay, and yes, I'm tired, so I'll be in my room."

The moment she closed the bedroom door, all the heavy thoughts and feelings which she had tried to banish crashed over her. She leaned on the door and stood there like she was pinned to it. Now, when she was finally alone, she wanted to release the chest pain tormenting her. She wanted to cry it out, but the tears wouldn't come.

She sat in the middle of the bed, took off the bracelet, and put it on the covers in front of her. She had no doubt Craig gave it to her because she looked like Eleanor. Now, other questions bothered her. Why was he protecting her from those guys? Where did he know them from? Amanda had never seen them in her life, but she knew they wanted something from her, and Craig knew what it was. How? What was the connection between Craig, those guys, and her?

Hanna said that Eleanor's death was an accident. How did she die? Was it possible that those guys had something to do with it? A strange thought crossed Amanda's mind. Maybe they wanted the same thing from Eleanor that they wanted from her, and they killed Eleanor because she didn't do it. Were she and Eleanor somehow connected? That would explain the resemblance. The thought scared her, and she gasped.

All this reasoning seemed ridiculous to her. Besides, even if some of her guesses were right, Craig, Hanna, and Ruben were the only people who could tell her which ones were. The fact that they knew something about her that she didn't, made her angry. She had to ask again.

She lay on her side and closed her eyes, and suddenly the tears rolled down her face. Some invisible ropes tied her to Craig, and she needed to cut herself free. There was a way to move on. Maybe Kimberly was right. Maybe Alec could help her with that. She had to give it a chance.

∼

AMANDA WAS LOOKING at her wrists. On the left one was the bracelet, shining with golden circles on the coins. She glanced at the coin with the roman number six and smiled. Slowly, her eyes moved up and stopped again. She was looking at her fingers now. On her right hand, she wore a ring. It had a coin, too. The coins on the bracelet had holes on the golden circle, but the coin on the ring, instead of holes, had shimmering diamonds. She lifted her hand to look at it closer, but something distracted her, some weak tapping.

Amanda woke up. She heard a knock on the door.

"Yes," she said with a sigh.

The door opened and Melinda walked in.

"Alec's here. I didn't know you were asleep or would've told him to come back later."

"What time is it?" asked Amanda, pulling her hair back from her face.

"It's five."

"Is Dad back?"

"No. He called, asked about you, and said he'll be late," said Melinda. She waited a moment, then said again, "Alec's here."

"I heard you the first time." Amanda sat up. "I'll be there in a minute."

Melinda looked like she wanted to say something, but just nodded and walked away.

Amanda swung her legs off the bed and sat. Her head felt big and heavy. Crying didn't make the sadness and pain go away. They had waited for her to awaken and now flooded back, making her eyes prickle again.

She picked up the bracelet from the bed and looked at it, thinking about the ring she had just seen in her dream. She was sure that such a ring existed. The hands she saw wearing the bracelet and the ring wasn't her hands. They were Eleanor's.

She took the bracelet and put it on the nightstand, then fixed her bed and went to the bathroom. After washing her face with cold water, she put on some makeup to cover the redness around her eyes and went downstairs.

Melinda was peering out through the open front door with a curious look.

"Where is he?" asked Amanda, stopping in the middle of the stairs.

"He said that he needed to get something from his car."

She heard the sound of a car door slamming, and a moment later Melinda stepped back. Beaming, Alec walked in, holding a big flat package in his hand.

"Hi. I brought your present, as promised," he said.

"Let's take it to my room," Amanda smiled.

Melinda, who was eager to see the contents of that mysterious package, sighed in disappointment.

As they walked into Amanda's bedroom, Alec looked

around. He had been there once before, and she knew he was examining the walls, trying to find a spot for the picture.

"Where do you want to hang it?" he asked, tearing off the brown wrapping paper.

"There." She pointed at the empty space beside the window.

"That's what I thought."

Alec tried the picture on the wall.

"Higher or lower?"

"It's fine like that," said Amanda.

He picked up a spiked hook that had fallen out from the package and pushed it into the wall, hung the picture, and adjusted it to perfection.

"Done," he said.

He stepped to Amanda's side, and they both looked at the painting.

"Thank you," said Amanda.

"Now," said Alec in a serious voice, "what's wrong?"

"Nothing." She shrugged. "Everything's fine."

Alec stepped to Amanda's dresser and looked at the photograph standing on it, Kimberly's present.

"Friends forever," he read aloud, then took it and showed it to Amanda. "That's how you look when everything's fine." He put the photograph down.

"You mean wet?"

"I mean happy." Alec approached her. "Something's bothering you. What is it?"

"It's nothing." Amanda turned away. "I feel better now."

"Then let's go out, get some dinner." He took her by her shoulders and turned her around. "Look at me."

She gazed into his gray eyes.

"I promise that I won't ask questions," he said, grinning.

"Sorry, Alec, I can't. My dad's leaving tomorrow, and I want to spend the evening with him." She had hours until her father's return and she wished she could go out, but she'd promised Ruben she'd stay home. "But we can still have dinner together," she said cheerfully. "Let's go downstairs. I'm sure Melinda has something tasty for us."

She was glad to have a reason to leave the bedroom. Amanda didn't want to be alone, and she was glad about Alec's company, but if they stayed in the bedroom too long, she was afraid he might break his promise and ask a question she didn't have the answer for.

Alec's hand slipped from her shoulder.

"Whatever you want," he said.

∽

RUBEN SAT across from Kimberly at the table in a small cafe.

"So you like history?"

"I'm not as good as Hanna, but, yes, I like it," said Kimberly. "I always wanted to be an archaeologist, to solve a mystery of the past. I can imagine how exciting it feels during an excavation to find ancient artifacts that tell you about life five hundred years ago or more."

"Yes, I know. Even I feel nostalgic every time we dig up treasure," said Ruben. Looking at Kimberly's widening eyes, he realized he'd gotten carried away and said something wrong.

"You found treasure?"

Usually, when Ruben brought up stories or facts from his past, he fit them into the life of a nineteen-year-old guy. Now he'd made a mistake, and it was too late to bite his tongue. He had to come up with an answer.

"No, not exactly. The thing is that I like archeology, too. I applied for permission to participate in an expedition to Romania. That's why I missed a year in college," said Ruben, embarrassed. He was almost five hundred years old; he was an antique himself and could tell her things she wouldn't be able to find in any book, but he had to come up with stupid stories and act like a regular teenager.

"I'm so jealous," said Kimberly. "What did you find?"

"A lot of things. I'll email you pictures." He changed the subject, "Romania is a very interesting country. I heard a lot of amusing stories about Dracula. Do you believe in the supernatural?"

"I'm skeptical about that. I believe in what I see, and I've never seen a vampire."

"Actually," started Ruben, who was going to say that she saw three of them yesterday, but luckily, he stopped himself in time. First, it seemed odd to him that he almost made the same mistake a second time, but then he caught himself on the thought that he wanted to be honest with her, he wanted her to know who he was. He smiled brightly and said, "Actually you're right, you have to see first."

It was late evening. They were sitting in the car in front of Kimberly's house. Her ginger hair shimmered under the headlights of the passing cars. She looked at the illuminated windows of her house, then again at Ruben.

"They're back," she said.

Ruben knew her family being back wasn't the only reason her voice wilted. She didn't want him to leave.

"Thank you," said Kimberly. "I had a very nice day."

"Me, too. I enjoyed every minute," said Ruben. He met her tempting glance, which had become so dear to him during these few days. His eyes went to her lips, which smiled at him so tenderly. Would it really be wrong if he. . . ? He leaned into her. No, it didn't feel wrong. It felt amazing.

~

WHEN RUBEN CAME HOME, he found Hanna sitting on the couch with a piece of pizza and a huge glass of coke in her hands. She was watching a movie, but when she saw Ruben, she put her coke down and pressed the pause button.

"How is she?" Hanna asked.

"A little upset, but she'll be fine." Ruben sat on the armchair.

"Did you guys go somewhere?" asked Hanna, biting her pizza.

"No, she wanted to go home."

"Then where the hell have you been? It's eight o'clock."

"Kimberly and I had lunch together."

"All right," said Hanna and stopped chewing, "Then?"

"Then we had dinner," Ruben said quickly.

Hanna stared at him.

"I guess not right away?"

He grinned.

Hanna swallowed and put the rest of her pizza back into the open box on the coffee table.

"May I ask what you did between meals?" she said, anger rising in her voice.

"We walked, talked. We had coffee in two different coffee shops. We had a very nice time. When we were sitting in a coffee shop, she asked me how long I'm going to stay here. When I said probably about a week, she asked when I'll visit again. To that," he raised his index finger, "I answered with a question. I asked her 'Do you want me to?' Then she looked at me with a sad smile and said, 'Yes.'"

"See what you did!" exploded Hanna, "Didn't we tell you to hold your horses?"

"I did," said Ruben, defending himself. "I told her it wouldn't be easy. That I'm Armenian, and I'm going to visit—"

"You did what?" Hanna yelled. "You're supposed to be our cousin."

"You wanted me to tell her that I'm Norwegian? Sorry,

honey, but do I look like one?" Ruben chuckled. "Hanna, relax, it's not like she said she loves me." The corners of his mouth moved downward in a grimace.

"You think this is funny? Ruben, this is not a game."

"You think I don't know that?" Ruben's face became serious.

"Do you? All those years you've been meeting girls, spending time with them, then disappearing. You're used to it."

"And you think it's easy for me?" shouted Ruben. He stood up, "You think that I never fell in love, that I don't know how it feels when somebody breaks your heart? Then think again, my dear cousin."

"You do?" All Hanna's frustration was gone. "And you never told me?"

"I'm sick and tired of it. What do you think happens to my heart when I watch the people I care about grow old and die? I also want to have someone who will love me and be with me forever."

"If you loved somebody, why didn't you bring her to Samson? When was this?"

"Why? Love is not enough. I had to tell her who I am, didn't I?"

"Ruben, I'm so sorry."

"Craig failed with Beth, but he found his Eleanor and she happened to be the one. His one and only," said Ruben, lowering his voice. "I like Kimberly, and I don't want to hurt her. The Book will be open soon, and if she tells me she loves me, I'll tell her the truth. Then we'll see whose heart is broken."

"Nobody's," said Hanna quietly. "Just make sure you want this. I know Kimberly, she's not amorous. I think she's falling in love. If she knows you really love her back—she'd do anything for you."

Ruben sat on the couch next to her.

"I know that you'll kill me for this, but," he looked at Hanna sideways, "I kissed her. I couldn't resist."

"Oh, shut up." Hanna sighed heavily. "You make me miss Ned even more." She got closer to him and dropped her head on his chest.

Ruben stroked her hair.

Chapter Seventeen

YEAR 1852

HANNA LAY on the warm sand of the beach, not far from the castle.

"It's been two years," she said.

"Don't worry, my love," said Edmond. "I'll wait as long as it takes. It only means that they care about you."

"I'll try to talk to them again."

"Don't be sad," he said, kissing her.

∽

HANNA KNOCKED on Eleanor's bedroom door.

"Come in. You're back," said Eleanor as she saw Hanna in the doorway.

She sat with a book in her hands on the large bed, resting against its tall, walnut headboard.

"Yes," said Hanna.

She pushed aside the edge of Eleanor's dress and sat on the bed.

"That was quick. Where did you two go this time?"

"Nowhere. He didn't have much time. He needed to go back to feed the horses. So we just spent all the time we had on the beach."

"You seem disappointed. You didn't have a good time?" asked Eleanor with a note of surprise in her voice.

"Of course, I had a good time. I had a perfect time. But it was too short."

"Oh, I am sorry," said Eleanor, putting aside her book.

"We want to be together forever. Like you and Craig, like Samson and Gabriella. It's been two years, and Samson still keeps us waiting."

"Hanna, you know how much Samson loves you. He wants to make sure that Edmond is good enough for you."

"You've all met him, and you know he's good and brave and that we love each other. Gabriella likes him so much. She said she was so happy I found my love. His parents died, and he inherited everything when he was sixteen—a nice house, money. He could live happily in Louisiana—"

"Hanna." Eleanor smiled. "We all know the story."

"He left everything behind and moved here so he could be close to me. He even took that stupid job to show Samson he's not a slacker."

"You know what?" said Eleanor, "I think you should talk to Samson again. He and Gabriella went to plant lilac shrubs near the bridge."

"You're right; maybe if I push hard enough he'll do it." Feeling stimulated, Hanna stood up.

"Do you want me to come with you?" Eleanor asked, standing up, too.

"No. But keep an eye on your bracelet. I'll call you if I need support."

Hanna looked at the freshly-planted shrubs and then crossed the wooden bridge, heading to Gabriella's garden. As she neared the small open place, she saw Samson lying on the bench with his head on Gabriella's knees. She stopped for a moment to watch them. She was amazed by the way they looked at each other, that after all those years their relationships hadn't become a habit or simply attachment. They were still deeply in love, the same as they were more than a hundred and fifty years ago when Hanna saw them together for the first time.

"Which one is it?" asked Samson, sitting up.

"It's Hanna," said Gabriella, smiling.

Hanna walked up to them and stopped behind the bench.

"You planted lilac," she said.

"Yes. What is it, my dear? You look sad," said Gabriella. She looked up at Hanna and put her hand above her eyes to block the bright glare of the setting sun.

"I'm not sad. I feel sentimental and jealous." She bent down to Samson, put her arms around his neck, and pressed her cheek against his. "It's been two years. Why won't you turn him?"

Samson beamed.

"So that's what this is about. And I, like a fool, of course, thought that you missed me that much."

Gabriella laughed.

"This is not funny," said Hanna sulkily. "Don't you want me to be happy, too?"

Samson took her hand, led her around the bench, and pulled her down on it between him and Gabriella.

"That's exactly what I want. That's why I needed to know more about him so that I wouldn't have to stop his . . ." Samson beamed again. "You know."

"You're evil." Hanna frowned.

"Stop teasing her," said Gabriella, taking Hanna's hand.

"My little Hanna," said Samson softly, "you know how

much I love you. You know I'd do anything for you. You needed enough time to check your feelings. I waited four years before I turned Gabriella because I wanted her to be sure she was ready to take such a serious step. And I also wanted Edmond to grow a bit older."

Hanna noticed that Samson was speaking in the past tense—needed, wanted. It gave her some hope, calmed her down.

"He is older. He's twenty now," she said in low voice. "I'm afraid. What if something happens to him?"

"Nothing will happen to him, my dear," said Gabriella.

"The boys just got home," said Samson, looking toward the castle.

"I think we should go back," said Gabriella.

"Everyone," said Samson into the nowhere, "gather in the great living room."

When Samson, Gabriella, and Hanna returned to the castle, everybody, except Fray, who hadn't shown up for two months now, was waiting for them. Eleanor was curled up next to Craig on the brown and golden striped sofa, and Ruben and Riley sat on the tall chairs next to the big fireplace. Gabriella and Hanna stepped forward and sat on another sofa, across from Eleanor and Craig.

"Good," said Samson, looking at them. "We're all here because we have one very important decision to make." He glanced at Hanna. "Hanna wants me to turn Edmond. We've known him for two years, and all this time we've been watching him, learning about his past."

"What?" Hanna stared at him.

"Yes," beamed Ruben. "And I have good news for you. He didn't kill his parents, they died from natural causes."

Everybody laughed. Hanna scowled.

"And now, when we know almost everything about him," continued Samson, "I think it's time. If anyone disagrees . . ."

But Hanna was already hanging on his neck and kissing his cheeks.

"…then you should say it now," finished Samson when she let go of him.

Delighted, Hanna hugged Gabriella, thanked her brothers, then turned to Eleanor.

"You knew, didn't you?"

"Yes. But I wasn't allowed to tell," said Eleanor apologetically. "We decided two days ago, but we've been waiting for Riley to come back."

"Can I bring him now?" Hanna asked Samson.

"You can tell him. But give him a couple of days to say goodbye to his mortal life."

"It's all right, he can say goodbye here," said Hanna, and in a split second, she was gone.

A few days later Samson Mountney's family had one more member.

∼

TODAY

Hanna, who was still sitting with her head on Ruben's shoulder, looked at her ringing phone. She picked it up.

"Amanda."

"I need to talk to you," said Amanda.

"Is everything all right?" Hanna asked, straightening up.

"Everything's fine."

"You want me to come over?"

"No. I want to talk to all three of you."

Hanna looked at Ruben, who stared back at her.

"Okay. Ruben will pick you up."

She hung up.

"What is it?" asked Ruben, gazing at the stupefied Hanna.

"She wants to talk. You said she was upset." She spoke in slow motion, her hand with the phone in it still hanging in the air. "How upset was she?"

"Not very. She wanted to know what's going on."

"What did you say?" Hanna asked, putting her phone down.

"I said she has to wait. Why? Is she angry or something?" asked Ruben.

"Her voice was calm but very demanding. I don't think she wants to wait."

"We need Craig. Call him," said Ruben, heading to the front door.

∽

CRAIG WALKED into the living room.

"She's not here yet?"

"No," said Hanna.

"What do you think she wants to talk about?" Craig asked.

"I think she's coming to get answers," said Hanna, "I know, it's my fault. It's because of what happened yesterday."

"Yes, it brings up a lot of questions," said Craig, "But it's not just that. She can feel things she can't explain, and it bothers her. We can't tell her the truth. She won't believe a word, and it'll only scare her more. But we can't keep her in the dark, either. We have to tell her something, or we'll lose her trust."

The front door opened. Amanda walked into the living room, followed by Ruben.

"Hi," she said, throwing a quick glance at Craig.

"Hi," said Craig. The coldness in her voice alarmed him. "Hanna said you wanted to talk."

"Let's sit down," said Hanna.

She and Amanda sat on the couch and Craig and Ruben in the armchairs across from them.

"I have some questions," started Amanda. "You said that I have to wait." She looked at Ruben. "Sorry, I can't. I need some answers right now." She turned to Craig. "Those guys who are after me—I've never seen them in my life, but you knew that they'd come, and you know what they want. So, I was trying to find a connection between you, them, and me, and I got nothing. That's why I came to you. It seems you're the one who can give me answers. I want you to tell me how you knew they'd come and how you know what they want."

Hanna and Ruben looked at Craig, but he didn't look back. He was staring at the floor and tapping the side of the armchair with his fingertips. Then he suddenly leaned forward.

"We know what they want because we want the same thing," he said calmly.

"What?" Amanda's eyes widened.

"Craig." Ruben cleared his throat.

"She has the right to know," said Craig in the same tone.

Amanda was stunned by such an unexpected answer. She needed time to digest that information, and they waited patiently.

"You said I can trust you." She turned to Ruben.

"And I'm saying it again. We're on your side."

"Hanna." Amanda looked at her. "How long have you known this?"

"Always," said Hanna, bravely looking back.

"You said you're protecting me? You all lied to me?" Amanda's eyes shone with tears, and she stood up. Turning her back to them, she took a few steps away.

"Amanda." Craig stood up, too.

"Don't," snapped Amanda.

"We didn't lie to you," Hanna said. "We just didn't tell you the whole truth."

Amanda turned back. Her eyes were dry again.

"What is it you need from me?"

Craig took a deep breath.

"We need your help."

"What are you waiting for?" She gazed at Craig. "Tell me what it is, and I'll do it."

"It's not that easy. To do it, we need one very important thing, and we don't know where it is."

"And those guys, do they know?" asked Amanda.

"Yes," said Craig.

"Then why are you keeping me away from them?"

"Because they don't care about you, and when you do what they want, they might hurt you."

Amanda stepped toward Craig.

"You mean they might kill me."

Craig looked down.

"Is that what they did to—did they kill Eleanor?"

Craig's eyes flew up at her.

"Amanda," said Hanna, slowly rising.

"How did she die?" Amanda asked with trembling lips. "Is that what happened?"

"We won't let anything happen to you. We will protect you," said Hanna.

"Like you protected her?"

Craig's eyes dimmed, and he looked away. Ruben stood up.

"No. That was different," he said. "They were the reason she died, but they didn't kill her."

"I knew it," whispered Amanda. "I could feel that there was a connection." She paused for a second, then said, "And I don't think it's the only one. I have one last question."

Craig knew that it was the one he feared the most, and his heart throbbed.

"Why do I look like her?" Amanda asked carefully like she was afraid to hear the answer.

"It's just a coincidence," said Craig.

He was lying. He had to. The answer to that question was very complicated, and if he told her, he would have to tell her everything. But right now it was impossible.

Amanda didn't seem convinced, but she didn't say anything. She turned around and headed to the front door.

Craig, Ruben, and Hanna exchanged anxious looks, then Ruben started toward the door too. But Craig stopped him.

"No. I'll do it."

The whole way back to her house they didn't exchange a word. Craig didn't dare look at Amanda, but he could feel that she was still angry. He knew this conversation answered some of her questions, but it also sowed the seeds of new ones, which would grow very soon and torment her even more, and all he could do to help her was find the house.

When he stopped the car, Amanda looked at him.

"I'm sorry," she said. "Those questions about Eleanor were . . . I know how painful it must be for you, for all of you. But this stir suddenly started around me, and I have no idea what's going on. It freaks me out."

"It's all right," said Craig, keeping his eyes on the windshield.

She pulled out something from her pocket, and when she opened her hand, he saw the bracelet laying in her palm.

"I had a dream today," said Amanda.

"What dream?" Craig asked, turning to her. "What did you see?"

"I saw the ring."

Craig's mouth went dry. He swallowed.

"I saw Eleanor's hands. She wore the bracelet and the ring." Amanda handed him the bracelet. "Take it."

"No."

"I look like her." Amanda's voice broke. "That's why you gave it to me, right?"

"No." He closed her palm. "I gave it to you because it belongs to you."

Craig regretted what he'd just said, but it was too late to take it back.

Amanda stared at him.

"I don't understand."

He looked into her eyes, which he missed so much.

"You will," he said quietly. "When this is all over, you will."

Chapter Eighteen

YEAR 1852, JUNE

SAMSON AND FRAY stood in one of the castle bedrooms. The man lying on the bed was in transition.

"I have rights too," yelled Fray. "I am just as old and immortal as you are. We've been in this together for centuries, but you never let me do this. Every time I choose somebody, you stop the transformation."

"I have to. You know the rules. Four days have passed, and he is still in transition. I can't wait any longer. I did the same when I chose the wrong person."

"Give him a chance."

"A chance to do what? Steal the dagger and kill my family in their sleep? It's not just my rules. The golden text describes the person the moment his blood drips into the pentacle. Do you know what it said about him? It said that he is unstable, aggressive, and has killed people." With those words, Samson pulled out his dagger and stuck it into the man's chest.

Fray growled like an animal.

"I could have done it right away," said Samson. "I waited this long because I wanted you to see it yourself. I can't bring someone like that into our family. It will put them in danger."

"Our family?" Fray cried out in fury. "They are not my family, I didn't choose them—you did."

"Then make the right choice. Bring someone good, and I'll turn him for you. Why do you always pick someone like this?"

"Because they're fun. Because they don't have rules and they do what they want. They don't have a mission to protect the world forever!"

"Killing people is not fun."

"If I were able to turn people, I would have an army by now, take over country after country. If you would listen to me, we could be kings of the world. And all we have is your family."

"You would have an army of killers. We are not killers, and we are not invaders. We are Hunters. We have been given this power to protect people from supernatural evil, not enslave them. You need to calm down before you say more stupid things, things you'll regret tomorrow," said Samson.

He returned to his study. He knew Fray wasn't going to regret what he'd said, that it was Fray's true desire to create an army of immortals. And that made Samson anxious.

He was cleaning the blood from his dagger when Gabriella entered the room.

"How did he take it?" she asked.

"This time it was much worse," Samson answered.

He stuck the dagger in the sheath and put it in his table drawer.

"Don't worry, he'll come around."

"Will he?" said Samson, irritated. "He says things that shouldn't cross his mind in the first place."

"People say things when they're angry. He doesn't mean them."

Samson walked to her and sighed. "No, I think, deep down, he does."

"Every family has its trouble maker. We'll deal with it."

Samson hugged her.

"Thank you, my love, I feel better."

"Liar," laughed Gabriella.

"You always make me feel better," said Samson, but his voice was sad.

"No, not this time." Gabriella became serious again. She pulled back and looked at him. "You're still deeply concerned."

"You're right, I am," said Samson, letting go of her. "I can't do what he asks me because it's wrong, and he knows it."

"It's just his temper. I'll go to him."

"I don't think that's a good idea."

"He's hurt. Maybe he wants to talk to somebody. He has to let his pain out." Gabriella walked to the door, then looked back. "Or he'll just run away again to look for comfort somewhere else, and God knows how that will turn out."

Fray was in a fury. Samson didn't want Gabriella to be alone with him. Now that he knew how Fray felt about the family, Samson didn't trust him. Just in case, he decided to keep his ear on the conversation.

Gabriella knocked on the door.

"Leave me alone," Fray yelled.

She opened the door and walked in.

"It's you. I said leave me alone," he said harshly.

"I'm not going anywhere until I talk to you."

"And say what? How sorry you are? That's what you said last time, isn't it?"

"I was sorry last time, yes, because last time I thought your choice was just a mistake, that you found a friend and you didn't know he was bad. But right now I feel sorry for you because I can see how lost you are. You knew that he was bad, and you brought him anyway. Why did you do that, Fray?"

"Maybe he is bad for you, but to me, he was exactly what I needed."

"He was a killer."

"How do you know? Because Samson said?"

"Because the Book said."

"I don't know what the Book said—I can't read those golden pages, and I don't see the reason why I should believe Samson?"

"The transition took too long. . . ."

"Oh, the rule," said Fray ironically. "It's his rule, and I don't believe in it, either."

"Why do you think he would lie to you?"

A note of frustration entered her voice.

"Isn't it obvious?" Fray laughed viciously. "He wants me to know who's the king in this castle." He raised his voice. "He and I have been in this boat from the beginning. For two hundred years we made our decisions together, and we chose Riley together. But then he came up with those rules, and he never asked me when he turned Ruben, or you, or Craig, or Eleanor."

"Because that small boat became a ship, and every ship needs a captain. He had to take the responsibility."

"Yeah, but I don't like his code. I am a First One, too, and I'm sure there are some things in that Book about the First. There has to be, and he just doesn't want to tell me. Maybe he is the Keeper of the Book, but Higher Powers made me as strong and as immortal as him, and I have the right to choose my people, to have my own ship, to build my own kingdom."

"So that's what this is all about—power." Gabriella took a deep breath. "Sorry, but we are all you've got. Samson was chosen by Higher Powers. they didn't make him the Keeper of the Book by accident."

"No. They made him the Keeper of the Book because he woke up first."

"I don't think that was a coincidence, either," said Gabriella sharply.

Fray hissed. Samson could only imagine the expression on his face.

"Listen," said Gabriella. "I didn't come here to fight. I wanted to talk and I'm glad you expressed your feelings. Maybe not today, but I hope tomorrow you feel better."

She left the room.

Samson began pacing. Everybody in the castle knew how impulsive and tough Fray was, but he was the only one who knew how dangerous Fray was becoming. Those aggressive thoughts weren't something new; they had been in his head for centuries, and if before he presented them to Samson in small portions, with time he was becoming more open about his ideas, what the two most powerful men in the world could do to change it. They all lead to destruction on the way to building their own empire.

"Sorry it didn't go as I hoped," said Gabriella as she returned.

"I know. I was listening," said Samson.

"But he let out some steam. Maybe that will help?" she said in an uncertain voice.

"Don't feel bad. That's how he is, you know that."

"Maybe when Riley and Craig come back, they can talk to him."

"Gabriella, you heard him. There's nothing we can do. He's six hundred years old. We can't change him. Besides, he hates Craig. He thinks that everything changed after I brought him into our family, that I trust him more. And that's true, I won't deny it."

"I can't blame you."

"I heard a noise. Was he packing?"

"He was looking for something."

"Did he find it? What was it?" asked Samson.

"It was a picture. A picture of some woman, just her face. Do you think he has someone?"

"I don't know. But if he does, why didn't he ask me to turn her?"

"Maybe he doesn't love her enough to spend eternity with her?" said Gabriella.

"Or maybe he is afraid of what the Book will tell me about her. Maybe he's afraid the transition will take so long I'll have to stop it."

"Oh, God," gasped Gabriella. "What if that's the reason he's so exasperated?"

"Not the major one, but it might be one of the reasons, yes."

Gabriella walked to the sofa and sat down, visibly disturbed.

"Has he said all those things before?" she asked after a moment. "Those things about the kingdom?"

"Yes. But before he called it our kingdom, because he needed me, because Fray was sure I was the only one who could turn people."

"But you are the only one."

Samson looked down. He took a deep breath and stepped to the Book.

"Actually, that's not true."

"Samson," whispered Gabriella. "No."

"The Book doesn't say that only the Keeper of the Book can turn people. It says that only the First One is strong enough to pull out the power and immortality from the Book." Samson looked at Gabriella. "If Fray finds out, we are all doomed. We will end up fighting our own kind."

"But it's on the golden pages," said Gabriella, terrified. "And nobody else knows about it. There's no way he'll find out."

"No, nobody else knows. All this time I kept it a secret. But I'm telling you now because the situation is becoming very dangerous. Upset people can be unpredictable. You heard him.

What if one day he becomes so desperate, wants to turn somebody so badly, that he tries to do it himself, hoping for a miracle? We have to be careful. From now on, we have to keep an eye on him and the Book."

"Are you going to tell the others?"

"No. Not yet." Samson started pacing again. "I trust all of them, but I'm afraid their behavior will attract his attention. If everybody starts watching him, he'll notice it, and it will infuriate him even more. It will put all of you in danger." He stopped. "He has the dagger, Gabriella."

"He wouldn't do that. Otherwise, the Higher Powers wouldn't have made him a First."

"Everybody who is turned by Higher Powers is a First. Through the Book, they transfer a part of their own power. It's irreversible. That's why the dagger can't kill us. They made me the Keeper of the Book and gave me a choice. They warned me, but I didn't listen. They didn't choose him—I did."

"You couldn't let your friend die. You did the right thing."

"Yes, we were friends for six years, but I never really knew him. I didn't know that he had so much anger in him. It's not even anger—it's violence. When he was killing those monsters, he wasn't just fighting against evil, he was enjoying it. When he could just easily stake or knife them, he preferred to torture them and then rip their heads off. He never cared about victims. And then he became more and more impatient with us. Every time he and Riley are fighting, I expect him to take out his dagger."

"No. Maybe he is irascible, but he is not a killer. He'd never do that to us."

"You always believed he is better than he seems." Samson looked at her fondly.

"I'll watch him. I'm around him more than anybody else. He's used to my attention."

"If you notice something, don't act, don't say anything, just tell me."

Gabriella stood up.

"Don't worry, my love, I'll be careful."

"He'll probably leave for a while." Samson walked to her and locked his arms around her. "We'll see what happens when he gets back."

"Everything will be fine," said Gabriella quietly, laying her hands on his shoulders.

Samson's hands crept up her back.

"My Gabriella," he said, kissing her neck. "I love you so much," he whispered into her ear.

"I love you more," she said. Her lips touched his cheekbone and then moved to his lips.

∽

FRAY, who was standing behind the door, slipped down and sat on the floor. His heart was about to jump out of his chest, and he thought if somebody looked at him now, they'd see sparks shooting out of his eyes.

He came to throw the bracelet at Samson and tell him not to call him and not to try to find him, that he was leaving, that he hated them all and didn't want to stay with them under the same roof.

But he heard his name, he heard them talking about him. What he had just discovered changed everything. He wanted to burst in and yell that he had known Samson was hiding something from him, that he had known that, as a First, he had to have some privileges, that all this power wasn't given to him just to make it easier to kill monsters; it had to have some other use.

But he stood up and disappeared as quietly as possible. In two seconds, he was in his room. He needed to think this through. If he told Samson he knew he could turn people, Samson would hide the Book. He'd lock it up somewhere and guard it day and night. Fray would not have a chance—he'd be alone against seven. He needed a plan. For now, he had to act like nothing had happened and do what Samson expected him to do.

He packed his valise and left.

∾

JOANNE STOPPED the horse at the outskirts of a small village.

"This one will do," she said, looking at the farmhouse standing alongside the road, then turned to the five horsemen behind her, "Dinner time."

She put spurs to the horse and galloped toward the big yard.

She dismounted in front of the porch and looked into the small panes of the window.

"Children." Joanne took a deep breath and closed her eyes. "I like children. I like their warm tender skin and fresh, delectable blood." She opened her eyes again and went up the wooden staircase. "You four wait here. Gregor, come with me."

Gregor, not very tall but a broad man with a square face, was Joanne's most trusted minion. More than fifty years ago, she saved him from the gallows after he was sentenced for the murder of his own parents. Joanne met him before the execution. When he asked her who she was, she said she was his salvation. She drank his blood enough to leave him conscious, then made him drink her own. As good as dead, he dropped to the floor.

When Gregor woke up at the graveyard, he remembered the choking rope around his neck. Looking up at Joanne standing beside him, he asked if he was really alive.

"You died," said Joanne, "then you came back to life. It wasn't a long journey, but during it you lost something, something that is very important for humans, but means nothing to us."

Gregor stood up.

"What was it?" he asked.

"The moment you died, your soul left your body. You lost it forever."

Gregor shrugged.

"I don't think I ever had one."

Joanne smiled.

"That's what I thought. Otherwise, I wouldn't have picked you."

"I feel different."

"You are different. You're a vampire now, a creature of the night. Serve me well, and you will live forever."

He never betrayed or disobeyed Joanne. She valued his devotion and loyalty, and that was why when the Hunters came after her eleven years earlier and Fray told her to take only one of her men and run away, Gregor was the one she chose to save.

Joanne knocked on the door, and seconds later it opened.

"Good evening," she said politely.

"Good evening, lady," said the moon-faced woman in a white bonnet standing in front of her.

"My name is Joanne Murray. I'm sorry to bother you, but we've come a long way and run out of water. Would you please help us?"

A little girl came running after her mother and grabbed her around the legs. She looked up at Joanne, and her small mouth fell open.

"Of course. Come in," said the woman.

"Thank you," said Joanne.

The moment they stepped inside, into a small anteroom,

Gregor grabbed the woman and put his hand over her mouth. The little girl looked from one to another, and her lips pouted. Joanne bent to her and took her hand.

"Don't be afraid," she said softly.

But the girl glanced up at her struggling mother, who looked back with wide-open, terrified eyes, and the corners of her trembling mouth went down. The child sobbed once and then burst out crying.

Holding the girl's hand, Joanne opened the next door and went forward.

At the head of the long dining table sat a man with a short beard and long hair tied at the nape. Seated in benches on either side of the table were two blond, curly-haired boys, watching their father drill holes into a long, thin piece of wood with the tip of a narrow knife.

All three of them looked at Joanne. Unlike his wife, the man wasn't very welcoming.

"Who are you?" he asked.

"Oh, you'll find out soon enough," smirked Joanne. "Gregor," she called.

Gregor came in, shoving the woman before him. The man stood up.

"Don't do anything rash, or we'll kill her faster," said Joanne. "Gregor, let her go."

Gregor pushed the woman, and she fell onto her knees. The man clenched his fists and dashed toward Gregor. He punched Gregor in the chest, but nothing happened. He might as well have punched a wall.

Gregor beamed. His mouth opened, the sharp teeth protruding like a trap. He idly lifted his hand and punched the man in the face. The man swayed, his eyes dimmed, and he fell on his back. Blood flowed from his nostrils down his cheek.

"I changed my mind," said Joanne. "We'll kill him first. Throw him outside, the boys are hungry."

"No," cried the woman. She crawled to Joanne's feet. "Please, please."

Her sons ran to their blubbering sister, now sitting on the floor, and pulled her away.

Gregor didn't need to be told twice. He grabbed the man by the scruff and dragged him outside.

"Now," said Joanne. She bent slightly to the weeping woman. "I heard there's a witch in this village. Who is she? What's her name?"

The woman stared at her with eyes full of fear.

"Witch? What witch?" she asked, sobbing. "We didn't do anything wrong."

"Tell me, or . . ." Joanne gazed at her rabidly, then pointed at the girl. "Or I will rip her head off."

Both boys froze in horror.

"Oh no, oh, God, no." The woman wept again. "It is . . ." She sobbed. "I think it's Ms. Cocker . . . Rebecca Cocker."

"How can we find her? Where does she live?"

"Behind the forge. It's a small house."

The door opened, and Joanne looked up to see Gregor returning.

"I'm done. You can have her," she said, then snarled and stepped toward the children.

***

"Mmm, that was delicious," said Joanne with relish.

Wiping her chin with a white handkerchief, she glanced once more at the bodies surrounding her, and then went outside where another bloodless body, with several bite marks, lay on the ground.

"Throw him inside and burn down the house," said Joanne, mounting her horse. "Gregor, let's kill that witch and go home." In her nearly two hundred and fifty years, Joanne never had a home. When she was a little girl, her mother was a servant on a small estate. They had a roof over their heads until one day the mistress's cat stole Joanne's food—a little piece of meat which Joanne herself had stolen from the kitchen. When she found the thief beside the woodshed, swallowing the last bit and licking her mouth with her rough, pink tongue, Joanne took the ax beside the stump and chopped the cat's head off.

The mistress threw them out. That was when the wandering began. Many things had changed since then, but not that. Even though the reason was now different, she was still running from place to place. There was fun and satisfaction, but it didn't last long, and every month or two she had to find a new nest.

Until now.

Now Joanne had a home. It was a big house with a marble floor and columns, eight bedrooms, and big and small living rooms, the house, which Fray built for them at the edge of the forest, not far from Williamsburg. Joanne had always loved flowers and, even though she couldn't enjoy the beauty of their colors and the dew shimmering under the sunlight, she was delighted with her small garden in the backyard.

After Fray came into her life, Joanne didn't have to run anymore. She now knew how to protect her home. Fray told her about the Book and the Map. As he said, there were two ways for Hunters to find them, and both involved the Map. The first way was witches, who, after detecting monsters, performed the ritual to summon the Hunters. The second way was Fray himself. Using the Map, Samson could locate the Hunters. In the chest beside the Book, he kept vials with the dry blood of each family member. All he had to do was sprinkle a small pinch of it onto the Map. It would create a red line straight to that person.

Years ago, when Samson put the empty vial before Fray

and asked him for blood, Fray refused to fill it. "What if I don't want to be found?" he said.

Since Fray wasn't a problem, Joanne's intention was to kill every witch in the surrounding area, to secure the place.

She hadn't seen Fray for weeks, and she was pleasantly surprised to see him coming down the wide marble stairs when she entered the house.

"You're back." She smiled.

"Did you miss me?" Fray asked, clutching her in his arms.

"Tighter," whispered Joanne, closing her eyes.

"You did," Fray chuckled.

She stroked his lips, and he looked at the small bloodstains on her gray, silky gloves.

"Did you have fun?" He asked.

"Yes. I killed the witch. No witches in a hundred miles. They will never find us."

"Excellent."

Fray's deep voice was full of excitement that Joanne had never sensed before. Her hand slipped to his chest and she felt his racing heart.

"How was your trip?" Joanne asked.

Fray stepped away and began pacing.

"I went to the castle, and guess what I found out."

The front door opened.

"The horses are fed, Ma'am," said Gregor, coming inside.

Fray stopped.

"You and him," he said, pointing his index finger at Gregor, "will pick young men and women from those villages and turn them."

"You want us to make more vampires?"

"Yes, and as soon as possible"

"And you want *us* to pick them? But you've always done it yourself."

"There's no time for that now. And it doesn't matter.

They're going to die anyway." The tone of Fray's voice became sharp and his face changed. He looked angry now.

"Fray, what's going on? Are we in danger?"

"No, they are." He gritted his teeth. "Because I am going to destroy them. He lied to me all this time, and he's going to pay for that. I'll make him suffer. I'll show him who's king."

"How?"

"I'm going to steal the Book. This is a perfect time for that. Right now there are only three of them in the castle—Samson, Gabriella, and Riley. The rest are in Paris. Then they are going to spend a month in London and come back sometime in September. We'll be done long before that. I have a plan, but we'll need more men."

"Then what? Fray, they'll hunt you down. You are invincible, but what about us? What about me?"

"You're not going to die, Joanne," he whispered, looking at her with jubilance. He walked closer and put his hands on her arms. "Your life is about to change. I will make you the strongest vampire ever."

Joanne's eyes narrowed.

"Are you saying that you can—"

"That's exactly what I'm saying. I'll take you to the sun." Fray let go of her and began pacing again. "He's been hiding it from me all these centuries. I will show them who I am . . ."

But Joanne wasn't listening anymore. She walked to the window, looked at her roses, and smiled

Chapter Nineteen

TODAY

THE LONG AND restless night after the conversation with Craig, Hanna, and Ruben didn't pass fruitlessly. Amanda made two decisions.

She was not going to blame Hanna for disloyalty just yet. What if she had serious reasons for not telling Amanda the whole truth? Amanda's first decision was to wait a little bit longer, as they had asked her to.

She still didn't know what was going on, and she still didn't understand why they couldn't tell her, and the connection between all of them still remained unclear. When Craig said the bracelet belonged to her, it made everything even more complicated, and the questions began to multiply. But there was one thing that became absolutely obvious after Craig said that the three of them wanted the same thing that those bad guys wanted from her: Craig only liked her because she looked like Eleanor, and he protected her because he needed her. Amanda herself was nothing, she was just an instrument and Eleanor's shadow. That conclusion led Amanda to her second decision—she had to stop thinking about Craig and move on.

Her dad's bedroom door was open, and Amanda saw him

standing beside the bed and packing a small suitcase. Bright morning light filled up the room through the fully open windows.

"How do you feel?" asked Amanda, walking in. "Nervous?"

"A little," he said, smiling slightly. "How are you? Did you sleep well? You seem a bit—"

"Hanna's waiting," called Melinda from downstairs.

"Coming," answered Amanda, then turned to her father again. "I am absolutely fine."

"Sorry for being so late yesterday. We didn't have much time to talk," he said. He added two ties to the suitcase and locked it. "Call me if you need something."

"You're just leaving for a few days."

"I know," he said softly. "But I've always hated leaving you alone."

"Dad, I'm not a kid anymore, and I'm not alone. I'm with Melinda."

"You know what I mean."

"I know. I'll miss you too." She hugged him. "Now," she said cheerfully, letting go of him, "don't you have important things to worry about? Catching the train, for example?"

∽

THE MOMENT AMANDA got in the car, Hanna turned off the radio.

"Amanda, I'm so sorry," she started. "I know you're upset."

"I'm not angry with you."

"You're not?"

"No. But if you'll keep talking about it, I will be." Amanda stretched her lips in artificial smile and flapped her eyelashes.

Hanna couldn't help but laugh.

"It's nice to see you in a good mood again," she said,

though it wasn't clear to her what could bring about such a dramatic change.

When they arrived at school, Kimberly was already waiting for them, leaning on her car and texting with a happy grin on her face.

"She's glowing," said Amanda anxiously. "Did you know that Ruben asked her to lunch yesterday?"

"Yeah," Hanna sighed. "They had lunch, then dinner, and they even kissed. I know, Ruben told me."

"But you said that . . ." started Amanda.

"I did. But he says he likes her. Believe me, I wasn't exaggerating. It's really reckless," said Hanna, and she pushed the car door open.

"You look good," said Amanda when Kimberly approached them. "Did you have a nice time yesterday?"

"It was perfect, and you'd already know that if you'd check your messages. I sent you at least five." Kimberly shook her head.

"You did?" Amanda began searching for her phone in her small leather satchel.

"Why didn't I get one?" asked Hanna, looking at her cellphone.

"You're a lesbian and wouldn't understand my interest in a man," smirked Kimberly, patting Hanna's back.

"You can read mine," said Amanda, raising her eyebrow. "It's fascinating."

Hanna took Amanda's phone, and they followed Kimberly to the school entrance.

"I don't know why you need archaeology," said Hanna sardonically after she had read all the messages. "You should write novels."

Looking at Kimberly's back and wagging between groups of students, a few of whom were still bandying words about Saturday's party, Hanna reached her locker. Only then did she turn around and realize Amanda wasn't with them. She started cursing herself when she saw her walking down the corridor with Alec. He held her around the shoulders, and she leaned into him in a way that was decidedly more than friendly. Sudden pain, like if somebody poked her in the heart with a blunt object, stopped her breath. She heaved a sigh. She glanced at Kimberly who was standing beside her and looking in the same direction.

"I guess she made up her mind," said Kimberly with glee.

"Oh, I'm sure you put your bit in it. What happened yesterday after I left?"

The bell rang, and students began to move toward their classrooms. Kimberly closed her locker and turned to Hanna again.

"That's right, I gave her some advice," said Kimberly.

"So this is your work?"

"Actually, it's yours. She was crying, Hanna."

Hanna's shoulders slumped.

"You're right. It's my fault."

"Maybe what I said somehow influenced her decision, but I know her. She would never listen to me if she still had hope," said Kimberly, and she walked down the already empty corridor.

"Wait a minute. You knew about. . . ? I knew because… She didn't tell me. Nobody tells me anything. She told you?"

"She didn't have to. As I said—I know her." Kimberly climbed the stairs. "Come on, Hanna, we're late."

During lunch, Hanna and Kimberly sat at their usual table beside the window, but Amanda's seat remained empty. She and Alec took a place in the corner, three tables away. They talked and laughed, but what irritated Hanna most was Alec's hand, which was constantly moving, stroking Amanda's cheek, fixing her hair, playing with her fingers.

"Stop staring," said Kimberly, poking into her salad. "Eat."

At that moment Alec's hand landed on Amanda's knee.

"I'm not hungry," said Hanna, pushing aside her plastic tray.

"You look like a spying, jealous husband," chuckled Kimberly. "Stop it."

"Don't you see what's going on?" said Hanna, letting out her frustration, "This is a cry of despair. She doesn't like him. She's just trying to hurt . . ." Hanna looked at Kimberly sideways. "You know."

"No," said Kimberly, swallowing, "she's just trying to move on."

If Hanna could, she would leave now, but she needed to keep an eye on Amanda. She had to endure this very unpleasant, though not entirely unexpected, turn of events the whole day. When Amanda walked to her locker without Alec at the end of the classes, and Hanna was sure that this agonizing day, which seemed much longer than usual, was finally over, it became worse.

"Kimberly, remember that double date you were talking about?" said Amanda

"Yes," said Kimberly, avoiding Hanna's gaze.

"Alec wants to take me out tonight. I thought if you and Ruben don't have plans, we could go together."

"Good idea. I'll ask him," said Kimberly. Hiding behind her locker door so Amanda couldn't see her face, she looked at Hanna and soundlessly mouthed, "Sorry."

"No, wait," protested Hanna, "you can't," she said staring at Amanda, and this time not because she was concerned about Alec, but because the word "out" sounded very ominous to her.

"Why not?" asked Amanda who, unlike Kimberly, knew what Hanna meant, "I can if Ruben is coming."

"It's not enough," said Hanna pointedly.

"Not enough for what?" asked Kimberly.

"It's nothing." Hanna waved her hand dismissively. "Forget it," she said thinking that she could talk to Amanda on the way home when it would be just the two of them.

When they exited the school, Kimberly's searching eyes stopped at the parking lot, and her face shone with a smile. Leaning on the metal barrier, Ruben beamed back. Taking off his sunglasses, he walked toward them.

"Hello, ladies," he said, then put his arm around Kimberly's back and kissed her temple.

Hanna's heart melted. Looking at Ruben, she smiled approvingly.

∽

"AMANDA, YOU CAN'T DO IT," said Hanna as soon as they got in the car. "It's dangerous. Ruben alone can't protect all three of you."

"Then it will be a bit more work for Craig. He can stay around like he did when we went to the party." Amanda shrugged.

"Why are you doing this?"

"Doing what?"

"Trying to hurt him," said Hanna.

"Because—" started Amanda sharply, but then she looked away and continued in a less irritated tone. "It has nothing to do with him. I just want to have fun. You told me yesterday that I can die at any moment. So why not?"

Hanna knew that it wasn't what Amanda was going to say, but if she dug into it, it would become hard and complicated like it was yesterday.

"Wait until Ruben picks you up," Hanna said. "Can you do that for me?"

Amanda nodded.

As Amanda walked into the house and shut the door behind her, Hanna called Craig.

"Where are you?"

"At the gas station. There are two more houses I want to check."

"You'll have to do it tomorrow, Craig. Come back, we need you." Skipping the details about Amanda's day with Alec, Hanna told him about their plans for the evening.

"Alec? Who invited Alec? And why can't you go?" asked Craig.

"Craig, I don't think you understand."

"You have something more important to do? What can be more important than that?"

"Craig! Ruben is going on a date with Kimberly—"

"Date? I didn't know they were dating."

"And Amanda . . . she is . . . it's a double date."

There was silence, and then Craig hung up.

∼

THE FRONT DOOR slammed and Craig walked in. Passing by Hanna sitting on the couch, he flung his car keys on the coffee table, marched to the cabinet, took out a crystal glass, and poured himself a whiskey.

"Craig, I'm so sorry," said Hanna, looking at his dark face. "It doesn't mean anything. She's trying to hurt you because she's angry."

Craig took a swig from the glass.

The front door slammed again. Ruben stormed into the living room and flung a newspaper on top of Craig's car keys.

"Two people were found dead in the park. Both bodies were drained of blood."

"Oh, no," whispered Hanna.

"We need to do something," said Ruben.

"Really?" said Craig sarcastically. "Like what? Wait, I know—go on a double date. That will make things much better."

"If you want, I can stay at home and leave the two of them alone," said Ruben harshly.

"No. She wouldn't go without one of us," snapped Craig.

"That's right," Ruben snapped back. "As she said to Kimberly, if we don't go, then she and Alec will spend the evening at her place. And since her father is in LA right now and Melinda is not her mother, they will literally be left alone. But if you think that Alec is gay, or such a gentleman—"

"Stop it," shouted Hanna, standing up. "This is serious. They're going out. Wherever it is, it's a public place, and the vampires won't need an invitation. We don't know how many there are, and they might show up all together."

"We need a plan," said Craig, and they all sat down.

Chapter Twenty

ALEC INVITED AMANDA, Kimberly, and Ruben to go to O'Malley's. The bartender was his friend's brother and he could provide them with drinks. Consequently, sitting on the soft couches in the quiet corner of the bar, Amanda and Kimberly were drinking light cocktails that looked like orange juice, and Alec and Ruben were having martinis that looked like icy water. Ruben, who preferred a glass of whiskey, was trying to finish his drink before it got diluted by melting ice.

"Are all three of you going to the same college?" asked Alec.

"Planning to," said Amanda

"So Amanda, you also like history?" asked Ruben.

"Actually, she likes to write," interjected Kimberly. "And, no, I don't mean a diary," she continued, ignoring Amanda's reproachful gaze.

"What do you like to write about?" asked Ruben.

"It won't interest you," said Amanda, blushing.

"Try me," Ruben insisted.

"It's—" Amanda shrugged. "It's a fantasy about older times."

Ruben stared at her.

"Hanna knows much more than what's in school books," said Amanda. "She's told me so many fascinating stories. It got my attention."

"I think that a love of history runs in Hanna's family." Kimberly smiled. "Ruben's already been on an archaeological expedition."

"So." Ruben cleared his throat. "So you'll need some history classes." He turned to Alec, who sat glued to Amanda. "I heard you're into football."

"Yes," said Alec, "but not in terms of career."

He leaned forward, still holding Amanda like he was afraid she'd run away. The thought that she probably would, amused Ruben, but the circumstances that would make her do it weren't funny.

"Photography is my real ambition," said Alec, leaning back again and pulling Amanda along. "Did you look at my website yet?" he asked her, laying his free hand on her crossed legs.

Ruben could hardly restrain the desire to break Alec's arm or make a hole in the line of his shiny teeth.

"You are just like Hanna," whispered Kimberly into his ear while Amanda and Alec were talking.

"What do you mean?"

"I mean your reaction," said Kimberly, and she nodded toward Alec and Amanda.

Ruben took a deep breath.

"I'm sorry."

Kimberly's face was too close to his. He kissed her. It took a moment before she pulled back.

"Feeling better?" she asked, opening her eyes.

"Relieved." He smiled.

∽

MEANWHILE, Craig and Hanna sat in the opposite coffee shop, looking at O'Malley's entrance through the window. It was Monday evening, and there wasn't much going on outside. A few parked cars and random passersby rushed to their destinations.

The young waitress with a pointed face and blond, thinning hair added coffee to their cups.

"This is the fifth one," said Hanna. "My stomach's gurgling." She looked up at the waitress. "Can I have some pie?"

"What kind would you like?" asked the waitress in a high-pitched voice. "We have blueberry, apple, and raspberry."

"Raspberry, please." Hanna looked at Craig. "Would you like some?"

"No," said Craig to Hanna's reflection in the window.

The waitress nodded and left.

"Maybe they don't know she's here," said Hanna, pushing away her coffee cup.

"Or maybe they have a plan," said Craig.

The waitress came back with the pie.

"Thank you," said Hanna. As she took her first bite, she noticed Craig squinting at the part of the street which was out of Hanna's view, behind her.

"Where are your car keys?" he asked.

Still chewing, Hanna pulled them out of her pocket.

"Run," said Craig.

But Hanna leaned to the window and looked out, following Craig's gaze. She choked. Not far from the coffee shop stood Mark beside a big, black Jeep, and men were coming out of it.

"Three, four, five," counted Hanna. "Craig." She looked at him, terrified. "There's six of them."

"Hanna," Craig squeezed her hand, "everything will be fine. Just stick to the plan."

"Can we kill them now?"

"You have my blessing." He looked out again. "If they propagate with that speed, we won't be able to keep the situation under control. I won't let them take her."

Hanna stood up.

"Wait," said Craig. "It's too late. You needed to run when I told you. They found my car."

"We shouldn't have brought your car," said Hanna.

"It doesn't matter. Car or not, they would've known we'd be somewhere near. Damn! One of them is coming. We can't let him come inside. He'll see us and call others. Let's go."

Hanna went out of the door first and the vampire, who Hanna recognized as the one who she'd hit in the nose the other night, was just a step away.

"There you are," he sneered.

It happened in a matter of seconds. When the vampire turned his head toward the Jeep, he noticed Craig coming out of the coffee shop from the corner of his eye. He turned back abruptly with a savage expression on his face, and Hanna was sure that he was going to roar. Instead, she heard a rattle and saw a stake sticking out of his chest. She ran in the opposite direction of the Jeep and crouched behind a parked van.

"There he is," she heard somebody's voice.

"Travis. He killed Travis," yelled another one.

Hanna peeked out. Craig was going toward the Jeep, dragging the dead vampire behind him. She pulled her hood on and headed to O'Malley's. As she reached the door, she glanced back at Craig. Afraid to think what would happen next, she walked in.

She quickly approached the table she was looking for. Ruben stood up.

"Ruben, what is it?" asked Kimberly

"Go with Hanna," he said and stormed off.

"You stay here," Hanna said to Alec, who looked confused.

"I don't understand," said Alec, frowning.

"Come on," Hanna gazed at Amanda and, pulling Kimberly by the hand, went toward the bar.

"Amanda." Alec stood up, too. "What's going on?"

"I'll call you," said Amanda and hurried after Hanna.

"What do you think you're doing?" asked one of the bartenders when Hanna headed to the passage at the left side of the bar.

"We need to use the back door," she said.

"Let them go," said Alec's acquaintance.

The three of them rushed to the metal door at the end of the corridor. They came out at the side of the building, where Hanna's car was parked behind the dumpster. Hanna opened the car door, but at that moment Amanda glanced at the street.

"Oh God," she gasped and froze.

Craig was lying on the ground, struggling to get up, but one of the five men standing around him kicked him, and he fell again.

"Amanda, get in the car," whispered Hanna.

But now Kimberly was staring in the direction where two other men were holding Ruben. He made an effort, lifted his legs, and hit the third one in the knee. The man bent forward. When he restored his balance, one fist hit Ruben in the jaw and the other one in the stomach. Kimberly screamed.

"Rub—!"

Hanna put her hand over Kimberly's mouth and pushed her into the back seat of the car, but it was too late.

One of the vampires looked toward them.

"Crap!" Hanna raged. "They heard us."

Amanda slipped into the front seat.

"There. There's the girl," yelled one of the vampires, and he rushed toward them.

Hanna started the engine and drove the car straight at him. He flew back on impact. Kimberly screamed. Hanna turned to the right and sped away. In the rearview mirror, she saw two vampires jump into the black Jeep and follow them.

"Seatbelts, put the seatbelts on," said Hanna.

"Hanna." Amanda looked at her. "Craig…"

"You knew that this would happen," snapped Hanna. "I hope you're having fun."

"He lied to me. You all lied to me. I was angry," said Amanda sharply. "We have to do something."

"In case you didn't notice, right now there's a car behind us, and it's coming after you."

Hanna looked in the mirror. The black Jeep was only two cars away.

"They're too close," she said. Without dropping speed, she turned into the alley. "We'll go to our place—it's the closest." She took the house keys out of her pocket and handed them to Amanda. "When I stop the car, run. They can't get into the house. The moment you're in, you're safe. Kimberly, do you hear me?"

"What the hell is going on?" shouted Kimberly, coming around from the shock.

"Kimberly, please just do what I say. I'll explain it to you later."

"Did you see what they did to them?"

"Craig and Ruben were trying to buy us time, distract them so we could leave unnoticed, and we blew it. So, I'm begging you to do it right this time. Open the door and get into the house. That's all I am asking."

When they got to the house, Hanna stopped the car with its front to the porch. The moment Amanda and Kimberly ran up the porch stairs, she heard the screeching of brakes. Hanna put the gear in reverse and drove into the Jeep, blocking its door. She got out of the car and ran to the front door, where Amanda and Kimberly were waiting for her, holding it open. But before Hanna reached it, she heard a blast of air. One of the vampires appeared behind her and grabbed her around the chest.

"Hanna!" screamed Kimberly.

Amanda snatched a small horse statue from the stand in the hallway and ran out.

"Amanda, NO!" cried Hanna.

There was another blast, and the second vampire clutched Amanda in his arms. She dropped the statue, and it shattered into pieces.

"Got you," laughed the vampire.

Hanna jerked, trying to free herself. She swung her head backward, hitting the vampire in the face. And then again. The vampire took a step backward, then forward, moving Hanna along with him.

But then Kimberly screamed again.

"Brian!" called the vampire holding Hanna.

Brian fell to the ground, and another tall, sturdy man appeared behind Amanda.

"Riley?" said Hanna, astonished.

She felt that the grip of the hands holding her weakened, and she clung to them. The vampire, who was trying to get away, struggled to shake her off. But Riley was already behind him. He snapped his neck, and the vampire collapsed.

"Oh, God, Riley." Hanna's voice broke.

"Hello, sister," said Riley.

She hugged him tightly around his neck.

"It's all right. She's safe," he said and kissed her head. "Get them inside. I'll take care of this."

He pulled back, but Hanna leaned into him again, carefully took a stake out from the inner pocket of her jacket, and put it in his hand.

"I think it's too late for conspiracy," sighed Riley. He turned his back at Amanda and Kimberly so that they wouldn't see what he was holding, and staked the vampire.

Amanda and Kimberly were staring in horror at the two dead men lying on the porch, whose bodies were getting pale and shriveling right in front of their eyes.

"You killed them," muttered Kimberly.

"They were already dead," blurted Hanna.

Amanda slowly raised her head and looked up at her and, when she turned her gaze to Riley, the expression on her face changed to surprise. She closed her slightly open mouth and swallowed. Then she touched her wrist, where the bracelet was supposed to be.

"Hello, Amanda," said Riley warmly.

"Hi," said Amanda and looked away.

Hanna glanced at the empty street.

"Riley, put the bodies in the Jeep before somebody sees us," she said. "We have to hurry. They have Craig and Ruben. I'll go bring more . . ." She was about to say "weapons," but she looked at a terrified Kimberly and stopped. She put her arm around Kimberly's shoulders. "Let's go inside."

The three of them went in. Hanna closed the door and turned off the porch light. She hurried upstairs to her room, took her handbag which had her gun loaded with wooden spikes, then opened the closet. At the bottom was a small wooden box. She lifted the lid and pulled out two stakes.

"You'll have to stay here tonight," she said to Amanda and Kimberly when she returned to the living room. "We'll drive you home in the morning."

"You never told us you have another brother," said Amanda.

"He's my cousin."

"Hanna, he killed two men," said Kimberly, staring at her with wide eyes.

"He saved us. Kimberly, those men . . . they're not men. You saw what happened to them afterward." Hanna sighed.

"They're killers. They came after Amanda. Amanda." She looked at her for help.

"Seriously?" Amanda looked askance at her, then shook her head and dropped into the armchair.

"They looked like zombies," said Kimberly.

"I thought you didn't believe in the supernatural," said Hanna with irony.

"Are you saying that they're . . ."

"They're not zombies. They're something else."

"Stop it," said Amanda. "You're freaking her out."

"Her? What about you? It doesn't scare you?"

"No. But it brings up a lot of questions," said Amanda with sarcasm. "Do you want me to ask them now?"

The front door opened.

"It's done," said Riley, walking in. "So, where are Craig and Ruben? Where are we going?"

"I'm not sure," said Hanna. "We can check the place where we left them, but the. . . the attackers probably took them somewhere else."

"I think I know where that is," said Riley. "How many were there?"

"Six. Those two came after us." Hanna paused.

"So there are four," said Riley.

"No. Craig . . . there are only three now."

Amanda and Kimberly gaped at Hanna.

"Oh, God," Kimberly gasped suddenly. "They'll kill them. They'll kill them both."

"Kimberly, they'll be fine," said Hanna. "I promise, Ruben won't have a scratch on him. You'll get him back as new and shiny as he was."

Riley looked at Hanna inquisitively.

"Yeah." Hanna sighed again. "They're dating."

"Guys, time is running," said Amanda impatiently.

"Right," said Riley. "I have bad news. There are seven more of them."

"Oh, no," whispered Amanda. She leaned forward and covered her face with both hands.

"What? How do you know?" Hanna asked.

"I've been tailing them for a week. Tonight they came here. There's a house beside the grove, and that's where they're supposed to meet the others. I was coming to tell you."

"Riley, what are we going to do?"

"First, I want to know how this happened. She shouldn't be outside after dark. What was Craig thinking?"

"It wasn't his fault," said Amanda, "It was me. Hanna warned me, but I didn't listen."

Riley thought for a moment, then took out his cellphone and made a call.

"Hello, Melinda. It's Riley."

Amanda, who was blankly staring at the antique vase standing on the coffee table, blinked.

"Yes, I'm here," Riley was saying. "We have a problem. . . . No, she's fine, she's here with us."

Amanda gazed at him, then at Hanna.

"Melinda?" Kimberly asked, pointing her finger at Amanda.

Hanna pressed her lips together and looked down.

"They have Craig and Ruben," Riley said into the phone. "We'll need your help. All right. We'll pick you up."

"What the hell is this?" Amanda jumped to her feet. "Is this a joke? What does Melinda have to do with anything?"

Hanna and Riley exchanged a glance.

"Melinda is . . ." started Riley.

"Riley, no," protested Hanna.

"Hanna, they're coming," said Riley, and his face hardened. "That means they're going to make a move, and we have no idea what they're planning. We can't afford any more mistakes." He turned to Amanda. "After your mother died, we put Melinda into your house to look after you. All these years she's been trying to keep you safe, the same as Hanna and Craig. What happened today is unacceptable. It puts you and everybody around you in danger. You have to be careful."

Amanda's eyes filled with tears. Riley's gaze softened. He walked to her and put his hands on her shoulders.

"We all care about you. I know that you're scared and confused, but it will be over soon. What you are going to do is very important. It's important for all of us. Believe me—you want this to happen. You'll see." He smiled.

"I don't even know what it is I have to do."

"You will. When the moment comes—you will."

Amanda nodded.

"When you say 'important for all of us'. . ." said Kimberly.

Riley looked at Hanna. "I don't think I can answer that."

"We'll see what happens," said Hanna.

"Hanna, let's go." Riley headed to the front door.

"I still don't understand," said Amanda. "How can Melinda help?"

Riley looked back.

"She knows some tricks. Melinda is a very special and powerful woman. Otherwise, we wouldn't entrust you to her."

Amanda nodded again, then stepped to Hanna.

"Hanna, I'm so sorry," she sniffed. "God, I hope they're all right."

"We'll fix this," said Hanna. "Now listen. Close the door after us and don't open it to anybody."

"Like they can't break in if they want to," said Kimberly, eyeing the windows.

"They can't," said Hanna. "You're safe as long as you're in the house. Whatever happens—don't let anybody in and don't step out."

"Don't worry about us. Just be careful," said Amanda.

AMANDA AND KIMBERLY stood in silence for a moment after Hanna and Riley left.

An image of Melinda, sitting on the edge of her dying mother's bed in the hospital, flickered in front of Amanda's eyes. Then she thought of Riley. When he looked at her, she felt the same tumult she had experienced during the conversation with Ruben. She trusted him the moment she saw him. Why? Why didn't Riley, who just killed two men in front of her eyes, seem like a killer to her? Maybe because she trusted Hanna? No, it wasn't just that. Amanda didn't think Riley was a killer because something was telling her that it was the right thing to do. Hanna said those men were already dead, and they looked dead. Within a minute they had changed and looked as if they had died months ago. *They can't get into the house, the moment you're in, you're safe*, she remembered Hanna's words. Who were those men? Were they . . . The tumult came back, and Amanda's heartbeat rose. She knew the answer and, no matter how crazy it seemed, she was sure it was the right one.

Kimberly went to lock the door.

"There's no need for that," muttered Amanda the moment she turned the key. "They can't come in unless you invite them."

"Very funny," grumped Kimberly. "I am freaked out enough without your nonsense."

Even though Amanda hadn't meant to say them aloud, the words just pushed themselves out. What surprised her most was that they didn't sound like nonsense to her. Amanda was absolutely certain that those two bodies, which a little while ago were lying on the porch, were dead vampires. Riley just killed two vampires.

Kimberly went to the kitchen and looked out the window.

"They took the Jeep. What do you think they're going to do with the bodies?"

Amanda walked into the kitchen and sat at the table.

"I don't know," she said absently.

Stunned by her discovery, she reversed in her mind everything that had happened in the past few days, looking for more proof. *It was just a piece of wood,* said Hanna when Amanda asked if Craig was pressing a knife against Mark's back the night after the party; *She shouldn't be outside after dark* Riley had said just a moment ago.

Kimberly sat down across from her. "Amanda, what's going on?"

"Huh?" said Amanda, a little startled.

"I'm lost in conjectures. I have so many questions that I don't know where to begin."

"Join the club."

"You keep saying it's your fault. You know something."

"Don't you see? They got hurt because they were trying to protect me. So whose fault is that?"

"But those guys, they haven't always been here, have they?"

"No, I never heard about them before. It started on my birthday. Remember at the lake you said you heard noises?"

"Yes."

"Somebody was watching us."

"But Hanna said—"

"I know. She lied, okay? She didn't want to scare us. But I was there when she told Craig about them. She said that there were two pale guys in hoodies . . . Pale," she repeated, amazed, then she remembered the look Craig and Hanna had exchanged at that moment.

"Pale? Those men Riley just killed, they were pale too, really pale."

"They're all pale," murmured Amanda, like she was talking to herself.

"I understand now."

"You do?" Amanda stared at her.

"If she knew someone follows us. . . I mean, that explains Hanna's behavior. I understand why she was always so careful and suspicious," said Kimberly, pondering.

"Yeah," sighed Amanda. "Since then I couldn't go anywhere without Hanna, or one of her family."

"And you have no idea what this is all about, what those guys want?"

"No. But I have this feeling. It's like I know, but I just can't remember."

"Do they know? I mean, Hanna and the others."

"Yes."

"Then why won't they tell you?"

The answer to this question, which Amanda herself had been seeking all this time, was now clear.

"Because it's something bizarre, unusual, and they're afraid I won't believe them and it'll only frighten me. They think I'm not ready for it. Kimberly, they don't know how to tell you, but you can't go anywhere alone either."

"Why?"

"Because you're my friend. You heard Riley. Everybody around me is in danger. Thank God Dad is not here. How would I explain this to him?"

"That's why Ruben. . . He's watching after me." Kimberly looked confused. "Amanda, is he just trying to protect me?"

"No. He told Hanna he really likes you."

"He did?" whispered Kimberly with a weak smile. It disappeared a second later. "Do you think they'll be all right? Riley just killed two of those men. If the others find out . . . Why would Riley do that?" Kimberly's voice was angry now. "He could have just knocked them down. He seemed like a normal guy, but he acted like a cold-blooded killer. He snapped those men's neck so deftly like he's been doing it his entire life."

"Kimberly, Riley is not a killer. He did what he had to do."

"What makes you so sure? You don't know who he is. You just met him."

"Does Hanna look like a killer to you, or Ruben, or Craig? Even Melinda is in on this with them. I don't know how to explain it to you." Amanda struggled to find the right words. She could see now why it was so difficult for Hanna, Craig, Ruben, and now Riley, to answer her questions. "Trust me on this, okay?"

Chapter Twenty-One

"MY POOR AMANDA," sighed Melinda after Hanna told her what happened. "You scared the hell out of her."

"We scared the hell out of Kimberly, but Amanda," said Hanna, looking back at Melinda from the front seat of the car, "she was in shock at first, but when she looked at Riley, her face changed."

"She clutched her wrist," said Riley puzzled. "Why?"

"She was wearing the bracelet on that hand," said Hanna, then suddenly she realized why. "Riley, she felt the connection, she felt the connection between you and the bracelet."

"My poor girl," said Melinda again. "Those feelings are haunting her, and she can't understand what they mean."

Riley stopped the car at the edge of the grove and turned off the engine.

"It's here," he said, pointing at the road. "Around that bend."

"Melinda, what are you planning to do?" Hanna asked.

"I am going to seal the house and make them unwelcome again. They'll pop out of it like champagne corks. To do so, I need to get inside first. I could disable two or three, but there are too many. If they all come out together, I won't be able to stop them."

"I think we can help you with that," said Riley. "This is their car; they won't expect us to come out of it."

"No," said Hanna. "But they'll probably be very curious if they think the two vampires who chased us got Amanda and are bringing her to them."

"Let's just hope that all ten of them don't come running to satisfy their curiosity."

But then they looked at each other.

"Actually that would be perfect," said Hanna.

"Right."

"Can we do that?"

"Let me think." After a moment, Riley spoke again. "There's a clearing in front of the house and a grove behind it. You two walk there from here. When you reach the house, find a place to hide, as close as you can. I'll put the bodies on the seats, stop the car in the front yard, and run. If not all of them, I'm sure most of them will come out to look at their dead friends. It'll be very risky to get in through the front door, so look for an open window or some backdoor which we can use. Let me know when you're ready."

"Take this," said Hanna, and she handed him a stake.

Hanna and Melinda rounded the turn and kept close to the trees as they went down the road. Now they could see a big one-story house standing in the middle of the large open space. Another black Jeep and Craig's car, which Hanna assumed Mark used to get here, were parked in front of it. Nobody was inside or near the vehicles. The porch light was on, and Hanna could see that two benches standing on either side of the door were empty, too.

Hanna and Melinda got closer to the backyard. They squatted behind the bushes stretching along the low fence and peered into the darkness. Music and voices came from the house. The voices got closer, and the next moment, they saw two men coming out from a hole in the ground under the house wall.

"What is keeping them so long?" said the first vampire. "It was two of them against a couple of girls."

"I don't know. That Hanna chick . . ." said the second vampire. He took the last puff from his cigarette and threw it away. "I would love to torture her myself, make her squeal like a pig."

Hanna looked at the closed windows, at the tightly shut curtains behind them, and took out her gun.

She stood up.

"Hey, did you just say my name?"

The vampire turned to her, and she pulled the trigger. The wooden spike hit him in the chest but missed his heart. The vampire roared.

Standing beside Hanna, Melinda stretched out her arm toward the second vampire and punched the air with an open hand. The vampire flew back, hit the wall, and fell in the hole on the ground where he'd come from. Hanna jumped over the bush and ran to the first one, who lay on the grass moaning in pain. He was trying to pull out the spike, but the piece sticking out was small and thin and his weakened fingers slipped. With a stake in her hand, Hanna bent over him.

"I would love to torture you too, honey," she said playfully, pushing the wooden spike deeper, "but I don't have time for that shit." And she thrust the stake through his heart. The moaning stopped.

Hanna ran to the second vampire and found him lying senseless on the stone staircase. Behind him, at the end of the stairs, yellow light streamed from the slightly open door.

"Basement," said Melinda, standing a few steps down.

"Yeah."

Hanna pressed the gun against the vampire's chest and

shot him. Then she took out her phone, stepped away from the stairs, and called Riley.

"Two down," she said. "We can go in through the basement in the back. The front yard was clean." Hanna hung up.

∾

RILEY DROVE into the front yard, came out of the Jeep, and looked around. There was nobody outside. He pulled the dead vampire's body from the passenger seat closer to the wheel and pushed his head into the horn.

The screech broke the surrounding silence. Riley ran. When he reached the corner of the house, he stopped, leaned against the wall, and waited.

Two men showed up at the porch.

"They're here. Go tell Mark," said one to the other.

"Stop that beeping, you moron, we heard you," rumbled the vampire. He remained on the porch. He waited a moment, but when the sound didn't stop, he went down to the car.

"Are you drunk?" he shouted. He opened the door and looked into the back seat, where Riley had put the second body.

The house door opened again, and three other vampires came out.

"Steve," called one of them, "Mark's asking if they have the girl."

"They're dead," yelled Steve and pulled back the head lying on the wheel.

The blaring stopped.

"What?"

"Paul and Brian, they are both dead," snarled Steve, and the rest of them hurried toward the Jeep.

Riley rushed to the backyard.

HANNA AND MELINDA dragged the vampire's body out of the way. Hanna was about to open the basement door when they heard another voice, which Hanna recognized as Mark's.

"Bill. Bill?" he called. "Where the hell are you?" Then he kicked somebody. "Still unconscious."

Hanna heard a jab, followed by a short groan.

"You'll be the first one to die," said Mark. "The moment the daggers get their powers back."

Hanna grit her teeth. Melinda's eyes sparkled with anger. She headed to the door.

"Mark, they're back," said another voice. Hanna grabbed Melinda's arm, stopping her.

"Did they bring the girl?" asked Mark. "And where the heck is Bill? Why did he leave these two here alone?"

"Who cares? Nobody will come after them. That Hanna—she's alone now."

"Damn. I just stabbed him, and look at his blood," said Mark.

"Yeah, it dries really fast."

Melinda looked at Hanna, but Hanna shook her head. Just then car horn stopped beeping. She waited for Riley to appear. If he hadn't come yet, it meant that many of them were still inside the house and could arrive at Mark's side any second.

"They're dead, Mark," somebody bawled inside. "They're both dead."

"Dead? How did she do that? That little bitch," Mark growled.

Hanna caught a noise behind her. She looked back and saw Riley.

The voices and sounds of footsteps inside the basement grew fainter.

"Let's go," said Hanna. "I don't think we have much time."

She opened the basement door and went down the wooden staircase. She took a few steps to the left, toward the shelves packed with plastic boxes, and looked behind them. In the middle of the big room, she saw Craig. He was hanging from the ropes twisted around his wrists, fastened to the pipe running along the ceiling. A knife stuck out of his chest. Beside him on the floor, Ruben lay with one stake in his stomach and another between his ribs. His hands and feet were bound with tape.

Melinda gasped. Riley knelt beside Ruben and carefully pulled out the stakes. Hanna ran to Crag and tugged the knife from his heart. Craig jerked and gulped for air. Judging by the bloody holes on his shirt, he had been stabbed several times.

"Craig," whispered Hanna, "Craig, it's me."

Craig's eyelids quivered. He slightly opened his eyes and closed them again.

"I'll need one minute," said Melinda.

She took four candles from her handbag, placed them in the corners of the room, and then lit them with a wave of her hand. Hanna and Riley cut Craig free and put him on the floor beside Ruben, who was coming around and now moaning.

They heard footsteps above and Mark's voice.

"Then how did they get here?" he asked.

"Maybe Brian was still alive, maybe he died after he stopped the car," said another voice.

"And he drove all the way with a stake in his heart?" said Mark, frustrated. "I would agree if I had a brain like yours."

"I'll lock the door," Riley whispered, and he climbed the stairs running up along the wall.

"Terra, aer, aqua et ignis." Standing in the middle of the room, Melinda began muttering the incantation, *"Uti tuus potestatem libero hoc domus de malo. Per malo foras . . ."*

"I hear noises," said Mark. "Turn off that music," he shouted.

"It's probably Bill," said the other vampire.

"Bill wasn't . . . She is here," snuffled Mark.

Footsteps sounded near the basement. Riley locked the door and pressed his back against it. There was a blow, then another and after the third strike, the door swung open. Riley flew down over the stairs and hit the opposite wall.

"Sic volo. Sic loquor," kept muttering Melinda.

"I knew she couldn't be alone in this," said Mark, coming down with two other vampires behind him.

Melinda gazed up at them, her eyes burning with rage.

"Not welcome," she said and raised her hand. "Out."

Mark's hands flew to his throat. He was choking. His body hit the handrail and then, like a bullet, ricocheted to the wall. Choking and hissing, vampires behind him bounced back and disappeared from the view. A ruckus erupted upstairs.

Controlling Mark's body with her hand, Melinda squeezed her fingers into a fist, which made Mark curl. She opened her hand again, slightly pushed the air in Mark's direction, and he was gone. The banging stopped.

Coughing up blood, Ruben broke the silence. Hanna lifted his head and gently put it down on her lap. Melinda knelt beside Craig.

"Amanda," he said, wincing in pain. "Where is she?" Breathing heavily, he pulled himself up and sat, leaning against the stone wall.

"They're at our place," said Hanna. "They're fine, thanks to Riley."

"Riley's here?" asked Ruben in a husky voice.

"Hi there," said Riley. "I'll go check the house."

Melinda went upstairs too and soon came back with a bowl of water and a towel. She ripped the towel into pieces, and she and Hanna began to clean the blood from Craig and Ruben's healing wounds.

"What do we do now?" asked Hanna, glancing at Melinda.

"I'm sure they're still around. So we wait until sunrise."

"Yeah, their cars are still here," said Riley, coming back.

"That's fine." Hanna took Ruben's hand. "Your lungs are damaged. They'll need time to heal. And you have to heal completely. I promised Kimberly that your beautiful, tanned skin would remain wound and bruise free."

Hanna, holding the towel by its wet corner, cleaned the fresh blood around Ruben's now smiling lips.

"Let's take the guys upstairs and put them on something more comfortable," said Riley.

∽

AT NEARLY TWO o'clock in the morning, Hanna called Amanda. Kimberly asked if she could talk to Ruben, just to hear his voice and make sure he was all right.

"Sorry," said Amanda. "Bad signal. I lost her."

"What did she say?"

"Everything's fine, but they can't come home yet. Something is wrong with the car. She said Riley can fix it, but it's too dark. They have to wait until sunrise."

"Do you think she's lying?" Kimberly asked.

"No. Why would she?" said Amanda, who was sure that Hanna was hiding something, or hiding from someone, and they were waiting for sunrise when it would be safe to come out. She also couldn't exclude the possibility that Craig and Ruben were injured badly enough to be taken to the hospital. Her heart skipped a few beats at that thought.

Kimberly lay down on the couch.

"I think she's lying," she said sadly. "Ruben's probably hurt. He's in pain and can't speak."

"Let's hope for the best." Amanda cringed in the armchair. If something happened to them, it would be her fault, it would be because of her selfishness.

There was nothing else to do but wait until morning. Kimberly closed her eyes, and a few minutes later Amanda heard her deep, even breathing.

Amanda felt strange. With Kimberly asleep, it was like she was alone in the house. That awkward sensation made her look around as if she were seeing everything for the first time.

It was Craig's home, where he touched everything. Where he listened to music, watched TV, read a book, where he ate, where he slept. Amanda stood up and walked to the stairs. She knew which of the bedrooms was his, and even though the thought of intruding in such a private space made her feel embarrassed, she couldn't resist the temptation to see it.

She pushed the door open and stood in the doorway looking into the dark room. The strip of light coming from the hallway fell across the large bed with a dark wooden frame.

Amanda stepped inside and closed the door. Now, only moonlight glimmered through the gap between the curtains on the tall windows, illuminating the room.

She walked to the desk not far from the arch in the wall and pushed the small button on the table lamp. Beige tiles shone from the room beyond the arch, and she could see the edge of a white bathtub sticking out.

Amanda looked at the desk. Next to the closed laptop there was a stack of printed maps. She picked up a few and looked through them. They were images of roofs surrounded by trees. On each of them was written the address and road number. Craig was looking for some place, and it had nothing to do with hiking. What was he looking for? Was he trying to find that important thing he had talked about?

No. She wasn't going to think about that right now. She wasn't there to search or detect. Still, there was one thing Amanda was hoping to see in this room: a picture of Eleanor. Her eyes moved around, but there were no pictures in the room at all; not on the desk, not under the lamp on the nightstand, and nowhere on the walls.

Amanda put the maps down. On the back of the chair, standing in front of the table hung Craig's shirt. She took it, glanced at the bed again, and approached it. Her hand stroked the soft, coffee-colored cover. She lifted it and slipped under. The moment her head touched the pillow, her eyes filled with tears. Pressing the shirt to her chest and inhaling the familiar, thin scent of aftershave, she closed her eyes.

Chapter Twenty-Two

YEAR 1852, JUNE

EIGHTEEN YEARS HAD PASSED since Eleanor had been turned, but when she looked into Craig's eyes she had the same breathtaking feeling as when she first saw him. He said, and she could see it in his tender look, that he felt the same way.

She loved her new family, and she regularly visited her old one, watching them from behind the trees and keeping an eye on her daughter. She couldn't stop thanking Gabriella and everybody else for saving her life, giving her a chance to be with Craig, and to be able to watch her little Margaret grow up.

Two years after Richard buried her, he got married. Leaving his part of the sawmill to his daughter, he sold the house and moved to England, leaving Margaret with Eleanor's parents. Eleanor was happy that Margaret was living in her parents' house and that Richard didn't take her to England with him, but the thought that her child would grow up without a mother and a father caused her pain. The only thing that made her feel better was seeing how much her parents and her brothers loved and cared about Margaret.

SHE STOOD in the dark narrow alley in Paris, looking at the low window. The room behind it was poorly illuminated by a single candle.

She bent down. Peering through the panes of the sooty glass, she could see only shadows, outlines of male and female figures.

"We have to leave before somebody finds us," said a female voice.

"Nobody is going to find us here," said a man. "I bet they don't even have relatives. Nobody's going to miss them."

"That man tasted horrible. Let's go find something else."

Not far down the alley a door creaked, and Eleanor heard heels clicking against the cobblestone street.

"Eleanor," called Hanna. "There's nothing in there."

Eleanor looked back.

"I hope the boys are luckier than us, I hope they found them, because I don't want to be late for that ball. We are in Paris," Hanna said excitedly, stretching her hands to the sky full of stars. "The best city in the world. I want to go shopping, and I want to dance at the ball . . ."

"They're here," said Eleanor.

Hanna's hands fell down.

"Where?"

Eleanor nodded toward the window.

"I think the people who live here are already dead," she said quietly.

"Oh, no."

They ran around the iron railing and down the stone stairs.

Hanna lifted the edges of her gown and kicked in the shabby door. Splintering into different directions, it fell down. The woman standing behind it hissed.

"Look what you did, idiot," she shouted at Hanna, pointing at the torn skirt of her dress.

"You're not going to need it anymore," said Hanna scornfully. "You better worry about your head."

There were no bodies in the room. Beside the stove under the opposite wall, Eleanor saw a half-open door. She hurried toward it.

Another woman and a man stood in the dark corner near the window.

Vampires could move as fast as Hunters. Hanna stood in the doorway so nobody could escape.

"Look at the bright side, Sheena," said the second woman. "Those girls look delicious."

"Yep, our blood is special," said Hanna, gazing at her. "Come and taste it."

At that moment, a man flew out from the other room and flopped face down on the floor before Sheena. She jerked.

"What's wrong with you?" she yelled. "Pull yourself together, Albert." She looked down at the man.

Keeping Hanna in view, Albert stood up. His hand slipped into the pocket of his drab olive coat with a fur collar. He retrieved a white handkerchief and wiped his bleeding nose.

Somebody roared in the second room, then came a choking nose. The second woman glanced at the room's door.

"Owen is still having fun," she said. Her upper lip crept up, exposing her fangs. She moved forward, but the man standing beside her grabbed her by the arm and pulled her back.

Hanna was holding a stake in her left hand under the cloak. The man kept staring right at that spot. She looked down. The tip of the stake was sticking out.

"Are you looking at this?" Hanna raised her hand.

Sheena laughed loudly.

"Isn't she adorable? Look at her little stake."

Hanna stepped to her. Albert darted to the gap formed

between Hanna and the way out. Hanna lunged after him, caught him by the neck, and threw him back to Sheena's feet.

"I didn't say you could leave," she said in a cold voice.

Sheena growled. Thin blue veins began spreading on her face, looking gray under the dim candlelight.

"Come here, you little bitch, I'll rip your head off," she said and swooped at Hanna.

Hanna clutched her by the throat and hurled her down. Sheena crashed onto the floor, wheezing. Hanna flipped the stake in her hand and stuck it deep into the vampire's chest.

The other woman gasped. The man standing beside her, who hadn't said a word all this time, spoke.

"I felt your power the moment you stepped in. You are one of them, aren't you?" He wasn't angry or scared. He was bemused. "You are so young," he whispered.

"So you've heard about us," said Eleanor darkly, coming out of the second room. She looked at Hanna. "They are dead. Man, woman, and baby."

She pulled the chair from the corner and smashed it into pieces with one blow of her foot. She picked up the sharp pieces and threw two of them to Hanna.

"Let's finish this," she said.

Albert, who was still sitting on the floor, crawled backward. Eleanor grabbed him by the throat and lifted him up. Hanna stepped over Sheena's body and walked to the other two vampires. She made the first strike and then the second. Albert's screams stopped, too.

Eleanor and Hanna stood on the street again.

"The baby was only a few months old," said Hanna.

"Yes," Eleanor sighed.

Craig, Ruben, and Edmond, following the witch's instructions, were separately searching other parts of the town.

"We have to let them know it's done," said Eleanor. She

pushed her ring first to the coin with her number then Craig's and Ruben's coins.

Hanna sent the message to Edmond, and silently they headed back to the hotel.

∼

ELEANOR WAS SITTING in front of the wide oval mirror and staring into it with an absent look. Standing behind her, Craig bent and kissed her neatly gathered, dark-brown curls.

"We were too late, Craig," she said, subconsciously fingering the diamond leaves of the necklace she held in her hands. "We couldn't save them."

"Eleanor, you have to stop thinking about that," said Craig, looking at her reflection. He gently took the necklace out of her hands and put it around her neck. "You and Hanna just killed five vampires. Imagine how many people you saved today."

Eleanor stood up. She wore an ivory, silky gown with golden embroidery around the décolleté and on the edges of the sleeves, lowered below the shoulders. A lush skirt emphasized her thin, corseted waist even more.

"You look amazing," said Craig.

"You, too," said Eleanor, stroking the lapel of his black dress coat.

She took his arm and they went to the living room, where Hanna, Edmond, and Ruben were waiting for them.

"Oh, Hanna, it's gorgeous," said Eleanor, looking at Hanna's peach dress with ribbons.

"So. Let's go have fun," Ruben beamed. "I hope Madame de Lécuyer has a few pretty girls for me."

"Just don't break the rules," Hanna admonished. "Remember—you can't pursue them after the dance."

Ruben spread his hands.

"Then what's the point of dancing?"

"She's right," Craig smirked. "You don't want to disappoint Madame de Lécuyer. Gabriella wouldn't like it."

Carlotta de Lécuyer was a friend to Samson and Gabriella. More than twenty years earlier, her carriage was attacked by vampires on a countryside road, and Samson and Gabriella saved her from, as she thought, robbers. In gratitude, she invited them to visit her in Paris. The first ten years, they visited Madame de Lécuyer and her husband every time they were in France. But as time passed, their meetings became impossible and they kept in touch by less and less frequent letters. The last one Madame de Lécuyer received right from the hands of Eleanor and Hanna, who introduced themselves as Samson and Gabriella Mountney's daughters. She was very pleased and kindly invited them with their fiancés and friend to the upcoming ball.

Eleanor sat on the sofa in a small room festively decorated with flowers. She looked into the large hall between the pinned-up velvet curtains. Big chandeliers, sparkling with crystal pendants, brightly lighted it. The small orchestra was placed on the balcony of the second floor.

Hanna and Edmond were dancing the waltz, and not far from them Eleanor saw Ruben. He was dancing with some elderly woman and looked like he was in pain. Eleanor smiled.

"He looks desperate," she said to Craig as he walked into the room. "What happened? Nobody else wished to dance with him?"

Craig glanced into the hall.

"Oh, that." He smiled too. "Monsieur de Lécuyer introduced him to his sister. She said that Ruben is lucky she wasn't already engaged for this dance."

Madame de Lécuyer, a not very tall woman with a rounded figure, entered the room with an envelope in her hands.

"Eleanor, darling," she said, sitting next to her, "this

morning I received a letter from your mother." She handed the envelope to Eleanor. "Since she didn't know which hotel you're staying in, she sent it to me. I hope it's good news."

Eleanor opened the letter. When she read it, she felt happy and sad at the same time.

"Margaret is getting married," she said, looking up at Craig. "The wedding is at the beginning of August."

"We have to go back," said Craig. "Don't worry, my love, we'll make it in time."

"So, it's good news," said Madame de Lécuyer. "But you seem a bit sad."

"Oh, no. I'm just emotional," said Eleanor.

"You look like your mother," said Madame de Lécuyer, and her hazel eyes softened. She took Eleanor's hand. "Gabriella's eyes and hair are darker, but you look like her."

Eleanor nodded and looked down.

"I'm sorry she couldn't come," added Madame de Lécuyer. "I miss her, and I would be delighted to see her again."

Those words made Eleanor miss Gabriella, too. They had been apart before, and for a much longer time than now. She didn't understand why, but suddenly an inexplicable longing washed over her. She felt anxious. She wanted to go home.

They had planned to spend another month in London, but Eleanor told the others about the letter and about her and Craig's decision to return to America.

"I'm coming with you," said Hanna. "Can't wait to see Margaret as a bride."

After half a minute of discussion about how they had all seen London, that London was not going anywhere and they had an eternity to visit it again, everybody went to their rooms and began packing.

Chapter Twenty-Three

YEAR 1852, JULY

GABRIELLA WAS SITTING on a bench in her garden, in front of a small pool with a bronze, wide garden urn in the middle. She was reading.

Around the low, white wall of the pool grew dandelions. They broke out through compacted earth and happily swayed their little yellow heads under the warm breeze. It was quiet. The only sound came from bees buzzing over blooming shrubs of pink azaleas and white camellias.

The high sun bit Gabriella's bare shoulders. She stood up and headed toward the castle. As she crossed the little bridge leading to the green pathway between the big old oaks, Eleanor's and Hanna's coins on her bracelet shone with green lights.

The door to Samson's study was open, but he wasn't there. Just in case, Gabriella checked their bedroom, too, and then went back downstairs.

"Lucy," she called.

The dwarf Lucy, and her husband Henry, along with a middle-aged woman named Sophie, worked and lived in the castle.

"Yes, Ma'am?" Shuffling her feet, Lucy came out from the kitchen.

"Have you seen Samson?" Gabriella asked.

"He said that if you asked, then," said Lucy slowly, "I should tell you that he's in the stable."

"You could just say that he's in the stable." Gabriella shook her head.

"He is in the stable, Ma'am," said Lucy after Gabriella, who was already walking out the front door.

"Samson," called Gabriella, walking into the stable.

A bundle of hay moved toward her, and only the tip of Henry's head sticking from behind it proved it didn't move by itself.

"I'm here," said Samson, rising between the horses Gray and Grace.

Gray was Craig's black Frisian steed, and Grace was Eleanor's, an Arabian horse with a dark chestnut coat and black tail and mane. Craig bought her in Egypt as a present after Eleanor's transition.

"She needs new shoes," said Samson, patting Grace.

"I have news," said Gabriella, stepping aside from Henry's path. "The girls are coming back."

"The boys, too," said Samson. "All three of them."

"I supposed so." Gabriella smiled delightfully. "Ruben is probably just a victim of circumstance, but Craig and Edmond wouldn't part from their ladies." Then she added, "I hope they'll keep it that way forever."

Samson approached her.

"Just like us," he said. "Doesn't matter how many years pass, I will never be parted from you."

He kissed her forehead, and they walked out from the stable.

"Maybe I should light the fireplaces in their rooms?"

Henry asked, catching up with them. "It's not cold, but it'll make it cozy."

"Thank you, Henry," said Gabriella. "That would be nice."

"Did you send a message to Riley?" asked Gabriella when they returned to the castle.

"No need for that. He's not far. He said he'll be back before dinner," said Samson and went up the stairs.

Gabriella started towards the kitchen but then stopped again.

"Samson."

Samson looked back.

"What is it, my love?"

Gabriella hesitated.

"Have you heard from Fray lately?" she finally asked.

Samson shook his head. She looked down and walked away.

Sophie and Lucy were sitting at the kitchen table and having tea with biscuits.

"Sophie, would you please change the bed sheets in Hanna's, Eleanor's and Ruben's bedrooms?" Gabriella said.

"Of course, Ma'am." Sophie stood up.

"No no, finish your tea first." Gabriella turned to Lucy. "They're coming home, and since you have to cook for the whole family, it would be better if you started earlier."

"Don't worry, Ma'am, dinner will be on time," said Lucy, dipping her biscuit in the tea.

"I'll help her, Ma'am." Sophie smiled.

"Thank you."

"Ma'am," Lucy called when Gabriella was already on her way out, "you said the whole family. Does that mean I need to count Mr. Wald, too?"

"No. Fray is not coming," Gabriella answered without looking back.

THEY SAT around the dining table, eating, drinking, talking, and laughing. They discussed the upcoming wedding, then the hunt, and then Hanna and Eleanor told about Madame de Lécuyer, about how nice she and her husband were, about their invitations to dinners and the ball. Craig joked about Ruben's dance with Monsieur de Lécuyer's sister, which made Riley laugh until he choked. Edmond, who had become part of the family only a few months ago and had never been in Paris before, was absolutely fascinated by the city. He talked about how much he learned during the trip, about meeting a witch for the first time, and the way he learned to track vampires. Hanna noticed that Samson was carefully listening and nodding approvingly.

When they started talking about stores and presents, the ladies quickly thanked Sophie and Lucy for dinner and disappeared.

In Gabriella's bedroom, Hanna and Eleanor unpacked, one after another, presents they had bought for her. Gabriella's bed was covered with gowns, fabrics, hats, shoes, and little jewelry boxes.

She picked up the dark blue silky gown.

"This is gorgeous."

She walked to the big rectangular mirror and held the dress to her body.

"Put it on," said Hanna. "I want to be sure it fits." She and Eleanor helped Gabriella change.

"Marvelous," said Eleanor, adjusting the folds.

"It looks perfect," said Hanna, excited.

"Thank you, my dears. Samson and I are planning a trip to New Orleans. I'll wear this gown to the theater."

"It's getting dark," said Eleanor, after they helped Gabriella change back into her purple satin dress. "Time to go. I can't wait to see Margaret. The weather is nice, and I hope they're having tea in the backyard. That would be the best view I could get."

"I'll come with you," said Hanna. "I haven't seen Margaret in ages."

"Your daughter is getting married," said Gabriella, sitting down on the ottoman in front of her dresser. "How do you feel about that?"

Eleanor pushed aside the skein of fabric from the corner of Gabriella's bed and sat down.

"A little weird. We look the same age," she said.

"You know you're a bit older than you look." Gabriella smiled.

"I just want to be sure they love each other."

"They do. I've seen them together." Gabriella glanced at Eleanor. "There's something else. Something bothers you."

"It's just . . ." Eleanor looked down at her lap. "I just wish I could be with her," she said in a low voice. "It's a very important day of her life, and I can't even congratulate her. If only I could hug her once."

Hanna knelt before her, took her hand, and kissed it. Gabriella sighed.

All three of them went to the smallest living room, where the men with glasses of the brandy Ruben had bought in Paris gathered around the fireplace. Gabriella joined their company, but Hanna and Eleanor headed to the stable, saying they'd be back soon.

∼

A HUNDRED YARDS AWAY, at the edge of the woods, Fray stood and looked at the castle.

"What the hell are they doing here?" he hissed, staring at

Eleanor and Hanna coming out the front door. "They should be in England. Damn it! It means they're all back."

"Hmm. So, what do we do now?" asked Gregor, standing beside him.

He was looking in the same direction, but because of the enchantment around the castle, he could see nothing but trees on the hill.

Fray knew that every evening after dinner Samson checked the Map. By that time, Fray arranged a witch to do a summoning spell showing a great danger. Since Fray expected only Samson, Gabriella, and Riley to be in the castle, he was sure all three of them would have to go hunt down the monsters. Now, he didn't know what to expect.

He kept his eyes on Eleanor and Hanna as they galloped away, and by the turn they took, he assumed that they must be going to Eleanor's parent's house. It would be at least two hours before they came back. So, now there were two less Hunters in the castle.

"It doesn't change anything. Just stick to the plan," said Fray darkly, still deep in his thoughts. "If the witch spills enough blood, they'll all go."

"Oh, she will. Joanne will make sure of that."

∼

TWENTY MILES AWAY, in the forest beside a small village, Joanne stood above the witch sitting on the ground.

"It's time. Do it," she said roughly.

The witch, a dark-skinned woman with a kerchief around her curly black hair, looked up with a gaze full of hate.

"What are you staring at?" Joanne shouted. "Isn't it your job? We are vampires, and you're a witch. So call them, call the Hunters. Do what you have to do."

The woman grabbed a twig and scratched a circle around

her, then lit the candle and put it in the middle. She unfolded the piece of cloth in her hand and took from it a pinch of black powder. Sprinkling the earth with the powder, she closed her eyes and whispered:

Guardian Hunters, fast and strong,
Come to the place where we belong,
No harm to come or death to befall,
Guardian Hunters, save us all.

She took the knife lying next to her and cut her palm. Dripping the blood into the middle of the circle, she continued:

I summon you to stop the evil on these grounds,
I am entrusted to your care

"That blood is not enough." Joanne bent to the witch. She sank her fangs into the woman's throat, and then pushed her head down, letting the blood stream into the circle.

∽

GABRIELLA LIT MORE candles and sat on the sofa.
"So." Samson, turned to her. "Did you like your presents?"
"Oh, I hope you did," said Edmond. "After what I went through."
"You?" Gabriella looked at him with surprise.
Ruben chuckled and looked at Riley.
"He actually decided to go with Hanna and Eleanor when they went shopping."
Riley and Gabriella laughed.
"I didn't know," said Edmond, pushing his blond curls back from his forehead. "I've never shopped with a woman before. It was a new experience."

"It wasn't just an experience, brother." Ruben took a sip from his brandy. "It was a lesson."

"Once I joined them, too. In Vienna," said Craig, beaming. "When, half an hour later, they were still standing beside a table of ribbons, I said that I urgently needed a newspaper and disappeared."

"All right," said Samson, smiling. He stood up. "Duty calls."

"So, you are not drinking anymore?" Ruben added more brandy to his own glass. "Good. More for me."

"Don't get too happy." Samson put his glass on the small rectangular table beside Ruben. "Fill it up. I'll be back in a minute."

Craig's and Riley's glasses landed with a thud beside Samson's. Ruben chuckled and pulled out another bottle from behind his chair.

Samson went to his study and unfolded the Map lying on the chest. The Map looked like a thin but large book. Continents were divided into parts, and each part had its own page.

He looked at Africa, then he checked the European countries. America was on the next page. When he opened it, he grabbed the Map and hurried to the living room.

"I'm afraid the party's over, boys," he said, walking in.

Everybody put down their glasses and stood up at the seriousness in his voice. Samson headed to the round table beside the window, and the others cleared it up, removing the book lying on it, the candelabrum, and the vase of flowers. When Samson put the Map down and opened it on the right page, they all looked at the red stain, which grew right before their eyes.

"I've never seen anything like that," said Riley.

"Me either," said Samson.

"Oh, God," gasped Gabriella. "This looks like a massacre."

"To create that kind of stain takes a lot of blood," said Samson. "One witch can't do it."

"So you think there's a few of them?" Craig asked.

"Very likely. But instead of guessing, we better go and see what's going on." He pointed at the stain again. "This is beside that Cold Stone village. Let's go get those vampires."

"How do you know they're vampires?" said Edmond. Everybody looked at him. "Sorry, I just wanted to ask."

"And we're listening. Ask away," said Samson.

"Can the Map show that, too?"

"No. But the sky can. There's no full moon tonight. And since there are no trolls in America, most likely, it's vampires. There are other kinds of monsters, of course, but we haven't seen them for centuries. Let's hope it stays that way." Samson looked at Riley, Ruben, and Craig. "The situation is unusual. So get your weapons, you're all coming. Edmond, come with me." He said and headed back to his study.

As they entered the room, Samson stepped to the large glass doors. Behind them, attached to the wall and placed on the stands in a special order, were weapons of different kinds and shapes that had been collected for centuries—knives, swords, axes, bows, and arrows.

Samson picked the seventeenth-century single-edged Chinese Dao sword and handed it to Edmond.

"You don't have much experience yet, and if you get attacked by many of them at once, it will be easier to just chop their heads off. Think you can do that?"

"Yes, sir," said Edmond, taking the sword. "I decapitated a goat once."

Samson smiled.

"You never take your dagger with you. Why?" Edmond asked when Samson took a sword, too. "It can easily kill anything."

"For security reasons. We move fast and anything can happen. One wrong move and it can as easily kill one of you."

"I didn't think about that."

"Go get your stakes, you'll need them too," said Samson, closing the glass doors.

Gabriella wished them good luck. As they one by one walked out of the door, she stepped to Samson and kissed him.

"I am the luckiest woman in the world, who doesn't have to worry even if she sends her husband to war."

Samson looked at her tenderly.

"But you still do," he said.

"You notice everything, don't you?" She smiled.

"I love you," whispered Samson.

"I love you more," said Gabriella, and she kissed him again.

~

"WHAT'S TAKING THEM SO LONG?" said Fray, irritated after waiting almost an hour. "The other two are probably on their way back already."

But then he saw figures coming out the front door. It was very dark now, and he couldn't discern who was who.

"One, two," Fray counted the silhouettes moving toward the stable. "Four. One is missing." A minute later, the fifth silhouette came out the door. Fray said with satisfaction, "It worked. They're all leaving."

~

FRAY COULDN'T TAKE Gregor with him; Samson was the only one who could open an arch in the veil. He waited another ten minutes to make sure that Samson was far enough, then stepped forward and disappeared. Gregor wondered what would happen if he tried to cross the invisible wall. He took a step, and then a few more. Nothing stopped him. But suddenly, he realized he was facing the woods. He turned to face the hill again and went towards it, but seconds later he was looking at the trees. And it didn't matter how many times he tried, every time he found himself moving in the wrong direction.

~

THE CASTLE'S front door slammed loudly.

Gabriella, who was having tea with Sophie, Lucy, and Henry in the kitchen, put her cup down.

"Who could that be?" Sophie asked.

"I have no idea," said Gabriella. "None of them could have returned so early."

"I'll go check," said Henry.

He jumped down from his chair and hurried to the hall. When he saw Fray at the top of the stairs, he opened his mouth to welcome him home, but Fray moved too fast and disappeared. Henry squeezed his lips together and went back to the kitchen

"It's Fray," he said.

"Fray is here?" Gabriella stood up, but then suddenly froze. "Where did he go?"

"He's upstairs."

There was a flash, and Gabriella was gone. Henry, Sophie, and Lucy ran to the hall.

Gabriella stopped at the second-floor corridor and listened. She heard a stir, and the sound of it was coming from the open door of Samson's study. She moved forward and stopped at the doorway.

Fray stood with his back to her. He was opening the wooden case on Samson's desk, the one Samson used when he needed to take the Book with him. Fray didn't turn around.

"Go away," he said.

"Just in case you forgot—this is not your room," said Gabriella coldly.

Fray looked back abruptly. His mouth was slightly open.

"It's you. I thought it was Sophie." He stared at her. "What are you doing here?"

Gabriella raised her eyebrow.

"I mean . . ." Fray glanced at the case, then again at Gabriella. "I saw you leave."

"You saw me? Are you sure it wasn't Hanna or Eleanor?"

"No. Not them." Fray's tone changed, became more irritated. "After. Ten minutes ago."

Gabriella's eyes narrowed.

"Were you watching us? Why?"

"Who was it? Did he turn someone?"

Fray didn't visit the castle often, and he had no idea that Samson's family had a new member. The last time he had shown up, Edmond had been in Paris. Fray came to ask Samson to turn the man he brought with him, but the moment Samson put his hand on the man's chest, he knew he would have to stop the transition. He knew what Fray's reaction would be, and telling him that he just turned somebody for Hanna wouldn't make it better.

"Yes. His name is Edmond."

"And he didn't even tell me," said Fray. "Why should he? I am no one."

"You are never here," said Gabriella, stepping forward.

"It doesn't mean that he can do what he wants," shouted Fray.

In the hall, the servants could hear their voices. It was clear that Gabriella and Fray were arguing, and it worried them. Henry carefully climbed up the stairs and hid in the corridor behind the pot with a bushy philodendron. He listened, trying to figure out the subject of the fight.

"He didn't decide it himself. We all agreed," explained Gabriella.

"I bet Samson turned him because he's a good boy," Fray said with irony.

"He is. You've seen him once. Remember the boy Hanna fell in love with?"

"Of course, love." Fray laughed. He went to the chest and opened it. "I hope you're all packed with lovers because Samson will not be able to do it again." He unclasped one side of the Book.

"What are you doing?"

Gabriella rushed toward Fray, but he roughly pushed her back, and she hit the table.

"It's my turn," Fray said with a savage expression on his face. "I will show you what the power is for."

"How did you. . . ?"

"How did I find out?" He stepped to her. "I was standing right there," he pointed his index finger, "right behind that door when he told you. I heard everything. He kept it from me for centuries. He'll pay for that. I'll destroy him."

He went to the chest again, unclasped the second side of the Book, and lifted it.

"I will not let you take it," said Gabriella with rage. She pushed her ring to the bracelet, first to the coin with her number and then to the clasp. Alarming rays of red light streamed up from all coins.

Fray put the Book in the case.

"It's not going to help," he sneered. "They're already half-way there."

"Half-way where?" Gabriella glared at him.

"Half-way to the Cold Stone." Fray laughed unnaturally. "Where my people did the ritual to fish them out of the castle."

Gabriella's blood boiled.

"It's all right," she said. "I'm still here."

∼

HANNA AND ELEANOR were already on the way back when both their bracelets shone, first with green and then with red lights. They stopped their horses.

"What the hell happened?" Hanna said, gazing stupefied at the bracelet.

"It was Gabriella," said Eleanor. "When we left, all of them were home. What could have happened?"

They stared at each other for a moment and then, without another word, spurred their horses.

∼

THE RED LIGHT coming from the bracelets shone in the darkness. Riley, Ruben, Craig, and Edmond had already stopped their horses around Samson before it extinguished.

"What could have happened?" asked Riley, looking at Samson's darkened face.

"I don't know. But it's something serious if Gabriella decided to call us. We have to go back."

"All of us?" Ruben asked. "What about the vampires? If several witches came together to summon us, it must be something really bad."

"I can't imagine what could be so urgent," said Craig, pondering. "Nobody can even get close to the castle."

"Maybe the Map showed something else," said Riley doubtfully. "Something . . . I don't know . . . more important."

But Samson didn't say anything. He was thinking.

"No," he said suddenly, moving his eyes from one to another. "There are no witches. There is only one witch, who is wounded, and she is bleeding right into the circle. She's probably dead by now."

"Are you saying she did the ritual right where she saw the vampires? Why would she do that? They never do that," Craig said.

"That's the question. Why?" said Samson, still deep in his thoughts.

"If she's there, and they can see her doing the spell," said Edmond, "wouldn't they drag her out from the circle? I mean, to stop the ritual."

"They don't know about the ritual," Riley answered. "Many of them don't even know we really exist. She was just a snack."

"He knows," whispered Samson, staring at Riley. "There is only one man who knows about the ritual and who can also enter the castle." His eyes burned with fury. "He can because he is one of us."

"Fray?"

"Why would he do that?" Ruben asked.

"This is a setup and Gabriella is in danger. To the castle! All of you!" Samson yelled, already speeding away.

∾

FRAY CLOSED the case and headed to the door.

"Put the case down," said Gabriella, standing in his way.

"Step aside," said Fray, putting his free hand on the dagger hanging on his belt.

"Put that case down," Gabriella insisted.

Fray lifted his hand to push her away, but this time she was ready for his move. With one hand she caught his arm in the air, then clenched the other one to a fist and punched him in the jaw.

Fray flew back and hit the weapon cabinet. The glass doors shattered into pieces.

His bleeding lips smiled.

"You know you can't take me," he said, wiping them with his palm.

"It doesn't mean I won't try."

Fray put the case down, grabbed Gabriella by the arm, and turned her, pressing his chest to her back.

"I can rip your head off," he whispered viciously into her ear.

"No, you can't."

Gabriella jerked her hand away and elbowed him in the stomach. He cringed just for a second, then turned her around and punched right into her chest. The blow threw her out of the door, and she slid down the corridor wall.

Henry, who was still crouching behind the philodendron, jumped. He shut his mouth with both hands, suppressing the gasp.

Fray picked up the case, took a step, and then stopped, looking around. He walked to the chest and glanced in it. Then he approached the table.

"Missing something?" Gabriella asked, stepping into the room again.

"Where's the Map?" he asked.

After everybody had left, Gabriella watched the Map in the small living room, so she could tell Samson if any changes occurred while he was within reach. And the Map was still there.

"Why do you need the Map? To spy on us?"

"Where is the Map, Gabriella?"

"Samson took it with him," she said without hesitation. "You made such a mess on it. It looked like there were dozens of vampires." She watched Fray as she spoke. He was looking for the Map on the bookshelves. "They could go to other places for food. Too many for Cold Stone; it's not that big, after all."

"Many?" He turned to her. "You haven't seen 'many' vampires." His lips quivered from excitement. "I'm going to make armies of them."

"Have you lost your mind? You're a Hunter."

"I was once. But I freed myself about two centuries ago, around the time I started sleeping with vampire women. I've learned a lot about them since then. They're real and honest, and the most important thing is that, unlike you all, they appreciate me and they're loyal to me."

Gabriella's eyes widened with every word.

"It's okay," said Fray, looking around again. "I'll take the Map later. For now, I'll just kill as many witches as I can."

Henry heard Fray's footsteps closing to the door and he ran down the stairs, where Sophie and Lucy waited for news with terrified expressions on their faces. But before they could ask anything, Henry shushed them, pressing a finger to his lips and pushing them back to the kitchen. He left a narrow gap in the door when he pulled it, and all three of them leaned to it, peering through.

There was only one thing Gabriella could do.

She didn't move when Fray walked past her. But as he went out the door, she rushed to the desk and opened the drawer where Samson kept his dagger. She pulled it from the sheath. Gabriella knew the dagger wouldn't kill Fray. But if she managed to stab him in the heart, he would be seriously injured and disabled for a while.

Samson had a secret room in his study. It was meant for the Book Keeper, and nobody knew about its existence but her. The room was behind the bookshelves. The button to unlock it was in the weapon cabinet. She had to push the button and then pull the shelves open. It was the perfect place to hide the

Book and herself until the others returned. But first, she had to catch Fray before he disappeared. She ran out.

Fray was already in the hall. Gabriella's silhouette flashed on the stairs. She stopped behind him and raised the dagger.

But Fray had felt the blast. When Gabriella stabbed him he was turning and, instead of the heart, she pierced his side. When she pulled the dagger out, blood gushed from the wound onto the marble floor. Fray roared from the pain and dropped to one knee. She grabbed the case and ran back to the study.

Gabriella reached the weapon cabinet and pushed the button. But at that moment she heard the blast, too. Fray took her by the arm and turned her around, and she saw the dagger in his hand.

∽

"WHAT IS YOUR PLAN NOW?" Fray roared and stuck the dagger into Gabriella's heart. "Slice me with a sword?"

Gabriella's lips parted, but there was no sound. The case and Samson's dagger slipped out of her hands. Her big black eyes blinked once and then closed. Swaying slightly, she fell face down onto the glass-covered floor.

Fray put his dagger back in the sheath, then opened the case and threw Samson's dagger in it. He wanted to look for the Map, but he'd lost a lot of time; the others could show up any moment. He took the case and hurried away.

∽

AS SOON AS FRAY LEFT, Henry, Lucy, and Sophie came out from the kitchen. The women ran upstairs, but Henry went to close the open front door. He glanced out and saw Fray slightly bent to one side, heading to the woods.

As Henry shut the door he heard screams, coming from the second floor.

He walked into Samson's study. Sophie and Lucy sat on the floor beside Gabriella's body, crying. Henry's shoulders began shaking. He covered his face with both hands and dropped to the floor, too.

∽

HANNA AND ELEANOR jumped down from their horses and rushed to the front door.

"Oh God," gasped Eleanor the moment they walked inside.

Both of them were staring at the red stain on the floor.

"The blood is dry," said Eleanor. "Whoever it is is healing."

"Why is it so quiet?" asked Hanna. "I don't like this."

Following the blood drops, they went up the stairs and walked into Samson's study. They looked at Gabriella lying on the floor and then at the sobbing women.

"What happened?" Hanna asked, glaring at the floor.

But Sophie and Lucy only sobbed harder.

Eleanor knelt beside Gabriella and turned her face up.

"Stop crying," said Hanna without turning her eyes from the huge red stain on Gabriella's chest. "She'll be fine," she said, her voice trembling. "She probably just cut herself."

Tears ran from Eleanor's eyes. There were small scratches on Gabriella's face from the broken glass. Stroking them, she looked at Hanna.

"They are wet, they are not healing, Hanna," she sobbed. "They are not healing."

"NO!" Hanna yelled. "No. She will be all right." Her whole body was shaking. "What happened?"

"It was Fray," muttered Henry, coming forward.

"Fray did this?" Hanna gulped for air. "Did Samson go after him?"

"He doesn't know. They weren't home when this happened?"

"When *did* this happen?"

"Only a few minutes ago."

"He couldn't have gone far."

Hanna's eyes burned with fury. She jumped to the weapon cabinet and grabbed the biggest double ax from the wall.

"Which way did he go?" She gazed at Henry.

Eleanor looked at her, alarmed.

"No." Henry shook his head. "Don't go."

"Which way?" Hanna shouted.

Henry looked at her mad eyes and sighed.

"That way." He pointed his hand to the hill.

Hanna stormed out.

Eleanor jumped to her feet, grabbed another ax, and ran after her.

~

RILEY, Craig, and Ruben each in turn asked Samson what was going on as they hurried home. Why would Fray, the Hunter, kill a witch?

"He wanted to lure us out of the castle," Samson said.

"The stain was big, but that didn't mean all eight of us would go," said Ruben. "He knew we wouldn't."

"You're right. That's why he chose the moment when he thought there were only three of us. The last time he came you were in Paris, and we told him you were planning to go to London after that."

"But why would he do it?" Craig asked.

"I don't get it, either," said Riley.

"He wants the Book," said Samson.

"What? Why?" asked Ruben.

"Oh, God," whispered Riley, "Gabriella will try to . . ."

"I know," said Samson, and for the first time in many centuries, there were notes of fear in his voice. "All I can do is hope that she won't."

Samson's heart was hammering. He couldn't wait to get closer to the castle so that he could speak to Gabriella. The moment they crossed the familiar field, which was only a mile from the castle he whispered,

"Gabriella," and then held his breath.

He waited a couple of seconds and then called again, "Gabriella, my love, answer me."

But there was no answer. His heart trembled. Horrible thoughts and feelings, which had chased him the whole way, became stronger and more real. Trying to push them away, he told himself that she might not be in the castle, and he began looking for reasons that could make her leave.

But none of them were good enough. The only real possibility was that Fray really had been in the castle, had taken what he'd come for, and she'd run after him. That horrified him even more. He spurred his horse harder.

Samson jumped down from the horse before it stopped, and he entered the castle. Riley, Craig, Ruben, and Edmond stepped in right after him. When they saw the blood on the floor, they froze and looked at Samson. His hands shook and his look went blank. He stepped over the bloodstain and jumped to the second floor. The others did the same.

When he burst into the study, they all heard a wild cry.

"NOOOO!!!"

"Oh, no." Riley gulped for air.

"Gabriella," gasped Ruben. He leaned to the wall and slipped down, covering his face with his hands.

Craig clenched his teeth, but tears filled his eyes. Edmond stood in the doorway with a shocked look on his face.

Samson fell to his knees beside Gabriella. His jaw trembled. Holding her by the shoulders, he lifted her and pulled her closer to his chest.

"No," he whispered. "Gabriella, look at me. Please, please." He stared at her. "My love, open your eyes."

He kissed the scratches on her face like he was trying to heal them. Then he touched the big red stain on the carpet and rubbed his fingers. They were wet.

He pressed her to his heart, tears dripped from his eyes.

"FRAAAY!" he roared madly, "I'LL RIP OUT YOUR HEART!"

"I doubt that. But I already ripped out yours," he heard Fray's gloating voice.

"He heard me." Samson turned to the others. "He is not far."

His hand slipped under Gabriella's legs, and he lifted her and put her on the soft, velvet couch.

The expression on his face was wild.

"When did he leave?" He asked in a rigid voice, looking at Henry sitting in the corner.

"Four, five minutes ago," said Henry, wiping his nose with his sleeve.

Samson looked at the empty chest, then went to his table and opened the drawer.

"He took the dagger," he said, looking into it.

"Gabriella took it," said Henry, and everybody stared at him. "He was leaving with the Book, and she stabbed him. But I looked. It's not here. He must've taken it after."

"She stabbed him?" said Samson, astonished. "You'll tell me everything later. We have to hurry!"

"You better, sir," said Henry. "You didn't notice, but your axes are missing, too."

They all looked at the weapon cabinet.

"Why would he take the axes?" Riley asked.

"He didn't. Hanna and Eleanor did. They went after him."
"What?" Craig gasped.
"Oh, God," muttered Edmond.
"HANNA!" Samson screamed, "COME BACK! NOW!"
"NO!" yelled Hanna in response.

Craig, Edmond, Ruben, and Riley ran out, and Samson stormed after them.

∽

THE WIND WHIPPED Hanna's face, wet from the tears. She heard Samson's voice full of pain, and it squeezed her heart, if it was possible, even more.

She and Eleanor galloped down the hill. From the darkness of the woods, they came out to a meadow, where the weak light from the crescent moon made the view more clear.

To decide which way to go, they circled, sniffing the air for Fray's scent. But the scent they found, and which was becoming stronger and stronger, wasn't Fray's or some mortal human's.

"Vampires," said Eleanor.

"Do you see them?" asked Hanna, peering into the darkness between the trees.

"No," said Eleanor.

"I can't define the direction. It's like the scent is everywhere."

"Yeah. That means we're surrounded," said Eleanor.

The horses neighed and reared up. Nearly thirty vampires came out from the woods and stood in a circle around Hanna and Eleanor.

"What the hell is this?" said Hanna, glaring at them. "We don't have time for this."

Hanna spurred her horse to pass through. But one of the

vampires jumped forward, grabbed the bridle, and pulled the horse aside, stopping it.

"Where are you going, girl?" said another one. "Don't you want to have some fun?" He smiled, showing his sharp teeth.

"They have no idea who we are," whispered Eleanor, rolling the axe in her hand.

"No," said Hanna.

If they killed one, the others wouldn't run. They'd attack, and then she and Eleanor would have to fight all of them. But the vampires were in her way, and she was too angry. She leaned forward and grabbed the one who was still holding the bridle by his clothes.

"Do you know who I am?" she asked, piercing him with a gaze. "I am a Hunter." She pushed him away. "Step aside or we'll kill you all," she said, staring furiously at the crowd.

"Fray warned us that you'd say that, that you'd try to scare us," said a tall, broad vampire, stepping to her.

Hanna and Eleanor glanced at each other and gritted their teeth.

"You shouldn't have said that name," hissed Hanna.

She swung her ax and chopped the vampire's head off. Silence fell on the meadow for a second, and then, screaming and roaring, the vampires ran at Hanna and Eleanor. Eleanor led her horse against them to one side and Hanna to the other. The vampire's bodies fell down one after another. But they were too many.

Usually, when Hanna and Eleanor hunted, they wore their slinky hunting clothes. Now, their dresses were restricting their movements. The vampires encircled the horses and clung to Hanna's and Eleanor's skirts and legs, trying to pull them down.

Hanna jumped down from the horse, grabbed one of them, and spun him around, knocking down a few others.

Eleanor freed her legs, stood on the horse's back, and jumped over the crowd, landing behind it.

Many of the vampires had knives. Hanna and Eleanor had several cuts, and blood covered their torn dresses.

Suddenly, many hands at once clutched their fingers around Hanna's arms and pulled her back.

A moment later, Eleanor was surrounded, too. Growling vampires dragged her to a tree and pressed her to it, trying to force her arms around the trunk. One of them wrestled the axe out of her hand and swung it above Eleanor.

But another hand snatched his wrist and yanked the axe out of his grip. Standing behind the vampire, Craig turned him around and chopped off his head. Two others opened their mouths and hit the ground, choking, staked by Ruben.

With his Dao sword, Edmond chopped off the hands holding Hanna. Riley sliced their owners with a sword, one after another.

Hanna saw Samson crushing the rest of the vampires and ran forward. She grabbed one of them and pulled him away from Samson. She turned the vampire around and, staring at his young, terrified face, yelled, "Where is he? Where did he go?"

Everybody looked at her. They had never seen Hanna so full of rage and hatred.

"I don't know," said the vampire, cringing in fear.

"Don't lie to me!" Hanna raised her axe above his head. "Where did you come from?"

"Two . . ." the vampire put his hand between him and the axe. "Two days ago I woke up in some church. An old, abandoned church. . . . But I don't know where it was. They brought us here in covered wagons."

"Who's 'they'?"

"Fray and one other. His name is Gregor."

"How long did it take to get here?" asked Riley, stepping closer.

The vampire shuddered.

"I don't know . . . five, maybe six hours."

Riley pulled him out of Hanna's hands and snapped his neck.

Samson looked at Hanna with eyes full of sorrow. She met his gaze, her lips trembling and tears streaming down her cheeks. She flashed to her horse, jumped on it, and sped toward the castle.

As Hanna returned, she ran to Gabriella and Samson's bedroom. She looked at the blue dress lying on the armchair. Choking from the pain in her chest, she began madly sweeping the presents from the bed. When it was empty, she gazed at it for a moment, then, sobbing, went to the study.

Hanna knelt before the sofa and took Gabriella's hand. She kissed it, and then pressed to her cheek.

"You were my mother," she muttered, burying her face in Gabriella's side. "I can't do this again."

Somebody entered the room. She looked back and saw Samson. She ran to him, and he hugged her. Hanna felt his wet cheek and wept harder.

The others were standing in the hall around the dry bloodstain.

"Lucy," said Craig, "could you bring us a cup, please."

Lucy, wiping her nose with her apron, went to the kitchen.

"It's here," said Ruben, coming back from the small living room with the Map in his hand."

"Oh, thank God," sobbed Eleanor.

After they scraped as much blood as they could from the floor and collected it in the cup, they headed to the library. Craig noticed that Riley wasn't with them. He turned around and saw the closing front door. Ruben was looking in the same direction. They exchanged a sad look and bowed their heads.

∾

THROUGH THE DARKNESS, Riley ran toward Gabriella's garden. When he reached it, he threw himself face down on the grass beside the lilac shrubs, and let out the pain he couldn't suppress any longer. His big, strong shoulders shuddered.

∾

SAMSON, with Gabriella in his arms, walked into their bedroom and put her on her side of the bed. Without taking his eyes off of her, he went around and lay down next to her. He stroked her soft black hair, kissed it, then buried his face in her neck and cried.

Chapter Twenty-Four

TODAY

AFTER A FEW SECONDS of falling through the darkness, Amanda hit something soft. When she opened her eyes, she wasn't screaming anymore, but her mouth was still open. She sat up and looked around. She was in the same bedroom of the same old, abandoned house from the dream she'd had a few nights ago.

She sat there for a moment, listening to the silence, then stood up and went to the hallway. Amanda looked at the doors but didn't check them, since she already knew what was behind them. She took the stairs, which, as she also already knew, lead to the living room. But after a few steps, Amanda stopped. She suddenly realized that, yes, it was the same place, but it wasn't the same dream.

She ran down the stairs, then stopped again. Even though everything looked absolutely the same, Amanda had a strange feeling that this time she wasn't alone. The front door was closed, and the key was in its place. When she looked at the floor, she saw that the dust was disturbed in all the same places where she'd walked last time. She even saw her footprints to the armchair, where she'd sat when she felt dizzy.

Her eyes stopped at the end of the room opposite the front door, where heavy curtains covered, as she thought before, big windows. But, when she approached them and pulled the curtains open, she saw wide doors to the backyard. The key was in the keyhole. She unlocked the door and stepped outside.

It was dawn. The first rays of sunshine touched her face. The sensation of their warmth and the smell of the blooming, though entirely neglected garden, was unbelievably real. Not so far away, surrounded by tall grass, stood an old table with chairs around it. Then, a little bit farther, she saw a bench. She stared at it for a moment, and suddenly her eyes prickled. She felt that inexplicable tumult like she'd experienced when she looked into Craig's eyes. Only this time it was stronger. The pain in her chest and the tears on her cheeks felt real, too, and it scared her. She wanted to wake up. She closed her eyes, hoping that when she opened them, she would be in her bedroom again.

She heard a weak moan. It sounded like somebody in pain. The moan came from the house. She followed it to the living room. To her left, she saw a door beside the fireplace. She went toward it. With each step, the moan grew louder. She opened the door and walked into a large library. And after a few quick steps, she saw it. It lay on a stand that stuck out from the bookshelves—a big, closed book with an iron cover.

Something erupted inside Amanda, spreading heat all over her body.

She gasped. She knew it was the book that cried for help, and she knew it was calling her and only her. She ran to it, but at that moment something pulled her back, and she fell into the darkness again.

Amanda opened her eyes and realized she was in Craig's room. A terrified Melinda stood beside the bed. Behind her, she saw Craig.

Amanda panicked. She wanted to run, to hide. But when she got out of the bed, Melinda stopped before her.

"What did you see?" she asked.

Amanda looked at Craig's exhausted face and then down at his shirt, cut in several places and covered with blood.

"Is that blood? Oh my God, Craig, I'm sorry. . . I. . ."

"Amanda, I'm fine," said Craig.

"Amanda, honey, what did you see?" Melinda asked again.

"Nothing," she said, breathing heavily.

"We need to know," said Melinda, insisting. "Otherwise, we won't be able to protect you."

"I was in that house again." Amanda glanced at Melinda. "Remember? I told you and Dad a few days ago. It was the same old, dusty house." She wiped the cold sweat from her temple with the back of her hand.

"Those dreams you see—they're very important," said Craig, his voice anxious. "Did you notice any changes? Did anything attract your attention?"

"No," said Amanda, staring at the blood on his shirt again. "Sorry, I need to go to the bathroom."

Melinda stepped aside, and Amanda ran out. On the stairs, she bumped into Ruben. Her eyes froze on his shirt, which was also torn and covered with blood.

"Don't worry," said Ruben. "I'm fine. And he's fine too."

But she could see the pain in his eyes.

She ran past him to the downstairs bathroom.

The fact that Craig saw her in his bed was embarrassing, and the sense of guilt for the blood on his and Ruben's shirts was unbearable. Her stomach clenched from those horrible feelings. She sat on the edge of the bathtub, her hands wrapped around her, trying to calm her nervous shivering.

She didn't remember falling asleep. Worry had kept her awake the whole night. When the light coming from the window became brighter, she decided it was time to get up. What happened next was a mystery to her.

∼

"IT'S A MAN. I could feel him," said Melinda.

"How did you know she was here?" Craig asked, picking up his shirt from the bed.

"I sensed the energy the moment I stepped into the house. The same energy I felt the other time. That son of a bitch is too strong. I barely pulled her back."

"I think she saw something. She just didn't want to tell."

"I think so, too. You scared her with your pretty look. You better change, and then, if you want, we can try again."

"No," said Craig. "Not now. She's in shock. She needs to rest."

"You, too. Get some sleep, get your strength back. Who knows what's going to happen next?" said Melinda.

With a sad smile, she looked at Craig absently staring at his bed, and walked away.

∼

AMANDA, Hanna, and Kimberly ditched school. After the restless, stressful night, they all needed some sleep.

"Are you hungry?" Melinda asked as soon as she and Amanda got home.

"No," said Amanda, avoiding her eyes.

"Amanda," said Melinda, shifting from foot to foot, "you probably have questions for me."

"I do," Amanda said, looking down. "But not now."

"All right." Melinda stepped closer and hugged her. "I just want you to know that I love you."

But Amanda didn't hug her back.

"Then you're probably the only one," she said coldly.

"That's not true." Melinda pulled back.

"Did you see what I did to them?" Amanda yelled suddenly. "That happened to them because of my selfishness."

"It's because you were hurt, and you didn't know how dangerous those men are."

"You don't have to call them men. I saw everything. I know what they are." Amanda gazed at Melinda, determined to fend off her questions.

But, to her surprise, Melinda didn't ask anything. She was nearly smiling.

"I knew you'd figure it out."

"So it's true. That blood," she said startled, "Craig and Ruben . . . were they—"

"No, no." Melinda hastened to reassure her. "It was just a scratch."

"Hmm," scoffed Amanda. "You need to stop lying to me. All of you."

"They were hurt," said Melinda. "But they are fine now."

Amanda nodded and bowed her head.

"I failed them and disappointed them, and, like that wasn't enough, this morning I embarrassed myself even more."

"Amanda . . ."

"No. Don't," said Amanda, and she went up the stairs to her room.

As she walked in, her phone rang. It was Kimberly.

"Amanda, what happened? When they came back, Melinda said 'it's happening,' and she and Craig ran upstairs. Then you ran out."

"When they returned, were you asleep, too?"

"No."

"Then why didn't you wake me?" moaned Amanda.

"I was going to. I just wanted to make coffee first. Why?"

"Why? Because I fell asleep in Craig's bed, that's why."

"Really?"

Amanda could feel that Kimberly was smiling, and she furiously pushed the red button.

She lay on the bed and stared at the wall where sunlight disappeared and reappeared again and again from behind cloud after cloud drifting across the sky.

Amanda thought about her dream. The image of the book was in front of her eyes, and its call for help echoed in her head. Craig said her dreams were very important, and she knew why. She was sure now that her mission was to help the book, to open it. Why was it important to Craig and the others? Why was it important to the vampires? What was the book's purpose? Her dream didn't have answers to those questions.

If only Amanda knew where the book was. If the book was real, and she had no doubts that it was, then the house could be real, too.

"Oh, God," she gasped, "it is."

She remembered the printed maps on Craig's table, the roofs surrounded by woods. Then she remembered Hanna, who showed too much interest in her dream and kept asking her for more details. Craig was looking for that house. She had to tell him what she saw this time. She had to tell him about the book.

Then another shock hit her. Her father had seen a book in his dream, and he even tried to open it. Why her father, and why her?

This was complicating everything even more. It was just too much. Amanda's head was exploding, and she was so tired. She didn't want to think about it right now. Hoping that maybe the next dream would give her more answers, she closed her eyes.

Chapter Twenty-Five

IT WAS NEARLY twelve a.m. Fray stood in front of the open window in a hotel room and gazed at the black BMW parked on the other side of the street. The young man sitting inside was looking in a newspaper through dark glasses.

Fray knew that he had been followed for the last few days, but now it was time to get rid of the tail. He stopped at Glendale, at this small hotel, before making his next step.

He walked to the table and opened the black case on it. On its one side two similar daggers were attached. He pulled one of them out of the sheath. The blade, which once had symbols on it, was now naked. The incantation was gone—it had disappeared the moment the Book was closed. He slowly stroked the blade with his fingers, feeling the cold, slick metal, and stuck the dagger back. Then he took out from the table drawer a small, fat, yellow envelope, closed it in the case, and left the room.

"I hope you enjoyed your stay, Mr. Wald," said a blond young woman playfully, standing behind the reception desk, and red spots began to spread on her round cheeks.

"It was nice," he said indifferently and looked around.

Nothing suspicious came to his attention. An old couple was sitting on the couch and examining a guide map, one male beside the entrance was frantically texting, and a bunch of people was heading to the exit.

He went outside, leisurely walked to the small parking place, and unlocked the door of his rental silver Honda with dark tinted glasses. After a moment of hesitation, he shut the door again and walked toward the black BMW. Fray put his hands on its open window and bent to the young man.

"You'll make a hole in that newspaper," he said in a casual tone. "What are you looking for? The weather report? I can assure you it will be hot."

"What is this, a warning?" said the young man, turning the page. "What are you going to do, Fray?" He pulled his glasses up onto his head and looked at him. "Kill us?"

"Very soon it'll become possible, and if somebody tries to double-cross me, I won't think twice," said Fray in a serious voice. "Tell Samson that he won't find it. He'll never put his hand on it again."

"Very soon? What makes you so sure?" The young man folded the newspaper and threw it on the passenger seat.

"I can see all the fuss over that girl, and the fact that Craig himself is guarding her is very conclusive. I never saw him around the candidates before. Maybe you should go help him and your Hanna because here you're just wasting your time." Fray walked away.

He got in his car and drove out of the parking lot.

He drove down Colorado Street. He could see in the rearview mirror that the familiar black BMW was only two cars away. When he reached Bethel Latino Temple, he switched on the right turn signal, and the two cars behind him slowed down. Fray turned into the big parking lot. The moment he pulled in, three similar silver Hondas with tinted glasses and the same license plates surrounded his car. Before the BMW caught up, all four of them drove out from the opposite exit, one after another—one car to the right, and the other three to the left, and to different directions at the crossroads.

Fray drove back to where he'd just come from, heading to the highway. He was going to Pasadena, and nobody was following him anymore.

∼

NED STOPPED his car at the parking lot and made a call.

"Samson, he did it," he said.

"All right. I'll take it from here," said Samson. "Go back to the hotel and wait for me there."

∼

FRAY STOPPED the car in the shade of the trees running along the boardwalk. When the car driving down the street had passed, he took his case and headed to the big, yellow house across the road.

When he knocked, the door opened immediately. Standing behind it, a small Chinese woman with no sense of life on her face bowed and stepped aside.

Fray walked in. Passing a Buddha statue on a stand, one of many traditional items in the house, he went to the small corridor. At the end of it, an open door to a large room waited for him.

A short, thin man, who was watering a bonsai tree, turned around.

"Good day, Mr. Wald," he said.

"I don't think it is. It didn't work."

"No," said the man, stepping forward. "Somebody interfered from the other side."

"So they know what's going on."

"Definitely," said the man. "It was a woman. She pulled the girl back. But the good news is, the girl knows. She knows it's there."

"You mean she saw it?" Fray asked.

"I am sure she did. She was overwhelmed. The thing you put in that house contains some enormous power. You and she are connected to it. I can feel it. When she got close to it, her emotions became too strong, so strong my hands were burning."

"So it is her," Fray muttered under his nose with a content smile.

"Do you want me to try again tomorrow?" asked the man.

"I'm not sure yet. She saw it. It means that she already knows what she has to do. Today I'll try plan B."

Fray opened the case, pulled the yellow envelope out of it, and put it on the table.

"Thank you for your service. I'll let you know if I need your help."

"I don't need the money," said the man, looking into Fray's eyes. "I want something else."

The man's tone was unusually cold. Fray frowned.

"Mr. Wald, I recognized you the moment you walked into my house."

"Have we met before, Wang? Because I would remember if we did."

"How can you? I was only nine years old when I first saw you. Twenty-five years ago, you came to my father and asked him to do the same thing that you asked from me. Twenty-five years is a long time, but you didn't change a bit. You look absolutely the same."

"What makes you so sure it was me?"

"We were poor then, and I could never forget the hand which gave my father that kind of money," said Wang. He looked at the mark above Fray's left wrist. "It's not a tattoo. I have never seen anything like that."

"You're right—it's not a tattoo, and, yes, I'm different," said Fray. "I've always been a legend, but people never knew when they met me that I was special."

"What legend?"

"It doesn't matter. So, if you don't want money, what do you want?"

Wang folded his hands behind his back.

"I want to be like you. I want to be immortal," he said firmly.

"Aha." Fray paused. "Just so you know—you will never be like me. I can make someone immortal, but as I said, I'm special. There is only one other person on earth who is like me and who has the same mark. And he is my enemy." He paused again. "You can be useful," he said, nodding. Then, after a lingering look, added, "I'll think about it."

∼

AT THE END of the same street, Samson sat in a car and kept an eye on the house.

As soon as Fray left, he drove forward and parked his car at the same spot.

When he knocked on the door, it took a while before it opened.

"Good afternoon," said Samson.

"Good afternoon, sir," said the small Chinese woman.

"I need to see Wang," said Samson.

"Just a minute," said the woman and closed the door.

A moment later the door opened again.

"How can I help you?" said Wang, standing in the doorway.

"My name is Samson." He noticed that Wang glanced at

his left arm, where half of the dagger mark stuck out from under the drawn-up shirt sleeve. "I am—"

"I know who you are," said Wang with tension.

"I need to talk to you."

Wang stepped back. Samson walked in and followed him into the big room.

"You recognized me by the mark," said Samson. "So he told you about me?"

"Only a moment ago, I asked him about the mark. He said there is only one other man who has it. And he also said that you are his enemy. I am a little bit shocked. Didn't expect to meet you so soon. To be honest, I didn't expect to meet you at all."

"That's true. We are enemies. Did he tell you why?"

"No. Actually, he didn't tell me anything. That he is immortal and he has a connection to that powerful thing, I found out myself."

"That thing?" Samson realized he was talking about the Book. His blood boiled. He didn't want to scare the man, so he tried to sound calm when he asked, "How do you know about that thing? Did he tell you?"

"No."

"Then how do you know?"

Wang looked at him, a little startled.

"Do you have any idea what you are helping him with?" asked Samson, barely controlling his irritation.

"Not exactly."

"That girl you keep teleporting for him is going to die if you succeed in holding her there long enough. After she does what he wants, he'll kill her."

"I didn't know that," said Wang indifferently.

"So I'm asking you—are you a killer?"

"What do you want from me?" Wang snuffled.

"Do you know where the thing is?"

"I can't tell you that."

"Did he tell you about *this* mark?" Samson showed him his right arm.

"No," said Wang, staring at it.

"Of course not. This mark means that *thing* is mine. He stole it from me, and I need it back."

But Wang didn't say anything.

"If you're afraid he'll kill you, I give you my word he'll never even know I was here."

"It's not that."

"Then what? He paid you to keep your mouth shut? I can pay you three times more if you tell me everything you know."

"It's not about money!" shouted Wang.

"Then what? Loyalty?" asked Samson. But then it hit him, "Oh, I see now. He promised you something, didn't he?"

"He said he'd think about it."

"You stupid man." Samson shook his head. "You have no idea what you're getting into. If you think that after he turns you, he'll let you go, you're wrong. I suppose you believe supernatural creatures exist. He's raising an army of vampires. You'll end up working for all of them forever, watching them kill people every day. And if you refuse to obey him, he'll kill you. He has that power."

Wang swallowed.

"I'm trying to stop him," continued Samson. "So if you know anything that can help me, say it before it's too late. That girl is very important to me. If you're not a murderer yourself, help me save her."

"If you're like him, that means you too have the power to make me immortal."

"Do you know why we have been given power and immortality? It has a purpose. Our mission is to fight and destroy supernatural evil."

Wang's face suddenly changed.

"The legend," he said, amazed. "You are the Hunters."

"We are. And it's I who allowed him to become one. He betrayed us and our mission. He's creating monsters and you're helping him. So, yes, I can turn you, but I won't."

"Then why should I help you?"

"Because if you don't tell me what you know, I'll have to kill you. That will at least stop one of his plans."

Wang breathed out with such rage that his chest heaved. His hands flew up, making a circle in the air. He crossed them, then outstretched them and punched the air.

There was an explosion. The stream of energy he sent at Samson ricocheted everywhere. The furniture jumped. The windows shattered, and pieces of broken glass flew in all directions. The pot with the bonsai tree crashed, and the tree fell on the floor, the same as the vase of flowers on the coffee table. The wooden frames of pictures rattled against the walls, and the room was full of noises of small objects falling down from here and there.

But nothing happened to Samson. Wang, who was thrown back, looked at him in astonishment.

"I don't think you fully understand my power," said Samson. "I am the First Hunter," he said, moving forward, "No magic can harm me."

Wang folded his hands before his chest like he was going to pray and closed his eyes. Realizing what he was going to do, Samson rushed to him. He grabbed Wang's hands and pulled them away from each other. To break his concentration, he lifted him and hit him in the nose with his head.

"Even if you teleport—," Samson threw Wang on the couch, "—I'll find you much faster than you think. I have witches, too, you know. I just need a personal item." He ripped a medallion with Chinese symbols from Wang's neck.

"No," cried Wang, holding out his hand.

"What? This thing is important to you? The thing that he

stole is important to me, and when my wife tried to stop him, he killed her. Tell me where it is," he put his foot on the couch and bent down to Wang, "and I'll give this back." He held the medallion by the chain before Wang's bleeding nose.

"It's in that house," said Wang, sniffing. "He put it there yesterday."

"That's impossible. We've been following him all this time. He didn't have it with him."

"Then somebody else did."

Samson pondered for a moment. He couldn't believe that Fray entrusted the Book to the vampires.

"What is his plan?" he asked.

"I don't know. But whatever it is, he's doing it today. I'm not a part of it, so you can leave me alone."

Samson took his foot down from the couch.

"If you touch that girl again, you are a dead man."

"I told you . . ." Wang tried to stand up. But Samson pushed him back.

"One more question. Where is the house?"

"I don't know."

"Don't lie to me." Samson glared at him.

"I only know it's in the woods, twenty miles away from Green Hill. I have a picture of one of the bedrooms."

"Twenty miles . . ."

"East. That's all I know."

Samson threw the medallion to him and hurried away.

Chapter Twenty-Six

THE ROOM WAS dark when Amanda woke up. She took her cellphone from the nightstand. It was 3.30 p.m. She rolled over and looked out the window. Gray clouds covered the piece of the sky behind its glass.

The green light was blinking on the side of her phone. She unlocked it. One call from her father and four messages from Alec.

Amanda sat up and called her dad.

"Hi, Dad."

"Hi, honey. How are you?"

"I'm fine."

"And school?"

"All the same. One and a half days didn't change much. How are you? Did they like your bridge?"

"The presentation went well. They said the whole project looks very interesting, but they didn't make their decision yet. It could take a couple more days."

She wanted to ask him about the dream, to see if he noticed something else in that house and if he had any idea what was going on, but it had happened so long ago. He'd probably told her all he remembered. Her questions would only distract him.

"But don't worry, honey, I'll be there for graduation," he added.

Graduation. It was only a few days away. And only a few days ago, it seemed so important, but now Amanda had almost forgotten about it.

"I'll keep my fingers crossed for you," she said.

"Thank you."

"Bye, Dad."

"Bye, honey."

As she hung up, she opened Alec's messages. They were full of questions. Amanda started to answer, but then stopped and put the phone aside.

The few hours of sleep hadn't made her misery go away. She felt crappy, and sitting alone in a dark room, attacked by heavy thoughts, wouldn't make it better. Alec was the only one who she didn't have to feel guilty with. He could at least temporarily distract her, and she could use some comfort right now.

She picked up the phone again.

"Amanda." She heard the alarm in Alec's voice.

"Hi. I just saw your messages. I was asleep."

"The three of you didn't come to school today. I was so worried."

"Everything's fine. We were up all night. We were too tired."

"I want to see you. Maybe we could meet, go somewhere?"

"Sorry. I'm still a little dizzy. But if you want, you can come here. We could look at your website together."

"Sure. I just need to finish something. I'll be there as soon as I'm done."

She was just getting out of the shower when she heard a knock.

"Who is it?" she asked, wrapping her towel tighter around her.

The door opened, and Melinda walked in.

"Not to disappoint you, but it's still me. As you know, there's nobody else in the house."

"I thought it was Alec."

"Alec's coming?"

By Melinda's tone, Amanda could tell that she didn't like the idea.

"Yes," she said, looking for fresh clothes in the chest of drawers.

"You haven't eaten anything since yesterday."

"I'll be downstairs in a minute."

Amanda heard Melinda's voice as she headed to the kitchen. She stopped at the end of the stairs and listened.

"My protection works," Melinda was saying. "If any dead man crosses within twenty yards of the house, I'll know."

She was on the phone. Amanda supposed that she was talking to Craig.

"She's fine," said Melinda. "She did. She slept for a few hours." There was a pause, then she said, "Don't worry, she'll get over it. Besides, Alec is coming. I'm sure he'll cheer her up." Melinda chuckled.

∽

"HI," said Alec when he walked into Amanda's bedroom an hour later. "Amanda, what's going on? Yesterday you just ran away."

"I'm sorry for yesterday," she sighed.

She turned away, but Alec took her by the arm and turned her around.

"Come here." He locked his arms around her. "It's okay.

We don't have to talk about it right now. But if you need help, I'm always here for you."

"I know," she said quietly.

Avoiding the gaze of his glittering gray eyes, Amanda looked at his chest. She put her hands on his arms, and through the soft fabric, she felt his hard muscles. Her hands moved up and laid on his shoulders. He gently pulled her closer. Her cheek was almost touching his face, and she could smell the freshness of his white shirt. He kissed her neck. One hand moved up her back and slipped into her long hair. Then he looked at her lips. Amanda closed her eyes, giving him permission. His soft fingers stroked her face up from the chin, and then he kissed her.

Amanda was grateful Alec didn't ask questions, for his understanding.

He lead her to the bed, and she lay down. Then she felt a weak pressure of Alec's body against hers and the tender touch of his warm lips. It felt nice and relaxing.

His heart hammered.

"Amanda," he whispered into her ear, "I love you."

"I know." She pulled up. "Alec, I'm sorry. I know this isn't what you expected to hear, but I need more time."

He nodded.

"I'll wait as long as you need," he said and sat beside her.

After a moment of silence, Amanda picked up the laptop lying on the floor next to the bed.

"Show me what you got," she said, smiling.

He opened his website and, clicking on the links, guided her through it.

"Alec, it looks awesome. Did you do it yourself?"

"All of it," he said proudly, then chuckled. "That's why it took so long."

"The paintings—are they here too?"

"No. Only the photographs." He clicked on the gallery and

put it on the slide show. "It's a lot, so just tell me when you get bored."

There were nice captures of football games, beautiful views of the ocean and mountains, pictures of rainy streets of New York, and sunny, romantic Italy.

"Have you been in Egypt, too?" Amanda asked, looking at the ruins of a pyramid.

"I traveled a lot," said Alec.

"With your parents?"

"No. With my uncle. Since I was twelve. I spent almost all my holidays with him, and every time he took me to new places."

Next were images of abandoned Buddhist temples. And then Amanda saw something that looked very familiar.

"Wait," she said when the picture changed. "Go back to the previous one."

"This one?"

"Yes," said Amanda. Her eyes froze.

"This is just some old house. I took it not too far from here when we went hiking with my dad. It was just standing in the middle of the woods."

"Not far? Where?" asked Amanda, staring at the porch of the house and at the tall grass around the angel fountain.

"Fifteen, maybe twenty miles away."

"Do you remember exactly where it is? Could you find the place?" she asked.

"Of course, I remember. It was the most historical moment of my relationship with my father."

Amanda slid down from the bed and began pacing.

"Amanda, what is it?"

"Give me a minute, please."

Her heart trembled. She was absolutely sure the house in the picture was the one from her dreams. The right thing to do was to call Craig, but what happened yesterday was horrible, and she wouldn't put them in such danger again. She needed to do what all of them wanted her to do and put everybody out of their misery.

"Alec, I need to go to that place. Can you take me there?"

"Sure. When?"

Tomorrow she would have to go to school, and after school Hanna, or one of them, would follow her everywhere. But nobody would expect her to go somewhere alone at this hour. Melinda said that there was protection around the house, so there were no vampires nearby.

"Now."

"Now? Amanda, it's in the woods. It's getting dark. Are you sure?"

"How far into the woods?"

"Five hundred yards or so."

"We can still make it. Alec, please. It's very important." She looked at him with pleading eyes.

"Are you going to tell me why?"

"I can't. Maybe after, one day."

"All right. Let's go," said Alec, and he stood up.

"Wait. Melinda won't let me leave. Let's go downstairs," she said, putting on a sweater. "I'll see what I can do."

But when Amanda and Alec walked into the kitchen, Melinda wasn't there. Amanda heard noises coming from the laundry room.

Her heart sank. For a second, she felt unsure about her plan. What if something happened to her? They had all tried so hard to protect her, to keep her safe. But then, the images of Hanna twisted in pain, and Craig's and Ruben's torn, bloody shirts flashed in front of her eyes again. What if something happened to them? What if they got killed? The vampires didn't need them. She wouldn't let it happen.

"Let's go," she whispered to Alec, carefully opening the front door.

∽

MELINDA HEARD a slam of a car door and then the start of an engine. *Alec must be leaving*, she thought. She turned on the washing machine and went up the stairs.

∽

CRAIG WENT TO THE KITCHEN, where Riley and Hanna, were having coffee.

"What did Melinda say?" Hanna asked. "Is Amanda all right?"

"She's fine," Craig said grimly. "She's waiting for Alec. I hope they don't plan new adventures for us."

"God! I hate that guy!" said Hanna. She put her cup down with a thud. Hot coffee jumped out and plopped on the table.

Craig's phone rang. It was Samson.

"Craig, I found out a couple of things. That house you're looking for is about twenty miles east. Did you look in that area?"

"Really? That's exactly where I was going to check."

"You'd better do it right now because the Book is already there."

"I knew it!" said Craig. "I knew she saw something today."

"Saw what?" asked Riley impatiently.

"Wait a minute, Melinda's calling." Craig put Samson on hold. "Melinda, what is it?"

His blood ran cold.

"Dammit, Melinda, how on earth . . . we're coming." He switched to Samson. "She's gone. She just ran away." He hung up and looked at Hanna and Riley. "Let's go, Melinda wants us to look at something."

∽

THE THREE OF them stared at the screen of Amanda's laptop, which still showed the picture of the old house in the middle of the woods.

"Craig, this is . . ." Hanna gasped.

"Eleanor's house," muttered Craig. "This is her husband Richard's house, where Samson turned her." His voice was low like he was talking to himself.

"Why would he do that?" Riley asked.

"To hurt me?" Craig shrugged. "I don't know."

"How does she know where to go?" Hanna asked.

"She doesn't." Craig clicked on the screen. "This is Alec's website. If he took this picture, then he knows where it is. We don't have time, we all— He looked around. "Where's Ruben?"

"On the beach. With Kimberly." Hanna bit her lip.

"Wonderful. Call him," said Craig sharply. "Riley, let Samson know."

"I'll come with you," Melinda said.

"No," said Riley, "you should stay here in case she comes back."

"She's not coming back," said Craig, and he stormed out.

∼

THEY SAT SNUGLY ON top of a hill watching the waves beat against the shore.

"You think it will rain?" asked Kimberly.

"No." Ruben glanced at the gray clouds. "They're drifting away." He kissed her ginger hair. "Maybe we should go. You didn't sleep enough."

"No," said Kimberly, cuddling tighter, "I have the whole night for that." She closed her eyes. "Ruben, I don't want you to leave."

His heart sank. He kissed her again.

"Have you heard about Eternity Road?" he asked.

"You mean the legend about the invisible wall? Everybody in Green Hill knows that story. They say the road is not too far from here."

"What else do they say?" Ruben asked, fixing his eyes on the horizon.

"Eternity Road leads to the invisible wall. Anyone who manages to cross it becomes immortal. A hunter who fights supernatural evil. But nobody's ever found the wall or even the road. It's just some old story."

"Imagine that the wall exists," Ruben whispered into her ear. "Imagine that you're standing right in front of it. Would you try to cross it?"

Kimberly looked at him.

"Would you?" she asked.

Ruben's cellphone vibrated in his pocket. He pulled it out.

"Hanna, what's wrong?" He slowly rose, drawing Kimberly along. "Eleanor's? I'm on my way."

"What is it?" asked Kimberly.

"It's Amanda. She ran away. I have to take you home." Ruben looked at her, thinking out loud. "No, I don't have time. It's closer for me from here. Kimberly—"

"I'm not going anywhere. I'm coming with you."

"Kimberly, you can't. It's too . . ."

"Don't tell me it's dangerous. I can't just sit alone and go crazy worrying. I'm coming with you," she said and headed to the car.

Chapter Twenty-Seven

YEAR 1852 JULY

TWO DAYS HAD PASSED since Gabriella's death and, dressed in her new blue gown, they buried her under a big oak beside her garden.

During those two days, everybody plotted the best way to punish Fray for what he'd done, for taking away from them someone so dear, someone who had been the heart and the soul of their family.

They also needed a plan to get the Book back. They all sat in the library waiting for Samson to tell them his final decision.

Meanwhile, Samson stood in his study in front of the window and absently stared into the yard.

Gabriella was gone. Fray had killed her. Gabriella was gone, and there was nothing Samson could do to bring her back. He had buried her, and it wasn't just a horrible dream. Everything around him lost its color, its meaning.

He couldn't imagine his morning without her, that when he woke up, she wouldn't be beside him, that they would never again watch the sun rise above the ocean together. The thought that he would never hear her voice and her laughter again choked him, and he gulped for air.

The castle would never be the same without his Gabriella. Nothing would be the same. For the first time in his entire life, he felt so empty and so tired that he wanted to fall asleep and never wake up.

But he wouldn't die, even if he could, because Fray was out there, and he, Samson, would find a way to rip his heart out as he had promised. It would take time—maybe years, maybe centuries. But he would not rest until he did it.

First, he had to find the Book. Gabriella gave her life trying to protect it. She knew that Fray's ambitions were against the mission, and she died trying to stop him. He had to do whatever it took to destroy Fray's plan. He had his decision ready but only one person could know the real meaning of it.

He took the Map and went downstairs.

As Samson walked into the library, he laid the Map on the table and opened it. Everybody stepped closer.

"As you know," started Samson, "we already used half of Fray's blood trying to track him down. And I'm sure he's counting on that because he knows how hurt and distraught we are.

"Realizing that he left his blood behind, he's been moving from place to place. His stops took just long enough to make the line on the Map disappear, knowing we'd have to use the blood again and again until we used the whole supply. That's why yesterday morning I decided to take a break. Besides, I'm sure those vampires we killed weren't the only trap he prepared to distract us, and his moves were probably leading us to new ones.

"We marked all the places where he stopped. The first time we checked, he was heading east, and then he turned north." Samson said, moving his finger from mark to mark. "The next time we looked, he was going east again. A few hours later, he made his longest stop here. Then he moved again, taking unexpected turns to confuse us. I checked on him an hour ago. He was back at the same place—the place where he made his first long stop." His finger made a circle on the spot. "And he's still here. This place is about five hours from us."

"You mean that's where the church is?" asked Ruben. "The place the vampire was talking about?"

"Yes. Otherwise, why would he go to the same place twenty-four hours later? Something's going on there. And we have to find out what it is."

"What if he cleans up the place before we get there?" Edmond asked.

"We'll follow him. We still have some blood. He's using the Book, I can feel it. Our mission is to see how much damage he has already done, find the Book, and bring it back."

"What kind of damage?" asked Craig.

"Using it how?" asked Riley.

Samson turned around and walked a few steps away. No one had asked him about the Book during the past two days. They were all in deep mourning, and all they thought about was finding Fray.

"Samson," said Hanna. "What is he going to do with it?"

He looked at them. "He can turn people."

"What?" Riley burst out.

"That bastard," Craig shouted furiously.

"Samson." Ruben stared at him. "After six hundred years, suddenly he can . . . "

"He always could," said Samson. "He just didn't know it."

"How did he find out?" Craig asked.

"When he was here last, he brought someone and asked me to turn the man for him. Right from the beginning, I realized the man was a killer, but I stopped the transition only on the fourth day, to show Fray I didn't have a choice. But he got mad anyway. Gabriella—" Samson took a deep breath. "She went to talk to him, to calm him down. He was shouting at her, telling her that he never cared about the family, that he hates us all. He said that, as a First, he has rights, too, that he wanted to build his own kingdom. He said he knew I was keeping secrets from him, that there are things in the Book about Firsts that I wasn't telling him.

"He was right. I have secrets. Not just from him—from all of you. There are some things that I can't tell you. What is written on the golden pages is meant only for me, for the Keeper of the Book. I told you as much as I could, and I should have kept it that way. But he was so desperate and so angry that it alarmed me. I was afraid one day he would just try to turn someone himself, or still the Book just to punish me. And I told Gabriella the truth."

"She knew," Hanna sighed.

"Is that the conversation he overheard? The conversation Henry was talking about?" Riley asked.

"Yes. I told her the Book doesn't say only the Keeper can turn people. It says that only the First has enough power to do it and, if there are other First Ones, then it's the Keeper's choice to tell them about it or not. Gabriella . . ." The pain in Samson's chest made him stop for a moment. Everything blurred in front of his eyes. He was having a meeting with his family, and Gabriella wasn't there. Saying her name and speaking about her in past tense made her death so real that he wanted to scream. He swallowed, and when he blinked and his vision became clearer, he saw that everybody was looking down.

"She said she'd keep an eye on him. When I warned her about the dagger and asked her to be careful," his voice became even lower, "she said that Fray would never do such a thing."

Hanna's eyes filled with tears.

"Now listen to me carefully." Samson's tone changed. It was sharp, and his eyes moved from one to another. "I know that you all are in a fury and you want revenge. Nobody wants to pay him back as much as I do. But you have to remember that he has both daggers, and I am not losing anybody else. Nobody moves, nobody gets near him without my order. Riley." Samson turned to him. "Do you hear me?"

They stared at each other.

"Yes," Riley said finally.

"We're leaving. Hanna and Eleanor, go change, pack your weapons and the things you need, it might be a long trip. The rest of you, prepare the horses."

Samson took the Map and went to his study. He walked in, put the Map down, and listened, making sure that all the men had gone.

"Eleanor," he said as soon as Craig stepped out the front door, "I need to talk to you."

∼

THE RIDE TOOK LONGER than expected. Finding the church wasn't that easy. They had to stop in a couple of villages to ask the inhabitants for help. People cursed the place and warned them to stay away from it, but in the end, they all pointed in the same direction.

Like dark shadows, they flashed across the field silver from moonlight, and then up the small hill. As they reached its top, they stopped behind the young trees.

The other side of the hill was much steeper. It sheltered a small village. Most of its houses were burned down.

"I think we're at the right place," said Samson.

"Yes." Riley sighed heavily.

At the edge of the woods surrounding the village, they saw the church. Before it was a small cemetery. A couple of dozen men stood between the gravestones. On one side of the church was a large barn, on the other side stood horses and covered wagons.

Samson listened.

"Is he here?" Craig asked.

"Yes. He's in the church," said Samson.

"How many do you think there are?" Ruben asked.

"Many," said Samson. "I want to see what's in that barn. Let's go."

They rode along the crest of the hill and then dismounted. Leaving their horses behind, they went down into the thick woods.

When they got closer, Samson stopped them. The big windows of the old church were boarded up. From the small one above the entrance came a faint light.

"Are the people inside, too?" Hanna asked.

"What people?"

"You said he's using the Book."

Samson could feel Eleanor's stare.

"He is," said Samson.

"Then what are we waiting for?" shouted Riley.

"Be quiet." Samson gazed at him.

"Is there somebody in the barn?" asked Craig.

"I don't hear anything. But there's something in there. Let's get closer."

But as they took their first steps, Samson stopped them again. Two men came out from the church. They carried someone toward the barn, holding the limp, unconscious body by hands and legs.

"Vampires," said Craig.

They waited for a moment.

"Now," said Samson as soon as the vampires walked inside.

Riley and Craig snuck into the barn before the others. They grabbed the vampires and, clamping their mouths, staked them.

All of them looked around and gasped. Except for Samson. He was looking at Eleanor, who stared back at him, terrified.

Nearly fifty bodies lay side by side on several lines of long wooden benches.

"That son of a bitch," said Riley.

"Samson," said Ruben, gazing at the pale faces of transforming young men and women, "these are not humans."

Astonished, Hanna looked from one to another. "What is this? How is it even possible?"

"It's much worse than I expected," said Samson.

Edmond stepped to one of the vampires, swung his sword, and jabbed the vampire's throat. The sword went through halfway and stuck. As he pulled the sword out, the wound began healing.

"It's not going to work," said Samson. "Only the dagger can break the enchantment, you know that. Their bones are like a stone right now."

"Excellent," roared Riley.

"What do we do now?" Ruben asked.

"We'll get rid of the ones in the cemetery. When we go inside, all of you will try to clear the way to the Book. Don't underestimate their power. Those vampires are about to get something they couldn't dream of, and they will fight for it until the end. I'll deal with Fray. Eleanor, you will be the one who has to take the Book."

"Why Eleanor?" Craig asked. "I can do it."

"No," said Samson. "Fray will be near the Book. He hates you and Riley most of all. He won't miss the slightest chance to kill you, so stay away from it."

"Samson," called Eleanor when everybody went to the door. "May I have a second with Craig?"

Samson nodded.

"We'll wait outside," he said, then turned to Riley. "Make sure the church doesn't have a backdoor."

Samson walked out last and closed the barn door behind him.

"WHAT IS IT, MY LOVE?" Craig asked, hugging Eleanor. "You're not scared, are you?"

"I am," Eleanor whispered.

"I'll be beside you. You are my life. I'll never let anything happen to you, you know that."

"I am scared for you." She looked deep into Craig's eyes.

There was so much she wanted to tell him. But there was no time for that.

"Don't be," said Craig. "Nothing is going to happen to me, I promise."

"I love you so much," said Eleanor. She stroked his hand and kissed it. "I want you to remember that."

She could see a sudden fear in Craig's eyes.

"Eleanor, is there—"

"Yes, there is something." She smiled to make his fear go away. "This might be a bad time for this," her fingers brushed his hair, "But I want you to kiss me. It will give me strength."

"THERE'S a small door on the other side. It's boarded up, too," said Riley.

"Good," said Samson, keeping his eyes at the cemetery. "We'll split up. Riley, Craig, and Edmond— go to the left. Hanna, Eleanor— you stay here and prepare your arrows. Ruben comes with me. Remember— quick and quiet."

As Hanna and Eleanor saw shadows from both sides streaking off toward the cemetery, they took their first shot. Two vampires hit the ground. But then the fight began in earnest, and it was impossible to aim. They put down their arrows and took out the stakes. As they moved forward, they saw a few vampires running to the church door.

The next second, Hanna and Eleanor stood before them.

"Where do you think you're going?" said Hanna and knocked down one of them.

The second vampire swung his fist. She dodged under his hand then rose sharply. Before he could make another move, she stuck the stake into his chest. Hanna grabbed the first one, who was trying to escape, but instead of staking him she began furiously beating him up.

"It's all . . . because . . . of you. . . . It's all . . . because . . . of you. . . ." She sent blow after blow into the vampire's face.

Eleanor killed two others and looked at her bitterly.

"Hanna," she called, stepping closer, "Hanna."

"It's all . . . because . . . of you. . . ." Hanna kept hammering the vampire's face.

Eleanor dragged her back. She staked the unconscious vampire and turned to Hanna, who glared madly at the shrinking body.

"Hanna." Eleanor hugged her. "You have to be strong. I need you strong."

"I am strong. I am stronger than ever," said Hanna with a shaking voice.

Hanna's shoulders shuddered. Eleanor hugged her tighter.

"Listen to me. I know you're in pain. But the thing is, this isn't over yet. I want you to be strong so you can handle what's coming next."

"What do you mean?" Hanna pulled back.

"Nothing." Eleanor shook her head. "It's just . . . things are crazy right now. We have so much to deal with."

Edmond showed up beside them. "Hanna, are you all right?" he asked, taking Hanna's blood-covered hand.

Eleanor was glad for his appearance.

"It's not mine," said Hanna. "Don't worry, I'm fine."

Samson kicked the church door, and it crashed to the floor with a bang. They stepped in.

The room seemed much bigger than it looked from the outside. It was packed with vampires waiting for their turn. On the long stone altar lay a man, and on the other side, Samson saw his case with the Book in it. It was placed on the stand for prayer books. Fray, who was standing between the stand and the altar, slowly turned his head.

"Samson." He rounded the altar. "What took you so long? No, wait, I know. The funeral," he said. "Sorry I missed that."

Riley clenched his fists.

"I'm not up for a small talk," said Samson in a stone voice. "I'm here to take what is mine."

"Are you ready to lose more members of your precious family?"

"You are not my family."

Fray laughed. "You know that you can't kill me."

"Everything in its time," said Samson, stepping forward.

He grabbed the vampire closest to him and hit him in the chest. His fist went through and came out from the vampire's back. Samson pulled his bloody hand out and threw the body to the growling crowd.

"Sorry," he said, "I didn't know that your army is so fragile."

"When my army wakes up—" started Fray furiously.

"That will never happen," said Samson, and he jumped.

He landed in front of Fray. Fray swung his fist, but Samson hit him first. He noticed the dagger wasn't on Fray's belt.

Riley jumped into the middle of the crowd and began crushing them. Craig, Eleanor, and Ruben wedged into the swarm of raging vampires.

Samson tried to jostle Fray away from the Book, but it didn't work. Fray kicked him a few feet away. Samson jumped up and punched him in the jaw, then kicked him in the stomach. Fray flipped and fell face-down across the man lying on the altar.

Samson grabbed Fray by his clothes and pulled him up. Fray clung to the body lying beneath him and dragged it along. He jerked his head backward, hitting Samson in the face, knocking him off balance, then turned around and hurled the body at him.

Riley was getting closer to the Book. He was now fighting on the stairs before the altar, attacked from all sides. Standing back to back, Craig and Eleanor put down half of the vampires surrounding them. Edmond, who was fighting between the wall and the line of pews, was swinging his sword madly right and left, but the vampires were too many, and they were punching him and pulling him from side to side. Ruben was making his way to Edmond to help him. Hanna was furiously fighting under the opposite wall and at the same time, she was trying to lure the vampires away from the altar.

Samson held Fray with one hand and punched him over and over. Then he spun around and kicked him away from the Book. Roaring, Fray jumped up and flipped. Still in the air, he pulled the dagger out of his long sleeve. He landed behind Samson, and when Samson turned around, Fray thrust the dagger deep into his heart. Samson shuddered. His legs weakened, and he fell to one knee.

"It hurts, doesn't it?" rasped Fray. "Your Gabriella stabbed me. So she got what she deserved."

Samson saw Riley fighting right behind Fray, and he pulled himself up. Fray turned to Riley, raising the dagger. Samson grabbed him and pulled back. The dagger slid down Riley's back, cutting his clothes. Riley looked over his shoulder. He saw Samson falling and hauling Fray with him. But Samson's grip wasn't tight enough, and Fray was on his feet again. Riley saw the blood on Samson's chest. He rushed toward Fray and punched him so hard that he flew to the wall and collapsed.

Eleanor jumped behind Riley and closed the case. Craig

and Ruben covered her flank, protecting her from the vampires coming up the stairs.

"Ralph, take her. NOW!" Fray suddenly yelled, staring as Eleanor ran down the stairs with the Book.

Everybody looked at Eleanor, who held the case with both hands. Craig, Ruben, and Edmond stood around her. But all the remaining vampires ran toward Hanna. They grabbed her and pushed her against the wall. One of them pulled the second dagger from behind his back and put it against Hanna's heart.

"Hanna!" screamed Edmond, and he jumped over the line of the pews.

"Edmond, stop!" yelled Samson.

Everyone froze.

"One more move," hissed Fray, "and she dies."

Eleanor stopped and turned around.

Fray pointed at Edmond. "Bring that one to me."

Two vampires took Edmond under his arms and led him to Fray. Edmond didn't resist. Fray flipped the dagger in his hand and put it against his heart.

"You think I'm stupid?" Fray glared at Samson. "I knew you'd find me sooner or later. Look at your Hanna."

A few vampires held Hanna, stretching her arms and pushing her shoulders against the wall. Others stood before her. Ralph, the vampire who was holding the dagger, smirked. Hanna glared at his bloodshot eyes and spat in his face. Ralph growled and jerked her head by her hair.

"Don't touch her!" roared Edmond.

"Quiet, Romeo," said Fray and then turned to Samson. "She was always a firecracker, your Hanna. You love her like a daughter. So if you don't want to bury her too, you'll do as I say."

Samson knew they didn't have a choice. He looked at

Hanna, then at Edmond, and then his eyes stopped at Eleanor. His heart sank.

"Step back to the door," said Fray sharply. "All of you, except Eleanor. Go." He gazed at Samson.

Samson looked at Riley standing at the end of the stairs and nodded to the door. Clenching his teeth, Riley obeyed. Samson went after him.

"I said all of you," Fray barked, staring at Ruben and Craig.

Ruben stepped back, but Craig didn't move.

"Are you scared?" Fray sneered at him. "Don't be. I have a better target." He glanced at Hanna, then at Craig again. "Your Eleanor just has to do what I say."

Eleanor looked at Craig. "Go. Do as he says," she whispered.

Craig stepped back.

"Eleanor, come forward," Fray said.

Eleanor turned to Samson. They looked at each other for a moment.

"Eleanor, I am so sorry," said Samson quietly.

Eleanor nodded once. Then her sad eyes looked tenderly at Craig. "I'm sorry, my love," she mouthed, then smiled weakly.

"Eleanor." Craig started toward her.

Samson grabbed his arm and pulled him back.

"You *are* stupid, Fray," said Samson, trying to distract Fray from Eleanor's actions. "You're raising monsters, and you thought I would let you get away with it?"

Eleanor moved her hand, and the case opened. The Book fell onto the floor and Eleanor knelt before it.

Riley gasped, predicting the next move. He gazed at Samson, his mouth open. Fray had the same expression on his face.

Eleanor pulled up one side of the heavy cover of the Book

and with great effort, using all her power, pushed it down against the yellow pages, rustling in protest.

"NOOOO!" Fray screamed wildly.

"ELEANOR!" cried Craig.

The Hunters shuddered. Rays of shimmering silver-blue light came out of their chests and flew into the Book. They couldn't move. Through the wall streamed about fifty other blue rays, coming from the barn.

Fray stared at the dagger. One by one, its symbols disappeared.

"Eleanor, NO! Please," Hanna cried.

When the Book was almost closed, sharp iron teeth, like small arrows, popped out from the iron clasps. They pierced Eleanor's hands and her blood flowed, soaking the pages. Two rays of glittering light came out of Eleanor's chest----one blue and one red. As they slipped into the Book, it clicked shut.

The Hunters could move once again. Tears rolled down Samson's face. Screaming Eleanor's name, Craig ran to her, and she fell dead into his arms.

Chapter Twenty-Eight

TODAY

AS AMANDA and Alec took off, Alec pulled out his cellphone.

"I have to tell my mom I won't be home for dinner."

He touched the screen a few times and then put the phone away.

"You didn't write anything," said Amanda.

"No." Alec smiled. "I sent the old message."

"Does it say I'm sorry that her son will starve because of me?"

Alec beamed.

"We can buy some donuts at the gas station if it'll make you feel better."

While Alec was paying for the donuts, Amanda looked around the gas station. Her eyes stopped on the big flashlights.

"I have two of them in the trunk," said Alec, approaching her. "I have a compass, too," he added jokingly. "Donut?" He handed her the open paper bag.

"Thanks."

She followed him back into the car.

She watched the trees flashing away behind the car window and thought about Craig. Surely, Melinda had already told him that she was gone, and he was going crazy not knowing where she was. He probably hated her right now.

"Are you still with me?" Alec asked "Amanda, you look worried, and a little scared. Just tell me what it is. Maybe I'll be able to help."

"I'm fine, and you're already helping."

Amanda's phone vibrated.

"Is it Melinda?" Alec asked.

"No, it's Hanna." She turned the phone off.

"That house . . . have you ever been there before?" Alec asked after a moment of silence.

"No."

"But you recognized it. It means that you've seen it. Where? Another picture?"

"Not exactly." Amanda paused. "You'll probably think I'm crazy, but the thing is—" She glanced at him. "I've seen it in my dreams."

"You're not crazy. Dreams can be very important."

"I just want to make sure it's the same house."

"And if it is?"

"Then I need to do something. Don't worry, it won't take long."

"Do what?"

"You'll see when we get in."

Alec looked at her, a little puzzled.

"You want us to break in?"

"Yep," said Amanda, nodding. "I hope you have some tools in that trunk of yours?"

"Sure." Alec grinned.

∽

CRAIG'S HANDS clutched the steering wheel. The image of Amanda falling dead was freezing his blood. Was that how it was going to end? He couldn't let it happen. Not again.

"She turned off her phone," said Hanna from the back seat.

"How much do they have—seven, eight-minute head start?" Riley asked.

"Something like that," said Melinda.

"We'll catch them. Besides, in her dreams, or whatever it was, the house was empty. You said there was no vampire around Amanda's house. So it's possible they have no idea what's going on."

"Fray wouldn't just leave the Book without somebody guarding it," said Craig. "Maybe the house is empty, and maybe Fray is not there right now, but the woods are probably full of vampires, and any of them can have the dagger. I'm sure he's prepared surprises for us."

"That's what scares me," said Hanna. "We're like blind kittens."

"He's had a hundred and sixty years to plan this day, and we are not mind-readers," said Riley, "All we know is that the Book is not opened yet. We have to get there before the blue light hits our chests."

∼

AS AMANDA and Alec came out of the woods to the front of the house, she stopped.

"I can't believe this," she muttered, staring at the fountain.

She walked through the tall grass and up the porch stairs. Screwdriver in his hand, Alec stepped to the door.

"Wait," said Amanda.

She suddenly remembered that in her dream she never

locked the door. She approached it and pushed the handle. The door opened.

"If I'd known that it was open when I came here…" said Alec.

"It wasn't," whispered Amanda. Her own words made her shiver. "This is impossible," she said as they walked in.

Everything felt exactly the same—the silence, the smell of the dust, the chill and moist air.

The sun was already behind the hill, and the faint light of dusk, falling in through the doorway and the gap between the heavy curtains, weakly illuminated small portions of the room.

Amanda's eyes froze as she looked at the floor. She switched on the flashlight and examined the stairs. And then she heard it, that weak, plaintive moan calling for her. She closed her eyes, listening.

"Amanda, are you alright?" Alec asked.

Her eyes flew open.

"Alec, is this real?" she said, looking at him. "I mean, this isn't a dream, is it?"

"Okay. You know? This is becoming a bit creepy."

"A bit? I've never been here, and you see these spots on the dust? Those are my footprints," said Amanda, pointing at the floor.

"What? If you've never been here, what makes you think they're yours?"

"I just know," she said, stepping forward.

"So what are we looking for?" asked Alec.

He turned on his flashlight, too, and followed her.

∼

RUBEN DROVE off the highway and hit the brakes, stopping the car on the dirt path.

"Is it here?" Kimberly asked, eyeing the woods on both sides of the road. "You said house. I don't see any house."

"Kimberly, I have to run," said Ruben. "Take the car and go back, please."

"So let's run," said Kimberly, stepping out of the car.

"Kimberly," called Ruben.

She slammed the door.

"Kimberly," Ruben got out, too. "It's getting dark."

"Yeah, we'll need flashlights."

"You have to go back, please."

"Ruben, we're wasting time."

The climb wasn't very steep and they moved pretty fast. Ruben always had a stake on him, and now it was his only weapon. With Kimberly beside him, the stake was poor comfort. Ruben clutched her hand at the slightest noise and stopped to look around.

Luckily, he didn't find anything suspicious. As soon as they saw outlines of the house, Ruben slowed down.

"Wait," he whispered a few feet away from the clearing, pulling Kimberly closer.

That view brought a sad smile to his face. For a moment his memory drew him back in time, showing him images of the day when he allegedly hunted the vampire who attacked Eleanor, then the day when Gabriella sent him to check on one-year-old Margaret while Craig and Eleanor were in Egypt.

"Look," said Kimberly, pointing at the house.

Through the open door, Ruben saw two strips of light swaying from side to side. Vampires didn't need flashlights since they could see in the dark as well as humans in daylight.

"It's them," said Ruben.

AMANDA TURNED her flashlight to the left of the fireplace.

"You see that door?" she said to Alec. "That's a library."

She walked ahead and glanced out at the garden as she passed by the backyard door.

"Does it look familiar, too?" Alec asked.

"Yes. Especially that bench" sighed Amanda.

She stepped into the library.

"Maybe you were here when you were little," said Alec, following her. "And you just don't remember?"

"You're forgetting the footprints. I know they're mine, and I don't think that I had feet that size when I was little."

The moan in her head was too loud now.

The curtains were tightly shut, plunging the room into darkness. Amanda pointed the flashlight at the desk with an oil lamp, then she moved it toward the bookshelves and stopped on the protruding stand with the book on it.

"There it is," she whispered. "Can you hear it?"

"Hear what?"

"The moan."

"No. I hear nothing. Is that why you're here? You want this book?"

"No. I'm here because the book wants me," said, Amanda getting closer. With each step, her blood grew warmer and her pulse beat faster.

"Okay, creepy again."

"Sorry, I mean . . ." she held out her hand. "I think I have to open it."

"Amanda!" she heard Kimberly's voice. "Amanda, where are you?"

Amanda lowered her hand.

"Kimberly?" she gasped, looking at Kimberly and Ruben as they walked into the room. "How did you find me?"

Ruben gazed at Alec.

"What were you thinking, bringing her here at this hour?"

But then he saw the Book. He turned his glittering eyes on

Amanda. "You knew it was here. You saw it in your dream this morning."

They heard several footsteps, and Ruben pulled out the stake stuck into his belt.

"You should have told me," said Craig softly, stepping through the doorway.

Riley, Hanna, and Melinda entered the room behind him.

"I—You said, when the time came, I'd know what to do. When I saw this book, I knew what I had to do. I thought if I . . . I didn't want you to get hurt again."

Craig stepped closer and took her hands.

"Nothing can hurt me more than losing you," he said.

His eyes were fixed on hers. They were warm and full of love. She knew that what he said was true. With his finger, he wiped away a tear from her cheek.

Alec frowned.

Craig put his hand on the Book.

"Craig," she said, "Can you hear it?"

"No, my love. You are the only one who can."

His words and his voice touched something buried deep inside her, somewhere in her soul. And that something was rising.

She looked at the Book.

"You can do it now," said Craig. "It will hurt just for a second. Don't be afraid."

"I'm not." She smiled. "Not anymore."

Amanda glanced at Riley, Hanna, Ruben, and Melinda. Their warm eyes gazed at her. She placed both her hands on the side of the Book above the protruding sharp teeth and, biting her lip, she pressed her palms against them. Trickles of blood flowed on the iron, and the teeth crawled back. Amanda heard the click and the moan in her head stopped. Beaming, she looked at Craig and pulled aside the cover.

The soft yellow pages rustled, and two shimmering rays of

light came out of it—one red and one blue. They rose slowly, then with full speed flew toward Amanda and hit her in the chest. Amanda flew back and fell unconscious into Craig's arms. Hanna shrieked with joy. Craig kissed Amanda, his eyes soaked with tears.

Craig carried Amanda to the wide velvet couch and put her on it. Standing behind the couch, Alec glared at him.

Another two blue rays came out of the Book and flew away after their owners—Samson and Fray.

"What happened?" asked Kimberly in a shaky voice. "Craig, is she all right?"

"She's fine," said Craig, kissing Amanda's forehead. "She's sleeping."

The rays of blue light were coming out from the Book one after another. The next one hit Riley, then Ruben, Craig, Hanna, and one more, which flew away to find Ned. The Hunters shuddered, backed up, and then lurched forward again.

Melinda sat next to Amanda. Her smiling lips trembled.

"My girl, my little girl," she said, stroking Amanda's hair.

Kimberly's mouth was open, but she couldn't say a word. Ruben hugged her.

"I'll explain everything to you later, all right?"

"All right." Kimberly nodded.

The next moment, a large number of blue lights burst out from the Book and stormed away. That, and a weak rumble coming from under the house, erased the happy expressions from their faces. There was another rumble, which sounded like somebody was trying to start a lawnmower, and then an old-fashioned chandelier shone with a yellow light, swallowing the luminous circles of the flashlights.

They heard several heavy footsteps.

"Melinda." Craig looked at her.

Melinda jumped on her feet.

Fray appeared in the library doorway, smiling viciously, with vampires behind him. One of them was Mark.

Melinda raised her hand.

"Shaary murum." She hissed the words.

Fray stepped into the room, but the vampires hit the dense air and stopped. Fray's smile vanished. "What? You're just going to hide here?" he said, then gazed at Amanda.

"You're not going near her," said Craig, glaring at him.

"She's not my concern."

"No? Then why did you choose to bring her into this house? The last time I came here was in 1948—"

Kimberly's mouth fell open again. Alec stared at Fray.

"—And there were people living here," Craig said. "What did you do to them?"

"I didn't kill them if that's what you're worried about. I bought this house and everything within five hundred yards of it."

"Why?" Craig asked again.

"Because I love nature. I even afforested all open places," he said artistically. But then Fray's face became ominous. "You're right. I brought her here, to this place, because that's where your Eleanor died once and where she had to stay dead." His sparkling eyes pierced Craig. "She closed the Book. She took away my powers," he shouted. "That love of yours destroyed one hundred and sixty years of my life, and your Amanda will pay for that."

"No," snapped Riley. "You're the one who has to pay. You killed Gabriella, and we'll make you pay."

"Glad to see it still hurts."

Kimberly's eyes widened further. She swallowed, staring at Fray from behind Ruben, who stood protectively in front of her.

"Who is this?" Fray asked, gazing back at Kimberly. "I see. A new love story. I hate to disappoint you, Ruben. The best chance you have is to watch her get old, wrinkle, and die as somebody else's wife. Or she can die much sooner."

"Shut your mouth," roared Ruben. "If you touch her . . ."

"What? What are you going to do?"

The vampires standing behind the protective veil laughed.

Riley launched forward and punched Fray right in the mouth. Fray staggered back. Riley slipped closer and kicked him in the stomach. Fray flew out of the doorway and crashed into the crowd behind him.

They heard the backyard door slam with a bang.

"Already on the floor?" said Samson, walking in with Ned.

"Look who's here," said Fray, straightening up. "Kids, daddy's home."

"Walk away, Fray," said Samson.

"I can't. You see, I have something here, and I'm not leaving without it."

"It's not yours."

"Listen to me," Fray said through gritted teeth, "I killed for that Book once, and I won't hesitate to do it again."

"Really?" Samson stepped closer and grabbed Fray by his clothes. "I don't see the dagger. I wonder where and how deep you hid it this time."

Fray hit Samson's hands from beneath. As he freed himself, he sent a blow into Samson's chest. In the moment of impact, Samson clutched Fray's arm. That helped him keep his balance and at the same time, his other hand punched Fray in the ear. Riley and Ned moved toward the vampires.

"Don't step outside that door," said Ruben to Kimberly. As she nodded and sat down by Amanda's feet, he ran out of the library.

"You stay here, too," said Craig to Alec.

He took the chair in the corner, struck it with his foot, and picked up the broken legs. Hanna, who had her bag with her, pulled out her gun.

"Stay away from him," said Craig.

"That plan didn't work that well last time," said Hanna grumpily. "They wouldn't play the same game twice. I'll try to catch that filth, Mark."

She rushed out.

"Melinda, is this room safe?" Craig asked.

"Yes. I sealed the windows, too. I'll stay here just in case."

Craig glanced at Amanda once more, then at the Book, and left the room. Melinda closed the library door behind him.

In the living room, Riley fought three vampires, and Mark was one of them. The moment Hanna came out of the library, Mark flew out the window. She grabbed the vampire running at her and threw him aside. The body hit the couch, kicking up a cloud of dust. She shot him, then dove into the window. Ned rushed after her.

Ruben fought beside Riley. He kicked one of the vampires toward the garden. The vampire flew out, crushing the shabby backyard doors. Ruben picked up a couple of sharp pieces of wood and ran after him.

The living room was covered with vampire bodies. Craig staked the last one inside and ran to the front yard.

Samson and Fray were tussling in the empty fountain pool. Samson holding Fray by the neck was slamming his head against the angel statue.

"Where is my dagger?" he asked with rage.

"I told you—I don't have it on me." Fray finally grabbed Samson's hand, pushed it away, and dodged to the side.

All at once, Fray's and the vampires' cellphones rang.

"You know," said Fray, breathing heavily as the ringing stopped. "I'll just walk away as you asked me."

Suddenly, the vampires began running away in different directions. There was a flash of a shadow and Fray was gone, too.

The Hunters stared at each other.

"Something's wrong," said Samson. He looked at Craig. "Where's the Book?"

"It's inside, in the sealed room." Craig froze. "Amanda."

He rushed into the house. Everybody ran after him.

Craig pushed open the library door. Amanda was asleep on the couch, just as he had left her. Looking terrified and crying, Kimberly sat on the floor next to Melinda, who lay in a puddle of blood.

"Oh, no," Hanna gasped, "Melinda!" She knelt beside her. "Melinda!" Hanna called again, shaking her.

Melinda stared back at Hanna with glassy eyes. She was dead.

Craig rushed to the couch to make sure Amanda wasn't hurt.

"Kimberly." Ruben had just come in from the backyard, and he ran to her. "Are you all right?"

Sobbing, Kimberly nodded and buried her face in Ruben's chest.

"The Book is gone," said Craig, gazing at the empty stand.

"How could this happen? You said the room was sealed," said Samson.

"Nobody came in. I was in the living room until the last vampire was out of there."

"Last what?" Kimberly stared at Ruben.

"I'll explain everything later."

"Kimberly, what happened?" Craig asked.

Kimberly wiped her cheeks and looked at everybody.

"It was Alec."

"Alec?" Craig and Hanna burst out at the same time.

Only then did they look around and realize that Alec, who they had all forgotten about, wasn't in the room.

"He walked to Melinda," Kimberly said. "He said, 'So you're the witch.' He was so arrogant, so . . . different," she sobbed. "And then everything happened so quickly. He pulled out a knife—"

"What knife, how did it look?" Hanna asked.

"It was beautiful . . . something was written on it with gold . . ."

"That son of a bitch," roared Samson. "So, that boy was his plan B."

"He tricked us again," said Riley in frenzy.

"Melinda knew Alec. She knew he was human. She probably didn't protect herself," said Craig.

"Alec, that bastard." Hanna shook her head.

"He seemed like a nice guy," said Kimberly. She wiped her eyes. "After he killed . . . after Melinda, he stepped to Amanda. He bent to her with that dagger. I was so scared he would . . ." She sobbed again.

"Kimberly, I'm so sorry." Ruben hugged her tighter.

"But he didn't do it," Kimberly continued. "He whispered, 'See you soon,' then he took that book and left."

"He had the dagger because he was supposed to kill Amanda. But he didn't dare," said Craig.

"Ruben and I were in the backyard and the rest of you were at the front," said Riley, "He walked by with the Book in his hands and nobody noticed him?"

"He didn't go out," said Kimberly. "He went there." She pointed at the stand. "Behind that."

Riley stepped to the bookshelves. He grabbed the stand and pulled it. The whole line of the shelves moved. The bottom didn't touch the floor, but the sides made a scraping noise. Behind it was a staircase. At the end of the stairs was a massive iron door. Riley ran down and rattled it. It was locked.

"You think we should chase the others?" Ruben asked Samson.

"No. They're gone, and we don't have time for that. He

had his plan, we have ours. We have a job to do, and we need to start as soon as possible."

"What about Melinda? What do we do?" Craig asked. With a deep sigh, he knelt beside Melinda and closed her eyes.

"We can't take her back," said Samson. "She was stabbed. The coroners will call the police. We'll take her to the castle."

"What about her family?" Kimberly asked.

"We are her family. She doesn't have anyone else," said Samson with sorrow.

"Oh God," whispered Hanna. "Amanda."

"Yes," said Ned. "She'll wake up and . . ."

Hanna looked at him. They hadn't even had time to say hi to each other. Ned approached her and they hugged.

"We're leaving," said Samson. "Ruben, take your friend home and then come to the castle."

"No, I'm not leaving her alone in a town full of vamp—" Ruben glanced at Kimberly. "She's coming with us."

"Are you sure?" Samson looked at him, perplexed.

"I'm sure," said Ruben.

With a wondering expression, Samson glanced at Craig, then at Hanna. They both nodded approvingly.

"Let's go, then," he said.

Riley put Melinda in Samson's Jeep, and they took off. Craig drove behind them with Ned in the passenger seat and Amanda in the back seat with her head on Hanna's knees. Right after them were Ruben and Kimberly in Hanna's car.

∾

KIMBERLY WAS DEEP IN THOUGHT. For the last week, things had been happening around her. Strange, scary things. But what happened now was absolutely surreal. Alec, whom she'd known for almost a year, and who, as she thought, was a nice guy, had killed Melinda right in front of her eyes. Then Craig and the others started talking about vampires as if they really existed. A few minutes ago, when Ruben took her in his arms and carried her out of the house, he stepped over pale, shrunken bodies on the floor, on the porch, and all over the front yard.

"Kimberly, are you all right?" Ruben said. "Say something."

"I thought Amanda was joking," muttered Kimberly.

"Joking? Joking about what?"

"About vampires. She knew that those guys who were chasing us yesterday were vampires."

"Really?"

"Yes. She said 'They can't come in until you invite them.'"

"So, she figured it out."

Kimberly could hear the satisfaction in Ruben's tone.

"Kimberly, you're in shock. I know that this is too much to handle."

"Alec killed Melinda," she whispered, mostly to herself.

"I'm sorry you saw it happen." Ruben took her hand.

"Shouldn't we tell the police?"

"No. Alec is far gone."

"The police will find him."

"Yes, they might, but then they will find us, too. We have to deal with this ourselves, and we will, I promise."

Kimberly looked blankly at the road.

"Where are we going?" she asked when all three cars slid off the highway to the narrow, dirt road.

"To my home. We're almost there."

The cars drove up a hill.

"I don't see any houses," said Kimberly, looking at the surrounding woods.

"Kimberly, do you trust me?"

"Yes," she said, but it sounded like a question.

"You've already been through a lot today," said Ruben

softly. "What you're about to see might shock you as well. But I want you to know you are absolutely safe."

"Are there more vampires?" she asked, a little startled.

"No, no vampires." Ruben paused. He turned to her, and his warm look reassured her. "Remember our conversation on the beach?" he asked.

Kimberly nodded. "I said that I don't want you to leave."

Ruben smiled.

"And I don't want to leave. That's why I brought you here. I want you to see something."

All three cars slowed down. Samson pulled his Jeep aside and stopped. Ruben stopped the car, too. Only Craig kept driving, and after a few yards, right in front of Kimberly's eyes, his car vanished.

"Where did they go?" Kimberly clutched Ruben's hand. "Ruben, they're gone." She turned to him, blinking. Ruben didn't seem surprised at all; he was still smiling. Kimberly's lips slowly parted. Even though her mouth was open, no sound came out, and she wasn't even breathing.

"I want to ask you again," said Ruben. "Do you remember our conversation at the beach?"

"Yes." Kimberly breathed out loudly, "The legend." She saw Samson get out of the car.

"Kimberly, right now our car is parked on Eternity Road, and this is it, this is the invisible wall."

"It can't be. Are you saying that the legend—"

"Give me a minute," said Ruben in a low voice, looking through the windshield, and she saw that Samson, who was standing fifteen yards away, nodded.

"He couldn't . . ." Her wide eyes were staring at Ruben. "That's impossible."

"You'll find out much more after you've crossed this wall."

"Wait. Ruben, if I cross it . . . I'm not ready."

Ruben's smile became even wider.

"You're not going to become an immortal hunter just by passing through the wall. It's not that simple."

"No?"

"Not until you choose to." He stroked her cheek. "Are you ready now? Samson's waiting."

"What is he waiting for?"

"People can't cross the wall on their own. He is the only one who can let you through."

Kimberly was overwhelmed. Her temples pulsed loudly, and her cheeks were on fire.

Ruben held out his hand, and she clutched it tightly.

"We're ready," said Ruben, looking at Samson.

Samson raised his hand, and his lips moved. The picture behind his palm changed, and seconds later Kimberly saw an arch emerging in front of their car with a completely different view behind it.

Ruben hit the gas and sped into it.

Over the next few seconds, a million questions crossed Kimberly's mind. But there was one that spoke out louder than all the others. That question made her shiver. It made her turn to Ruben and peer at him more closely. She looked at his young face, his hands, at his neck, and his tanned smooth skin that showed in the gap of the unbuttoned collar of his shirt.

Was Ruben immortal?

"This is my home," said Ruben as he stopped the car before the castle.

His voice awakened Kimberly from her deep thoughts. She looked around.

"It's beautiful," she said, mesmerized by the spectacular view.

She looked at the yard first—at its fountain, its neatly trimmed bushes, at the colorful flowerbed, and at the statues standing beside the benches along the edge of the green court.

Kimberly turned her gaze to the stately castle. She looked

up the walls of its tower, then at the cells of windows and at the small and big stone balconies. Then, her eyes moved down to the large, brown wooden door and stopped at the slender elderly woman standing on the low, wide front stairs.

"Who is that?" she asked.

"That's Amelia Cox. She manages the household."

Samson's car stopped beside theirs. He came out of it, opened the back door, and took Melinda in his arms. Ms. Cox opened the front doors, and he carried the body into the castle, Riley in tow.

"Poor Melinda." Kimberly sighed heavily.

"Let's go inside," said Ruben.

As they passed the front door, Kimberly noticed big pentacles on the dark brown wood. Inside she saw Hanna and Ned coming down the marble stairs that ran along the wall.

"Hanna, is Amanda okay?" Kimberly asked, stepping forward.

"She's fine," said Hanna, hurrying to her. "It's you I'm worried about." She hugged Kimberly. "How are you?"

"I don't know yet. Very confused. So much has happened."

"I'm glad you came with us. Let me introduce you to someone. Kimberly, this is my boyfriend."

"So you're not a lesbian?"

"Edmond." The young man held out his hand, "You can call me Ned."

"I'm Kimberly," she said, taking his hand. "It's very nice to finally meet you. Now, at least one of my million questions has been answered."

"Let's go. I think it's time to take care of that million," said Ruben. He put his hand around Kimberly's back and led her to the stairs.

Chapter Twenty-Nine

YEAR 1852

AFTER THEY BURIED GABRIELLA, they all gathered in the library and listened to Samson tell them his plan.

"We are leaving," he said at the end, "Hanna and Eleanor, go change, pack your weapons and things you need, it might be a long trip. The rest of you go prepare the horses."

Eleanor walked into her room. As she opened the weapon's chest, she heard Samson's voice.

"Eleanor, I need to talk to you."

A minute later Eleanor entered the study.

Samson stood beside the window, staring at the ocean.

"Samson," Eleanor called.

He turned around.

"You wanted to talk to me?" said Eleanor.

Samson stepped to his desk. "You better sit down," he said, pointing at the tall chair on the other side of it.

But Eleanor didn't sit.

"This is serious, isn't it? This is something bad."

"Yes." Samson sighed. "Eleanor, we're in big trouble," he said, folding his hands behind his back.

"What is it?" Eleanor asked anxiously.

"Downstairs, I said that Fray can turn people."

"Yes." nodded Eleanor.

"The thing is, I don't think that he's going to turn people. From what Henry told me, I understand he's going to turn vampires."

"No," gasped Eleanor. "Is that even possible? Vampires don't have a soul."

"They don't need one. All they need is fresh blood. The absence of a soul will make the process much longer than usual, but in the end, they will wake up strong and invincible. Their cuts will heal even faster. Sun, fire, or stake wouldn't be dangerous to them anymore."

"Then we have to find Fray before he—"

"It's already too late. He's used the Book, I can feel it. He knew we would try to track him down, and if we found him, he might lose the Book. As I said, a couple of times his stops took much longer than was necessary to make the tracking line on the Map disappear, and they happened at the same place. If that place really is that church, there might be more vampires there."

Samson's words surprised Eleanor more and more. When he paused, she asked the question bothering her.

"Samson." She looked at him with bewilderment. "I'm a little confused."

Samson nodded but didn't say anything.

"Why are you telling this to me?" she asked. "Why not Riley, or Craig, or Ruben? Why me?"

"Because, if it already happened, if Fray already turned them—then there's only one thing left to do, and you are the only one who can do it."

"I don't understand. Do what?"

Samson walked to the window again and stood there, looking out.

"Samson, if there's something I can do, I'll do it. Just tell me what it is," Eleanor said.

Samson looked at her. "Eleanor, you know that I love you. You are my family."

"I love you, too. And I respect you and trust you." Eleanor looked straight into his eyes. They were full of pain. "If we're talking about our feelings, then I think what you need me to do is very dangerous. It might kill me."

"It *will* kill you," said Samson.

Eleanor felt the air streaming inside her through her open mouth. Her entire body froze. She didn't feel anything. It was like her heart froze, too.

"If he's already turned them and they're transitioning, then only a dagger will be able to stop them, and we don't have any of those. It doesn't leave me a choice. You will have to close the Book."

Eleanor scarcely heard Samson. His voice was muffled as if there were a thick barrier of glass between them. She had to die. She thought about Craig, imagined him holding her lifeless body. She'd never see Margaret again. Hanna had just lost Gabriella, and losing Eleanor as well would crush her. She stared at Samson.

"Craig," she whispered. Her lips were shaking.

"Craig can't know. Nobody can know. I'll explain everything to them later. Eleanor, I just lost Gabriella, and I would never wish for anybody to go through what I'm going through right now. But we are Hunters, and we have a mission to stop the dark powers. There is a chance we'll get the Book back, but I don't think we'll be able to get the daggers. He knows that we'll go after him, and I'm sure he's prepared. If we let those transitioning vampires wake up, not only will we never be able to get the daggers and forever witness their violence, but there's also a big chance that they'll kill you all."

Eleanor nodded.

"I understand," she said, and her voice was strong again. "I'll do it. I'm a Hunter, and I'm ready to do my duty. I have only one question. You said I'm the only one who can. Why? Is there something special about me? What is it that I have and the others don't?"

"A daughter."

"Margaret?" Eleanor froze again.

"Don't be frightened. She's safe. And keeping her safe will become our number one priority. Eleanor, when I said that I'm not losing anybody else, I meant it. Any of us who closes the Book will die. Myself included. I would do it in a heartbeat, but then the Book would remain closed forever. Only the same soul and the same blood will be able to open the Book again. You are the only one who has a child. Your bloodline will continue. One day you'll come back, and the day you turn eighteen, the age you became a Hunter, the Book will recognize you the moment your blood spills on it."

"Reincarnation," whispered Eleanor.

"Yes."

"When?"

"I don't know. It can take ten, twenty years, maybe much longer. We failed, and we'll be punished for that. You'll come back when you're allowed. The moment you open the Book, it will give you back everything—your memory, your feelings, your experience. It will give you back your life, and you will be the same Eleanor again."

∾

TODAY

AMANDA OPENED HER EYES.

She lay on a large soft bed. In front of her hung a portrait. A portrait of her and Craig. She was wearing a long emerald, silky gown with a full skirt, embroidered with rhinestones. Her dark brown hair was gathered up, and a few curls hung down her neck. Over her silky gloves, she wore the ring and the bracelet with golden coins. Standing beside her, Craig wore a black dress coat with an ivory vest, white shirt, and a brown puff tie.

Amanda sat up and looked to the side where the whisper of the ocean was coming from. Craig stood with his back to the open balcony door. Behind him, the thin curtains swayed from the breeze. Her eyes met his warm, tender look.

"Craig." Her legs slipped down from the bed.

"Eleanor," he whispered.

And as he stepped toward her, Eleanor threw herself into his arms.

Acknowledgments

I want to thank the four most important people in my life.

I can't thank enough my guide, my editor, my daughter Zara for her invaluable help, and her boyfriend Christian for his support.

And my daughter Dora and her husband Ewoud for always being there for me when I need them.

Also by Lana Melyan

LANA MELYAN

FORGED BY FATE

Trilogy

Book 1 — Wolf curse

Book 2 — Hybrid Born

Book 3 — Heir Chosen

THE WEIGHT OF MAGIC series

9 Episodes

1. The First Wave
2. The Legacy
3. The First Spell
4. The Family Tree
5. The First Fight
6. The Last Bell
7. The Sacrifice
8. The Last Secret
9. The Call of Blood

BELLS and SPELLS

Romantic Christmas adventure

Novella

Follow Lana Melyan on Amazon for new release alerts

Visit Lana Melyan's website lanamelyan.com to subscribe to the mailing list and be the first to learn about new releases and discounts.

Printed in Great Britain
by Amazon